# *Love Served Hot*

## Mellanie Szereto

amatoria press

Loved Served Hot
Copyright © 2013 Mellanie Szereto
Published by Amatoria Press

ISBN-13: 978-0-9911473-1-1
ISBN-10: 0991147316

Cover art by Dragonfly Press Design
Cover art and logos Copyright © 2013 Dragonfly Press Design

This story is a work of fiction, and any resemblance to real persons and/or events is coincidental.

# Dedication

Many hugs and thanks to Cheryl Brooks and Lynne Greeley for their invaluable feedback and to Judie Aitken, Judith Bastin, and Sandy James for their never-ending support on my writing journey.

Special thanks to the multi-talented Bethany Michaels for her fantastic cover design skills.

My sweet husband deserves mention for his patience with my writing schedule and his reminders about what true romance is. He's my very own hero.

To my readers—Thank you for choosing to spend time reading my books. I hope each one takes you on a wonderful trip inside my characters' worlds. Enjoy!

# Chapter 1

"Mr. Burault, many of the residents of Montgomery Crossing have restricted diets. Your sample menu includes undercooked meats, simple carbohydrate grains and vegetables, and desserts laden with refined sugar and saturated fats." Lilith Montgomery met the interviewee's haughty gaze and pasted on what she hoped was a polite smile. "Thank you so much for your interest, but I believe your ideas are better suited for an upscale restaurant."

The man had the nerve to look down his nose at her and regard her extended hand like a pile of greasy French fries. He tucked his chubby fingers behind his back without a handshake. "Humph."

*So much for trying to be nice.*

*Don't let the door hit you on the ass as you're leaving.*

Tuning out the dull clunk of the office door closing, Lilith sank into the chair behind her uncle's desk and turned her attention to her laptop. The résumé of the next—and last—chef candidate stared back at her.

*Graduate of the Culinary Institute of Chicago. Apprenticed under Chef Bernard Weiss.*

*Sous chef at The Westerfield House in Cincinnati for two years. Promoted to chef a little over a year ago.*

*Another overqualified, pompous jerk, no doubt.*

Why would someone with that background want to start up a private restaurant on the grounds of a retirement complex?

*Probably because he thinks it's an exclusive club, just like everybody else.*

She leaned forward and kneaded the knots of tension crawling up her neck.

*Uncle Wade, if you weren't recovering from gall bladder surgery, I'd give you a piece of my mind.*

Then she'd feed his toupee *du jour* to the paper shredder for placing the misleading advertisement.

*Yeah right. Like I could ever do something that mean to the man who rescued me.*

An entire day wasted on failed interviews had put her in a nasty mood. The last applicant would probably only add to it.

The phone buzzed.

Lilith almost ignored the receptionist's likely announcement that her next appointment had arrived, but the framed photo of her and Uncle Wade caught her eye as she swiveled toward the noise. She'd made him a promise.

Letting out a resigned sigh, she picked up the phone. "Yes, Wanda?"

"Your three-thirty appointment is here a few minutes early. Shall I send him in?"

*Tell him to go back to his* haute *cuisine kitchen and take all five of the previous applicants with him.*

"Yes. Thank you, Wanda." Lilith was better off getting the ordeal over and done before the weekend.

Wishing she'd had time to pop a fourth breath mint since tasting Burault's garlic-loaded Chicken Alfredo, she straightened her skirt as she stood. She slid her tired feet into her navy pumps and hoped she survived the trip across the room and back. Less than two hours of heels and business clothes, and then the weekend would be her savior. She rounded the desk as chef number six rapped twice.

The door swung open.

"Ms. Montgom'ry? I'm Flynn Hastings. Pleasure ta meet ya." A bare hint of Irish brogue colored the greeting, and tousled auburn curls framed a handsome face with bright blue eyes and a mischievous smile.

Her heart skipped a single beat before she reined in the foolish beast. She didn't need any more complications in her life right now, especially the fraternizing with a potential co-worker kind.

*Not that he'll want the job after I tell him the truth.*

She shook his offered hand, ignoring the giddiness in her stomach with the contact. A garlic overdose was probably the culprit. "Hello, Chef Hastings. Have a seat. I should clarify a few points about the position before we get started."

"Flynn, if ya don't mind." He followed her to the desk, waiting until she sat to lower himself into the chair opposite hers.

*At least he *has* manners.*

"Mr. Hastings—Flynn—we're looking for an experienced chef interested in running a small private restaurant. Although Montgomery Crossing encourages its residents to remain as independent as possible, we'd like to provide healthy meals for those who can't or prefer not to cook for themselves. The schedule will include breakfast and supper six days a week, plus brunch on Sundays. While the position requires a commitment of working every day, the hours are set at forty per week, with holidays as well as requested days off—within reason, of course." Surprised she'd held his attention through the disclosure, she gave him a full five seconds to voice his inevitable annoyance.

He nodded, as if encouraging her to continue.

Licking her lips, she suffocated a spark of hope. "Nutritional and dietary monitoring rank high in our goals for this endeavor. Many of our clients have medical conditions that require special care where meals are concerned. The facility has to cater to those needs."

She held her breath in anticipation of his relaxed expression morphing into a frown and narrowed eyes. So far, everyone she'd interviewed had expected to be managing the kitchen of an exclusive dining club. Uncle Wade had performed the shameless bait-and-switch trick.

*You old snake-oil salesman, you left me to deal with the fallout.*

Flynn jotted several notes in the portfolio on his lap. "Diabetics, cancer treatment patients, people with thyroid problems?"

Was he truly considering the job?

"Yes, plus several others. I have a list of all the current health issues for the residents if you'd like to see it."

He nodded again, not looking up from his pad of paper. "Sure. Then I'll need a minute to make a couple adjustments to my menu. How many people live in the complex?"

Slipping off her shoes, she stretched across the desk to hand him her most up-to-date printout. "We're at capacity with thirty-four right now. Eight couples and eighteen singles. Most of the special diets consist of healthier choices. I've been helping our residents with personal menu planning for the past five years, so they're better informed about what they should and shouldn't eat. A lot has changed regarding the perception of proper diet since they learned about nutrition in school. Oh, and we may have a few employees wanting to dine in the restaurant from time to time."

His crooked smile sent her pulse skittering as he scratched a line through one item and scribbled in a new one. "Registered dietitian or self-educated nutritionist?"

*Amazing. A chef who knows about more than just* preparing *food. And handsome as sin.*

She smoothed her palms down her skirt to calm her renegade hormones. "I have a master's degree in dietetics and nutrition."

"Excellent. You'll understand the reasons why I chose the entrées I did."

Pushing to his feet, he set his portfolio in front of her and then moved around the desk to stand beside her chair. His breath caressed her cheek, setting off the wrong kind of shiver. "Because of the relatively small number of patrons, I've limited the menu to four main dishes for the evening meal with a variety of sides. One meat, one poultry, one seafood, one vegetarian. The choices will rotate through the menu no more than twice a week, for a total of sixteen entrées. Each will be plated to order, whether the person makes his or her selections on site or in advance. They should have the same expectations they would from a full-service restaurant. And the menu will change seasonally, depending on what fresh fruits and vegetables are available."

Lilith tried to force her attention to the details on the page, but Flynn's woodsy scent distracted her mind as well as her body. "Do you mind if I take a look at this while you prepare your samples?"

"Not at all."

"Thank you. I'll have Wanda show you to the work area." Dialing the outer office, she weighed the pros and cons of hiring her last option. "Wanda, would you please escort Mr. Hastings to the kitchen?"

After an affirmative response, Lilith turned toward Flynn. A quick glance at his menu had told her most of the dishes required more prep than cook time. "Is an hour long enough?"

He was silent for several long moments, his stare a little unnerving. "An hour's fine. I look forward to hearing your opinion of my work."

Considering the narcissistic nature of all of the chefs she'd interviewed, his response put her senses on high alert. Either he genuinely cared what she thought, or he was sucking up to get the job because he'd been fired from his most recent one. His accent had also vanished.

*Did he really think I wouldn't notice?*

Uncle Wade's meddling voice popped into her head. *"Give the man the benefit of the doubt, Lily. Not every male is like that good-for-nothing, lying ex-boyfriend of yours."*

*Boy*friend. What an accurate description for the losers she dated up until a year ago. No wonder Flynn's teasing smile and pleasant scent had gotten to her. Her poor sex drive was tired of plastic playmates and solitary confinement.

She forced her attention back to the menu as he met the receptionist at the office door. The last thing she needed to see was a tight muscular ass to go with that irresistible leprechaun face, adorable mop of hair, and spotless white uniform. What she wouldn't give to share a breakfast of steel-cut oats and corned beef hash with her Irish chef.

*Be honest. Food has nothing to do with why you want to share breakfast with the man.*

The computer-generated spreadsheet was neat and organized—except where he'd handwritten the changes. The pencil marks resembled a doctor's illegible scrawl.

*Cyesslettubd ferlleftyckos? I can't wait to see what* that *is.*

Eying the clock on the wall, she swallowed a yawn. Thank goodness for Montgomery Crossing's monthly birthday party this evening in the clubhouse. No Friday night dinner to make for the whole crew tonight, and a couple of the night staff would supervise the shindig to be sure none of the residents got too carried away during the festivities.

Who knew what might trigger an episode for Norma Reed?

Lilith tried to shake off the disconcerting thought. Her dear friend was slowly succumbing to one of the debilitating illnesses that were a depressing reality of the job. No amount of planning could prevent the inevitable.

Leaving her shoes under the desk, Lilith forced herself out of the too comfortable chair and padded to her uncle's mess of a filing cabinet, hoping work would distract her. Although Wade had a system, she had yet to decipher it. Maybe by the time he returned to work, she'd have it figured out and reorganized. Her ridiculous fascination with Flynn Hastings might even disappear into a folder in the darkest depths of the metal drawers as well.

Instead of fixating on her friend's illness and a drool-worthy applicant, she pulled out the leases she'd discovered earlier and carried them to the copier. Creating a digital database was far more constructive than letting depression take hold or falling for another heartbreaker.

The scanner hummed as it copied last page in the pile, and Lilith couldn't help but compare the noise to her favorite vibrator. "Ah, Zippy, you know how to make a girl happy."

"Um, sorry ta interrupt."

The slight Irish lilt had returned, sending a spasm through her uterus. Leave it to the gods of perfect timing to bring Chef Flynn Hastings back to her office while she fantasized about a little self-indulgence.

"Wanda isn't at 'er desk, and the menu samples are ready except fer a few last minute details."

She'd have to settle for a delicious meal instead.

She gestured for him to lead the way. "What do you think of the kitchen setup?"

"Kudos to whoever designed it." Holding the door for her, his lips twitched as though he was trying not to laugh.

"That would be me." As she took a step past him, sexual awareness morphed into self-consciousness. The difference in their heights had grown from roughly eight or nine inches to at least a foot in the forty-five minutes since he'd gone to prepare his samples.

*Because I'm missing three and a half inches.*

Without slowing, she pivoted to re-enter her uncle's office. "Seems I forgot something."

"Forgetfulness is often the brain's subconscious way of surrendering to what the body wants." His words held more than a hint of amusement.

Moving the chair, she tried to reach her shoes with her foot. They slipped farther into the black hole beneath the desk. "I guess my brain forgot that I'm short and shouldn't go traipsing through the hallways in my stocking feet."

A dimple appeared in his left cheek as his mouth curved upward. "Petite, not short. And strange saying, that, especially nowadays when stockings are called socks." He cocked his head, looking even more like a giant irresistible leprechaun. "Unless you really are wearing stockings."

*Good gravy, I'm not touching that comment with a ten-foot four-leaf clover.*

His eyes had darkened to stormy blue, an instant warning to her that he might be willing to step over the line between acting director and interviewee. Just as quickly, his demeanor changed. "My apologies, Ms. Montgomery. That was unprofessional of me. It's been a long year, and, well…I'm sure you don't want to hear about it."

A sweep of color inched up his neck to contrast with his stark chef whites. He seemed to have as much trouble with women as she had with men.

Or did he?

More than one of Lilith's dates had used the "poor me" story to try for a piece of ass. She was better off ignoring the bait, especially with his part-time accent.

Finally resorting to ducking under the desk on her hands and knees, she grabbed her shoes and then slipped them on as she straightened. "Let's go taste those entrees before they get cold."

He stepped aside, gesturing for her to exit first. His light footsteps behind her belied his height and breadth. "I haven't dished up anything yet, in case you couldn't come to the kitchen right away. I don't use warming ovens."

Glad to have successfully changed the subject, she hurried along the empty corridor toward the dining wing. The sooner she finished the interview, the sooner she could pretend her feet weren't killing her. Each painful step reminded her why she hadn't gotten a business degree. Playing dress-up was a whole lot more fun when she didn't have to do it every day.

When they reached the dining room, Flynn led her to a table set for two. "If you'll have a seat, I'll bring out the samples."

She sat as he held the chair for her. The cloth napkin unfolded as she picked it up, and she spread it over her lap. "Thank you."

Giving a nod, he walked toward the kitchen, his uniform shifting with the movement of his long legs and far-too-indistinct backside. Some women swooned at a man clad in military or civil servant garb. Sure, firemen, policemen, and soldiers caught Lilith's eye, but a guy in whites held it.

Unfortunately, so had the loser wearing UPS brown the day he got fired. Then he'd lied to her about being employed for three months—until she'd caught him lazing on her couch watching afternoon talk shows when he should've been working.

She wasn't about to make that mistake again.

"Do you like lemonade?" Flynn stood poised to pour pale yellow liquid into a water goblet filled with ice and lemon slices.

How had he arrived back at the table without her realizing it?

*Lemonade?*

Her confusion must have shown on her face, because his eyebrows rose. "To cleanse your palate between entrées. Three servings of lemon sorbet might be a little excessive."

"Yes, of course." Why hadn't she thought of that? "Lemonade is fine."

*If I stop thinking about uniforms, my brain cells might function a little better.*

Strong hands gripped the handle of the pitcher and the goblet as he poured, the ice tinkling against the glass. His nails were clean and neatly trimmed, his fingers long and tapered. She forced down the request for him to hold up his hand for her to visually measure the distance from the tip of his thumb to his middle finger. Common sense had failed her in the past, and she refused to let sexual attraction dictate her social life ever again.

Had he not been the last applicant for the chef's job, she might've even considered telling him she'd already filled the position. As it was, she was stuck, and she'd have to keep a tight lid on her simmering hormones.

The image of a pressure cooker formed in her head.

*Not a good sign.*

# Chapter 2

Flynn strode into the state-of-the-art kitchen for a quick breather. Lilith Montgomery's curvy body and shamrock green eyes had almost made him say to hell with the job interview, he needed the woman more.

That was a lie, though.

He'd turned in his two weeks' notice to The Westerfield House almost a month ago. After finishing out his term, he'd packed up his apartment and moved to the other end of the state. Kent wasn't near the size of Cincinnati, but with its close vicinity to Cleveland, he'd figured finding employment would be a piece of cake.

Plenty of opportunities had come along. He'd been offered three head chef positions, all at highly respected establishments, with excellent pay— and *long* hours. After spending nearly eighty hours a week on the clock for more then a year, he'd proven cooking therapy was ineffective. Working himself to death wouldn't change what had happened. Nor would it make him forget.

*Gotta get my head in the game. No more wallowing in guilt and self- pity.*

He couldn't afford to blow this interview. Preparing meals for the residents of a small retirement community seven days a week beat the high-stress business of rolling out several hundred entrées in a few hours' time. Wanda, the middle-aged blonde behind the reception desk, had seemed friendly too. Employment at Montgomery Crossing was exactly what he needed.

Ms. Montgomery, on the other hand, fell into the "want" category. She'd even managed to set off his usually dormant Irish brogue twice. He had no reason to be nervous, especially since asking her for a date was out of the question.

Plating two modest servings of iron skillet-seared salmon on beds of rice, he added a sprig of fresh dill to each. He dropped a couple handfuls of pasta into the pot of boiling water and gave it a stir. The timer in his head set itself, the ticks so automatic he no longer had to check his watch.

He returned to the dining room to set a dish at Ms. Montgomery's place, reciting the information she'd likely want to know. "Entrée number one. Dilled Salmon with Spinach and Brown Rice Pilaf. High in Omega-3 fatty acids, complex carbs, and iron. Moderate sodium content. Most vegetables and fresh mushrooms can be substituted for the spinach. And it'll be served with a variety of sides."

The aroma rising from the table made his stomach rumble. Taking the seat across from her, he waited for her to taste the offering.

She lifted the fork to her lips. Several moments passed with no indication of her like or dislike of the fish. The only movement of her face was an occasional blink and rhythmic chewing.

A bite of rice followed, her reaction as stiff and bland as the first one. He might've expected unresponsive behavior from a food critic, but not from a potential employer.

Unable to restrain his need to know if the food warranted the lack of emotion, he flaked off a piece of salmon and settled it on his tongue. The texture was perfect—not tough or chewy. A mix of mild fish flavor, salt, black pepper, and freshly chopped dill spread over his taste buds. It tasted exactly the way it had the thousands of times he'd prepared it.

Could the rice be the problem?

He slid the fork under the grains, certain he had the right proportion of spinach to rice. Leaning over the plate, he lifted the bite to his mouth. The rice was firm but not crunchy, the spinach and seasonings adding enough hint of flavor to complement the earthy tone of the dish.

Taking a peek at his dining partner, he finished chewing. He'd no more than swallowed when she shuddered and closed her eyes. They opened again, staring straight at him with a slightly glassy look as she pulled in a shaky breath.

*Please don't tell me she's allergic to—*

"Oh my." She fanned her fingers at her face as she squirmed in her seat.

*No cayenne. No hot pepper sauce. No peppers, period—not even black in the rice—and only the lightest dusting of freshly cracked on the fish.*

Sifting through the ingredients in his mind didn't help identify the culprit. "Are you all right?"

Her tight smile didn't reassure him. She lifted her napkin to dab at her lips, not quite hiding her quick exhale. "Um, yes. I'm fine. Good. Shall we try the next?"

Wasn't she going to comment on the entrée? Or had she decided to wait until she'd completed the taste testing to evaluate the samples?

"Good" could've referred to the dish, couldn't it?

Pushing up from his chair, he paused before setting off for the kitchen again. The dish had been better than good, and he shouldn't put too much stock in her response. Confidence in his cooking skills had never been an issue for him.

*Drain and dish up the pasta.*

*Ladle the sauce.*

*Position the port.*

*Garnish.*

He was on his way in less than two minutes.

His judge slid her now-empty plate to the side and drained her glass.

*Empty?*

She had to have inhaled the rest of her salmon and rice while he was gone. That fact alone eliminated the possibility of a known allergy to the fish.

Her gaze seemed glued to the dishes in his grasp. "This must be entrée number two. Campanelle and Portabellas with Roma Tomato Sauce."

Flynn bit the inside of his cheek to keep from groaning aloud as he placed the pasta dish between her utensils. Her husky tone suggested she might prefer food to sex. A combination of the two would certainly be interesting.

*Just what I need—to lose this gig before I get it. Focus, damn it!*

He'd already risked making a bad impression with the stupid stocking comment, no matter how sexy her legs were. Adjusting the front of his chef's coat to hide his body's reaction to her voice, he refilled her glass and then rounded the table to sit opposite her again.

"Thanks." This time she hesitated a couple seconds before picking up her fork and knife. "Tell me more about the vegetarian selection."

Curious to see if her expression became an unreadable mask, he launched into a full description. "The pasta is made from chickpea flour instead of semolina. Higher protein, fewer carbs. Whole wheat or whole grain is another possibility, but I'd add a protein to the sauce to make up the difference. The ports are seared in olive oil for good fats. Freshly grated Parmesan for vegetarian, or without for vegan."

She held her loaded fork near her chin. "Chickpea pasta sounds fairly expensive and not readily available. What protein options would you use?"

"Cannellini works really well. Marinated and sautéed tofu is another. Black beans."

She gave a curt nod. The ruffled edge of the sauce-covered campanelle disappeared between her teeth. She looked more thoughtful than with the first entrée, her tongue sneaking out to lick her lips. Her fork clinked against the porcelain plate, and he held his breath for her verdict.

Her sudden gasp as she grabbed the edge of the table didn't bode well. The small squeak probably meant she was in pain, and her fingertips turned white from her death grip.

Stumbling out of his seat, he rushed to her side. "You're not all right. I'm not a doctor, but I'd guess acute appendicitis. Or maybe a really bad case of acid reflux."

She shook her head, sending her strawberry-blonde ponytail swinging back and forth. "Fine. I'm fine. Really. I just, um, bit my tongue." Her chest rose and fell in a steady rhythm as she straightened in her seat. "You're hired. Can you start work on Monday?"

The abrupt announcement and unexpected question should've made his day, but he could only gape at her. Her eyelids fluttered as if she was having a difficult time focusing, and she wanted to know if he could make breakfast for the residents of Montgomery Crossing on Monday morning?

"You're still interested in the job, aren't you?"

Was he?

While seeing her every day would likely test the control over his attraction to her, the idea of running a cozy restaurant for a few dozen old people appealed to him. His life would become his own again. He'd no longer have to deal with the conceited personalities of his peers. He'd have set hours and a new start, not to mention the ideal location.

He hooked his foot around the closest chair, pulling it closer to sit facing her. "Yeah, I'm interested. I can start Monday."

She seemed to relax, finally easing his worry about her health a little bit. "Good. You're a phenomenal chef. We can go over the details of the contract in the office."

"Give me fifteen minutes to clean up the kitchen? You can try the other two entrees while you wait if you like."

Reaching for the goblet, she seemed to consider his suggestion. "Oh, I'm not...very hungry. I ate a late lunch, and I'm on this...diet."

*Diet?*

Why in the world would a woman all of about five-foot-three and a hundred twenty pounds need to lose weight? He'd never understand the way the opposite sex viewed their bodies.

He shrugged, untangling his feet from the chair leg to stand. "Okay."

She did the same. "Would you like some help?"

Exactly what he didn't need—sharing close quarters with a female capable of tempting him to break his hard and fast rule about getting involved with his boss. He still wasn't entirely convinced she was feeling a hundred percent, but he'd rather she didn't find out how his body was responding to hers. "Thanks for the offer, but no. My mess, my cleanup. How about if I meet you in your office when I'm done? That way you won't get bored waiting on me."

He'd also be able to box up the rest of the food to leave with her. Half a dozen bites of rice and salmon and one of the campanelle wasn't enough to keep a bird alive.

Heading to the kitchen again, he gave her a brisk salute. "See you in a few minutes."

\* \* \* \*

Lilith hobbled along the corridor and into the office with her pumps dangling from her fingers. If she'd tried navigating with them on her feet, she would've collapsed into a boneless heap on the floor.

She dropped her shoes beneath the desk and fumbled through the stack of papers her uncle had labeled "Very Important" with a sticky note for the contract. It contained all the vital information she had to discuss with Flynn Hastings, including his salary—which couldn't possibly be generous enough.

The man was a gastronomical genius. One taste of his food had given her orgasms like she'd never experienced in her life. That she hadn't died from embarrassment at having them happen right in front of him was a miracle, because the most pleasurable event of her life had also been the most humiliating.

Her bikini top falling off as she climbed out of the pool at her only teenage boy-girl swim party now ranked a lowly second. Her prom date stepping on her gown and ripping off half the skirt in front of three hundred people slipped to third. Getting her period in Mr. Warden's fifth-grade health class fell to fourth.

Why did things like that always happen to her?

*"You know, Lily, sometimes shit happens. But it takes manure to grow a pretty flower."* Uncle Wade always managed to make her feel good about herself, especially when something traumatic bit her on the ass. Eventually, the ordeal would fade to a less noticeable odor.

She slid the single typewritten page from the pile, scanning the print to refresh her memory.

*Restaurant schedule. Vacation days. Pay scale.*

Nowhere did she find a notation about the consequences of a resident having spontaneous orgasms and dying from eating the food. Maybe she needed to rethink the job offer.

A knock at the open door set the butterflies in her stomach aflutter.

Flynn stepped into the room at her wave. A surreptitious glance at the front of his pants didn't reveal the half-expected telltale stain, a sure sign he hadn't come from eating his own food.

Did his secret ingredient only work on women?

Holding out a trio of waxy cardboard containers, he sat in the chair across from her. "The other two samples and the rest of the campanelle. In case you get hungry later."

"Oh, thanks." She'd have to make sure she was alone when she ate any more of his cooking. Partaking with the residents in the dining room would be tantamount to suicide if he agreed to take the job.

*No more public orgasms for me.*

She traded him the contract for the boxes. "I'm sure you'd like to read through this before you sign. It's pretty straightforward. Not too much legal jargon."

Giving a nod, he crossed his ankle over his knee and looked down toward the paper as he seemed to concentrate on every word in the binding document.

She busied herself behind the desk realigning Uncle Wade's all-important stack. Next, she alphabetized and straightened the lease files.

"I have a question about the last paragraph in section two." Flynn swung his foot to the floor as he leaned forward. He laid the contract on the desk, pointing to a spot near the middle of the page. "This reference to a housing option—what kind of option?"

Lilith almost whimpered aloud. How could she have forgotten about the on-site apartment clause in the agreement?

Clasping her hands in her lap, she forced her gaze to the dimple in his left cheek. "Montgomery Crossing has a limited number of employee apartments on the premises, let on a first-come, first-served basis."

She hadn't lied, even if she hadn't exactly invited him to apply for the housing option.

"Do you have a unit available?" His hopeful question defeated her vague implication that all of them were taken.

Not trusting her voice, she nodded.

"Can I see it before I make a decision?"

She cleared her tight throat. The top drawer slid out with a gentle tug, and she removed the set of keys to the only empty apartment. "Of course. Give me a minute to change shoes and put on a jacket."

He didn't move from his spot in the chair as she retrieved her running shoes and blazer from the coat closet. Even with her back to him, the itchiness crawling up her spine told her he watched her.

Why in the world had she ever agreed to be acting director during Uncle Wade's sick leave?

She double-knotted the second shoelace and then straightened to slip on her jacket. When she turned around, Flynn was fiddling with one of the buttons on his chef's coat. She was losing her marbles. He hadn't been watching her at all.

"I'm ready." *Or at least as ready as I'll ever be.*

He stood, the difference in their statures becoming obvious again. She was Sprout to his Green Giant.

"If you'll follow me, we'll take a quick tour of the grounds on our way to the apartment." At his nod, she walked at a controlled pace through the reception area and followed the hallway to the exit. The automatic doors whooshed open at her approach, sending a rush of goose bumps over her legs from the cool autumn air. "The sidewalk goes past the gardens and outdoor recreation area to Building F. The two buildings to the right of the courtyard house our couples, four in each. The two buildings to the left have six apartments each for singles, and the two straight ahead have six units apiece for singles, including the employee residences we added last year."

"Nice place." Flynn paused at the colorful profusion of hardy mums near the entrance to the covered patio. "A lot of attention to detail."

"Thank you. This is the last place a fair number of our tenants will live. We want it to be a pleasant experience." Not wanting to dwell on those who'd passed during the five years she'd worked there, she picked up her pace. "Each building has its own laundry facility and each unit a direct phone line to the office."

"What about utilities?"

The closeness of his voice reminded her that his stride was much longer than hers, and she barely resisted the urge to increase the distance between them by jogging ahead.

"Water's included. Electric isn't. Cable and internet are available for an additional monthly fee." Adjusting the keys in her grasp, she continued along the sidewalk toward the far end of Building F. Her heart rate increased with every step toward the last door.

"I saw parking at the other end of the sidewalk when I drove in. Is that lot for employees too?"

She gave a curt nod as she halted at apartment six, willing her hand to stop shaking. The deadbolt clicked with a quarter turn to the left. "Yes. A permit is required. I'll give you one when all the paperwork is done."

Inserting the key in the knob, she kept her eyes trained on the door.
*Please hate it. Please hate it.*

"You said this is the only vacant unit. Mind if I ask who lives next door?"

She crossed the threshold as she withdrew the key, holding on to the knob for dear life. "Um. I do."

# Chapter 3

Beige walls, floors, and curtains barely registered in Flynn's brain as he pretended to inspect the living room, kitchen, and bathroom. The place was like new and a hell of a lot more practical than the fifteen-hundred-square-foot condo he'd rented in Cincinnati—and his pretty boss lived next door.

His guide had encouraged him to explore the apartment at his leisure, but he hesitated at the bedroom doorway. By the locations of the exterior doors, the floor plans seemed to be mirror images of each other, meaning her bedroom would be on the other side of the wall from his.

How would he sleep with all of about six inches between him and her?

*Next door. I'm going to be living next door to a woman I want to* share *a bedroom with.*

He rubbed his fingers over the tight muscles in his upper back as he ventured into the last room. Even without furniture to gauge the size of the area, he had no doubt a king bed would fit, an absolute necessity for a six-foot-three man. He'd have to find a way to deal with his attraction to his employer, because he wanted the job, damn it. He *needed* the job, and screwing it up over a woman wasn't happening.

After a cursory check of the closet, he returned to the living room. "I'll take it. How soon can I move in?"

Ms. Montgomery's jaw twitched ever so slightly. If he hadn't been watching for her reaction, he probably would've missed it.

Was she having second thoughts about the offer?

"The apartment is ready, but you'll need to fill out the paperwork and I'll need to run a credit check." She lifted her wrist and glanced toward her watch. "I should have the report tomorrow morning. Or if you prefer, we can set up a payroll deduction for rent in lieu of the credit check. A nominal security deposit is required as well. As soon as the check clears, the keys are yours."

"Let's do the payroll deduction, and I can pay cash for the security deposit." After living in a motel for two weeks, he was more than ready to settle into something more permanent. Paying for another week of storage would be a waste of money.

"Oh, okay." She gestured at the exit. "Then we have a couple contracts to sign."

The quiet walk back to her office suggested she wished he'd said no to the housing option. Her spiel had been informational rather than enthusiastic, and she hadn't given him a move-in date even after he'd chosen the easiest route to finalizing the lease.

Did the thought of having a guy twice her size living next door worry her?

Or she could think he was a jerk after his earlier misstep.

Had his food saved him from falling victim to a "we'll-be-in-touch" dismissal?

The automatic entrance stole an opportunity to prove his manners by holding the door for her. Maybe he should've helped her into her jacket earlier. He sure as hell should've kept his mouth shut about the damn stockings. He was lucky she hadn't kicked him off the property for that suggestive remark—especially since she *was* wearing stockings. When she'd bent over to tie her shoes, he'd gotten a clear glimpse of the dark band circling her thigh through the back slit of her skirt. That slit had also drawn his eyes up to her magnificent ass.

She rounded the corner of the desk, putting the obstacle between them as she shuffled through some papers. A stapled packet of several pages slipped free. Thrusting them at him, she straightened the pile. "The lease. While you read through that copy, I'll prepare another with your name and the unit number to print out and sign."

Looking up from the document, he frowned. "Not that I think you're trying to pull a fast one, but I'd rather read the lease you're going to print out."

"A fast one?" Her fingers froze over the keyboard of her laptop, and her jaw twitched again. "Of course." Though her words were agreeable enough, they sounded tight and forced. Her gaze flicked toward a point on the wall behind him. "I'll have it ready in a couple minutes. Perhaps you can sign and date the work contract. You'll also need to fill out a withholding form."

The phone buzzed, and she almost jumped out of the chair. The woman really needed to relax. Stress or an ulcer, possibly even lack of food, had likely caused her pained reaction earlier. If she'd actually bitten her tongue, he'd broil his smelly gym socks for supper.

She snatched the receiver from its cradle. "Yes, Wanda?"

After several seconds of silence, she closed her eyes and lifted her hand to her forehead, her thumb and forefinger kneading the shallow furrows. "No. He charges an arm, a leg, and your firstborn for afterhours calls."

Flynn tried to go back to rereading the last section of the agreement, but her frustrated voice distracted him.

"I'll take care of it. You need to get home so Bob doesn't have a meltdown. Okay. I'll see you Monday." She hung up the phone and sighed. "Do you have a few minutes, Mr. Hastings? I have to make a quick phone call."

The "afterhours" reference suggested she had electrical or plumbing problems, and he had nowhere he had to be. "Sure. Take your time."

"Thank you." Taking a cell phone from her pocket, she pursed her lips. Then she tapped the screen several times and put the phone to her ear. "Hi, CC. It's Lilith. I'm sorry to bother you at the party, but I need your plumbing powers. Great, thanks. See you in a couple minutes."

Plunking the phone on the desk, she exhaled and set her fingers clacking on the keyboard. She let out a low growl and pointedly hammered on what had to be the "delete" key. After another clatter of typing, she stood, aiming toward a printer on the other side of the room. It spit out the last of a dozen sheets as someone knocked on the door.

She—*Lilith*—hurried to answer the summons. The door swung inward when she reached for the knob, the six-panel slab of oak conking her on the forehead. "Ow, ow, ow! Geesh, CC, I was about to let you in."

Flynn winced at the sympathetic twinge of pain.

A man wielding a plunger peeked around the door. "Oops. Sorry, Lily honey. You okay?"

With a hand to her head, she nodded. "Yeah, I'll be fine."

"Are you sure? Wade'll ban me from the office if you end up in the emergency room again." The bulldozer kissed the top of her head as he stepped into the room.

*Wade? Her husband?*

The idea of another guy—

*Wait a second. She said the employee units are for singles, and I'm moving in next door to her.*

*Boyfriend?*

*I'm better off if she has one.*

His insides begged to differ, though. He tightened his grip on the pen instead of rubbing at the faint ache in his gut.

CC winked at him. "Wade's her uncle, by the way."

Flynn clamped his lips together to keep from letting out a whoop of relief. Luckily, the action also kept him from laughing out loud at the old man's clothes. The orange high-tops might've been okay if they didn't have purple tights fitted to wiry legs coming out of them. The tool belt slung low on his hips would've been fine, if not for the wrestling uniform the same color as his shoes. The purple mask, however, was too much.

Ms. Montgomery—*Lilith. Lily*—had mentioned a party. Could it be a Halloween party? That certainly would explain the crazy costume.

She seemed to take the outrageous getup in stride. "Bonnie thinks she lost her earring down the sink in the locker room. Will you check the trap please?"

"'Course!" Patting the pipe wrench hanging from his belt, CC grinned. "You s'pose she'll give me a kiss for thanks?"

"A hug at the very least." She ducked as the plunger swung around toward her head. "I appreciate the help, CC."

"Any time. Good choice for the new chef. Decent looking and about your age. A little hoochie-coochie would do you good, Lily." With a salute, he exited the office, pulling the door closed behind him.

"Sorry about that." Her cheeks flamed as red as the spot in the middle of her forehead when she turned to face Flynn. "The residents here are notorious for their matchmaking attempts."

He shrugged. What else could he do? Tell her he agreed with the old guy that they should get together? "No problem. Contract is signed and withholding done. Ready to take care of the lease?"

The change of subject seemed to her liking since she strode to the printer and gathered the papers. She handed him the stack. "Yes. You asked about a move-in date. The keys are yours as soon as we're done with the signatures and security deposit. The amount is in section four. Oh, and we have a part-timer to help with cleanup in the restaurant. Will you need an assistant to help with prep?"

"A colleague of mine contacted me a few days ago about possibly taking on a student who needs an internship. The school will pick up the tab for his hours. I'd like to go that route, if you don't mind." Glancing up from the first page, he caught her touching her fingertips to the bump. The poor woman had to have a headache besides the welt. "Are you okay? I can get some ice from the kitchen."

She waved off his offer. "This is nothing. I'll down a couple ibuprofen when I get home. An intern is fine."

"I'll get in touch with my colleague on Monday."

A quick skim of the details had to suffice. His instincts told him he could trust her, and by the way she kept eyeing the clock, her workday had probably ended sometime between five and five thirty. The clock now read five fifty-five.

The "nominal" deposit was far less than he expected and well within the cash in his wallet, so he scribbled his signature on both the designated lines and initialed each section. Handing her the document and cash, he let relief settle over him. He'd found a position to allow the kind of structure that would balance his life again.

She signed the lease, her neat script looking incredibly feminine next to his. "I'll make a copy for you, write out a receipt for the deposit, and the keys are yours. Here's my business card, in case you have any questions or problems. I check my e-mail several times a day, but feel free to call or text if you need an answer right away. Oh, and you'll need a parking permit."

Five minutes later, he stood to leave, but reluctance held his feet in place as she gathered her shoes, purse, and the boxed leftovers. "I think I'll take a few quick measurements at the apartment before I go. Want me to carry something for you?"

Her eyes skipped from him toward the computer bag still laying on the desk. "Yes, thanks. I appreciate it. Would you mind taking the food? I'm afraid I'll drop it and miss out on…a real treat."

What had she meant to say? Didn't she eat meat? Could that have been the reason she'd cut off his taste testing halfway through?

He smiled, hoping she'd believe he'd taken her statement as a compliment, even if she'd only intended to keep him from knowing she'd likely toss the chicken and pork dishes in the garbage. That made her a considerate person in his mind, although he preferred honesty to a kind fib.

He waited for her to lock the office door and then walked with her down the hall and outside. Laughter and music came from the opposite end of the building. Lights shining through sliding glass doors revealed the party she'd mentioned. He almost missed Lilith's soft words for the background noise.

"I promise the residents aren't party animals. Quiet hours start at ten, but they're usually all home by nine."

Recognizing the path she'd led him along less than an hour ago, he kept pace with her. "I'm not much of a partier myself. Getting mellow in my old age, I guess."

Her laugh triggered a ripple of awareness in his veins as she stopped at unit five in Building F. "They tell me I need to learn to loosen up and let my hair down. I think you'll get on just fine with them."

Considering the sudden ease of their conversation, Flynn was relieved they'd reached her apartment. Another few minutes of walking and talking, and he would've revealed much more than she needed or wanted to know about him.

He handed her the containers of food. "Nothing wrong with cutting loose once in a while. See you around. I'll be the one hauling furniture and boxes tomorrow."

"Thanks. And if you need help, Kip the maintenance guy lives at the other end of the building in number two." Her tone suggested she'd resigned herself to him living next to her. She stepped through the open doorway.

"Good to know."

"Goodnight." The door closed, leaving him to stand there or move on.

Three steps to the right took him to his own apartment and his new opportunity. He wasn't going to waste it.

\* \* \* \*

Listening for another light thud from next door, Lilith paced her living room. She'd stashed Chef Flynn Hastings' third and fourth entrée samples in the fridge with the rest of the second, but only because she didn't want him overhearing her reaction to them—especially if they affected her body the same way the first two had.

He didn't plan on staying all night, did he?

She toed off her running shoes at the end of the couch before padding to her bedroom. If she had to kill time waiting for Flynn to leave, she could at least swap her work clothes for yoga pants and a hooded sweatshirt.

With her skirt in the basket of dry cleaning, she unhooked the clasps from her stockings, her interviewee's comment replaying in her mind.

*He couldn't possibly have known.*

Could he?

A soft *thunk* sounded. Was he finally gone?

A sprint to the living room sent her hose drooping around her feet, but she peeked through the blinds instead of worrying about her elephant ankles. Flynn passed her window as he sauntered along the sidewalk, glancing back over his shoulder and looking her in the eye. His cheeky grin made her stomach flip-flop, and she jerked her fingers free of the slats.

*Caught.*

Geez, he probably thought she was nosier than a stereotypical little old lady. She *was* behaving like one, even if spying to find out about the new tenant wasn't her motive. No, her reason won the prize for most embarrassing. She was jonesing for a foodgasm.

*Hey, at least I have a discerning palate.*

Food-induced orgasms brought a whole new meaning to safe sex, and she didn't need batteries, either—only a method to reheat her meals.

Flynn's masterpieces deserved warming in the oven rather than the microwave, so she headed to the kitchen, intent on her task. While she waited for them to heat, she'd finish changing clothes, pour a glass of wine, and read a chapter or two from the book a couple of her female co-workers had raved about a few weeks ago.

The handwritten labels on the two containers had Lilith shaking her head as she pulled the food out of the fridge. She had no idea what the pen markings said, or which was right side up. Giving up on trying to make sense of the scrawl, she popped open the first lid.

*A stuffed boneless pork chop. Apples in the filling? Hm…*

The second box held a lightly browned chicken breast tenderloin and a separate cup of lumpy orange relish of some sort.

*Fruit chutney?*

Lifting the plastic cover, she sniffed the mystery sauce.

*Mm, peaches.*

If these dishes didn't shoot her to the moon, nothing would.

With her dinner transferred to a casserole dish, she placed it in the oven to heat. Comfy pants and a glass of soft red were next on the agenda. Friday night at home alone didn't have to be lonely.

*Oops! Better set the timer.*

She finally settled at the table with her wine and her e-reader after a quick clothes swap. A few taps of her finger on the screen brought up the title.

*"Iced Latté."*

*Strange.*

Erin didn't usually go for stories so innocuous sounding. Romance was her addiction, not a title that gave the impression of a bunch of women sitting on the patio at Starbucks exchanging gossip.

Lil clicked open the file to enlarge the cover. A dark-haired man with intense brown eyes caught her immediate attention. He held a woman with skin the color of milk-diluted coffee in his arms, her expression suggesting she was more than willing to let him cover her in icing and lick it all off.

A giggle escaped. "Oh, Erin, you naughty girl."

Curious about the other book Erin had loaded for her, Lilith closed *Iced Latté* and opened the next in the list, *Just Desserts*.

"This oughta be good." She gave a snort of laughter as she tapped her finger on the thumbnail-sized cover.

A moment later, it loaded.

Auburn curls framing the face of a nearly naked man caught her eye first. Then the strawberry-blonde hair of his lover registered.

A disconcerting shiver raced up Lilith's spine. "My God! That's Flynn and me!"

Granted, the models were hardly identical matches for either of them, but the likenesses were a bit unsettling. She slid the e-reader away from her as she rose, her thoughts chasing her when she paced to the living room.

How in the world would she ever look at him again without wanting to see how his muscles compared to the man on the cover?

*I will not strip him naked. I will not* think *about stripping him naked.*

She'd been perfectly content with her boyfriend-free life for the past year. Only a fool would ruin it by letting a picture tempt her into abandoning her self-preserving choice.

High-pitched beeping called her from the next room.

Determined to put the book out of her mind, she rushed to the kitchen to take her dinner out of the oven. She and Flynn were officially co-workers starting Monday and neighbors as soon as he moved in next door. While he seemed nice enough and probably worked hard, she couldn't act on her attraction, tempting chef whites or not. She'd have to find satisfaction in the meals he prepared—and preferably in private.

She carefully scooped the entrees onto a plate, unwilling to forgo civility when her food demanded better of her. Any dish capable of triggering an orgasm deserved her best china, fine flatware, and a cloth napkin.

Ignoring the darkened screen of her e-reader, she sat down to test the potency of the chicken and pork entrées. A sip of wine did little to calm her skipping pulse. As many times as she'd seen to her own needs, simply diving into the steaming invitation to euphoria should've been a no-brainer. The enticing scents of delicately seasoned meat, tart apples, and sweet peaches had her mouth watering, but she hesitated.

She wiggled in the chair to get more comfortable. Cutting off the tip of the chicken tenderloin, she dragged it through the fruity puddle and then lifted it to her mouth.

*Insert.*

*Chew.*

*And...*

Nothing.

She swallowed the delicious morsel, waiting for the much-anticipated burst of physical pleasure.

Still nothing.

Another stab at the peachy chicken yielded a party for her taste buds and nothing more.

*The pork. I'll try the pork. I'm just too tense. Too expectant.*

A slice through the tender mix of boneless center-cut chop and apple stuffing sent a ripple of hope through her veins. She crammed a too-large bite into her mouth, ready for the overload of sensation in her inner muscles.

It didn't come.

*She* didn't come.

*Not fair!*

Not only had she made a huge mistake in hiring a stud of a chef, now his fabulous food didn't even make up for not getting to have sex with him.

Her body had proven once again that she wasn't normal.

# Chapter 4

Still pouting from her disappointing supper, Lilith washed, dried, and put away the few dishes she'd used. She certainly wasn't in the mood to read about lattés or desserts anymore.

Leaving the damp dishtowel on the handle of the oven, she retreated to the living room for her shoes and keys. A brisk walk on the grounds would boost her spirits and make her forget about food-induced orgasms, relationships, and romance—at least temporarily.

Cool air swept around her neck as she left her apartment, and she tugged up her hood against the cold. Putting her head down, she turned into the wind.

A shadow engulfed her, and broad shoulders filled her vision as she bounced off something solid enough to send her falling backward. She grabbed for her doorknob, but it slipped away too fast. The ground rose up to meet her, rattling every bone in her body.

"Oof!" Pain radiated through her hip, and she choked back a curse.

"Hold up, guys! Collision!" A faint accent tinted the hollered warning.

*Ah, hell. I should've just gone to bed.*

She curled up next to the exterior wall to keep from getting stepped on as well as knocked to the ground.

Flynn dropped the end of an enormous mattress and crouched in front of her, brushing her ponytail away from her face. "Are you okay, Lilith? God, I'm really sorry. I was walking backward and I didn't see you coming out the door. Please tell me you're okay."

He offered his hand, but she shook her head. "It only hurts if I move."

"Do you think anything's broken?"

*Yeah, my life.*

She straightened enough to make sure her legs still worked. "Just a bunch of blood vessels in my backside."

Grabbing her keys from the sidewalk, he frowned and then unlocked her door. "Hey, guys, can you balance this monster for a couple minutes? We've got a casualty."

"Sure thing, Mr. Hastings." A teenage boy appeared next to the near end of the mattress. "Want us to carry it in for you?"

"No, wait for me. I'll be right back."

Before Lily could protest, Flynn picked her up and strode through her open door straight to the bedroom. He eased her onto the bed, helping her roll to the side. The movement stole her breath, making any complaint impossible.

A second later, he jogged out of the room. "Give me about five minutes."

She tried to speak, but he was already gone.

Damn, her butt hurt like hell. Every joint and muscle in her body ached, and she wanted to cry from the irony. Her new chef had figuratively knocked her on her ass with his cooking and then he'd literally done the same with the accidental impact. She hadn't planned on him getting her into bed this way, either.

*Or at all.*

What else could go wrong with her life?

Cradling her pillow, she closed her eyes. Maybe if she stayed in this position instead of going to the bathroom for the bottle of ibuprofen, the pain would subside on its own.

"I'm so sorry, Lilith." The mattress shifted under the weight of her new neighbor. He slid her yoga pants halfway past her hips in a single movement. Smoothing his hand along her bottom, he followed her lower spine to her tailbone. "Nothing feels out of place here."

*Easy for you to say. You're not the one with your rear end exposed to a complete stranger.*

He traced the curve of her hip, gently pressing on the joint. "I don't think you broke any bones, but you'll probably be sore for a few days. Do you have an icepack or a bag of peas in your freezer?"

Unable to do anything but groan, she squeezed her eyes shut tighter.

"I know it hurts. This is all my fault." The bed shifted again. "Don't try to move. I'll go see what I can find."

Pain was the least of her worries. A thong did *not* count as underwear when accounting for the lack of coverage in the back—and he hadn't pulled her pants back up. Foodgasms in his presence didn't begin to compare to this mortification.

*Please let this all be a terrible nightmare.*

Heavy footfalls announced his return. "I found a bag of cranberries. Um, right side? Or did you land on your tailbone?"

Evidently, pretending she'd fallen asleep wasn't going to work. She braced for an ice-cold bag of fruit. "Right hip."

Something soft and slightly cool brushed against her skin, putting the mildest pressure on the sore spot.

"Not too cold? I wrapped it in a dishtowel."

"Fine."

"I brought a glass of water and some pain relievers, but I need to run to my truck for a straw. Will you be okay until get back?"

"A straw?"

"Yeah, so you don't have to try to sit up to drink. I'll be back as quick as I can." His fading footsteps and the click of her apartment door signaled his departure.

Her heart skipped a beat, and the tickle in her tummy warned her of impending complications.

*What have I gotten myself into this time?*

\* \* \* \*

Flynn let the chilly evening air fill his lungs as he stepped outside. Concern for Lilith's wellbeing had switched his brain from chef to med student in an instant, and once he'd been sure she wasn't seriously injured, awareness of what he'd done had hit him.

*Shit. She probably thinks I'm a damn pervert.*

Reaching his truck, he tried to focus on his task, but the image of her perfectly rounded ass in that lacy blue thong was seared onto his brain.

"Is the lady okay? You ready to go, Mr. Hastings?" The voices of his hired helpers from the back of the pickup brought him out of the lust-induced fog.

He rummaged through the glove box for his supply of paper napkins and straws. "Ms. Montgomery is hurting right now, but I think she'll be okay. Can you guys wait here for a couple more minutes? I need to help her take some pain pills."

The motel manager's son nodded. "Sure."

Flynn snagged a paper-wrapped straw before heading down the sidewalk, jiggling Lilith's keys against his palm. He'd have to find a way to make up for the accident. With the basic staples in his refrigerator and cupboards, he could cook her meals tomorrow so she could recover from the fall. He'd offer to run errands for her and do whatever menial Saturday tasks she normally did.

Hell, at this point, he could only hope she didn't fire him before he started his new job—because she'd never believe he hadn't copped a feel on purpose.

Letting himself inside her apartment, he tore the wrapper off the straw and went to face the music. Her eyes popped opened as he walked into the bedroom, the frozen cranberries still balanced on their shapely perch. She'd make a great patient for him while he played doctor.

*Priorities.*

He grabbed the pills and the cup of water from the nightstand. "Feeling any better?"

Her grimace spoke volumes.

"Here, take these." Holding the tablets to her mouth, he waited for her to allow him entrance.

She didn't argue, her lips parting so he could set the medicine on her tongue. Several sips of water followed. "Thanks."

"You're welcome. And again, I'm really sorry. You'll tell me if there's anything I can do for you?"

Her eyelids drooped. "Was an accident. Not your fault."

He begged to differ, but she was already falling asleep. Removing the cold pack, he set it aside to gently ease her pants up past her hip. By the time he folded the blankets from the other side of the bed over her, her breathing was slow and even.

Leaving the light on, he made a quick trip to the kitchen to return the cranberries to the freezer. Then he hurried to the door, locking it and pocketing her keys before jogging to his truck.

The boys had already climbed in the cab and fastened their seatbelts by the time he slid behind the steering wheel. They were quiet on the fifteen-minute ride to the motel, and Flynn handed them each a ten-dollar bill as they unbuckled. "Tomorrow morning at eight, guys?"

Both of his helpers nodded.

"And another twenty bucks each when we're done."

The boys grinned, and the motel manager's son gave him a thumbs-up. "Thanks, Mr. Hastings! We'll be ready."

When the boys disappeared through the lobby entrance, Flynn tightened the grip on his need to rush back to Lilith. She wasn't going anywhere, and speeding would likely get him a ticket.

The interminable drive allowed his mind to wander back to the moment he'd realized he had his hands on her silky skin. He couldn't explain his compelling attraction to her. Sure, she was pretty and smart. Her lack of pretense and almost shy—*No, not shy. Self-conscious maybe? Yeah.*—response to her plumber's teasing about getting laid spoke volumes about her social life. She was honest and unassuming, professional and polite.

*Okay, I admit it. I like her.*

Parking in the same space he'd claimed earlier, he tried to keep his pace casual and unhurried as he followed the sidewalk to her apartment. Liking her didn't mean he had to act on his feelings. They could be friends instead of lovers. He'd check on her, return her keys, and go to his new home next door.

Even as he unlocked the door, indecisiveness pitted his common sense against a growing foe.

Should he have knocked?

When was the last time a woman had affected him this way?

*Not since high school. And I can't let her do it now.*

He shut the door, careful not to let it clunk closed, and then laid her keys on the end table as quietly as he could. Four more steps took him into her bedroom.

Smothering the draw to lie down beside her, he sat down on the floor to study her relaxed features. The lamp on the nightstand cast a ray of surreal luminescence across her angelic face—the graceful bow of her mouth, her lightly freckled cheeks and nose, the delicate line of her jaw. The rosy lump in the middle of her forehead didn't detract from her beauty. It only served to remind him that she'd had a damn rough day, reinforcing his decision to behave himself.

Unfortunately, the chances of him maintaining a strictly professional relationship with her got more impossible by the minute. He was attracted to her on a physical level, but the more time he spent with her, the more he liked her ability to take things in stride. For all the crap she'd had to deal with in the few hours since he'd met her, she hadn't complained once. She was sweet yet tough.

*And let's not forget beautiful and sexy.*

His half-hard cock could attest to the latter.

He pushed up from the floor to turn off the lamp and retreat to the kitchen with the half-empty water glass. Watching her sleep wouldn't help her rest or make keeping his hands to himself any easier.

The layout of her kitchen was exactly opposite of his, and the spotless counters didn't surprise him. The e-reader on the round two-seat table was the single item that seemed out of place in the room—probably her version of clutter. When she'd searched the piles on her desk earlier, she'd straightened them as she finished. Neat stacks of files by the printer had all but confirmed his guess that she preferred organization to mess.

A scan of the living room revealed the same everything-in-its-place appearance. He could hardly offer to clean her apartment tomorrow if it was already clutter and dust-free. Even the bathroom had looked like she was expecting company.

*It's Friday night. Was she supposed to have a date?*

His stomach twisted.

*Over my dead body.*

The thought of some other guy putting his paws all over Lilith wasn't a pleasant one. Flynn had never been possessive where women were concerned, but this curvy little angel triggered something he couldn't quite identify.

*You know damn well what it is.*

He'd get over his infatuation soon enough, though, and going to his own apartment was a good start.

After a quick peek into the bedroom to be sure she was still asleep, he returned to the kitchen to switch on the light above the sink and turn off the ceiling light. Reaching to close the blinds, he braced himself with a hand on the table. A bright flash of color below his elbow made his breath catch in his throat.

*Yeah, let's knock her stuff on the floor. As if she doesn't have good reason for canning me already.*

He slid the e-reader away from the edge of table as he straightened, and the picture on the screen captured his attention. A double take assured him the woman wasn't Lilith, as the first glance had told his brain, but the resemblance was there. Words in some frilly font flowed across the image, naming the title. *Just Desserts.*

*A dessert cookbook?*

Did Lilith have a weakness for decadent desserts?

*Aha! Maybe chocolate's the way to go.*

He could stop for whatever ingredients he didn't have on hand after he cleaned out the storage unit in the morning. First, he had to choose a recipe, though. If he was lucky, she'd bookmarked a few favorites.

Sitting down, he tapped the arrow to turn several pages, finally arriving at chapter one. The opening read like fiction, with an introduction of the Lilith lookalike as she printed out flyers for a fundraiser bake-off featuring desserts. He continued reading through several more pages before a single point became obvious. This "cookbook" contained only one recipe—how to seduce with dessert.

The book might not include directions for a to-die-for German chocolate cheesecake, but it kept him interested enough to finish chapter one and begin chapter two. He never would've expected a prim businesswoman like Lilith Montgomery to enjoy a taste for erotic stories. She hid her wild side quite effectively under her conservative suit and simple ponytail.

Were stockings her way of rebelling beneath her conformist wardrobe?

Glancing at the page count at the screen and then at his watch, he dove into chapter four. He was almost a fifth of the way done already. Why not read the whole thing?

He was squirming in his seat by the first real kiss and wishing for a bucket of ice to pour down his jeans when it led to no-holds-barred sex. The use of lemon glaze, melted vanilla bark, and strawberry licorice ropes might've been hilarious if the scene hadn't been so damn sensual and thought provoking. To think he was thirty years old and had always settled for unflavored lovemaking. The happily-ever-after ending didn't hurt, either.

The images teasing his hyped-up libido all featured his boss. The book cover sure as hell didn't help in that respect. Speaking of which, he still needed to reset the story to the picture of him feeding Lilith.

With the e-reader back to its original place, he waited for the screen to darken.

*Too bad it has to stay a fantasy.*

Fate had thrown too many good opportunities at him today. A terrific job in his dream kitchen. Time to have a social life. A woman who sparked his interest. A boss he liked. A chance to recover from the last year. If he could choose them all, he would—but that wasn't a viable option.

He stood.

*Time to go.*

Walking through the living room, he clicked off the lamp as he aimed for the exit. His path took him past the entrance to Lilith's bedroom.

*One last check.*

She still lay in the same position, but her facial features were now masked in the dim lighting.

*Just go, you fool.*

He checked the end table to be sure he'd set her keys in plain sight. All the lights except the one above the kitchen sink were off. As he opened the door, he tested the knob from the outside.

*Locked. Now close it.*

The action took more effort than it should've, but the audible click gave him no chance to change his mind. Life wasn't always fair, and staring at her dark bedroom window wouldn't change that fact. She was only irresistible because he'd gone too long without a girlfriend.

*Dating the boss is a bad idea.*

Three steps put him in front of his own door. He shoved the key in the lock, trying not to wonder if he'd made a mistake by leaving her alone. She hadn't hit her head that he knew of, so a concussion was highly unlikely. Although the bump on her forehead could've caused—

*Knock it off. She's fine.*

He forced his legs to carry him inside and he kicked off his shoes as he headed for the bedroom. He still needed to spread sheets and a blanket on the mattress before he crashed. Another night in a motel room hadn't appealed to him in the least, but he'd figured on having all evening to make his bed, frameless as it was until tomorrow. If he hadn't let his curiosity about Lilith's taste in desserts lead him down the road to reading about sex with food props, he would've gotten the job done. Instead, the peek into her private life would haunt him for a long time.

He skimmed his hand along the wall for the light switch as he entered his new bedroom. Sudden brightness had him blinking away dancing spots. The wall he shared with his neighbor drew his gaze before he could stop himself. She couldn't be more than ten or twelve feet from him.

His fresh start had turned complicated.

Risking the job for a temporary fling was stupid. As ex-lovers, he and Lilith would face the stilted awkwardness of seeing each other day in and day out, with one of them the dumped party. He had no illusions that they'd fall madly in love and live happily ever after like the characters in her book. Life played by its own rules, and they didn't always make sense.

Ripping the tape off the top of the box marked "towels, sheets, and blankets," he got down to the business of making his bed and stocking the bathroom for his morning shower. A yawn had him digging a pair of boxers and a T-shirt from his suitcase.

His body had adjusted to non-restaurant time faster than he would've thought possible. Six years of working until midnight and sleeping in the next day had changed to early to bed and early to rise in the two short weeks since he'd quit his last job.

Had he known somewhere in the back of his mind that he wouldn't return to the kind of job he'd had before?

He rolled his shoulders to loosen his taut muscles.

Why else would he have turned down the other offers?

He *had* told Lilith the brain usually surrendered to what the body wanted. Of course, his philosophy could also apply to his attraction to her.

*My brain better be smarter than that.*

He stripped off his jeans and sweatshirt to put on the boxers and T-shirt, his thoughts still circling the dilemma. They kept at it while he brushed his teeth, as he turned off the light, and when he slipped under the covers. Rolling to his side to find a comfortable position, he gave in to the urge to place his palm against the wall between him and his boss. The most important issue that might pose a problem was she hadn't shown any discernible sign of being attracted to him.

*Well, damn.*

# Chapter 5

*Bzzzzz.*

Lilith groaned and smacked the snooze button.

*Forget snooze. Where's the stupid* off *button?*

How could she have forgotten to turn off her alarm before she'd gone to bed last night?

*The only day of the week I don't have to get up early for work, and I don't even get to sleep in.*

She rolled over and yanked on the blankets to bury her head. "Ow!"

Returning to her left side, she winced at the ache in her right hip. With the pain came the memory of last night's sidewalk crash with Flynn Hastings and his gigantic mattress.

*Oh God. He touched my naked butt.*

He must've tucked her in bed as well—and she'd slept through it. A quick assessment of what she wore beneath the covers confirmed he hadn't taken the liberty of removing her clothes. He'd also pulled up her pants at some point. She ought to be grateful for that, but waking up next to a hunky chef would've been better than apple pie and carrot cake for breakfast.

*I'll never learn, will I? Hormones and common sense don't mix.*

Giving up on going back to sleep, she eased out of bed, careful not to put any pressure on the sore spot. The walk to the bathroom hurt less than she expected, and a peek in the mirror told her exactly what part of her body she'd fallen on. A mottled patch of blue and purple the size of a softball adorned the side of her pale butt cheek. Green and yellow would likely join the rainbow in a few days.

*Wonderful. I won't be able to sit for a week.*

As she tossed the last of her slept-in clothes in the hamper, she twisted the faucet handle to hot and then waited for steam to rise from the shower. If the warm spray soothed the stiffness from her muscles, maybe she'd get to mark off some of her weekend to-do list. Laundry didn't require sitting. Nor did sweeping, and she could write bills standing at the kitchen counter. A trip to the dry cleaner, a quick stop for groceries, and a run to the post office would mean driving—and sitting. Unless her bruise healed really fast, errands would have to wait for another day.

Water sluiced over her skin as she washed and rinsed, soothing away some of the stress.

*The world won't end if I don't get everything done.*

She shut off the shower and grabbed her towel. After a gentle pat dry, she slid back the curtain and steadied herself with a hand against the wall to step out of the tub. With her luck, she'd fall and hit her head if she didn't hold on to something. Exactly what she didn't need—more bumps and bruises. A hunky Irish chef wouldn't be around to save her, either.

*Damn it. I have stop thinking about him.*

One of these days she'd have to learn how to stifle her attraction to men in uniform. Flynn might not be a bad guy, but she liked her simple life too much to add complications on purpose.

Donning her robe, she headed to the bedroom to get dressed. Her baggiest yoga pants called her name as she sifted through her dresser drawer. She certainly didn't have anyone to impress.

With laundry first on her list, she bent to slide the full basket out of her closet. As she grabbed the handle, a knock sounded on her apartment door.

*What now?*

She straightened, sending a jolt of pain through her backside. Another dose of ibuprofen was muscling its way to the top of her inventory of things to do.

Abandoning the dirty clothes, she hobbled to the front door. A peek out the peephole made her shoulders slump and her tummy somersault.

Her new neighbor stood outside with a casserole dish held out like a peace offering. He should've appeared less appealing with the flower-print oven mitts covering his hands, but nothing seemed to tone down his masculinity.

*I'll never survive seeing him every day.*

She opened the door and tried for a friendly greeting. "Good morning, Mr. Hastings."

The scent of brown sugar and cinnamon assaulted her nose, taste buds, and empty stomach.

He extended his arms, the hesitation in his expression weakening her willpower. "Just Flynn. G'morning. I brought breakfast for you. I didn't figure you'd be up to doing much with the sore hip."

How could she refuse the gift of such a thoughtful man?

"It's just a bruise. You didn't have to go to all that trouble."

"Yeah, I did. That bruise is my fault, and I plan to make up for it. Besides, breakfast was no trouble. I had to eat anyway." He stepped inside when she gestured for him to enter. "I'm cooking for you today and whatever else you shouldn't be doing. Your apartment is spotless, but you probably planned to wash clothes or get groceries."

Did the guy read minds?

Lilith led him to the kitchen—not that she'd risk eating with him in the same room. She might not have experienced foodgasms last night from his chicken and pork dishes, but she also hadn't imagined the contractions ripping through her reproductive system from eating the salmon and pasta he'd prepared.

Should she have waited until he'd disappeared into the kitchen yesterday instead of wolfing down the entrées as he walked away? What if he had to be present for those shockingly satisfying mini-orgasms to happen?

She wasn't about to subject herself to that embarrassment again.

*Now, the sexual kind of orgasm is a different story. He can give me as many of those as he wants.*

*No.*

*No, no, no.*

*Not going there. Under any circumstances.*

He set the dish on the stove and lifted the lid. "I hope you like oatmeal. I didn't have a lot on hand to make anything fancy, but Fried Steelies is one of my favorites. This is my grandma's recipe. I usually make a hash to go with it. No fresh corned beef, though. I need to pick up some supplies later. If you have a list, I'll get your stuff too."

She almost choked. "Um. Yes, I like oatmeal."

Hadn't she fantasized about sharing a steel-cut oats and corned beef hash breakfast with him?

*I'm in so much trouble.*

Pulling open cupboard doors and drawers, he took out a plate, a fork, and a serving spoon. "I'll plate it for you. Then I need to go get my helpers so I can finish cleaning out my storage unit. When I'm done moving in, I'll stop by to see what else you need help with."

Disappointment overpowered relief. He was leaving instead of eating with her, and he was coming back.

*Stupid confused hormones.* "You don't have to do that."

He set the plate and fork on the table. "I don't *have* to. I *want* to." He slid back the chair. "Come sit down and eat."

Obeying his request, she crossed the room to ease down onto the seat.

She flinched when her bottom made contact. "I have bills to write. I can eat at the counter while I work."

Flynn frowned at her. "It still hurts. You can stand to eat, but I'm coming back to help when I'm done. Three hours at the most. And you're welcome to seconds if you want more."

She reached for her dish to move it to the counter, but he beat her to it. He searched the cupboards again, this time pulling out a glass. The refrigerator got scrutinized next. "Orange, cranberry, or grapefruit juice?"

His generosity and thoughtfulness unnerved her. No man she'd ever been attracted to had offered to do things for her. They always wanted her to do everything for them or expected something in return.

Why did Flynn have to be so damn perfect? Or worse yet, what did he want in exchange for being nice?

She swallowed a sigh. Her ricocheting thoughts were giving her a headache. "Grapefruit please."

"Your wish is my command." He poured juice in the glass next to her breakfast. Then he snapped a business card down beside the plate. "I should get going. I told the boys I'd pick them up at eight. My cell number's there if you need anything while I'm gone."

"Okay. Thanks." Too confused by his behavior, she could only stare after him as he waved and headed through the living room.

Taking a bite of the fried oatmeal, she followed his progress toward the exit. A contraction tore through her middle when the lightly sweet flavor of brown sugar and steel-cut oats burst onto her tongue. She squeaked in response as the front door clicked closed, hoping the cry that wanted out stayed put until her magical chef was out of hearing range.

*Five, four, three, two, one.* "Oh my."

A shiver rippled through her veins, and she drew in a shaky breath. Maybe yesterday's uterine tremors during the tasting hadn't been a fluke. A drink of tart grapefruit juice acted as a quick jolt of reality. She cut off another crispy corner of the triangular piece of inch-thick oatmeal and tucked it in her mouth before she lost her nerve.

Hints of cinnamon powered through this time, but her body didn't react with a blissful spasm. She chewed, swallowed, and finally waited. Nothing—the same as her encounter with last night's chicken and pork samples.

*Well, that's interesting.*

Evidently, Flynn's food had the power to give her orgasms when he was present, but not when he was gone. She'd have to test that hypothesis again after she recovered from the latest attack of food-and-chef lust.

Would she have to hide in the pantry in the complex's kitchen while he was cooking for definitive proof?

She finished the serving he'd dished up for her, savoring every morsel. While she didn't have another foodgasm, she enjoyed the pleasurable dining experience. He was a fabulous chef, and the residents of Montgomery Crossing would love the new restaurant option.

*Hmm… Do all women react the way I do to his food?*

*Uh-oh. What if Mrs. Underwood's pacemaker short-circuits?*

Why did one solution always lead to another problem?

\* \* \* \*

Shooing the motel manager's son and his friend back to the truck, Flynn raised his fist to rap on Lilith's door. She hadn't seemed angry or upset about the mishap on the sidewalk. In fact, her attitude toward the accident surprised him. Most people would've been pissed off and ready to sue, but she'd downplayed his carelessness. If he was lucky, she'd allow him to make amends.

*See. I can do friends instead of girlfriend.*

He tapped on her door.

Several seconds passed before she answered. Her argument began before the door was fully open. "You know, I really don't expect you to—"

He put up his hand to halt her objection. "I feel bad for knocking you down. Let me soothe my conscience, okay?"

Shaking her head, she gave a dramatic sigh. "Okay. I suppose having some help isn't such a bad thing."

"Nope, help is good. I'm headed to the grocery store. I'll be glad to get whatever you need. Do you have a list?"

"Yeah. Come on in." When she limped toward the kitchen, he trailed after her. "Are you finished moving?"

"Yep." He stopped at the archway and leaned against the wall. "Do you need me to run any other errands for you?"

Her brief hesitation told him she did. "You don't—"

"I know I don't have to. I'm offering." He stuffed his hands in the back pockets of his jeans. "You shouldn't be driving if you can't sit comfortably."

"I'm not used to anybody taking care of me. It's usually the other way around." Wielding up a pencil, she jotted some notes on a notepad. "Are you sure you don't mind?"

A satisfied grin tickled his mouth, but he held it in. He'd won this round. That probably wouldn't happen often. "I'm sure. How'd you like the oatmeal?"

She opened the fridge and peered inside. "Different, but in a good way. Probably reheats better than regular cooked oatmeal. Have you ever tried it with a fruit compote topping?"

"Yeah. I've made a few different combinations. I think I like golden raisins and dried cranberries best, but a mix of peaches and pears is good, too. For the breakfast menu, plain oatmeal is one of the options, with a choice of toppings to accommodate the no-sugar and low-sugar diets." For the first time in months, he was excited to talk about food. Or maybe he liked talking to *Lilith* about food. She actually showed interest in the topic beyond discussing whether or not something on the menu would sell. "What else was on your agenda for today? I can carry your baskets to the laundry room if today is wash day."

She looked at him over her shoulder. "I only have one load. Most of my work clothes are dry clean only."

"I can drop off those on my way to get groceries—*after* I carry one basket of dirty clothes to the laundry room for you. Anything else?"

Closing the refrigerator with her knee, she added to her list. "Are you sure you have time to run errands for me? You must have boxes to unpack and furniture to arrange."

He moved away from the wall, grasping her by the shoulders to look her in the eyes. "I'm sure. What else is on your list, Lilith?"

She blinked up at him, and her muscles tensed beneath his fingertips. Her tongue slipped out to moisten her lips, triggering a crushing impulse to kiss her. She nibbled on her lower lip and caution seemed to dim the light in her eyes. "Stamps. I need stamps."

Dropping his hands and backing off, he squashed the urge to get closer. He shouldn't have touched her again. "No problem. I need to fill out a change of address form, so I can do that at the same time."

"Great." Her backward step suggested she agreed with his choice to put some physical distance between them. "Thanks."

He accepted the sheet of paper she tore from the notepad, careful to avoid making contact with her fingertips. A quick glance told him she'd included all the errands they'd discussed as well as a dozen or so items she needed from the store. "I should get going. Where's your laundry?"

"Um, in the bedroom." She started forward and then hesitated.

Was she afraid to squeeze past him?

*Maybe the attraction isn't one-sided after all.*

He shifted sideways to let her through the doorway and then followed her into the room where he'd felt her up last night.

*To explain or not to explain?*

"About yesterday. You know when…" *I pulled your pants down and pawed your ass? Geesh, no.* "I planned to become a doctor before I decided to go to culinary school. Four years of pre-med and a year of med. My first instinct was to check for injuries. I'm sorry if I offended you by…touching. I swear my intentions were purely medical."

*Too bad I let my dick intrude on my chivalry.*

She spun around. "A doctor? Really? I guess that explains your knowledge about nutrition and dietary restrictions in the menu. As for the other, I guess you were just, you know, doing what you needed to do. Nice to know I was in good hands." A pretty blush colored her cheeks, and she snorted a laugh. "Awkward choice of words. What made you change your mind?"

Unable to hold in a chuckle at her gaffe, Flynn let go of the tension in his shoulders. "My dad and my grandpa are both doctors, and I thought I had to live up to that legacy. I handled the classes all right, but my first year of med school taught me I wasn't cut out for the pressure of life and death decisions. I'm much more comfortable chopping vegetables than I would be slicing open patients."

"Your family was okay with you changing directions, I hope." She bent to lift a basket of laundry, but he slid it out of her reach with his foot.

"I'll get the basket. Where're the things that need to go to the dry cleaner?" Hefting the load, he turned toward the bed. "My oldest sister stuck up for me, although nobody gave me a hard time about quitting the program. They've always been supportive."

Pointing to another basket stacked full of neatly folded suits inside the closet, Lilith finally seemed to concede to his appeal that she take the day off. "The best kind of family to have. Besides, you're very good at what you do."

"Thanks." He leaned in to retrieve the clothes. Next to them lay a pile of sheer stockings, lace panties, and colored bras.

*Thirty-four double D. Damn.*

Her ruffly blouse and hooded sweatshirts disguised her breasts well.

He itched to rub the silky cups between his fingertips, and he had to clear his throat to speak. "What about the rest of the laundry in here?"

"Oh, shit. My hand washables." She grabbed the belt loop at the center back of his jeans. "Get out of there! You already saw my underwear and my ass. You don't need to know my bra size."

He pressed his lips together to keep from busting out laughing as he straightened.

*Too late, Lilith. And you can be damn sure I won't be forgetting it any time soon.*

"You looked, didn't you?"

Unable to lie to her, he shrugged. "I didn't mean to. The print on the band was laying there for anybody to see." He swiveled to face her. "It's just a number and a couple letters. No big deal."

She gasped. "*No big deal?* How would you like it if men's underwear had numbers for the length of your cock and letters to tell how big your balls are?"

Her blunt language surprised him, giving him another glimpse of her less-than-prim side. Temptation to drop his drawers and show her his eight double Bs almost won out over common sense. He needed to get the hell out of there before he offered to let her touch his bare butt to even the score. That was a surefire way to get kicked out and fired.

*Time for an apology.*

"You're right. I shouldn't have looked, and I don't think most men would want to advertise the size of their *packages*." He scooted the second basket out of the closet. "I'm thinking of testing a recipe I've been tweaking. Dark Chocolate Pound Cake. Want to be my guinea pig this afternoon?"

Her gaze went from hopeful to narrowed in a fraction of a second. "You're not trying to bribe me, are you?"

He hefted the baskets. "Damn right I am."

# Chapter 6

Clutching her keys, Lilith shoved her feet into her running shoes and rushed after Flynn, not an easy task between untied laces and his long strides. At least she was treated to an unobstructed view of his spectacular backside as she tripped along the sidewalk. The man filled out a pair of jeans and a T-shirt every bit as well as his chef whites.

She caught up with him only because he stopped halfway down the building. "I'm not going to fire you for looking at my bras. Not showing up to work on time and serving garbage for food? Yeah. Being disrespectful of the residents? I'll come after you with an iron skillet."

His left cheek dipped inward, betraying the amusement he almost certainly held back. "I don't doubt it for a minute. The bra thing was an accident, I swear. And it's not like I haven't seen women's underwear before. I grew up with three older sisters." He lifted an elbow toward the entrance to the laundry room. "If you'll get the door, I'll carry your basket inside."

She turned the knob and entered the lounge area, taking full advantage of the opportunity to talk about something other than her undies. "You can set it on the table next to the dryer."

He walked past her. "Nice place. I half expected a concrete floor, cinder-block walls, and a bare light bulb. Damn! These are real washers and dryers. Why not the coin-operated kind?"

She followed him into the adjoining tiled workspace. "Repairs and maintenance on the machines are included in the rent. It's easier than dealing with all those quarters. Besides, with only six of us in the building, we didn't really need commercial-grade equipment." Unlocking the cabinet marked with the number five, she wanted to hug him for turning the conversation to business—except then he'd be too close again. The bottle of detergent almost slipped from her grasp at the prospect. "Everybody has their own storage cabinet, so all you have to bring is your dirty clothes. I'm not sure if I told you, but the two smaller keys I gave you yesterday are for this lock and your mailbox."

"Okay, good to know." He took a step into the lounge area with her basket of dry cleaning. "I better get going. You'll take it easy while I'm gone?"

"You're doing half the stuff on my to-do list. I couldn't work too hard if I wanted to."

At the wave of her hand encouraging him to leave, he shook his head and walked out the door. The fit of the denim across his tight butt stayed with her while she loaded the washing machine and set it to wash. Checking the clock on the wall, she calculated a half hour and then limped back to her apartment.

*One item done on my list.*

She entered her kitchen, intent on crossing off "laundry," but the counter was bare. What had she done with her list?

*I'm going senile. Flynn has it.*

More likely, her brain was too preoccupied with his pheromones to think straight.

Since she repeated the same routine almost every Saturday, she didn't really need a piece of paper to tell her what to do. Crossing items off a list simply gave her a tangible sense of accomplishment—and reminded her to rely on herself.

*Laundry, bills, vacuuming. Grocery shopping, post office, dry cleaning.*

Flynn's volunteering left her with sweeping and paying bills. Breakfast had distracted her from doing the second, but she wasn't about to complain. If she hurried, she'd get both done before he returned. She might even have all her underwear, stockings, and camis washed in the sink by the time he finished his half of her chores—not that he hadn't already seen more of her and her underthings in less than a day than any man in the past year. Too bad she hadn't gotten any sexual satisfaction out of it. Of course, his food had given her a fair share, even if no physical contact had been involved.

Her poor body was so confused. It couldn't tell the difference between artificial orgasms and real ones. Maybe she needed to give up her plastic playmates *and* gourmet meals, in hopes of setting her uterus straight. Men had rarely satisfied her. When they had, it had been by pure coincidence and always a bit disappointing. While she had all the proper parts, they didn't seem to work very well with the opposite sex. Masturbation and toys had proven she wasn't completely incapable of achieving the ultimate high, and Flynn's cooking had hit the spot.

Perhaps the biggest problem stemmed from the worry that if she *did* have sex with him, the act wouldn't meet her expectations. Or that it would.

Could she fake enough pleasure to convince him, or any other man, she'd enjoyed their encounter?

*I need therapy.*

Unfortunately, the only sex therapist she knew was the retired Dr. France Ito in apartment 2C. Lilith had no desire to reveal her problems to a ninety-year-old woman who offered prophylactics and free advice on how to spice up sex lives to couples living in the complex. Confidentiality wouldn't be an issue if France remembered to turn up the volume on her hearing aide. More often than not, she didn't, though, leaving no conversation private to the ears of the well-meaning matchmakers and busybodies of Montgomery Crossing.

Pulling her checkbook and the past week's bills from the basket in the cupboard, Lilith set to work. Her sexual problems weren't on the list of things to deal with today.

A knock on her front door interrupted her halfway through the task, and she finished her signature before going to look through the peephole. CC's wife stood on the sidewalk.

Lilith opened the door. "Hi, Alice. How was the party last night?"

The pink-haired woman wiggled her hips. "Terrific! I won the limbo contest. 'Course it helps, me being only five feet tall. Mind if I come in for a quick visit?"

"Of course not." Lilith gestured for Alice to enter. "Wanda said the mammogram drive was a huge success."

Speeding into the living room at a power-walk pace, Alice fluffed her teased fuchsia hairdo. "Yep, but I didn't come here to talk about boobies. Well, I suppose I did, indirectly. Who's the hunk? And did you see any action?"

"Hunk?" A tickle in Lilith's tummy had her brushing invisible lint from her sleeve.

"Yeah, the hot guy who moved in next door to you. Boy, I'd like a peek or two at his abs. I bet he's ripped. Is he?"

"Uh, I don't know."

"You don't know his name? Or you haven't seen him with his shirt off yet? 'Cause I noticed him leaving here kinda late last night. *Long* after your bedroom light went out." Alice's twinkling eyes widened. "Is he good in the sack? Man, I'd leave the lights on with that fella."

"Alice!" Lilith straightened the lamp on the end table. "He's the new chef, and, no, I didn't sleep with him!"

"Well, hell, honey. Why not? And I already know you hired him to run the restaurant. CC gave us the scoop last night when he got back from the freelance plumbing job. What's his name?" The older woman leaned in close. "He's a hottie, but don't tell CC I said so. He thinks I shouldn't appreciate young studs. Like he doesn't ogle those girls in my Victoria's Secret catalogs, and I'd bet my next orgasm he talked Bonnie into a hug. God, I love that dirty old man."

The results of the interviews had obviously made the rounds. "His name is Flynn Hastings, and he's starting Monday morning. I had a little accident last night. He was just making sure I was okay. And hottie or not, he's my co-worker now."

Alice rolled her eyes. "So? I was CC's office manager when we started dating. And I know Wade would approve of a strapping Irish lad for his Lily."

"You don't understand, Alice." Lilith barely resisted stomping her foot. "He was the only one interested in the job that I was willing to hire. I'm not risking one of us having to quit when the fling is over. Not that I want to have a fling."

"I know that, Lily honey." Propping her hands on her hips, Alice pursed her lips. "You need to be hunting for a man you want for the long haul. Although taking a few test drives is a good idea. Nice to know what's under the hood. Anywho, this Chef Flynn Hastings—great name, by the way—he must be an okay guy if you decided to hire him."

"Yes, he's polite and considerate. A nice person. I think everybody will like him."

"What about *you*? Do *you* like him?"

Lilith's stomach somersaulted. "Well, yes. He's a nice man and an excellent chef."

Why couldn't she think of another word besides "nice"?

Alice gave an impatient-sounding grunt. "But do you *like*-like him? You would've shown him the exit if he was rude or couldn't cook worth a damn."

*Can I plead the fifth?*

How could she answer the question without making her attraction known?

"Come on, Alice. I have eyes. The man is good-looking and built. How could I not notice?"

Alice's mini-bouffant wiggled when she shook her head. "You're in denial, girl. You think you can't have him, so you won't even judge him like an eligible bachelor. I'm telling you, if you don't snap him up, somebody else will. Then what'll you do?"

The somersault in her belly became a full-twisting dive to her knees.

Lilith marched to the coat closet to retrieve her vacuum cleaner. "I'm not going after a man just to stop some other woman from getting him first. Besides, what makes you think Flynn even likes *me*? He might already have a girlfriend. Have you thought of that? Or he could be engaged, you know. It's not like men wear engagement rings."

Alice snorted, probably at the desperate attempt at reason. "Like I said, you're in denial. He stood staring at your closed door for a good minute last night after he left. The man is thinking about *you*, so he damn well better not have a girlfriend or a fiancée."

Snuffing out the immediate flicker of hope, Lilith unwound the power cord and dragged it by the plug to the nearest outlet. "It doesn't matter. I'm not getting involved with someone I work with."

With a shrug, Alice stepped toward the door. "Suit yourself."

"I'll put copies of the menu in the game room this afternoon." Tapping the handle release with her foot, Lilith waited for her guest to give her customary wave.

"I'll pass the word." Alice's right hand came up as she grabbed for the knob with her left. Two seconds later, she was gone.

Her words echoed in Lilith's head while she swept the living room and bedroom. *"The man is thinking about you."*

What would she do if he really did like her? What if he asked her out? Would she have the strength to decline?

\* \* \* \*

Shoving the truck door closed with his foot, Flynn thumbed the lock icon of his key—not an easy feat while holding six sacks of groceries in one hand while grasping three more and an empty laundry basket in the other. He walked along the sidewalk fronting Building C, hoping none of the straps on the cloth bags broke.

Almost an hour and a half had passed since he'd left Lilith alone with her laundry. Chances were the clothes were washed, dried, and folded by now. Even knowing her as little as he did, he didn't doubt for a second that she'd try to carry the full basket back to her apartment rather than wait for him. He'd probably hit the jackpot by getting her to let him help her with the errands and the trip to the washing machine.

She was used to being the one to offer assistance. She'd admitted as much. Accepting his help hadn't been easy for her, and she wouldn't do it often. That meant he'd have to take advantage of the rare opportunity to do so, to show her he was interested in friendship rather than getting laid.

He turned the corner to cut between the singles buildings, spying her swaying ass as she hobbled down the sidewalk toward her apartment. Damn, if she didn't have a stack of clothes in her arms.

*Independent is a hell of a lot better than needy.*

"Going somewhere with that laundry, lady?" He couldn't keep the laugh from his chastisement.

Whirling around, she nearly dropped the pile of clothes. "You weren't supposed to catch me in the act. I could've told you somebody else—"

"You would've lied to me?" He feigned a wounded expression as he closed the space between them. "I bet you never lie, except to keep from hurting someone's feelings."

She unlocked her door, pushing it open as she turned the key. "No, I wouldn't have lied to you, but I might've changed the subject so I didn't incriminate myself."

"Devious. You want your groceries on the table or the counter?"

"On the counter's fine." Her call from the bedroom struck an interesting chord.

They sounded like long-time friends or lovers with their comfortable teasing. She didn't seem like a woman he'd met less than a day ago, and the comfort level pushed too many of the right buttons.

He set the bags on the counter and then shifted his keys to his free hand. The sooner he got out of there, the better his chances of keeping his intentions in line. "Stamps are in with the bread and your dry cleaning will be ready on Tuesday."

"Thanks." Her quiet word of appreciation as she came out of the bedroom slowed his progress to the front door. "Will you let me make you lunch? You really didn't have to go to so much trouble."

He shrugged, not willing to start an argument over his offer of help. "No trouble. Lunch? I was supposed to be feeding you today, but sure. What time?"

"Twelve thirty? I'd like to go over the menu one more time. I promised the residents I'd have copies available in the game room this afternoon."

Why did the idea of a working lunch bother him? Was she just going out of her way to make him feel welcome?

He couldn't read the motive in her eyes, but maybe it was just as well. He couldn't act on an attraction that he wasn't certain existed.

*Act on the attraction? Didn't I decide not to mix business with pleasure?*

She was giving him a chance to build their working relationship, and all he could think about was getting personal. "I have the menu in a spreadsheet on my computer. While you make lunch, I'll make the changes we talked about yesterday and e-mail the document to you. That way you can print as many copies as you need. We could even put it into a menu template if you want."

Her frown confounded him.

Had he said something wrong?

Crossing her arms under her breasts, she tilted her head to the right. "Can I ask you something?"

He shrugged. "Yeah, I guess."

"Why are being so nice? And helpful? You're not even officially on the payroll until Monday."

The better question was why would she expect anything less from him.

"I'm taking the job seriously because I want to make a good impression. It's my menu we're throwing out there for target practice, but you made the decision to hire me. Everything to do with the restaurant reflects on both of us, even though I'm responsible for making sure the residents like what I present. Besides, I doubt you want to spend the weekend doing your job *and* mine."

"Technically, neither one of us is supposed to be working." She bit her lower lip, as though she was holding in a smirk. "I won't tell if you don't. And I appreciate your dedication."

The smile won, spreading across her face to light up her pretty eyes and make his heart skip a beat. His platonic intentions didn't stand a chance if he didn't get the hell out of there. He'd have to find a way to get over the infatuation damn quick if he expected to keep his dream job. A little distance from her would be a good thing.

Adjusting his grip on his grocery bags, he reached for the doorknob with his free hand. "I should dedicate some time to putting away my groceries before lunch. See you in about a half hour?"

She blinked at him, her mood seeming to dim. "Sure. Thanks for everything."

Not giving himself a chance to analyze the tightening in his gut or the apparent change in her disposition, he turned the knob and stepped outside. He pulled the door closed behind him, effectively ending the conversation until he returned. If he was smart, he'd find an excuse to avoid having lunch with her and simply plug his menu into the template and e-mail it to her. All she'd have to do is print as many copies as she wanted.

He jabbed the key into the lock of his own apartment door. The solution was easy.

As he entered his new home, he tossed his keys on the couch. No attraction to a woman he'd met less than twenty-four hours ago could be anything other than physical. Lilith was his ideal woman.

Why wouldn't he have that normal reaction?

So what if she was also intelligent and sweet?

Any guy who'd gone without sex as long as he had would want to get laid. He was more selective than a lot of men he knew, but the biological need was still there.

Entering the kitchen, he eyed the cluttered counter. He'd have to finish stowing his cookware and gadgets at some point. As he stocked the fridge and the cabinets, Lilith continued to invade his thoughts. Memories of her silky skin made his fingertips itch, and his imagination succeeded in imprinting a picture of her thirty-four double-D breasts on his brain. Real or not, the image provoked his long-neglected sex drive.

He closed the pantry. Lunch with Lilith was out of question. He'd end up kissing her.

*Uh-huh.*

Considering how much time he'd spent thinking about her since yesterday afternoon, a make-out session was likely a conservative estimate of what would happen if they tweaked the menu together on her couch.

Stepping back was a hell of a lot smarter than putting his hand in the cookie jar.

# Chapter 7

*When will I learn?*

Pursing her lips, Lilith chopped another handful of dried cranberries. She shouldn't have invited Flynn to lunch, even if her menu-related excuse was logical. His chef persona had weakened the immunity she'd built up against men. Although he seemed helpful, kind, and conscientious, he could easily have her fooled. He wouldn't be the first.

*Or the second.*

*Not even the third.*

She scooped the fruit off the cutting board and dropped it in the bowl. Next, she grated fresh orange peel on top of the cranberries and added a couple dollops of low-fat mayonnaise before gently folding the final ingredients into the mix of roasted chicken breast, chopped celery, and walnut pieces. With the lid snapped into place, she put the bowl in the refrigerator.

A quick stir of the leftover soup on the range kept her from checking the clock. She had plenty of time to send Uncle Wade a message about the new chef and not nearly enough time to get her hormones under control before Flynn Hastings returned.

Standing at the counter, she powered up her computer to e-mail the man who'd instigated the whole restaurant mess. If he hadn't raised her like his own daughter, she'd find incredible satisfaction in seeing his toupee-ed head on a platter.

She logged on and waited for the usual assortment of spam to appear. The list of new messages in her inbox popped up, the top one with a vaguely familiar address. She glanced to the subject line.

*Menu?*

Curious about the contents, she clicked on the e-mail.

*"Ms. Montgomery, something came up and I won't be able to come over for lunch."*

Disappointment stung before she could gather irritation at Flynn for cancelling. Of course he was leaving her in the lurch without the menu. She should've expected it.

With her fingers poised over the keyboard to hit Reply and type a scathing answer, she skimmed the rest of the message.

*"I put the menu into a template and attached the file. I've also included the plain document in case you don't like the design I used. Since the kitchen is missing a few ingredients I need early in the week, I'll pick them up and turn in the receipts. Call or text my cell if you have any questions. Flynn"*

A pair of paper clips with names next to them jumped out at her from below the "From" and "To" section. Maybe he wasn't irresponsible and inconsiderate, but she was still better off not seeing him on a semi-social basis.

She downloaded the files and opened the menu in hopes of finding something she didn't like about it. The large, bold print on a wheat-colored background would be easy to read. A loaf of whole-grain bread on a cutting board and a colorful mix of fruits and vegetables formed a pleasant border along the bottom of the page. The stupid thing was perfect—exactly what she'd had in mind.

*He* was too damn perfect.

No one was without flaws, though. His were simply well hidden.

Making a trip to her bedroom, she set the computer on the desk. If she had to eat lunch all by herself, she'd multitask by making a sandwich and ladling a bowl of soup while the printer spit out enough copies for everyone in the complex.

Alone didn't have to mean lonely. She was used to spending much of her free time in her own company. A man with a light Irish brogue and loads of charm was the last kind of complication she needed in her personal life.

*Crap. He even made me forget about e-mailing Uncle Wade.*

Yes, she was far better off having been pushed aside rather than getting involved with the new chef. She got the copies started and then limped back to the kitchen.

Taking a loaf of rye from the bread box, she focused on making her lunch. She'd have enough leftover chicken salad to last several days, avoiding the possibility of having to eat Flynn's food in front of him.

*Eat in front of him? Never again!*

He'd probably saved her the embarrassment of having an orgasm during their business meal. Sure, she enjoyed getting off as much as the next girl, but yesterday's experience had been humiliating enough to last several months. He wasn't exactly *trying* to make her body react like a naughty little sex fiend, though. In fact, other than the comment about stockings during the interview, he hadn't shown any romantic, or even sexual, interest in her.

Then why was the cancellation affecting her like a broken date?

*Because he isn't interested and I am. Ever the fool.*

If Flynn had stood staring at her door last night, he was most likely worrying about whether she planned to sue him for running over her with his mammoth mattress. The man probably preferred women with fewer curves anyway. He'd seen her naked butt and her bra size, and he'd carried her into her apartment. Even with his build, he wouldn't mistake her for a willowy woman.

Alice had been mistaken.

Topping the chicken salad with a few spinach leaves, Lilith slapped on the top slice of seedless rye and cut the sandwich into two equal triangles. She arranged the halves on a paper plate before ladling a serving of homemade lentil soup into the old chipped cereal bowl she'd used as a kid. Eating her own food alone hardly warranted breaking out the fine china. With no choice but to stand or lie on her stomach on the floor to eat, she opted to remain at the kitchen counter.

The printer clicked and hummed in the bedroom, the sound familiar and soothing. She bit into the sandwich. Comfort food took precedence over everything else at the moment. She didn't let life get her down often, but getting stood up was the last straw after a week from hell.

*Stood up? Right. That would imply I'm actually considering going out with Flynn—which I wouldn't—or that he'd invite me.*

Besides, Norma Reed's situation was far more dire in the grand scheme of things than whether or not Lilith had a date. The poor woman didn't deserve the horrible disease stealing her memories and the irreplaceable connection with her husband. Someday soon, Norma would become a shadow of herself, looking the same but ceasing to exist.

Taking another bite of sandwich, Lilith glanced toward the bedroom with teary eyes. The residents were expecting the menus, and dwelling on the unfairness of reality wouldn't change it.

She debated putting off e-mailing her uncle as she retrieved the copies. Her mood was hardly conducive to typing in a polite message. He deserved a few choice words, but not today.

*Best to get it done.*

*"Hi, Uncle Wade. I've hired a chef. He's agreed to start Monday. The contract is signed and the payroll withholding form completed. He opted for the employee apartment and has moved in. See you tomorrow*

*afternoon. Lily"*

Since short and to the point was her style, he wouldn't read any of her aggravation and frustration in the words. She clicked Send and waited for confirmation as she opened the freezer door. Hidden behind the bag of frozen cranberries Flynn had used for an icepack was the last slice of white chocolate-raspberry cheesecake from an impulse baking binge three months ago. She'd earned it, and she could work it off at the gym after her visit to Uncle Wade. Maybe by then her hip wouldn't hurt every time she moved.

After transferring the wedge of calorie-laden heaven to the fridge, she cleaned up her lunch mess and downed another dose of ibuprofen. A quick trip to the game room with the menus would give the pain medicine a few minutes to kick in so she could take a nap. She didn't have anything better to do since her to-do list had been hijacked.

The brisk fall air stiffened her already achy muscles, making her wish she'd forgone the drugs in lieu of a hot toddy once she returned to her apartment. She fought with the breeze to keep hold of the file folder of menus.

"Hello, Lily dear." Dr. Ito waved from one of the chairs on the covered patio. "Join me for a minute?"

Lilith nodded and hobbled through the gate to enter the sheltered area.

"I won't ask you to sit since Alice said you had a little mishap last night. Limping, I see. You should be home resting." The old woman tucked a few strands of silvery blue hair back into her long braid and tsked. "I'm of a mind to tell that young man he owes you a nice relaxing massage. An orgasm or two wouldn't hurt, either. A good release of endorphins would ease the pain. Much better than resorting to popping pills."

Biting the inside of her cheek to keep from groaning, Lilith cursed her pale complexion. "Um, I'm sure he's busy…unpacking or something."

"He left about twenty minutes ago. I watched him hurry down the sidewalk like a ghost was after him." Dr. Ito frowned. "He's a good-looking man. You didn't chase him off, did you?"

Why couldn't the people she adored stop trying to fix her up with every single guy that set foot on the grounds?

"We were supposed to go over the final draft of the menu over lunch, but he canceled. Does that sound like I chased him off? Not that I'm comfortable cavorting with someone I work with."

"Cavorting. Pish. I didn't mean for you to have a one-night stand with him. You're not exactly the type of woman to sleep around. You need a steady diet of faithful man and hot sex." The old woman reached into the pocket of her jogging suit and pulled out a strip of condoms. She forced them into Lilith's grasp. "Use these. You won't regret it."

Lilith stuffed them in her coat pocket. "Okay. Sure. I have to go now. Work to do."

Another *tsk* carried to her ears as she exited the gate. It banged shut behind her, sending her heart racing even faster than it had with the suggestion to invite Flynn into her bed. After dropping off the menus in the game room, she walked back home for her nap, taking the long way around the complex to avoid another helpful bit of advice.

*Bit of advice? More like order. How am I going to survive working with him five days a week and living next to him seven?*

She didn't possess the willpower to refuse white chocolate-raspberry cheesecake. How would she abstain from lusting after her new chef?

\* \* \* \*

*I can do this.*

Stopping across the street from his destination, Flynn took a few seconds to calm his nerves. Drew had seemed genuinely excited to hear from him, promising a spur-of-the-moment visit wouldn't interfere with his and the girls' plans. Little girl giggles in the background during the phone call had taken Flynn back to his childhood, to growing up with three of the best sisters a little brother could've had. Kate might not be with them anymore, but not a day went by that he didn't think of her. At least he'd finally come to terms with the regrets and guilt. He couldn't have saved her.

*Life isn't necessarily fair.*

He turned into the driveway of the two-story colonial, pulling in one last slow breath as he shut off the engine. Before he could open the door, two squealing voices shattered the silence.

"Uncle Flynn! You're here!" Ten-year-old Kristin yanked on the handle, jumping up and wrapping her arms around his neck when the door swung open. Her ponytail swept across his cheek, and he combed his fingers through it.

Little sister, Hannah, crowded in next to her, practically climbing on his lap. "Look, Uncle Flynn! I got my new front teeth!"

Closing his eyes, he gathered them both in a hug and savored the fact that they remembered him with such affection. He'd abandoned them when they'd needed him the most. "You sure did. I missed you. Both of you."

"Hey, munchkins, aren't you going to let Uncle Flynn get out of his truck?" Drew's teasing started the girls chattering again, and Flynn forced his eyes to meet Drew's gaze. The sadness had faded since the last time they'd seen each other.

The memory made Flynn's gut twist, and he tried to banish the reflection of the family interring his sister in the ground. After her burial, he hadn't bothered to say goodbye to his family. He'd simply walked out. Apologies for keeping her secret wouldn't bring her back or give him another day, week, or month with her.

The year of no contact had been hell, and he'd never get it back to enjoy all he'd missed.

Kristin and Hannah scrambled out of the way, allowing Flynn to slide out of the seat. He extended his hand to his brother-in-law. "Hey. How have you been?"

Drew took it, and the handshake segued into a slightly awkward hug with lots of back patting. He smiled as he let go and stepped back. "We're doing okay. You?"

"I'm getting there. I start a new job on Monday." The tightness in Flynn's chest eased a bit. "Mom said you're working from home now. Something about a remote office option."

Nodding, Drew gestured for Flynn to walk with him along the sidewalk, following the girls to the front porch. "I set up an office in the spare room. A couple times a month, I have to meet with my boss and clients for a few hours, but I'm here every morning to send the girls off to school and I'm here when they get home. I don't want to miss out on spending as much time with them as I can. Life's too damn short."

"Yeah." Flynn dropped onto the step beside his brother-in-law to watch the girls scoop the guts out their pumpkins, amazed by the changes in his nieces since last year. "Kristin's going to be tall like Kate. I can't believe how much she's grown. I'm sorry I wasn't here for them."

"You know Katie'd be pretty pissed off at you if she knew you stayed away so long." Drew's smirk surprised him. How could a guy lose the woman he loved, the mother of his children, and still have a sense of humor? "But I understand why you did what you did. We've all had to grieve in our own ways. Want a cup of coffee or something?"

*Hell, I'm wired enough without adding caffeine.*

"Nah." Flynn leaned forward to rest his elbows on his knees, a grin tugging at his lips as Hannah flung a handful of seeds and strings into the bucket next to her. "God, they look so much like her."

"Yeah. Makes me glad we didn't wait to have kids. I get to keep a part of her with me. You ever think about getting married and starting a family?"

An image of Lilith flashed through his brain.

Why would he immediately picture her when Drew mentioned marriage and family?

He gave Drew a sidelong glance. "Not really."

"You don't sound too sure about that." Drew chuckled. "Got your eye on a woman who isn't interested?"

"My boss is something else, but I'm not screwing up the new job for a shot in the dark."

"Probably a good idea for now, but don't cross her off the list just because you work with her. You never know when you're going to meet the right girl." After a long pause, Drew lowered his voice. "Kate wanted me to find someone else after she was gone. She knew how much I liked being married, and she didn't want me to be alone for the rest of my life."

"Does that mean you're dating?" Anger that Drew could move on so quickly after Kate's death warred with sympathy for the man who'd been left to raise their daughters by himself.

"No, not yet. I've been thinking about it. Meredith and Colleen have been helping out when Kristin needs a female to talk to, but they have families of their own to take care of. I'd like the munchkins to have a mother again. Not sure how to give them that and find somebody I can live with for the next thirty or forty years."

Flynn couldn't begrudge his brother-in-law wanting to have a woman around—for him *and* the girls. But, honestly, what were the chances Drew would find the kind of happiness he'd had with Kate a second time?

*I can't seem to find it once. Right place, wrong time. Right woman, wrong everything else.*

*Right woman? Geez, I've known Lilith for a day. Am I crazy?*

"Uncle Flynn, will you help me draw a scary face?" Kristin's request brought him out of the haze.

"I don't draw very well. Your dad's the one with that talent." He pushed up from the step and then squatted next to her on the sidewalk. "Besides, wouldn't you rather have a happy face?"

She grimaced at him. "Uh-uh. Halloween's supposed to be creepy. I want my jack-o-lantern to have fangs."

Popping up from the ground, Hannah flung her gooey hands around his neck and almost knocked him off balance. "I want mine to have a screamy face. You know, like he saw a ghost."

He steadied himself. "You believe in ghosts?"

Her infectious giggle made a smile tickle his lips. "No! You're silly!"

Laughing, he hugged her. "Yep. And now I'm sticky, too."

"Oops." She sobered as she unleashed him. "You're not mad, are you? I don't want you to go away again."

Guilt worse than he'd ever experienced in the last year flooded his conscience. He'd been a jackass for not considering Hannah's and Kristin's feelings when he'd cut himself off from them. "I was never mad at you, angel, and I was wrong to stay away. I'm not going anywhere. I swear."

Kristin propped her fists on her hips and narrowed her eyes at him the way Kate had done so often when they were growing up. "You better stay, or I'm telling Grandma you broke a promise."

Raising one hand to Kristin and the other to Hannah, he tucked in all but his two little fingers. "Pinky swear."

Both girls hooked their pinkies to his and nodded.

One fanged vampire and one screaming ghost-seer later, Flynn trailed after his nieces to wash off the pumpkin goo. More than once Hannah and Kristin reminded him of his promise, giving him a fair idea of how selfish he'd been during his mourning period. He hadn't been the only one going through a tough time, but he'd handled it much worse than the little girls who'd lost their mom.

Afternoon had changed to evening when he finally said good-bye and climbed in his truck to go home. Drew and his daughters waved from the front porch as Flynn backed out of the driveway, his headlights casting their shadows onto the wall behind them. Considering avoiding Lilith had been his motive for the visit, the day had turned out a lot better than he'd expected. The three people most justified in being pissed off at him had welcomed him back with open arms.

Tomorrow, he'd spend some time with the rest of his family and put more distance between him and his new boss.

# Chapter 8

"Hey, Lil. It's Erin. Bonnie and I are going speed dating tonight. Want to come with us? Call me!"

Shaking her head, Lilith deleted the voicemail message. Her co-workers might be adventurous, but she had no interest in desperate men wanting to get laid or find a maid. Being alone was better than being used.

She tapped in Erin's number, unable to completely ignore the invitation.

As usual, the call didn't even finish the first ring before Erin answered. "You're coming with us, right?"

Lilith frowned at the contents of her refrigerator. "Hello to you too. I'm feeling fantastic this afternoon. Thanks for asking."

"Don't be grouchy. You know, you'd wake up a lot happier if you had company in bed."

"I don't have time for a puppy." She pulled out the bottle of grapefruit juice. Wine would've been her first choice if she wasn't planning on taking more pain medication with her supper.

Erin grunted. "Ha-ha. I guess that means you're not going. If you're staying home by yourself on a Saturday night, the least you can do is read one of the books I uploaded for you. You might want to make a trip to the store for batteries, though. Mm-mm. I had no idea you could have that much fun playing with food."

The two titles Lilith had viewed last night had hinted at a food-related kink factor, but she doubted Erin had been ignorant on that subject before she'd read the stories. "Have fun tonight. If you don't show up for work Monday morning, I'll send out a search party."

"Ooh, send firemen. They're so skilled with their hoses."

Cutting off Erin's giggles, Lilith disconnected and pocketed her phone to make dinner. She hardly wanted for Flynn's Fried Oatmeal or the rest of his pasta dish after he'd bailed on her earlier, but throwing away perfectly good food went against her conscience.

*Damn it, I should just eat the stuff and return his stupid casserole dish already.*

He'd find his dish if she left it in the kitchen, and she wouldn't have to see or speak to him—until the workweek started. Then she wouldn't have a choice.

Placing the glass container and the carryout box in the microwave, she resolved not to truly enjoy her neighbor's attempt to placate her. His menu samples might be oven-worthy, but she was in no mood to haul out her iron skillet or dirty another dish.

Bitchiness had already set in, and she hadn't even gone out with the Flynn.

Why did she let men affect her? Shouldn't her life experiences have taught her to shut down her feelings around the opposite sex? Hadn't she done that rather effectively for the last year?

The microwave beeped, and she removed her high-carb dinner. Sure, both dishes were nutritious, but loading up on pasta and oatmeal would likely put her in a mental coma if she didn't go for a long walk after she ate.

*What does it matter? It's not like I have a hot date—except maybe with a book.*

When had she become a whiner?

With a fork in hand, she once again stood at the counter to eat. As she raised the first bite to her lips, a knock sounded. She dropped the fork back into the pasta container and stomped to her front door. If Erin and Bonnie thought they could drag her along on their escapade, they were out of their oversexed minds.

Twisting the knob, she yanked the door open. "I said I wasn't interested."

Harold Winters from 4E furrowed his thick gray eyebrows at her. "France is right. You need to play hide the sausage with the new guy."

*Oh my God! Do the residents have nothing better to do than discuss my sex life? Or the lack of it?*

She let out a slow exhale, trying not to let her shoulders slump to match her mood. "Sorry, Harold. I thought you were Erin and Bonnie. And fooling around with Mr. Hastings is asking for trouble, especially since I met him only yesterday."

He waved off her objection. "Margie and I have been burning up the sheets since the day she moved in here. Sex is fun and healthy. France even gave us some pointers on making it last longer. That's no easy feat at my age."

*Marge Galinski and Harold?*

Both of them were in their late eighties. If one or the other didn't come to breakfast, Lilith could certainly guess why. They were a nine-one-one call waiting to happen.

Before she could respond, Harold stuffed his fist into the pocket of his argyle vest and pulled out a medicinal-looking tube. "I'm telling you, Lily, you need to chill out and turn up the heat."

He handed her the tube and then winked as he spun on his heel and sauntered toward Building C. After slicking his hands over his thin silver hair, he knocked at Marge's apartment. A moment later, he stepped through the open door.

Even the single residents of Montgomery Crossing were getting lucky.

Returning to the kitchen, Lilith stood the tube next to her plate and took a bite of barely warm oatmeal. The flames on Harold's gift caught her attention, and she studied the label.

*Cupid's Flavored Warming Lotion. Raspberry Parfait. Turn up the heat!*

As much as she adored the senior citizens she interacted with every day, she could do without their advice. They had no idea how awful her choice in men had been since her first date in high school. She didn't doubt that nice guys existed, but they never came within kissing range of her.

Hungrier for a dose of dessert than dinner, she pushed away the plate and carryout box. They tasted okay, but she needed something indulgent. The cheesecake in the fridge would at least give her a sugar high, if not an orgasm.

She scraped the leftover triangles of oatmeal into the container with the pasta and carried the mix to the compost barrel outside the back door. The pungent aroma of decomposing food waste wafted out of plastic container as she dumped in the remains of her dinner. Closing the lid, she gave the barrel a spin to mix in the new material.

*There. I'm not wasting it.*

Back inside, she washed her hands and retrieved the slice of cheesecake. With her e-reader in one hand and the wedge of cheesecake in the other, she made a beeline for the bedroom, flicking off lights with her forearm as she left the kitchen. The rest of her evening would consist of white chocolate-raspberry decadence and a steamy book in bed, away from the depressing overcast sky and the real world.

Not bothering with the lamp, she settled on her stomach on the mattress. She rested her wool-socked feet on the pillow, propped herself up on her elbows, and tapped the screen of her endless library to light up a small area around her. The same cover that had unnerved her last night filled the page again. She closed it to open the other book Erin had uploaded.

*Iced Latté.*

The image of the exotic woman and her dark-haired lover popped up. Passion flared in the man's deep brown eyes, and his sculpted body invited exploration. No former boyfriend had ever looked at Lilith like that—or looked that good.

Flipping past several pages to the first chapter, she cut the tip off the wedge of her final serving of calcium, protein, and solace for the day. The opening line drew her in as she slipped the bite of cheesecake between her lips.

*"Calais Shepherd hesitated, unsure if she wanted to lick off every bit of chocolate frosting first or simply stuff all of John in her mouth."*

A snort escaped, but Lilith continued reading and eating, her disposition improving with every forkful and every paragraph. The heroine was strong, self-reliant, and smart, besides being beautiful. She didn't take any bullshit from her jackass landlord, and the woman had great taste in pastries. Too bad Calais also had a weakness for Kane, the guy who owned the cupcake shop down the block. His light-as-air amaretto frosting was the icing on her cake. When Kane started testing out flavors on Calais, Lilith hauled out Zippy.

Setting aside her e-reader, she put fresh batteries in the vibrator and tapped the remote's "on" button. The familiar sound sent her inner muscles into anticipatory trembling.

*Nothing like erotic-story foreplay to get a girl ready for playtime.*

For all their uniformed sexiness, none of her former lovers had been overly interested in elevating anyone's sexual readiness except their own. While a quickie was okay from time to time, she required more than a painful pinch of her nipple and a rough finger insertion in her vagina to get her juices flowing. No matter how many times she'd tried to encourage her men to spend a few minutes teasing and using soft touches, they hadn't listened or learned. Guys simply weren't trainable.

Zippy, on the other hand, always followed her directions to the letter.

Slipping out of her clothes, Lilith shivered and opted to don a tank top to keep the chill from distracting her. The thin layer between her fingers and her breasts would ease the sensitivity as well.

Why hadn't any of her ex-boyfriends considered that?

*Forget boyfriends. No one knows my body like I do.*

A light caress over her distended nipple sent another pulse of anticipation to her lower belly. Resuming her previous position on the bed to avoid her bruise, she slid Zippy underneath her to buzz along her inner thigh, nearing her clitoris without getting close enough to directly stimulate it. A release of fluids triggered a slight contraction and a hitch in her breath. Forcing her eyes to the screen, she continued reading as she moved the vibrating toy closer to its target and brushed her thumb over a nipple. The image of Kane and Calais engaged in food-play morphed into her and Flynn.

A little fantasizing wouldn't hurt anything, would it?

She'd never act on an attraction to him.

Impatient for the pleasure of an orgasm, she adjusted Zippy, gliding the tapered tip through her damp slit. She stopped at her clit and pushed the speed up a single notch. A quick rush of sensation rocketed from the bundle of nerves to her breasts, spreading goose bumps over her skin, but she backed off. Another second of stimulation would've driven her from turned on to hypersensitive. She'd learned to recognize the onset of sudden reversal years ago, and that spelled the end of any chance at achieving the ultimate high.

The best reason for staying the hell away from Flynn Hastings suddenly stared her in the face—or the crotch. She doubted she could take the disappointment, and he'd think she was impossible to please.

Disgusted with her stupid imagination, Lilith powered down Zippy and rolled to her side, draping her arm over her face to block out the light from her e-reader. The mood was gone. Her hot-and-cold body had decided on frigid again. She swallowed against the lump in her throat and squeezed her eyes shut to ease the stinging of hot tears.

Why couldn't she be normal?

She pushed up from the mattress, setting the now-dark e-reader on the nightstand and carrying her useless vibrator to the bathroom. By the nightlight, she removed Zippy's batteries and washed him. After she relegated him to the drawer, she brushed her teeth. Her hot Saturday night date with an orgasm had been a no-show, so she might as well take advantage of a few extra hours of sleep. Tomorrow, she'd cook Sunday brunch for the residents and spend the afternoon with Uncle Wade.

*Damn, I act older than anybody else in the complex. I guess it's time to get a cat or two.*

\* \* \* \*

Flynn had delayed going back to his new apartment as long as he could. He'd filled his gas tank, looked for a local place to get new tires for his truck before winter, and picked up a few specialty items at a whole foods shop he happened to see on the drive. With groceries in need of refrigeration, he now had no choice but to pull into the Montgomery Crossing parking lot.

*What do I say to Lilith if she's out walking? Do I tell her I went to visit family? Or was the explanation I sent enough?*

*Ah, hell. What if she didn't check her e-mail?*

Snagging the bag of groceries from the passenger seat, he got out of the truck. Several windows in the singles buildings were lit up, reminding him that he lived in a real community now. A couple women had waved at him as he left earlier, but he'd yet to have a conversation with any of the people he'd be feeding.

He followed the sidewalk to Building F, forcing his gaze forward when apartment 5F's dark windows caught his eye. At eight-thirty on a Saturday night, his boss was most likely out with her friends or on a date, like any single female her age. Either scenario fell under the none-of-his-business category.

In fact, everything about her did.

Keeping his eyes on his doorknob, he let himself into his apartment. Maybe in a few weeks, he'd start going out too. A woman in the grocery store had looked at him several times, giving him the impression she was interested, even if she wasn't really his type. Fifty-something cougars might be able to lure some guys, but Flynn had never been into no-strings affairs.

The bag slumped to the side when he set it on the counter, and he made a quick grab to stop the contents from dumping on the floor. He'd have to make a trip to the restaurant kitchen tonight to drop off the items he'd need early in the week. A call to the supplier Monday morning should mean a delivery no later than Thursday.

He dug an envelope out of one of the small moving boxes he'd yet to unpack and stowed the grocery receipt inside. To keep the envelope handy, he stuck it the front of the fridge with the only magnet—the one Kate had given him when he graduated from culinary school. The matching "Kiss the Cook" apron was in his bottom dresser drawer for safekeeping.

Checking his pocket for his keys, he picked up the bag and headed to the complex's main building. Lilith had assured him his apartment key would unlock the outer door so he could access the kitchen at any time.

*The menu. If I find copies in the game room, she had to have gotten the e-mail.*

Security lights lined the sidewalk and bordered the patio area, lighting his way to the double doors he and Lilith had used yesterday. A full turn to the right yielded a click.

He entered, relocking the door behind him before making the delivery to his new workspace. Switching on the overhead florescent lamps, he surrendered to a contented grin. He had his own kitchen, with practically brand-spanking-new appliances, storage cabinets, and counters. The best part would be working forty hours a week in the place.

He'd already promised his mom and dad he'd come to their house for lunch tomorrow, but Flynn planned to unpack his knives and his favorite pans in the evening to prepare for Monday breakfast. Taking a couple minutes to inspect the utensils his boss had stocked, he imagined his first day on the job.

*No bumping elbows because of too many people in the kitchen. No yelling back and forth to hurry up and get this, get that. No rush, rush, rush.*

His preparation of meals would move at a snail's pace compared to The Westerfield House. He'd actually get to enjoy cooking again—and he wouldn't have to scarf down his food without tasting it.

Reluctantly flicking off the light switch, he aimed for the far end of the hallway. The dining room was dark except for a couple glowing exit signs. An arrow on the wall a few yards down the corridor indicated men's and women's locker rooms and an exercise room to the left. The hall continued past an alcove with a loveseat and a couple armchairs. He finally came to a sunroom with tables and chairs, a set of shelves with stacks of board games, and a bulletin board with a copy of his menu tacked in place with a pushpin.

Lilith had gotten his menu and liked the template version he'd chosen well enough to use it. He'd have to check his e-mail for a thank-you, because she was the type of person who'd send one.

Satisfied that he hadn't given her another reason to be displeased with him, he returned the way he came. He double-checked the lock on the exterior door before setting off toward his apartment. His neighbor's windows were still dark, and he frowned at the little slice of regret in his gut. He'd done the right thing by canceling lunch. Spending time with his brother-in-law and nieces was a far better choice than tempting fate by seeing Lilith again.

He let himself inside apartment 6F, willing away the image of her that popped into his head. His med-school brain had cursed him with the unforgettable memory of running his fingers down her lower spine and over her perfectly rounded hip. Her lacy blue thong had almost done him in. He'd always had a weakness for her curvy kind of ass, but he wasn't about to let a single miscalculation screw up his new life.

*I made the right decision, damn it.*

# Chapter 9

Blinking her bleary eyes at the clock, Lilith groaned and threw back the covers. She had twenty minutes to get her butt over to the main building to start brunch. One of these days, she needed to stop working weekends on top of her Monday through Friday duties. Her sparse personal life didn't require time off, but she couldn't work on becoming a crazy cat lady if she never went to pick out a free kitten or two.

In the bathroom, she splashed water on her face and rolled on fresh deodorant in lieu of a shower. A simple braid would keep her hair out of the way while she chopped, mixed, and cooked. She scurried to find clothes. Skipping her favored hooded sweatshirt and exercise pants, she donned a sweater and forced her bruised backside into a pair of jeans.

With a minute to spare, she shoved her feet into her running shoes and slipped on her coat. As she pulled her front door closed, a single thought stopped her in her tracks.

*Keys! Damn it, I forgot my keys!*

She was cursed. It was the only explanation that made sense.

She growled as she gave her door a half-hearted kick. Then she marched toward Alice and CC's apartment to collect her spare key. With her luck, she'd interrupt them during one their role-playing sex games.

*Because I really need to see that again.*

She could deal with Alice in a Catwoman suit, but CC dressed as Tarzan in what barely constituted a loincloth crossed the line. The time they'd answered their door mostly naked and handcuffed together had made her wish for amnesia and brain bleach.

No wonder she had sexual issues.

As she raised her fist to knock, Alice popped her head out of a narrow gap in the door. Her fuchsia hair was parted down the center and gathered into poofy pigtails above her ears. A sickening sweet scent emanated from behind her. "You forget your keys, Lily?"

Giving a curt nod, Lilith held her breath. Was that smell supposed to be strawberries?

*Don't ask. Just get the key and go.*

Alice dangled the keychain through the opening, her arm naked well past her elbow. "I invited Flynn to brunch this morning. Hope you don't mind."

"Of course not." With her stomach somersaulting, Lilith snatched the key and pivoted to leave. "See you in about an hour."

A giggle followed her as she started toward her destination again. "We might be a few minutes late."

Lilith broke into a jog, as much to escape the too-much-information conversation as to make sure the meal was finished on time. Fumbling with the lock, she managed to let herself into the building without dropping the key. Picking up anything from the ground would be a major pain in the ass.

She released the second door, activating the automatic sliding mechanism, and then flipped on the hall lighting on her way to the kitchen. Her thoughts shifted to the menu she'd planned and the headcount for each of the dishes. At least she wasn't a bumbling idiot about remembering numbers.

At home in her state-of-the-art creation, she set to work preparing her usual offerings of scones and yogurt parfaits to accompany this week's featured vegetable frittata, whole wheat French toast, and her latest experiment, sweet potato hash with extra-lean, lower-salt ham. The aroma of steaming spinach and mushrooms blended with sautéed onions, freshly baked cranberry-orange scones, and a hint of cinnamon from the French toast. Lilith's belly growled as she loaded the last of the food items to deliver to the buffet table, but she ignored it. She'd eat while she cleaned up her mess.

She wheeled the cart into the dining room as the first of the residents lined up at the coffee urn. "Good morning, Walter. Are you and Harold watching the game together today?"

The lanky retired physics professor added a couple dribbles of skim milk to his cup. "Yesiree, Miss Lily. I'd ask you to join us, but sometimes our language isn't fit for a lady's ears."

His manners from a long-gone age were refreshing and entertaining. He'd likely be shocked if he heard the words that sometimes came out of her mouth.

"You're so thoughtful. I'm going to visit Uncle Wade after brunch. Shall I send him your best wishes for a speedy recovery?"

"Absolutely. Are those your delicious scones I smell?"

Transferring the dishes to the table, she nodded. "Cranberry-orange this time. I set a couple aside for Dorothy. Would you mind dropping them off at her apartment on your walk home?"

Walter set his mug at his seat. "Not at all. Isn't that cold gone yet?"

"She was feeling a little better Friday morning, but the doctor told her to rest and he'd check on her Monday. He was concerned about her lungs staying clear after that bout of pneumonia last spring."

Stepping up next to Lilith, Harold picked up two plates from the stack, handing one to Walter. "Sure is hell getting old."

She placed the last of the entrees on the table. "So is being thirty-something at times."

"Now, Lily, just because you're over thirty doesn't mean you're old. And so what if you were? Acting young keeps you young." Harold helped himself to a wedge of frittata. "No peppers, right? Those buggers give me terrible indigestion."

She let his veiled reference to her being too serious roll off her back. He meant well. "Spinach, artichokes, and mushrooms with Asiago."

"Walt, don't you love this sweet girl? She takes better care of us than our mothers did." Adding a scone and a helping of sweet potato hash, Harold winked at her. "I'm surprised some nice young man hasn't begged you to marry him."

Walter filled his plate, following his cohort down the table. "You mean like that fellow?"

Lilith followed the direction he gestured with his head as Flynn entered the dining room with CC and Alice. "Sorry to deliver and run, but I have work to do."

Pushing the cart through the swinging door, she ducked into the kitchen before she had a meltdown. She'd wanted to simply stand and stare at her edible new chef. He looked far too good in blue jeans and a formfitting long-sleeve T-shirt. She'd also wanted to stamp her foot and blame him for her failed orgasm last night. If he hadn't invaded her fantasies, she might've gotten a little pleasure from Zippy instead of having to toss him in the bathroom drawer. Her best bet was to hide out until everyone finished eating and went home.

Tomorrow at lunchtime, she'd scour the classifieds for free kittens.

\* \* \* \*

A flash of strawberry-blonde braid brought Flynn's attention to the entrance to the kitchen. He'd carefully avoided scanning the dining room for Lilith, but he'd recognize the shape of her ass and that distinctive hair color anywhere.

Had she left because he'd arrived? Or was she busy serving brunch to the group that had gathered outside the kitchen?

The woman with pink hair—Alice Carlton, the plumber's wife—nudged him up to the buffet table. "Lily puts out quite a spread for Sunday brunch. Grab a plate and load up!"

Two more women crowded in around him, one leaning in closer to whisper at his elbow as he reached for a scone. "Chef or not, you ought to set your sights on that young woman. She's a wonderful cook. I'm Marge Galinski, by the way."

Her companion leaned in on the other side. "I'm Vivian Underwood from 6E. Did you notice Lily has perfect hips for childbearing?"

Flynn bit the inside of his lower lip to keep from groaning, but that didn't stop the burning sensation on his ears. If he had to guess, he'd say his face was about the shade of Alice's hair.

He pointed to a serving dish of something orange with slices of caramelized onion and uniform cubes of ham in it. The shade was too muted for carrots. *Sweet potatoes?* "This looks good. Do you know what it is?"

Vivian scooped a helping onto his plate. "Sweet potato hash with ham. France and I got to taste it when Lily tested the recipe. It's delicious."

Using tongs, Marge set a slice of cinnamon-speckled bread beside the sweet potatoes. "And you have to try her French toast. I can't believe it's actually healthy. Now, don't forget to sample the frittata."

*Good thing I'm hungry.*

"Thanks, ladies. I think I'll get a cup of coffee." He'd have to drink the regular stuff if he expected to survive the meal with a roomful of busybodies with good intentions.

At the coffee urn, a bald man with what looked to be a permanent frown held out a full mug. A dingy gray beret hung out of his jacket pocket. "You'd think these old fools would mind their own business. I hear you're the new cook. Flynn something-or-other. I'm Lenny Bostwick, the resident grouch."

This time, Flynn had to bite his tongue. He took the offered brew, hoping it didn't slosh over the side from the effort not to laugh. "Flynn Hastings. Good to meet you, Lenny. I should go eat before my food gets cold."

Alice waved her arm in the air, gesturing for Flynn to join her and her husband. He could hardly pretend not to see her and make a run for the exit, so he sat with the couple.

A moment later, a tiny woman joined them, a round bluish bun bobbing up and down as she settled in the chair between Flynn and Alice. "Hello,

Mr. Hastings. I'm France Ito from 2C. We're so glad you decided to run the new restaurant. Our dear Lily spends too much time on work and not enough on play."

Alice patted Flynn's arm. "France is a retired sex therapist, but she's still happy to offer advice if you ever need any."

Flynn took a quick sip of coffee to hide his shock at Dr. Ito's occupation. The residents of Montgomery Crossing were an eclectic mix to say the least. "Nice to meet you, France. Thanks for the welcome."

She set a tote bag on the table and reached inside it. Her face brightened, and she withdrew her hand, placing the find next to Flynn's plate. "Be sure to use these. And they can't do their job if they aren't applied correctly. I have pamphlets with detailed instructions at home. Stop by anytime for a copy if you need one."

An accordion strip of Trojans slowly unfolded beside his fork. Evidently, no topic was off limits.

He stuffed the condoms in the back pocket of his jeans. "Oh, uh, okay. Thanks."

Focusing on the pile of food in front of him, he took a bite. Maybe if he kept his mouth full, nobody would attempt to continue the sex therapist's line of conversation. They seemed to take the hint, digging into their own meals.

The first taste of the sweet potato hash surprised him. He'd expected some sweetness from the potatoes and a bit of saltiness from the ham, but a subtle savory flavor gave it a balance that was as good as it was unique.

Moving on to the French toast, he cut off a slightly crusty edge and almost laughed at Lilith's ingenious use of whole wheat bread instead of white. She'd managed to add a healthy twist to the classic favorite, except hers didn't need a drop of syrup to make it edible. A touch of honey and cinnamon offered an alternative to the typically high-sugar breakfast food. She might've used egg substitute too, although it wasn't obvious from the texture or taste.

He downed a couple more swallows of coffee, careful not to scald his tongue and ruin his eating experience. The frittata was next, and it didn't disappoint, either. Neither did the seasonally flavored scone.

Marge was right. Lilith Montgomery knew her way around a kitchen. Flynn only hoped the clientele liked his cooking half as well.

Several more of the residents introduced themselves as he finished eating, each one trying to play matchmaker between him and Lily with all the subtlety of a freight train.

If his boss snuck into the dining room while he was eating, he didn't see her, and leaving before she made an appearance seemed like the best plan.

He said his good-byes as he carried his dirty dishes to one of the serving trays seemingly left out for that purpose.

Making his way along the hall, he strolled toward the main exit. His family deserved to have him arrive promptly after being absent for a year. They'd already forgiven him for being a selfish ass during his over-long mourning period. Now he needed to tell them they'd done right by abiding by Kate's wishes and allowing her to protect him one last time.

\* \* \* \*

Peeking out the door to the dining room, Lilith finally relaxed at the sight of the empty tables. She could clean up the mess in peace.

The cart rattled as she pushed it toward the buffet table, the metallic clanks echoing off the ceiling and walls. A single portion remained of each of the entrees, the last person through the line always making sure she got to sample what she'd cooked. The retirees she helped care for were also her most-treasured friends.

She made quick work of her duties before inspecting the dining room and kitchen a last time. Since she wouldn't appreciate arriving to anything less than a spotless workspace, the new chef deserved the same consideration. Flipping off the lights, she tried to brush off the bit of melancholy from having prepared and served her last meal for the residents.

*They're in good hands.*

Flynn's truck was missing from his parking spot when she unlocked her car forty-five minutes later, and her chest tightened just enough to notice.

Hadn't she told Alice the man might have a girlfriend?

Even if he'd simply gone for a drive, Lilith had no business speculating on his whereabouts. He didn't owe her an explanation.

Easing into the driver's seat, she winced at the pressure on her hip. She shifted to her left side and bit her lip all of the twelve-minute drive to the house where she'd grown up.

Uncle Wade met her at the mudroom door, his salt-and-pepper toupee sliding forward as he wrapped her in a one-armed hug. "How's my girl?"

Tsking at him, she returned the embrace. "I could've let myself in. You should be resting."

He scowled at her. "You need babies to take care of so you'll stop mothering us old folks. I'm fine."

His comment smarted, even though he meant well, and she clenched her jaw to silence a retort. Having been a bachelor his entire life, he had no right to lecture her on starting a family.

She tucked her hand in the crook of his elbow and guided him to the recliner in the living room. "Sixty-four isn't old. And I'm thinking of getting a kitten. Probably two. I wouldn't want the poor thing to be lonely while I'm working all day."

"You need somebody who can talk back to you, Lily. Cats might be good for listening, but what about when you want to hear another human voice?" He sat, grimacing a little as he settled in the chair. "Shouldn't these damn incisions be healed already?"

A stitch of empathetic pain zipped through her side. "The surgery was only a week ago. You promised me you'd take off the full four weeks to recuperate."

"But I'm going stir crazy! How am I gonna last another three weeks?" Adjusting his hairpiece, he frowned. "I have things to do, people to boss around."

"If you're trying to get me to let you stay at my apartment, it isn't happening. You're not setting foot on the grounds of Montgomery Crossing until the week before Thanksgiving, and then only if the doctor says you're allowed to go back to work." She gingerly dropped onto the couch adjacent to his chair as she plucked a fluffy pillow from the nearest corner. Then she gave him her best reproving stare, partly to chastise him and partly to cover the throbbing in her hip.

His chuckle was too familiar. "I've told you a thousand times. You don't have it in you to pull off that look. You're a sweet, mild-tempered girl who couldn't be mean if she wanted to be. And don't make me laugh. It hurts."

With the pillow against her face, she toppled over. The thick padding muffled her frustrated scream. Tossing the muffler into the other corner, she sighed. "I'm tired of being the nice one, the efficient one, the one with the perfect temperament. Good old reliable Lilith."

Uncle Wade sobered. "So, tell me about the new chef."

*As if that's an improvement in the topic of conversation.*

Schooling her expression, she propped up on her elbow. At least her butt didn't hurt in that position. "He understands the dietary needs of the residents, and his menu is creative and healthy. I think everyone will enjoy the choices he'll be offering."

"I wouldn't expect anything less with you doing the interviewing and hiring." The casual tone of his voice warned her the interrogation had just begun. "How old is he? Does he seem like a friendly sort?"

"Yes, he's polite. I'd guess he's about thirty or so based on his resume." She resisted the urge to elaborate on his background of pre-med, med school, and then culinary training. That much information might be construed as interest.

"You said his name is Flynn Hastings. Sounds Irish. He isn't some smidgeon of an ornery leprechaun like me, is he?"

A snort came out before she could stop it. "More like the Jolly Green Giant."

"Good-looking fellow, huh?"

Popping up to pace to the fireplace, she growled. "Not you too! I'm not dating someone I work with. Not that he's even interested."

A smirk lit up the green eyes that matched hers. "You sound a little disappointed. Could it be the lady doth protest too much? Perhaps you're suffering from a mild infatuation?"

Heat flooded her cheeks, and she attributed it to her temper rather than embarrassment. "I'm not infatuated with the man. If you're going to spend the afternoon provoking me, I'd just as soon go to the shelter to look at kittens."

Shaking his head, he grunted. "I only want you to be happy, Lily. You're too deserving of a good man and a family to spend your life alone and disheartened. But if you prefer not to talk about him, fine. You can catch me up on all the gossip. Harold and Margie ask about sharing an apartment yet? I wish we had an open unit in one of the couples buildings."

"No, they haven't asked." Was she the lone person in the entire complex who hadn't known about Mr. Winters and Mrs. Galinski before Harold had mentioned it yesterday evening? "John Reed started researching Alzheimer's facilities last week. Norma slipped out while he was in the shower on Tuesday, and Alice found her half a block down the road. He's hoping to have something set up no later than Thanksgiving."

"Damn. It's been a rough week, hasn't it?"

Lilith nodded, too choked up to answer.

*Harder than you know, Uncle Wade.*

Endless interviews and a cancelled work meeting were nothing compared to preparing to say good-bye to a dear friend. She'd gladly endure a hundred egocentric chefs and twice as many broken dates in exchange for Norma's wellbeing.

No wonder that slice of cheesecake had been calling her name.

# Chapter 10

Pushing through another set of crunches, Lilith focused on the dots of the tiled ceiling. Thankfully, the exercise room had been empty when she'd returned from the visit to her uncle. She probably would've hidden out under her blankets, pigging out on every crumb of comfort food in her apartment if it hadn't. She'd needed to be alone, to forget about the depressing realities of working in an aging community.

She shoved a loose strand of hair out of her face and flopped on the mat. Her abs burned and her ass hurt like hell, but physical pain beat thinking about a long-time friend losing herself. Within weeks, Norma Reed probably wouldn't recognize or remember half the residents—or worse, her devoted husband.

With a mighty effort, Lilith stood and ambled to the free weights.

*Front lifts. Side lifts. Curls.*

Bending at the waist, she added some Pilates moves, each muscle group getting a thorough session of repetitions. She'd likely suffer tomorrow, but what didn't kill her would keep her from having to buy new clothes the next size up.

She lifted her sweat-dampened tank top away from her lower back as she walked to the locker room. A few minutes in the whirlpool would serve to cool down and loosen her muscles. After a good soak, she'd go home and plan her workweek.

She had plenty to do with Uncle Wade out of the office, unlike when he wasn't recovering from surgery. By hiring a chef, her mostly part-time role as nutritionist and dietician would become all but obsolete. Flynn clearly knew how to provide healthy, balanced meals without her guidance. She'd basically given him half her job.

*Be honest. Uncle Wade created the job so I wouldn't have to make it on my own.*

Once he came back to work, her job title would look more like "cruise director" than "health management coordinator." With her experience, she could join a nutrition counseling service and teach patients about special diets related to their diseases and conditions. She might even make decent money at it—which was an important point since she'd have to find a new apartment and actually drive to work. By adding a few more classes at the hospital, she could supplement her income, if necessary.

She donned her swimsuit and then stood under the spray of the shower for a full minute. Wrapping a towel around her, she exited the locker room and hurried to the whirlpool. A glance toward the observation window gave her the all clear to drape the towel over the railing and set the timer on the wall. The exercise facilities were never busy on Sunday nights, but her shapely figure made her a bit paranoid about someone catching her breasts and rear hanging out in public.

Sinking into the bubbly water, she closed her eyes and imagined what her new job would be like. A pale, bald-headed woman about Lilith's age morphed into a young girl with an IV-drip hooked up to her arm. Another patient sported a nebulizer mask. The images weren't any better than watching her current clients grow frail and die.

* * * *

Tightening his arms around his mother, Flynn winced at the rush of guilt. "I missed you too, Mom. I'm really sorry—"

"Hey, what did I tell you?" She eased back to look him in the eye. "The only thing that matters is you're here now. I'm so glad to have my little boy home again."

He barked a laugh. "I haven't been little since I was eight."

"Would you prefer I call you my baby boy?" Tugging him down by the collar, she kissed his cheek.

He gave a fake shudder. "Baby? I'd never hear the end of it. I guess I can handle little."

She winked at him and returned to stowing leftovers from supper in the fridge as he continued rinsing plates and silverware to load the dishwasher. "I have a box for you from Kate. Remind me to give it to you before you leave."

The twinge in his gut lasted only a split second, but the dull ache stayed. "A box? What kind of stuff is in it?"

"I don't know. I wouldn't have felt right opening it. It seemed too personal. Too private. Take it home with you, and when you're ready, see what she left for you."

He nodded, not sure what to say. Half of him wanted to tell his mom to keep the box, but the other half wanted to go home with it right this minute. Indecision cramped his neck and shoulders.

What would Kate have put aside for him? How had she managed to prepare for her own death?

Closing the dishwasher, he pretended to check his watch. "I should get going. I have to be up early tomorrow for the new job."

The way his mom studied him sent another wave of guilt washing over his conscience. She'd always been able to read him, and she was damn well aware he was running away again. "Call me if you need anything, Flynn. And I promise it'll get easier. Go say good-bye to your dad while I get the box."

His footsteps seemed loud in the silent hall, even after spending all afternoon with a houseful of family. Everyone else had made quick exits shortly after supper, leaving Flynn the last to leave. He hadn't minded, though. Memories had been creeping out of the walls, and the earlier noise had distracted him from hearing the voices of the past that lived in his parents' house. Too many scenes were trying to play out in his head at once.

Was that why he was suddenly in a hurry to go?

His father was crouched in front of the fireplace adjusting the low-burning logs when Flynn stepped into the family room. Neither spoke as the slightly more wrinkled and grayer version of himself stood. A handshake became a hug, and Flynn waited for the chewing out he deserved.

"Are ye goin' home?"

Flynn straightened his spine as they parted. "Yeah. I start my new job tomorrow."

"Nice place, that Montgom'ry Crossin'." His da pursed his lips and furrowed his brow. "Yer mom's been happier t'day than I've seen her in a long time. Thank ye for that. Yer a good son."

The need to shake his head almost won, but Flynn stifled it, lowering his gaze instead. "I should've come home sooner."

"She wouldn'ta liked seeing ye angry. Ye chose the right time, and we're glad ta have ye home now. Let's go have a Guinness at the pub once yer settled."

Too tight-throated to answer, Flynn simply nodded.

He bit the inside of his lower lip as his mom brought the box and his parents walked him to the door. They didn't blame him for being selfish and holding a grudge, albeit a relatively short one in the grand scheme of things. They'd offered more support and love rather than telling him the truth—he'd taken his damn time making things right.

The shoebox rested on the seat beside him on the ride back to the apartment. He tightened his grip on it every time it threatened to slide away. Then he tucked it under his arm as he strode down the sidewalk from the parking lot to his front door, only setting it down on the couch to take off his coat.

*To open it or not to open it? Am I ready to see what's inside?*

He paced to the kitchen doorway and back, the box always in his sight. Curiosity and anticipation finally got the better of him, and he lumbered over to remove the lid. Inside, a stack of photos rested on a pile of tissue paper. He picked up the top one, sucking in a slow breath to still his shaking hand.

Young Kate held a baby swaddled in a blue blanket, her smile as bright as Flynn had ever seen it. He flipped it over to check for a date—not that he needed one. She'd been eight years old.

*"The very first time I held my baby brother. I'll miss him."*

His chest tightened at the familiar handwriting and simple sentiment.

Dropping the picture into the box, he replaced the lid and sat on the floor with his back against the couch. He cradled his head in his palms and closed his eyes.

*Okay, so I'm not ready. That doesn't mean I won't be tomorrow or maybe next week. One picture today. Another one in a couple days.*

A minute of absolute silence calmed his roiling stomach and jumpy nerves enough to go change clothes for a workout. He'd check out the exercise room Lilith had mentioned and burn off some stress.

*My knives and pans.*

Leaving the bedroom, he detoured to the kitchen and hefted the packing crate to drop off in his workspace. Unpacking wasn't the same as burying himself in cooking. It needed to be done in any case.

The hike to the main building was short but chilly, even with sweats over his shorts and muscle shirt. Winter was quickly chasing fall into hiding.

He balanced his load on his knee as he unlocked the entrance and relocked it behind him. Having already inspected the cabinets for empty storage space, he finished unpacking in a matter of minutes. He stowed the empty crate in the broom closet and then aimed for his destination along the dimly lit corridor.

As he neared the side hall leading to the locker rooms, he slowed. A couple feet past the turn, a broad yellow swath from the gym's picture window illuminated the main hallway.

Had someone else beat him to the punch?

Not really in the mood to socialize, he eased closer, careful to stay out of sight as he checked for occupants. The weight benches, ellipticals, and treadmills were empty. No one stretched on the mats. At the far end in the corner, a flash of movement had him jerking back and sent his pulse racing.

He peeked around the edge of the window again, this time frozen in place by the voluptuous outline of his boss—first from the side and then from the back. A swimmer-style suit left nothing to his imagination. She was, without a doubt, a generous-breasted 34DD. Her narrow waist accentuated the flare of her curvy ass. Even the nasty bruise on her hip didn't detract from the most mesmerizing body he'd ever seen. She wasn't long-legged by any means, but her thighs and calves looked toned and incredibly touchable, perfect for wrapping around his waist while he made love to her.

Turning from what must have been an adjustment to the spa controls, she all but disappeared into the tub—his cue to get the hell out of there before he did something incredibly stupid. He wasn't about to let his suddenly alert cock lead him down the path to the unemployment line.

Careful to move slowly, he backed away from the window. A cold shower crossed his mind, but he headed outside for a jog to the coffee shop. He'd watch or listen for Lilith if he stayed in the immediate vicinity of Montgomery Crossing and his apartment. A bedroom wall wasn't enough distance between him and the stuff of wet dreams, but a mile might be.

*I'll just keep telling myself that.*

The cold night air cleared his head a little, and he set off at a decent pace before the urge to go back could take hold. The steady *cush, cush* rhythm of his shoes hitting the sidewalk lulled him into a zone of five steps on an inhale, then five steps on an exhale. Each outgoing breath sent a wispy cloud into his face. Focusing on counting and the pavement ahead of him, he followed the streetlights north.

His muscles rebelled at the lack of warm-up, tightening with every block, and he paused at one of the tables outside the coffee shop to stretch. He leaned forward to lengthen his calf muscle and Achilles, dropping his chin to his chest. A pair of high-heeled boots stepped into his field of vision, and he glanced upward.

A cap of short blonde hair was ringed around the edge by a dark fringe of hacked-off strands. "You must be dedicated to be out running in this cold."

Shrugging, he avoided meeting her heavily lined eyes. The dark red color on her lips brought to mind vampires, especially under the eerie glow of the security lights.

"Join me for a cup of coffee? I'll even buy since I don't see a bulge anywhere there shouldn't be one." Her tone made him wish for an oversized trench coat—in addition to a cross and a wooden stake.

"No thanks."

"Are you sure? I'm Yasmina." She extended her claw-tipped fingers and shifted her stance, emphasizing her long, lean body.

He preferred women with a little more meat on their bones, less threatening fingernails, and names that didn't sound like they should be manning a pay-by-the-minute phone-sex line. Ignoring her prompt, he stretched his other leg.

"I bet you work construction with that body. Broad shoulders, strong biceps, tight glutes."

Amused by her determination, he opted for blunt honesty. "Nope. I'm a chef."

*If that occupation doesn't catch her off guard, nothing will.*

She scrunched up her over-made-up face. "You mean like a fry cook? Or one of those guys who cooks spaghetti at Olive Garden?"

*Is she for real?*

"No, like a went-to-culinary-school kind of chef."

Waving a hand at him, she frowned. "Oh my God. You're gay, aren't you?"

Flynn waffled between being offended for all the gay chefs of the world and relieved to finally find a way to rid himself of the unwelcome attention. "My girlfriend doesn't think so."

"Right. Like you have a girlfriend. What's her name?" She propped her fists on her nonexistent hips in obvious challenge.

"Lily. We're getting married Christmas Eve." The words were out before he considered his response. He wasn't usually much of a liar, but she seemed to believe him.

Spinning on her hooker heels, she shook her head. "Whatever."

The chance for a getaway had arrived, and he took it, setting off at a faster pace than before. Concentrating on his rhythm, he pushed the inclination to analyze why he'd used his boss as an escape hatch from his mind.

Although a layer of sweat coated his skin when he finally spotted the parking lot at his new home, his lungs were protesting against the constant intake of frosty air. He slowed to a walk as he approached the apartments, white puffs rising in front of his face to cloud his view.

Not willing to risk another collision with Lilith, he scanned the length of the buildings between him and his front door. Even with the sidewalk clear of pedestrians, a bit of caution wouldn't hurt. Seeing her might do him in after getting an eyeful of her curvaceous body at the gym.

A thorough perusal of the well-lit courtyard yielded no movement but the branches of the nearly leafless trees. More than likely, he'd been gone long enough for her to soak in the tub, get dressed, and go home. Besides, light now filtered through the blinds of her living room window, and they'd been dark when he'd headed to the main building for a workout.

He increased the length of his stride, finally letting out a relieved sigh as he closed his door behind him.

Then he spied the box he'd left on the couch.

The impulse to put it someplace he didn't have to see it didn't come. In fact, looking at old photos of his sister might prove an effective distraction from the other woman invading his thoughts.

*A few minutes of stretching and a shower first.*

He'd gotten too damn good at procrastinating over the last year, especially with the amount of practice he'd had. Every opportunity to put in more hours had been an excuse not to call his family or visit them. He was lucky they'd welcomed him home at all after treating them like the enemy for so long.

*Forget the shower. I'll take one in the morning. And I can stretch while I'm looking at pictures.*

Grabbing the shoebox, he sank onto the floor. As he raised the lid, Kate smiled at him from the cherry rocking chair his mom and dad still had in living room. She'd been the best oldest sister a boy could've had. He loved Meredith and Colleen, but Kate had always known when to hold him back and when to let him go. She'd apparently believed he wouldn't be able to handle the truth of her illness.

*And maybe she was right. I sure wouldn't have wanted me around if I was dying.*

Setting aside the picture that had sent him running out the door, he studied the next one in the pile without picking it up. The memory forced his lips into an upward curve. He sat behind the steering wheel of Kate's red Beetle, with her riding in the passenger seat. He'd been fifteen at the time, and she'd been teaching him to drive. Colleen had used that photo to blackmail him into keeping quiet after he'd seen her making out in the back seat of her boyfriend's car after a football game—not that he would've actually told their parents.

He flipped over the picture as he lifted it from the stack, hoping for another of Kate's notes.

*"What's in front of you is just as important as what you see in the rearview mirror. Live every day like it could be your last."*

His smile slipped. "I'm sorry, Kate. I've wasted the last fucking year."

Glancing into the box, he spotted the corner of what seemed to be an envelope beneath several more photos.

Had she wanted him to sort through the keepsakes in some particular order? Or could he skip reminiscing over snapshots of the past until after he looked at the contents of the item demanding his attention?

He slid the envelope free, carefully breaking the seal and withdrawing a folded piece of paper. It had to be a note from his sister, but apprehension edged in again, stalling his effort to open and read the message.

With the lid in place again, he carried the note and the box to his bedroom, setting them on the nightstand before grabbing his boxers off the covers. Maybe a good night's sleep would give him the kick in the ass he needed to face what was certain to be a lecture from Kate about moving on.

# Chapter 11

"If I was fifty years younger, I'd sneak in the kitchen and jump his bones."

Flynn barely held in a hoot of laughter when Alice Carlton's voice carried through the server door. He'd hoped to hear comments on his food, but conversation at the closest table had centered on him and Lilith every time he'd had a chance to listen in on Vivian's, France's, and Alice's chitchat—and they weren't shy about speaking their minds.

"Good luck getting Lily out of that office for a meal, let alone chef a la mode." A peek out the porthole window told him Vivian had made that comment. "Wanda said she's been on the phone with every Alzheimer's facility from here to Cleveland, making appointments for John to check them out."

France shook her head. "Poor Norma. I can't even imagine how horribly confused she must be sometimes."

Since they didn't seem inclined to even mention yesterday's breakfast and supper or today's breakfast, he had no idea whether they liked his food. They ate it, but that didn't necessarily mean they enjoyed his meals. After the way they'd sung praises over Lilith's brunch, he'd figured he'd get plenty of yeas and nays without asking. If nobody gave him any feedback by the end of the day, he'd ask his patrons to fill out comment cards. Considering the restaurant-style setup, he probably should've had those available on all the tables with his first meal.

*Something to work on between the breakfast and dinner shifts. Maybe before I interview interns.*

His schedule was filling up, but being busy was better than spending too much time overanalyzing his mixed feelings about reading Kate's letter. A day and a half later, he still hadn't unfolded the paper, let alone read it.

*Tonight. I'll read it tonight.*

Shifting his gaze to the buffet table, he forced his brain back into kitchen mode. A couple serving platters needed refilling, and until he chose an intern, he was responsible for prepping, cooking, and serving. He was damn lucky to have part-time cleanup help.

A quick check out the window for passersby preceded his trip out to the dining room. He nodded at the matchmakers. "Top o' the morning to ye, lassies."

The greeting earned him a trio of wicked grins, and Vivian fanned herself with her napkin. "Good morning, Flynn dear. Don't you haul that lovely Irish accent out too often. I have a pacemaker, you know."

"Yes, ma'am. I'll save it for St. Paddy's Day."

Her eyes brightened. "I traveled to Ireland once a long time ago. Kissed a pair of blarney stones and found a pot of gold."

The women erupted into raucous giggles.

Short on words, he made his delivery and returned to the kitchen. If the women had been that outspoken in their younger years, they must've driven the guys crazy. A lot could be said for romance and wooing, which was more his speed. He'd never been into being aggressively pursued or pursuing.

Unfortunately, the one female he was most interested in showering with flowers and compliments was also the one who'd sign his paychecks twice a month. She'd been mostly out of sight but not out of mind for the past two days. He still wasn't entirely convinced Lilith had been okay with him cancelling lunch on Saturday. Her response to his e-mail hadn't given him a clue.

*"No problem."*

Those two words could've meant simply that. Or they could've held her impossible-to-read anger, sarcasm, or irritation. At least she hadn't fired him under the cover of darkness and gloom Monday morning.

The crowd in the dining room cleared out a few minutes before eight, leaving Flynn to debate dropping off what amounted to room service at his employer's office.

*Wanda can take the food into Lilith. I don't have to see her.*

He boxed up the extra muffins, setting aside a pair each for his boss and her receptionist. By taking a late breakfast to them both, no one—especially him—could read anything into the action. He was simply being friendly and trying not to let food go to waste.

*Yeah. And I can remind them about helping themselves to the carryout portions in the fridge.*

A quick stop in the office confirmed what Alice had said. Lilith's door was closed, meaning he wouldn't catch a glimpse of her even if he wanted to. Wanda's smirk as she thanked him suggested she saw through his excuse, but she promised to see that Lilith took time out of her busy schedule to eat.

After retrieving his laptop, he retired to the dining room to design comment cards and wait for his apprentice applicants.

By the end of the day, Flynn had an intern and enough positive comments from the full house at supper to assure him his menu and food were acceptable to the patrons. As he strolled home from the kitchen, he couldn't help but notice his next-door neighbor's windows were dark. A backward glance told him Lilith was still holed up in her office.

Why should he care if she spent more than fourteen hours a day on the job?

*I'm not her keeper. Or her protector.*

Being attracted to her was normal. She was a beautiful, intelligent woman.

Why wouldn't he have sex on the brain around her after seeing her in a swimsuit?

Going inside, he leaned on the door to close it and tipped his head up to stare at the shadowed ceiling. Logic wasn't working.

He flipped on the light switch on his way to the bedroom and stripped off his whites to trade them for a T-shirt and shorts. A workout might relieve some of his sexual frustration, but he'd put off reading his sister's note for too long already. He'd also likely see the source of his frustration if he went back to the main building.

*Just what I don't need—another hard-on, with no relief unless I take matters into my own hands.*

The box was still on his nightstand. All he had to do was take off the lid, unfold the paper, and read.

Sitting in the middle of the bed, he sucked in a fortifying breath and set the shoebox on his lap. Opening it was no harder than resisting the female who slept on the other side of the wall. In fact, it was a hell of a lot easier. He set the lid on the covers beside him.

*Now pick up the envelope.*

That task took a little less effort.

*Take out the note.*

*Unfold it and read it.*

Familiar handwriting drew his gaze to the lined paper. He stared at the distinctive feminine script, studying word after word and swallowing hard against the lump in his throat.

*"Dear Flynn,*

*I'm glad you're finally reading this. It means you've forgiven me—and yourself. You couldn't have done anything to save me, and I couldn't disrupt your life by telling you the truth.*

*How much time has passed since I died? Six months? Nine months? A year? Drew says I'm crazy to think you'll need that long to heal, but he doesn't know you like I do. I bet you'll spend ages working until you drop, too hurt to let yourself grieve. It won't help. The family is there for you. And don't you dare blame them for keeping my secret. They thought I should tell you, but I made them swear not to. You're doing what you were meant to do, what you love to do. I couldn't interfere with that by sharing all this pain and suffering with you.*

*Are you ready to move on now? You'd better be. If you turn me into a ghost because you're my unfinished business, I'm going to haunt you for the rest of your days. I want you to be happy, to find some nice girl-next-door type who deserves you and have a family of your own. Will you do that for me?*

*I love you, Flynn, and I'm sorry. This is my last chance to try to protect you. Please don't hold it against me. Never settle for less than what you want. Live your life to the fullest and without regrets.*

*Think of me with happiness in your heart. Kate"*

Tears stung his eyes, but he didn't try to blink them away. For once, he let them flow.

\* \* \* \*

Annoyed and frustrated didn't begin to describe Flynn's mood on Friday night.

His job was perfect. He'd enjoyed the relaxed atmosphere of preparing two meals a day for the same small group all week. They'd even invited him to their Halloween party, although he'd had to refuse since he'd already promised his nieces a fun evening of trick-or-treating in their neighborhood.

The problem stemmed from Lilith's obvious avoidance of him.

A boxed portion of last night's salmon had vanished from the refrigerator sometime between Thursday night cleanup and Friday breakfast prep, and everyone else in the complex had dined in the restaurant. Even Wanda had joined the residents for supper. The only box of Chicken Marsala had been missing Thursday morning. Wednesday had arrived with no more Pasta Primavera in the fridge.

Did the boss dislike him so much that she didn't want him to know she liked his food?

Every night about ten, her front door clunked closed. A couple minutes later, the bathroom faucet would run, and then she wouldn't make another noise until shower sounds carried through the wall at five in the morning. Otherwise, he didn't see, hear, or talk to her.

That didn't stop him from imagining her long wet hair half hiding her full breasts and water droplets rolling along the curves of her fabulous ass. Something had to give before his balls turned blue. Cold showers had been a temporary fix at best.

He grabbed his keys on his way out the door and set off jogging down the sidewalk to the parking lot. Luckily, traffic was light and he arrived at Drew's house as the first few costumed kids hit the streets to beg for candy. The girls would've given him hell for being any later.

*No distractions tonight. I'm here to spend time with Hannah and Kristin.*

Donning his coat, he climbed out of the truck and then grasped the handles of the grocery bag he'd filled with Reese's Cups and Kit Kats. The least he could do was contribute to the chocolate supply his brother-in-law would hand out. Whatever was left, the girls could divvy up between them.

Flynn slipped the ape mask down from its perch on top of his head as he strode to the front door. He pressed the doorbell and waited.

It swung wide, revealing a pint-sized queen and a Drew-sized Darth Vader holding out a cauldron of goodies.

"I told you it was Uncle Flynn, Daddy." Hannah curtsied at Flynn. "You may call me 'Your Majesty.' Nobody ever lets me be the boss, so I decided to dress up like a queen for Halloween. That way I get to tell everybody what to do. Kristin! Hurry up!"

Drew flinched when she yelled for her sister again then skittered up the stairs toward the bedrooms. "Are you sure you want to chaperone? Not that I mind the offer."

Even in the heavy-breathing, monotone voice, Drew sounded like a man in need of a little peace and quiet.

"It'll be fun. Besides, you sound like you could stand a break." Flynn set the candy on the hall table as he slid the mask upward.

Lifting off the Vader helmet, Drew rubbed at his temple. "I've been assigned this pain in the a—, um, *rear* project. An entire advertising plan, logo, and the whole deal right after the first of the year. I'm already on deadline for campaigns this month and next month. I have another small package due a couple weeks after that, and I haven't had a vacation since Kate and I took a few days together before she got sick."

Flynn's problems were trivial compared to being a single father, sole breadwinner, and recent widower. "Have you asked my mom about taking care of the kids for a week, or even a weekend? And Merie and Colleen probably wouldn't mind helping out more. I can stay with Kristin and Hannah for part of a day if you need some time to work while they're off school for the holidays."

"Everybody's been great about offering to watch the girls, but I just don't know if I can go someplace without them. I'm trying to be a good dad."

"You're a great dad." Stepping closer, Flynn lowered his voice. "I started going through the box of stuff Kate left for me. She wanted me to be happy, and she'd be pissed off if she knew you were trying to juggle all this pressure on your own. Kristin and Hannah will be fine without you if you need some down time. Just say the word."

Drew nodded. "You're right. Speaking of happiness and down time, do you still have the hots for your boss?"

Every muscle in Flynn's jaw tightened. "I don't want to talk about it."

"What? She has a boyfriend? She blew you off?"

He shook his head. "I doubt she has time for a guy, considering how many hours she works. She's been in the office every morning by five thirty, and I usually hear her apartment door close about ten o'clock at night when I'm getting ready for bed. I haven't talked to her since Saturday. I haven't seen her since she was climbing in the hot tub Sunday."

A smirk slid across his brother-in-law's face. "Hot tub, huh? She was in a swimsuit? I'm guessing you liked what you saw."

The image of Lilith's shapely body invaded Flynn's brain again. "I'm only human."

"And she hasn't shown any sign of interest? Well, I guess not if she's working sixteen hours a day. That probably means she isn't seeing anybody, though. Have you considered going out with somebody else? You know, to get her out of your head."

"Won't work. Believe me, I've tried looking at other women, but they aren't doing anything for me. I don't know how much longer I can maintain a strictly professional relationship with her. She's exactly what I want." Flynn rubbed the back of his neck to ease the stiffness. "Other than being a workaholic."

Drew adjusted his hold on the helmet. "You don't suppose she's putting in all those long hours to avoid you, do you? Maybe because she's having a hard time keeping things professional herself?"

"Ha! I should be so lucky. She won't eat when I'm serving dinner, but she'll sneak into the kitchen for leftovers after I finish for the night. I think her actions speak for themselves."

"Be careful about jumping to conclusions. Woman logic doesn't work the same as guy logic. And sneaking suggests she's afraid of running into you. Sounds a lot like you. Worried about crossing the line and not being able to go back." Sliding on the helmet, Drew effectively ended the conversation as Kristin's and Hannah's voices echoed in the hall.

"We're ready, Uncle Flynn!" A witch with a green face and a warty nose cackled at him from behind the Munchkin queen. "Let's go!"

Darth Vader chuckled. "Flynn, I am their father, but you're a flying monkey."

Flapping his arms, Flynn walked to the door. "Lead the way, ladies."

They'd gone no more than a block before Kristin pulled him to the edge of the sidewalk as they approached the next house. "Tyler lives here. You should wait at the end of the driveway this time. His parents got divorced last year, and his mom wants to get married again. She tried to get Daddy to go out on a date with her. I don't like her."

Not sure how to respond, Flynn simply nodded and handed her the flashlight. She evidently wasn't too keen on the idea of Tyler's mom replacing her mom or becoming her aunt.

Hannah frowned. "I don't like her, either. Besides, we already picked out a nice lady for Daddy to marry."

The girls walked side by side up to the house, leaving him to ponder that enlightening tidbit. Telling Drew probably wasn't in anyone's best interest.

Both of Flynn's nieces were frowning when they returned, Hannah digging in her bucket when she stopped in front of him. "She gave us those yucky fruit-flavored Tootsie Rolls."

"We can throw them away when we get home." Kristin switched the flashlight to the hand with her candy stash and then reached out to hold hands with her sister. "Come on. We still have two more blocks to go."

"Okay." Hurrying to keep up with her much taller sibling, Hannah looked up at Flynn. "Do you have a girlfriend? You should get married and have babies. I like babies."

Talking and asking questions seemed to be among her favorite things as well.

"Nope, no girlfriend. I've been thinking about this woman I met recently, though. She's pretty and smart. And she enjoys helping people." His stomach did a jumping jack with a half twist. "I like her, but I'm not sure she likes me."

With every minute that passed, the resolve to keep his distance weakened a little more.

Stopping at the next driveway, Kristin gave him what he could only figure was the "smart female, dumb male" look. She cocked her head to one side, raised her eyebrows, and pursed her lips. "You'll never know if you don't ask her. You could give her flowers or cook something special for her. She might even kiss you."

Hannah lifted her scepter into the air. "I command you to kiss her and live happily ever after, Uncle Flynn."

Why couldn't life have the simplicity of a six-year-old's royal decree?

He shoved his hands in his jacket pockets. "I'll think about it. Now, scoot."

Turning toward another ranch house, they both grumbled as if they knew he wouldn't follow their advice. How could he, though, when Lilith hid in her office all day and locked herself in her apartment at night?

The suggestion ate at his insides for the rest of the walk around the neighborhood, and he declined Drew's offer of a warm drink, citing his early prep as an excuse to go home. Too keyed up to get ready for bed, Flynn headed straight for the main building and his kitchen. Preparing a double batch of steelies to fry for breakfast would provide him with an activity more constructive than lying awake, wondering what to do about his infatuation.

Once again, the lights in the office glowed through the blinds. Lilith worked as many hours as he had before the move.

Was she burying her troubles in long hours and no social life?

*Sorry, Queen Hannah. Looks like a kiss and happily ever after are a no-go tonight.*

# Chapter 12

*Breathe. And stop looking at Flynn's broad shoulders.*
*Damn it! Not there, either!*

Removing her fingers from the slats, Lilith let the blinds snap closed. She shouldn't have watched her chef cross the courtyard from the main building to the employee apartments. His worn jeans practically glowed white under the security lights lining the sidewalk, triggering a not entirely unwelcome twinge between her thighs and a spike in her pulse.

Almost a week had passed since she'd seen or talked to him face to face, but the attraction hadn't waned. In fact, the less she saw of him, the more he snuck into her thoughts.

At least he'd finally left for the night. Now she could sneak down the hall for supper.

Why had he come back? And what had he been doing in the kitchen until nearly ten o'clock?

She swapped her pumps for hiking boots and grabbed her sweater from the closet. A quick glance at the desk reminded her she'd have to log a couple hours tomorrow to finish scanning the last of the housing contracts. Her life was a smorgasbord of fun.

*Quit your bitching, Lil. The alternative isn't any better.*

Erin and Bonnie had invited her to an all-male review. They'd even offered to pay her way, but ogling mostly naked men with a couple hundred other women wouldn't do anything except compound her problems. She'd still have to rely on her battery-powered playmates, because picking up a stranger for a one-night stand wasn't on her bucket list. Neither was having her heart stomped on again.

The eerie silence in the hall had Lilith wishing she'd simply gone home to make her own dinner hours ago. She had plenty of supplies on hand, and nobody had ever complained about the food she prepared. Yet, two issues persisted. First, cooking for one was a pain in the ass. Second, she was dying for one of her chef's delectable creations. Her obsession with a certain handsome Irishman was beside the point.

She flipped on the switch inside the doorway, flooding the industrial kitchen in light. The sudden brightness made her see spots, but she hurried toward the refrigerator Flynn used to store the single-serving portions. If she found a container of his fabulous Campanelle and Ports with Roma Tomato Sauce to reheat for her late-night supper, at least one of her cravings would be sated. The other would have to go unsatisfied, no matter her sexual frustration.

With the stainless steel door wide open, she scanned the contents. After more than a week of trying to decipher Flynn's scrawl on notes he left with Wanda, Lilith had finally learned to recognize a few key letter combinations—hopefully enough to read some of the identifying marks.

He'd written a date on the front lip of each box, narrowing down the possibilities. The top shelf held the newest selection of entrees, and she pulled out containers one by one to study the names. Printed labels had her breathing a sigh of relief. She'd hired a man with phenomenal cooking skills, an amazing body, and a good dash of common sense.

*Baked Tilapia. Raspberry Chicken. Apple-stuffed Butterfly Chop.*

Any of those main dishes would send her taste buds to heaven, but her stomach was set on pasta, so she continued her search. She found several containers of rice, vegetable, and legume sides. Disappointment and impatience added to her irritation, and she debated removing every damn box.

*Come on. He had to have some left. All I want is one measly serving.*

Almost ready to give up, she reached for the last box.

*Camp and Ports.*

*Hallelujah!*

Not even bothering with a plate, Lilith popped the waxy cardboard box into the microwave and set the timer. As the food heated, she organized the top shelf of the fridge, lining up the containers in their original positions. Flynn may have told Wanda that she and Lilith should help themselves to the single portions, but late-night raids seemed wiser than asking him for carryout at mealtime.

The microwave beeped as she pulled a disposable utensil packet from the cabinet at the far end of the kitchen, and her belly grumbled at the momentary delay.

She lifted the lid to allow the steam to poof out in an aromatic cloud. Her mouth watered with the rising bouquet of tomato sauce, Italian herbs, and portabella mushrooms. Too bad she couldn't finagle an orgasm or two from the meal.

*I seriously need to get some new toys.*

She shoved the plastic fork handle through the wrapper and then poked a piece of bell-shaped pasta. A few quick blows on the steaming forkful ensured her taste buds would survive to enjoy every bite of supreme deliciousness.

A mix of tart and earthy flavors exploded on her tongue with the first taste. She groaned, closing her eyes to recall the memory of her first time sampling the dish. Her uterus contracted a fraction to tease her, but the sensation faded as she swallowed. If she wanted another foodgasm, she'd have to hide in the pantry to eat while Flynn slaved over the stove. A peek at him during her closeted snack would bring her the ultimate in dining pleasure. Of course, remaining silent might be an issue—not to mention that kind of behavior would bring a whole new level to perversion.

She freed the knife from the package and cut off a generous piece of mushroom. Pairing it with a ruffled bell, she shoved the bite between her lips and savored heaven. With her talented chef off-limits, his divine food would have to meet her needs.

Cutting a smaller portion of the flavorful port, she rationed the remainder of her supper.

What were the chances of finding another serving on one of the other shelves?

\* \* \* \*

After pressing a sticky note to Lilith's office door, Flynn followed the hall toward the exercise room in hopes of burning off some energy. Cooking sure hadn't helped. A meeting with her tomorrow might give him a clue whether or not she had any interest in him.

He was too damn confused about his feelings to go another week without seeing or talking to her. Hannah's decree kept circling his thoughts, and his wavering determination to avoid Lilith had finally crumbled.

Was a kiss from her worth risking his job?

Too bad staying away from her had him lying awake night after night thinking about everything from the kinky dessert story he wanted to do to her. The bedroom wall they shared wasn't thick enough to suppress his fantasies of drizzling lemon glaze over her seductive curves and licking it off. He'd even opened the package of licorice ropes, unable to get the image of her tied to his bed with them out of his head.

While he'd only resorted to taking care of his own sexual needs once since seeing her in the hot tub, the urge had been almost continuous.

Having a normal work schedule gave him a lot of free time to spend thinking about his hot neighbor. No wonder he hadn't missed dating for the last year—he'd had no time to imagine spending hours naked in bed with a woman like Lilith.

A glance toward the dark dining room brought him up short as he strolled past. Light filtered onto the carpet from beneath the serving door to the kitchen and through the porthole window.

Had he forgotten to flip off the switch when he left earlier?

He'd been distracted enough.

He backtracked down the hallway to the other entrance. As he lifted his hand to push the door open, a noise came from the other side.

*Was that a moan?*

*Geesh. Please don't tell me old people are having sex in my kitchen.*

*And why do I smell tomatoes and basil?*

Hesitant about whether or not to enter, he strained to hear another sound.

"More. I want more."

Was that Lilith's voice? Did she have a guy in there with her?

*Not if I can help it!*

He shoved the door open and stepped into the room, shading his eyes against the brightness. A squeak brought his attention straight to the woman in question, her face half hidden behind a tipped-up carryout box. Only her wide green eyes were fully visible. She lowered the container, revealing flushed cheeks and a dab of red sauce on her chin.

He strode into the kitchen, grabbing a towel on his way to the sexiest female he'd ever met. Wiping away the drop of sauce, he bit the inside of his lip to hold in a combination of lust and amusement.

She liked his food.

*No, she* loves *my food.*

The week of not showing up for meals in the restaurant had nothing to do with his cooking.

Was she avoiding him because she wanted him as much as he wanted her?

Hope built in his chest—and lower.

Her gaze skittered away from him. "I was hungry. I didn't have time to eat supper. You said I could help myself whenever…"

He took the licked-clean box from her to set it on the counter. "I did, and you can. Did you enjoy it?"

She nodded slowly, the tip of her pink tongue snaking out to lick the corner of her mouth. "It was delicious."

The sensual action could've been involuntary, but it sent an electrical charge straight to his dick, either way.

Was she delicious too?

The need to know proved too much, and he leaned in closer for his own taste. Sounds like those she'd made deserved to be induced by something a hell of lot more interesting than campanelle and ports.

Soft, full lips met his, stealing his sanity and making his heart race. She raked her fingers through his hair, tugging him against her full breasts as her tongue slipped between his teeth.

Wrapping his arms around her, he held her in place, letting the mixture of spices from the entrée and the sweet flavor of Lilith feed his hunger. He rubbed his tongue over hers, relieved to finally be able to kiss her. Barely keeping a tight rein on his reaction, he rocked his hips forward, rubbing his erection against her hip. Damn, but he wanted to be inside her.

*I* need *to be inside her.*

Her hand closed over his butt, guiding him away from her hips and to her center. She arched against him, and a growl escaped him.

Stiffening, she jerked out of his hold, her hand moving to cover her mouth as she panted. "Um…I—you…"

She scurried out of the kitchen, leaving him Super Glued to the floor.

Why did she have to confuse him and make him horny as hell every time he saw her? What had he done wrong? Did she think he was going to ravage her against the center island?

As much as he wanted to strip off her prim blouse and knee-length skirt, he wouldn't have let things go past the kissing and groping stage. Never in his life had he had sex without protection, and he wouldn't have let it happen with her—especially when he wasn't even prepared.

He snorted.

*Like I was really just going to play with her nipples and cop another feel of her ass.*

She probably had on a pair of sexy stockings again. If she hadn't put on the brakes, the adage about a first time for everything could easily have come to pass—because common sense would've flown out the window.

He limped to the sink, turned the cold water on full blast, and stuck his head under the stream. The spray sent dribbles down the back of his shirt, making him shiver. Unfortunately, the icy dowsing did nothing to shrink his hard-on.

His willpower had deserted him, and more than likely, she'd call him into the office for that meeting tomorrow to fire him for crossing the line.

Why hadn't he kept his mouth—and his dick—to himself?

He'd ruined a perfectly good working relationship and screwed up the best job he'd ever had for one kiss.

*A damn fine kiss, but still only a kiss.*
*No happily ever after.*

She might've gotten caught up in the moment with him, but the moment had ended all too soon. Based on her reaction, she couldn't want him as much as he wanted her.

Turning off the tap, he reached for the towel. No amount of cold water would fix this, and an apology probably wouldn't, either. A week of trying to resist her had failed. He had limited choices.

*I should quit and go start packing now. Maybe Drew'll let me stay at the house long enough to find another job.*

He dried his hair, fumbling with the words he'd use to tender his resignation. His best bet was to slide it and the apartment keys under the door before she arrived at her office in the morning. He'd save them both a boatload of embarrassment.

The necessity of a clean kitchen drilled into his brain from his training, Flynn disposed of the empty box and utensils and then wiped down the counter. The microwave oven was next, followed by a quick assessment of the rest of the room. Lilith had limited her mess, like he would've expected after seeing her living space. Leaving the damp towel on the rack to dry, he switched off the lights and slinked to his apartment to make a phone call.

He skimmed through his contacts as he unlocked the door, tapping on Drew's number to connect instead of allowing his eyes to drift to his neighbor's dark windows. Her whereabouts were none of his business or concern, especially since she'd as good as rejected him. Too keyed up to sit, Flynn paced from one end of the living to the other.

His brother-in-law finally answered on the third ring. "Hey, Flynn."

"Hey, Drew. Do you mind if I stay with you for a few days?"

Several seconds of silence preceded a response. "No, I don't mind. What's up?"

Dropping to the couch, Flynn grunted. "I need a place to crash while I look for a new job."

"You got fired?"

"No, I'm quitting." The words left a nasty aftertaste in Flynn's mouth.

"Quitting? I thought you were excited about this position. What happened?"

Flynn leaned forward to rest his elbows on his knees. "A major misstep. And I love the job."

"That doesn't tell me what happened. Did you have a disagreement with your boss? You've only been home for about an hour."

"No, not a disagreement. I kissed her."

Drew's snickering hit a nerve. "Hmm. I guess she slapped you. At least you know the attraction isn't mutual."

"She didn't slap me! She kissed me back and then she…ran away." An all-out laugh in his ear had Flynn pushing to his feet to pace again. "Thanks for the support."

"Ah, come on, Flynn. She probably wouldn't have run away if she didn't like you—and the kiss. Maybe she's embarrassed, or she could think getting involved is a mistake. Women can be hard to read."

"You don't say."

"Sounds to me like quitting is *your* version of running away. You're not sure how she feels about you, so you want to cut your losses before she can tell you she isn't interested."

"Wait a minute. Whose side are you on? All I wanted was a bed for a few nights, and you're making me the bad guy."

"You're welcome to stay here, but you might try looking at the situation from her point of view. She hired a damn good chef to run her restaurant. I doubt she wants to jeopardize that for a couple kisses and a—"

"Okay, okay. I get your point." After kicking off his running shoes, he stalked to the kitchen. "You think I should pretend it didn't happen?"

"Play it by ear. If she doesn't mention it, don't bring it up. Give her a chance to figure out how she wants to handle your working relationship—and if she thinks having a personal one is okay."

Flynn's stomach somersaulted. "What about what I want?"

"Do you know what you want?"

Massaging his tense forehead with his fingertips, Flynn closed his eyes. He didn't have an immediate answer to that question. "I'll let you know if I decide to come hang out at your house. Later."

He ended the call, setting his phone beside the range and bracing his hands against the edge of the countertop.

*What* do *I want?*

Besides the obvious—Lilith naked under him—he wanted to spend his days cooking for and talking to the residents of Montgomery Crossing. They were nice people, if a little eccentric, and he enjoyed their company. Now that he had free time, visiting his family was a top priority. He needed more than a career, but the personal life he craved included a woman who could take the job he liked from him. Having it all seemed impossible.

Could he live without her so he could have the rest?

Maybe another week of keeping his distance would convince him that she wasn't the only girl in the world, assuming she didn't toss his ass off the property when he showed up for work in the morning. Then those seven days wouldn't matter, because he'd be busy looking for a new job.

# Chapter 13

With the last of the housing contracts filed, Lilith slid the drawer of the cabinet closed and checked the clock. She'd managed to sneak into the office while Flynn was in the kitchen serving up Saturday breakfast, averting an awkward meeting. His sticky note on the door had caught her off guard, though.

Had he left the request for a meeting last night or this morning? Before or after the kiss?

Why had she given in to the craving for his food? Better yet, what the hell had possessed her to act like a sex-crazed teenager?

*Why did he kiss me?*

Deep down, she hadn't expected Flynn to be like all the men she'd dated. He'd seemed kind and thoughtful.

*Remember the voice of experience?*

*Or I could remember what* actually *happened.*

Flynn may have initiated the kiss, but she'd put up no resistance. He wasn't any more to blame than she was. She'd allowed her bad judgment to take control when she should've known better, and he'd behaved like any normal guy.

Now she simply had to wait until he left to visit his family to go about her weekend business of laundry, housecleaning, and running errands. If Alice hadn't come to the office to ask if Flynn had invited Lilith on his outing, she might've been stuck doing paperwork all day to avoid him. She wasn't about to trust herself to have a private meeting with him.

Plopping down in the chair, she crossed her arms on the desk and lowered her head to the makeshift pillow. Exhaustion tried to pull her into sleep, and she teetered on the edge from a week of long hours and disconcerting dreams. Surrender took less energy than prying her eyes open.

A rapid set of knocks had her jerking upright and sent her heart pounding. She checked the clock. Only a couple minutes had passed, but the fogginess in her brain suggested she'd been asleep for far longer.

"Come in." She straightened and ran a hand over her hair to check for loose strands. Caught between hoping Flynn had stopped by to set up the meeting and dreading that she'd have to face him after last night, she clenched her fingers together on her lap.

The door swung inward, and a well-dressed woman stepped into the office. Her smile seemed affected, like she had little reason to be happy. "Miss Montgomery? I'm Eliza Langley. We spoke on the phone yesterday."

Relief mixed with disappointment as Lilith pushed to her feet. "Yes, hello, Mrs. Langley. Come in and sit down."

"Oh, it's 'Miss.' I never married." She crossed to the nearest chair and sat. "Please call me Eliza."

"And I'm Lilith." Lilith retrieved a move-in packet from the drawer and offered it to her visitor. "As I told you yesterday, Montgomery Crossing will have two singles apartments available within the next few weeks. You'll find a floor plan with the lease information, a list of amenities and activities, and an application in the envelope. Does your father have any special medical conditions or illnesses we need to be aware of?"

Eliza shook her head. "No, he's quite fit for a man of eighty-four. He just doesn't like living by himself in a big house anymore. He'd been trying to talk my mother into moving to a smaller place before she passed away last year."

"I'm so sorry for your loss." A pang of sympathy burned in Lilith's chest for a long moment. "Would you like a tour of the grounds?"

"Thank you, and a tour sounds wonderful." Eliza joined Lilith when she rose to put on her jacket. "I appreciate your taking the time to meet with me today. Having to look for an apartment for an elderly parent isn't something I really ever thought about until recently. It's a bit of a role reversal, isn't it?"

Gesturing for Miss Langley to precede her, Lilith locked the door behind them. "That's probably the comment I hear most often from those in your position. Do you have siblings to help with the packing and moving?"

"My brother and his wife live in Texas, so I'll be handling the arrangements by myself. I don't mind, though. My dad and I have always been close, and I understand how hard it must be for him to be alone." Eliza paused as they went out the exit to the courtyard. "This is lovely. My father loves to garden. Will he be allowed to pull weeds and mulch the beds?"

"Absolutely. We added the flowerbeds because so many of the residents enjoy gardening. It keeps them active, and they like maintaining their own yard. We even have a small garden plot for vegetables and herbs."

"Terrific! He's going to love living here. I guess Dad and I need to fill out this application and get the wheels in motion."

"I'll be glad to hold one of the apartments for a few days while we handle the paperwork." Continuing along the sidewalk, Lilith pointed to the buildings that would have empty units as soon as Harold and Marge moved into John and Norma's place. "Apartments 4E and 6C have the same floor plan as mine. I can show it to you if you like."

"Only if it isn't an inconvenience. You live on the premises?"

"Not a problem." Lilith dug the keys out of her pocket and led Miss Langley to her door. "This building accommodates six employees and has the same setup as the resident singles. I moved in about a year ago. Two of the cleaning staff, our maintenance man, one night nurse, and the chef in our new restaurant also live here."

Inside, Eliza followed her through the living room to the kitchen. "You've put a lot of work into making this a great place to work as well as live. Your parents must be very proud of your accomplishments."

Reluctant to take total credit, Lilith led her to the bedroom. "My mom and dad died when I was twelve, and my uncle came to take care of me. He owns and manages Montgomery Crossing. I'm acting director while Uncle Wade recovers from surgery."

Eliza's face paled, and she reached for the bedpost as her knees seemed to give out. "Wade? Wade Montgomery?"

Lilith guided her to the edge of the mattress to sit. "Are you okay?"

Her guest's whisper had Lilith straining to hear the words. "I knew a Wade Montgomery a long time ago."

The man she'd known had to have been more than a casual acquaintance, and Wade Montgomery was hardly a common name.

Had he broken Eliza Langley's heart?

Careful not to bump the framed picture of her parents, Lilith picked up the photo of her and Uncle Wade, holding it out for Eliza to see. "This was taken a couple months before my mom and dad died."

Somehow, Miss Langley grew even paler. "Did he...did he ever get married?"

*What did you do, Uncle Wade?*

"No. He became my legal guardian. We're all the family we have."

Eliza buried her face in her palms, muffling her words but not making them completely unintelligible. "Except for your cousin, Garrett Langley Montgomery."

\* \* \* \*

*Tan blazer in with lights. Navy pants go in darks.*
*Wait! Dry clean only.*
*Head is stuck in spin cycle.*

Tossing the pile of dirty clothes back in the basket, Lilith picked up her cell phone for the tenth time since Eliza Langley had left. While Lilith had no intention of dropping the bomb on Uncle Wade, she was tempted to cancel her scheduled visit.

How in the world would she sit and have a normal conversation with him, knowing what she did about his past?

The red-haired, green-eyed boy in the picture could easily be her cousin and Wade's son.

Did her uncle have any clue that he'd fathered a child?

Wade Montgomery wouldn't have walked away from his flesh and blood, not after the sacrifices he'd made to raise her. He'd never hinted at regrets for the choice he'd made. If anything, he seemed thankful for the opportunity to be a father to her since he'd remained a childless bachelor all his life.

Miss Langley hadn't shared the details of her relationship with Wade or the conception, and Lilith didn't want to know—not without hearing his side of the story.

*When did melodrama sneak in and take up residence in my quiet, uneventful existence?*

After shoving the basket back in the closet, Lilith traded her yoga pants and sweatshirt for jeans and a sweater. As distracted as she was, she'd turn her light-colored clothes blue and purple with red spots. Maybe her brain would be able to handle laundry in a few days.

Fifteen minutes later, she parked in the driveway of her childhood home. Uncle Wade's warm welcome and comforting hug at the mudroom door did nothing to ease the urge to spill Eliza Langley's secret.

"How are you doing, Lily girl?" He frowned as he lit the fire under the teakettle on the stove and touched his fingers to the empty crown of his head. Then he stirred the contents of the soup pot on the front burner. "Forgot to put on my hair today. You're working too hard, aren't you?"

She shrugged and inhaled the hearty aroma of Mulligan Stew. "I'm doing what has to be done. John needs help finding a place for him and Norma, so I spent most of the week making phone calls and setting up appointments. Harold and Marge asked about leasing John and Norma's apartment after they move, meaning we'll have two vacant singles soon.

And Betsy's mammogram showed a suspicious mass. She had to go in for a diagnostic on Thursday afternoon. Results should be available on Monday."

"Damn, I hope the cancer isn't back. Chemo just about did her in last time." Pulling his phone from his pocket, he tapped away at the screen. "Hm. Cut flowers or a potted plant? Ah, pink calla lilies. Perfect."

Lilith filled the tea ball and then placed it in the pot, her jittery nerves calming as her uncle's actions reminded her why she adored him so much. He was thoughtful and bighearted. A man as caring as him would've taken responsibility for Garrett if he'd known about him. Miss Langley had seemed sincere, but she could've lied.

Couldn't she?

*He deserves fair warning, no matter what the truth is.*

The teakettle whistled, and Lilith poured hot water over the tea to steep while she waited for him to complete the order. "Uncle Wade, I need to talk to you about something important."

He slid a pair of chairs out from the kitchen table and gestured for her to sit adjacent to him. "You're not going to start in on leaving Montgomery Crossing to find a *real* job, are you? Because I won't accept your resignation, young lady. Everybody there depends on you for too damn many little things to put them all on paper. *I* depend on you."

Guilt seeped in to keep her worry company. He might not have guessed what she wanted to discuss, but he'd hit on a subject that had crossed her mind more than once since her visit with him last Sunday. He had all the makings of an annoyingly good parent.

She dropped into the seat. "Fine, I'll stay. But that isn't what I want to discuss. A woman came to pick up an application and tour the grounds today. She said she knows you."

"I know lots of people. What's her name? And I assume that means we'll have only one empty unit once we do the switcheroo."

"Yes, she thinks her father will enjoy living there. Her name is Eliza Langley. She has brow—"

"I know what she looks like." He stood so fast, his chair tipped over backward and banged on the tile floor. Pacing to the counter, he took two china cups from the cabinet and poured the tea. His hands fisted and unfisted several times before he removed the lid from the sugar bowl. He stood without moving for a full minute. "She's the reason I never married."

"I'm so sorry. I'll tell her something came up, that the units aren't available." Lilith rubbed at the hollow ache in her chest. Evidently, she wasn't the lone Montgomery to have bad luck in love—and she'd invited the enemy to come for a visit. "Please forgive me, Uncle Wade. She asked to see you, and I gave her your address. She's supposed to be here in a couple minutes."

Opening the lower cupboard, he removed a bottle of Jameson. He added a splash to the teacup on the right. "Care to join me, Lil?"

*Skip the tea and pour me a glass.*

"You shouldn't drink if you've been taking the pain pills the doctor prescribed." At the narrowed gaze he cast over his shoulder at her, she pushed back her chair and stood. "Forget I said that. What the hell do I know, anyway? Pour a couple fingers for both of us, and don't bother with the ice."

"Yer a fine Irish lass, ye are, Lily. And I quit taking the pain pills ten days ago. I didn't like feeling fuzzy headed." He pushed the tea aside and tipped up the bottle into a pair of highball glasses, the two fingers' worth ending up closer to three-quarters full. "Shall we adjourn to the livin' room until the heartless wench comes callin'?"

Ready to pickle her own problems as well, Lilith gave a decisive nod. "I don't think I'll be driving home tonight. Do you mind if I stay in my old room?"

He handed her a dose of forgetfulness and offered her his arm. "This is your home. You'll always be welcome whether I'm living here or not."

The ding-dong of the doorbell made her jump.

Downing a hefty swallow of whiskey, he detoured to the front door. "Excuse my profanity, Lily girl. It's sure to be dandy."

Eliza had to have done something truly horrendous for Uncle Wade to resort to swearing at a woman. He'd never so much as raised his voice at a female, let alone resorted to offensive language.

He swung the door wide and opened his mouth as if to speak. After several seconds, he gestured for the person on the porch to come inside. "I feel fine, but the doctor says no lifting for another three weeks."

A trio of teenagers entered, Lilith recognizing one of them as the boy from a few houses up the street. He gave a casual wave. "Hi, Miss Montgomery."

She smiled, too relieved to do more than return his wave.

Pointing at a sealed box near the window, Wade patted the other boy on the back. "I appreciate you picking up my donation. Did you sign me up for one of those Christmas tree names? I want to shop for a twelve-year-old girl, same as before."

The young woman nodded and held out a package wrapped in foil. "Yes, Mr. Montgomery. I'll drop off her wish list as soon as they're posted. These are for you. My mom and I made cookies to help you get better quicker."

"Thank you, lassie. Tell your mother I said hello."

Trooping out the door with the box, the visitors left and Uncle Wade seemed to watch them go until they were out of sight. Finally, he shut out the chill.

His expression turned thoughtful. "Nice kids. I would've liked to have had one or two myself, but I'll never regret being ma and da to you, Lily. You saved me from a lifetime of sorrow."

Tipping up her glass, she washed the lump in her throat down with a swallow of whiskey. "Stop it. You're going to make me cry."

His offer to buy presents for a girl the age she'd been when her parents died had already set them in motion.

He was quiet as he sat down beside her on the couch. Would he still have the same attitude if he knew the woman who'd broken his heart might've given him that gift?

*I hope, for your sake, she isn't lying, Uncle Wade.*

Lilith took another sip, leaning her head against his shoulder. Without him for support, she would've crumbled long ago.

"I loved Eliza." His soft voice held no bitterness or contempt now, only sadness. "Too bad she didn't love me. I suppose that's how relationships go sometimes, though. Ready for supper?"

"Sure." Setting her drink on the end table, she rose. "She's late. What will you do if she doesn't show up?"

He followed her to the kitchen. "Keep living. I may not have found someone else to love, but I haven't stopped looking and hoping."

His statement hit too close to home, and she dished up their stew instead of commenting. He'd probably pester her about having a social life and spending time with people her own age. Then he'd tell her that the right man was worth waiting for, and she needed to be ready when he showed up to sweep her off her feet. For having loved and lost, Uncle Wade was far too optimistic about finding The One.

An hour passed, and then two.

At ten o'clock, Lilith drained the last few dribbles from her second glass and got up to check the locks. When she shuffled back through the living room, her uncle was switching off the lamp.

He gave her a gentle hug and a kiss on the cheek. "Sleep well, love. Do you want me to go with you tomorrow?"

"Thanks for the offer." Trying for a smile, she shook her head. No one should be subjected to her presence on the most depressing day of her year. "I'll be fine. Goodnight, Uncle Wade. I love you."

She hurried up the stairs to her old bedroom before he could contradict her, because she had no idea whether she'd ever reach "okay."

# Chapter 14

Surrendering to a yawn, Flynn parked in his assigned space and cut the engine. He'd stayed at Merie's house later than he'd intended, but a year was a lot of missed time to make up for.

He pulled on the handle to get out, careful not to bang his door into his next-door neighbor's car—except her car wasn't there. Had Lilith finally taken a little time off from working eighty hours a week?

Saturday seemed to be her laundry, housekeeping, and errand day. Maybe she was making a late-night grocery run.

*Or she could be avoiding me again after last night.*

They'd both become experts at steering clear of each other, and their kiss had complicated matters even more. As much as he'd tried to put it out of his mind, the feel of her lips against his had invaded his thoughts almost constantly for the past twenty-four hours.

That single kiss had held more passion and desire than he could ever remember sharing with any other woman. His willpower to resist her was weakening, and he wanted it all—the job, the time for family, and the girl. Every part of his life seemed to be falling into place.

Was she one of the pieces that had been missing? How could he find out without jeopardizing the new job he truly enjoyed?

He caught himself eyeing the unlit office window and then her dark apartment windows. She wasn't home. He should be grateful he hadn't crossed paths with her on the sidewalk, because chances were pretty good he would've begged her for another kiss.

*And a night in her bed. Or a week. Maybe longer.*

His sex drive might've gone into hibernation when he'd been working himself to death, but it was awake and raring to go now. If sex had been all he needed, he might've been able to convince himself to hook up with some stranger in a bar, but he wasn't interested in a one-night stand.

Something about Lilith made him want more.

She was gorgeous and alluring, but her interaction with the residents fascinated him every bit as much. She'd do almost anything for any one of the people who lived in the retirement village. Her flight response from their kiss convinced him she'd also been hurt by someone—probably a guy who'd taken advantage of her sweet nature.

Inside his apartment, he kicked off his shoes and shed his jacket. With brunch on the menu tomorrow, he could afford to stay up a little later, but he got ready for bed. His habit of rising before the sun would wake him early, and he had a quick errand to run in the morning before heading to the kitchen.

The shoebox drew Flynn's attention as he slipped under the covers. Since reading Kate's letter, he'd managed to get through a few pictures a day. Somehow, the stack of photos had dwindled down to the last one. Tonight, the layer of tissue paper was coming out of the box.

Gently lifting out the print, he tilted toward the lamp to study the scene. It could've been from any number of family get-togethers, if not for the dull quality of his sister's smile. Actually, all of her looked different. She was thinner, her eyes not as bright and her hair limp and faded.

How had he not noticed?

Death had already started taking her away, and he'd been too caught up in his own world to even see it.

He turned the picture over.

*"I can't tell you I'm dying. I want to see your smile. Are you happy, Flynn? Make the most of your opportunities to discover true happiness."*

Each successive message had gotten more philosophical, urging him to live for every moment of his life. She'd paraphrased more than a dozen clichéd sayings in one way or another, every one telling him to stop and enjoy the roses.

*Or the Lily.*

Was he making a mistake by distancing himself from Lilith Montgomery?

The worst she could do was can his ass if he asked her to consider going out with him. The best that could happen was she'd consent to a date and they'd fall crazy in love.

He didn't particularly want to start another job search, but what if he missed out on connecting with the love of his life?

Setting aside the photo, he moved the box to his lap to remove the crumpled tissue paper. A rectangular-shaped package rested in the bottom. He lifted it out, tearing away the wrapping. A book landed on the bed beside him, its worn back cover vaguely familiar.

He picked it up, examining the front before opening it to the first page.

Kate's handwriting looped and swayed across the paper.

*"To the best little brother a girl could have. Happy reading! (As if you haven't read most of it already) All my love, Kate"*

Flynn's insides ached, but a laugh escaped. She'd given him her diary—the one she'd caught him red-handed sneaking back into her dresser drawer when he was nine. Lucky for her, he'd sucked at learning cursive writing. He could read it now, but writing it so anyone could read it was a lost cause.

Carefully flipping pages, he scanned the opening line of the first entry.

*"Younger brothers are almost as bad as younger sisters…"*

\* \* \* \*

Flynn blindly patted the air until his fingers touched wood, and then he smacked at the snooze button. The alarm buzzed on. Forcing his eyes open, he tried again, grateful when silence replaced the jarring noise.

Staying up until almost two had been a bad idea, no matter how absorbing his sister's diary was. She'd shared her most private secrets with him, but he should've rationed them instead of devouring the whole damn book. The insight made understanding why she hadn't told him about her illness much easier, even if her secret had caused him more pain than he'd ever known.

Of his three older sisters, only Kate had known about the miscarriage their mom had suffered before he'd been conceived. The need to protect and shelter him made sense now. If their positions had been reversed, he probably would've been scared of something terrible happening to his youngest sibling too.

He rolled onto his back to stare at the ceiling. The security lights still shone in the courtyard, their rays filtering in through the blinds, sending flecks of light to dot the surface. The night-sky pattern served as a reminder of the hour his wake-up call had come.

Four hours of sleep wasn't near enough, but he got up anyway. While he showered, he could rehearse the proposition he'd finally decided on in the wee hours.

He liked Lilith, and telling her was the next step in moving on with his future. Sitting around waiting for her to acknowledge his existence could take weeks or months. Life was too short to take the passive approach. He'd worry about what to do if she rejected him when it happened.

*If it happens. Gotta think positive.*

Twisting the knob to hot, he turned on the water for a steaming shower. Every line he recited seemed too practiced, and he finished washing and shaving with no clue how to say he wanted to get to know her on a personal—romantic—level.

Asking her out to dinner was ridiculous when he could prepare a meal for her. Inviting her to his apartment for a meal might give her the idea that he was more interested in getting laid than eating or getting acquainted. With their work schedules, neither of them had coinciding free time until at least seven o'clock most evenings. He'd probably scare her off completely if he invited her to his parents' house for Sunday dinner for their first date.

Still racking his brain for a plan, he grabbed his keys and headed to his truck.

Half an hour later, he stashed the bouquet in his fridge, traded his street clothes for chef whites, and locked the door behind him. Brunch prep was up next.

Turning to follow the sidewalk to the main building, he nearly plowed over Lilith.

She stepped backward and shoved her fingers through what looked like sleep-mussed hair. Her cheeks were flushed peach under the yellowish glow of the courtyard lights. She wore the same green sweater she'd been wearing when he'd spied her leaving yesterday.

Nibbling on her lower lip, she waved and ducked into her apartment before he could even wish her a good morning.

His stomach dove to his knees. No, he hadn't heard her come home last night, but he'd been immersed in the diary. Her attire, messy hair, and full blush spoke for themselves. She'd spent the night with a lover, and Flynn was shit out of luck where she was concerned.

That well-loved, just-rolled-out-of-bed look would've had him dragging her back for another round. He also would've found a way to spend the entire day with her.

*Too bad I'll never have the chance.*

He'd fallen for a woman who wasn't available. Not for a second had the notion crossed his mind—not when she buried herself in work almost every day. She'd barely left her office in the week and a half since he'd met her.

Why would the possibility that she had a boyfriend enter his head?

Reality had sucker punched him right in the gut.

Frozen in place, Flynn struggled to set his feet in motion. Calling in sick wouldn't exactly constitute a lie. His chest hurt, his stomach had tied itself in knots, and all the hope he'd fostered since making the decision to pursue Lilith had splattered on the sidewalk at his feet. Working for her would be purgatory. Living next to her without being able to admit his feelings would drive him insane.

*No wonder she ran away when I kissed her. A boyfriend. Shit.*

Shaking off the disappointment, he strode past the gardens. As much as he preferred a quick cutting of ties to a drawn-out two-week notice, he couldn't justify leaving the friendly group of seniors to fend for themselves. His boss hardly had time to cook for them. He'd search the web for job openings—again—between drafting his resignation and feeling sorry for himself. Then he'd call Drew about the spare bedroom.

*Back to square one. Well, maybe square two. I'm home with the family.*

An hour of chopping, whisking, and sautéing didn't work its usual magic. If anything, his mood worsened. He *hated* the thought of quitting a job he loved, and he'd been stupid to fantasize about his boss.

*I know better than to mix business with pleasure. Why did I let my dick talk me into thinking about her as a woman?*

"Hey, Flynn! The natives are getting restless out here!" Alice stood inside the server door, her hands perched on her hips.

He loaded the last of the serving dishes on the cart. "Sorry. I'll be right out."

"What's gotten into you? Nursing a hangover like Lily?"

"A hangover?"

Alice nodded.

Lilith didn't seem like the type to get drunk.

Grasping the handle, he rolled the cart toward the exit. "No hangover for me. I stayed up late reading last night."

"Reading's good. At least she spent the night at Wade's instead of driving home. Getting behind the wheel of a car when you're tipsy is something I don't tolerate." Alice held the door open for him.

*Wade's? Oh, yeah. Her uncle.*

Relief triggered a jump in his pulse.

*Stop right there. Maybe she isn't sleeping with some loser, but that doesn't mean I should. Damn, I need to think about this some more.*

"You're right, Alice. Drinking and driving don't mix."

*Like business and pleasure?*

"It's about time Lily let her hair down a bit. What with doing her own job and Wade's too, I'm surprised the poor girl hasn't collapsed." After walking with Flynn to the buffet table, Alice transferred a platter to the serving area. "The boss man should be back to work in a couple weeks, though. That gallbladder of his won't be giving him any more trouble."

*The boss man?*

"Lilith's uncle manages Montgomery Crossing?" Flynn flexed his fingers to loosen their grip on the handle. They were almost numb from squeezing so hard.

"Owns and manages. Lily's acting director while he recuperates from surgery. Didn't she tell you Wade'll be back in the office by Thanksgiving?"

"No." Another loophole tempted him to toss out his reasoning for not getting involved with his enticing neighbor.

"With all the stuff she's had to juggle, I'm not surprised she forgot to mention it. Then again, she probably thinks she can use that excuse to ward off my matchmaking skills. I'm telling you, Flynn. You two need to get cracking. There're sheets to set on fire and a happily ever after to wrangle into submission."

He tried and failed to suffocate a chuckle. "Sheets to set on fire?"

Moving the last of the brunch items to the table, Alice waggled her eyebrows at him. "Yeah. And mattresses to burn. You should've seen the sparks a-flying when you and Lily met on the sidewalk this morning. I'd suggest keeping a fire extinguisher handy. The whole place is liable to go up in flames with the first kiss. Or has Lily already gotten on base with you?"

His face had to be bright red. Still, he wasn't one to kiss and tell. "Thanks for helping, Alice. I'd better get back to work."

Her humming followed him all the way to the kitchen.

*"Flynn and Lilith sitting in a tree, K-I-S-S-I-N-G. First comes love. Next comes marriage. Then comes Flynn with a baby carriage."*

They hadn't been in a tree for that first kiss. Their meeting of mouths had happened less than ten feet from where he stood—and sex would've come next if she hadn't slammed on the brakes.

Lust was blurring the line between emotional and sexual attraction, but love, marriage, and a baby carriage didn't scare him. He could handle those—and an affair that ended with one or both of them singed would be a hell of a lot worse than the scenario featuring another man that he'd imagined earlier.

Indecisiveness dogged him through refilling the tray of rolls and pulling the second dish of scalloped apples from the oven. He pushed through the server door to make the last delivery.

"You feeling okay, Flynn?" Harold furrowed his thick gray eyebrows as he added milk to his coffee. "You're not having woman trouble with Lily, are you? 'Cause I got a bit of advice for you there. Apologize, whether you think you're right or wrong, buy her flowers and chocolate, and tell her she's special. That'll fix damn near everything."

Giving a nod, Flynn kept his mouth shut. He'd learned to listen and agree during the last week, his advisors' advice coming from decades of experience. They didn't need to know about the state of his and Lilith's strange hot-and-cold association, either. Neither of them seemed to know what they wanted.

Harold leaned in closer. "An orgasm is always good too."

Did all seventy-, eighty-, and ninety-somethings have sex on the brain?

"I'll keep that in mind." Flynn wouldn't forget receiving that pointer from a man more than twice his age.

Retreating to the kitchen again, he gathered the pots, pans, and bowls he'd used and washed them. Too much nervous tension was pumping through his veins to stand around waiting for the meal to end.

*She doesn't have a boyfriend.*

*She isn't the person who signs the paychecks.*

*She wouldn't have kissed me if she wasn't interested, would she?*

Logic dictated she had to like him, even if she had the same misgivings he had about dating a co-worker. Her avoidance of him could be explained by Alice's revelation that Lilith was covering hers and her uncle's jobs.

Hadn't he started out trying not to cross paths with her because of the working-together issue?

*Okay, I'll go for it. The worst she can do is reject and fire me.*

He rushed through cleanup, packaging the extra servings and stowing them while his kitchen helper cleared the tables and rinsed the dishes. They had the dining room ready for Monday breakfast in record time.

Ten minutes later, Flynn made a quick stop to change his clothes and retrieve the bouquet he'd bought earlier. Then he headed out his apartment door.

# Chapter 15

Lilith worked her fingers into her gloves and frowned at the gray sky as she climbed out from behind the steering wheel. The wintery clouds fit her mood much better than the colorful autumn wreath she'd picked up from the florist's shop yesterday. Between the hangover, Eliza Langley's games, and today's errand, her weekend was shaping up to be the worst of the year. The only redeeming event had left her confused, conflicted, and in need of a new vibrator.

*I should've left as soon as Flynn came in the kitchen. Kissing him was a mistake.*

She'd made a bigger mistake grabbing his ass and grinding her lower belly against his erection. The size and shape of what he hid under his whites was no longer under speculation.

A faint spasm rippled through her lower belly.

*It was a shiver. I'm just cold.*

A dose of reality had more than likely cured his case of lust this morning. Having her handsome neighbor catching her looking like something from *Night of the Living Dead* was sure to have destroyed any spark of interest he might've had in her.

She carefully lifted the wreath from the hatch, balancing the ring of grapevines, bittersweet, and mums against her leg to close the back door. The clunk aggravated her lingering headache.

The annual ritual always put her in funk for a couple days anyway, memories of that fateful day still vivid in her mind. Uncle Wade had come over to stay the evening with her while her parents went out to dinner to celebrate their twentieth wedding anniversary. To this day, she couldn't eat pizza, having taken the first bite right before the doorbell rang to announce her mom and dad had died in a car accident ten minutes after saying good-bye to her.

She hefted the wreath and walked toward the plot she could probably find with her eyes closed—not that having her eyes open helped. Tears had blurred her vision the second she'd shut off the car. The sight of the wide headstone acted as an "on" switch to her grief, and her once-a-year cry seemed to get her through until the next time.

Under the spreading branches of the leafless maple, she leaned the decoration against the marble base, leaving the names and dates uncovered. She dropped to her knees to trace the etched lettering. "Bye, Mom. Bye, Dad. I love you too."

The tears flowed faster, dribbling down her cheeks to drip off her chin. Although the sorrow didn't reach as deep as it had when she was twelve, the emptiness in that corner of her heart still amplified the loss and the chill spread to the rest of her body.

Too bad the numbness didn't dull the pain.

\* \* \* \*

Counting the stones, Flynn followed the paved path up the hill to the twelfth marker on the left. He stepped off the blacktop into the brown grass, moving close enough to read the inscription.

*Kathryn Hastings-Fulton.*

He replaced the withered bouquet in the metal vase with the fresh flowers he'd bought that morning and then stuffed his hands in his jacket pockets. Luckily, rain from the night before had filled the holder since he hadn't thought to bring water.

"You probably thought I'd never come back, didn't you, Kate? I just needed some time to get my shit together. You didn't have to keep the truth from me, but I understand why you did. You always did your best to protect me from the hard stuff. I appreciate that, and I'm proud to say you were my big sister."

The words hadn't stuck in his throat like he'd expected them to, and the same sense of relief he'd experienced visiting Drew and the girls settled over him again. He was finally getting his life back on track.

*Took me long enough, didn't it?*

"I met somebody. I'm not sure how things will go, but I'll give it a shot. She's smart and pretty, and she's nice to everybody. Well, except me. She mostly ignores me. I think she's upset because I kissed her. You'd like her."

Crumpled brown leaves rustled across the ground in front of him, the gusty breeze sending them past the headstone and toward the path.

"Love ya, Kate. I'll be back soon. Oh, and thanks for the box of stuff. I think I'm okay now."

He turned to head to his car, but muffled crying drew his attention to the other side of the path. A woman hunched over a wreath with orange, yellow, and white flowers, her shoulders heaving beneath her strawberry-blonde hair.

*Lilith?*

Why would she be here?

He crossed the pavement, hoping for a closer look.

Another gust blew hair into her face, and she tucked the loose strands behind her ear, giving him a clear view of her silhouette. If this Irish beauty wasn't Lilith, she had a twin.

He closed the gap between them. His chest tightened as he read the names on the headstone where she knelt. The man and woman buried there had to be her parents, and by the dates, today was the twentieth anniversary of their passing. She couldn't have been more than about ten or twelve years old when they'd died.

Empathy compelled him to kneel beside her. The desire to hold her came from more than simple compassion. Affection made him fold his arms around her, gathering her against him. "I'm so sorry for your loss, Lilith. I wish I could make it better."

She looked up at him, her cheeks pink from the cold and her eyes red from crying. Her lips trembled as she blinked at him.

He fell for her a little more, and he let his heart guide him. "I'm here for you. What can I do to help?"

Twisting toward him, she clutched at his shoulders. A whisper carried to him on a gentle breath. "Kiss me."

Elated that she seemed to want what he wanted, he lowered his mouth to hers, gently pressing his lips to her cool skin. She didn't panic like she had the first time, and he took the kiss deeper, tracing the seam of her lips to ask for entrance.

She opened for him, meeting his tongue as he glided inside for a taste. Instead of the flavor of pasta, a hint of dark chocolate and mint tempted him to explore every inch of her seductive mouth. His intent for a slow exploration transitioned to a wild mating of tongues as she sucked and nipped at him, sending his control to the edge.

Tossing aside her gloves, she worked several of his shirt buttons free and rubbed her cool palms over his chest and along his neck to his back. The touch of her hands on his bare skin had his cock trying to bust his zipper. He cupped her breasts through her coat and debated his options. Stripping her down to make love to her out in the elements, especially on her parents' grave, was out of the question.

Easing away from her mouth, he pulled in a lungful of air. "My car's down by the—"

Her body stiffened against him, his voice seeming to break the spell. "No, I can't. This is a mistake."

She scrambled to her feet, meeting his gaze for a moment before looking away. The next second, she beat a hasty retreat down the hill, fleeing like she couldn't escape fast enough. As much as her body was obviously telling her yes, her mind was still saying no.

Did he have the patience and the desire to wait her out? Was he willing to accept that she might not want to be with him?

*She wouldn't have kissed me if she didn't feel anything. Casual sex isn't her style.*

*Ah, Lily, I wish you'd give me a chance.*

A car door slammed and an engine cranked over to inform him she'd reached her car and was leaving him alone to analyze her actions and reactions. He might've grown up with three older sisters, but they'd given him little insight into why women behaved the way they did. What made sense to women didn't have to be understandable to guys. Merie or Colleen certainly wouldn't refuse to give him advice on the subject. The biggest issue was keeping them from blabbing to the entire family that he was thinking of getting serious with a woman.

Flynn almost jogged to his car to shadow Lilith home, but giving her space was probably a wiser choice. If he crowded her, she'd likely push him even farther away. If he left her alone, she'd wonder why he hadn't chased after her. The situation was no-win from an immediate perspective. No matter how helpless she'd appeared today, she was strong, and he'd score more points by letting her be independent than treating her like a weak little girl. In time, she'd see that he wasn't out for a casual fling, that he respected and cared for her.

Her gloves bunched in one hand, he folded up the collar of his jacket against the wind and stood. "You'd be proud of her, Mr. and Mrs. Montgomery. She's a wonderful person."

"Damn right she is." The low voice coming from behind Flynn sent his pulse hammering in his veins, and he jerked his gaze over his shoulder. A man not much taller than Lilith shuffled up to the plot, holding what looked like a thatch of fake red hair to his head. "You must be the new chef. Hastings, right? Flynn Hastings. Good Irish name. I'm Wade Montgomery. What were doing kissing my Lilliputian?"

*Wade Montgomery. Lily's uncle.*

*He saw us kissing. Shit.*

Not sure where to start, Flynn replayed the older man's words in his mind. A burst of laughter burst out of his throat. "Lilliputian? You don't call her that to her face, do you?"

"You think I have a death wish?" Eyes nearly identical to Lilith's sparkled with what Flynn could only assume was amusement.

"No, sir. Yeah, Flynn Hastings, the new chef. Um, the kiss. Well, it just sort of happened."

"Does that mean you like her? Or are you just trying to get in her pants? Because if that's the case, you better find yourself some other girl. I've had it with boys messing around with my Lily's heart."

Flynn turned toward Wade to extend his hand, meeting the man's intent stare. Not about to admit wanting to get in her pants, Flynn smiled and offered the next best thing—the other truth. "Nice to meet you, Mr. Montgomery. Yes, I like her a lot."

Ignoring Flynn's outstretched hand, Wade slapped him on the back. "Good. Lily needs a boyfriend who'll treat her right."

Flynn could hardly disagree with Lilith's uncle, but achieving boyfriend status would take more than passing a note to her in the hall asking her to go out with him. "She hasn't been very receptive to being anything other than casual acquaintances."

"Ah." Wade reached up to adjust the patch of hair again. "Giving you a rough time, is she? I don't blame her after the last loser she dated. You have your work cut out for you."

Nodding, Flynn debated asking the man for help, but pushed the idea aside—at least for now. Showing her he was a nice guy would take some time, and outside pressure could easily backfire. "She's worth the effort."

"I think I like you, Flynn Hastings. When you get back to Montgomery Crossing, send Alice to make sure Lily's okay. Twenty years hasn't done much to heal the pain of losing her parents." Mr. Montgomery rested his hand on the top of the marble headstone. "Oh, and don't you dare tell her I was here. She'll raise hell if she finds out I haven't been home playing invalid."

As protective as she was of the residents, Flynn could well imagine how she'd react if she knew her uncle had been out gallivanting instead of staying home to recover from his surgery. "I won't say a word—not that Lilith won't be avoiding me like the plague anyway. Take care."

Walking to his car, he couldn't help wondering what excuses she'd use to stay in her office until after supper this week. He'd probably be lucky to even catch a glimpse of her for days.

How long would he have to wait before she finally trusted him not to hurt her?

She was worth waiting for, but he hated the thought of weeks or months passing by as he watched for a sign that she might not reject him again.

Although he'd planned to drive to his mom and dad's from the cemetery, he detoured for a stop at the apartment. He had a task for Alice Carlton, and the old gal would be tickled hot pink to know he'd crossed paths with Lily. She'd tried all last week to get Lilith to the restaurant so she could play cupid. Even her husband, CC, had conspired with the day nurse to get the workaholic out of her office. Nothing had worked—yet.

Lilith's car was parked in her usual space, and Flynn followed the sidewalk the long way around the complex toward the couples' buildings. As he approached the Carlton's apartment, Alice exited the front door and set off at a steady pace, trained right at him.

"Hey there, Flynn. Think you can keep up with me?" She shot past him, and he pivoted to catch up to her, taking two short strides for every three long ones of hers. "You look like a man who needs a bit of advice. Lily still avoiding you?"

He shrugged. "Sort of, but I don't really need advice so much as somebody to check on her. She was at the cemetery today, visiting her mom and dad's grave. She's having a really rough day."

"Then why don't you go comfort her, offer her those broad shoulders to cry on? Bet you could think of a cure for that hangover too."

He should've expected nothing less than bluntness from Alice. "Hmm. I don't know her very well, and I think she'd probably rather talk to a woman."

"You tried to help her, but she ran away like a scared kitten, huh? Okay, I'll stop by her apartment. Don't you worry that handsome head of yours." Alice winked at him. "Might drop a good word or two about a young man she ought to get to know better. You two would make the cutest little redheaded babies."

While Flynn wasn't opposed to having children, Alice was jumping the gun a bit. "No kids until after the wedding. I'd kinda like to have my wife to myself for a couple years."

"Ha! You think she's your Miss Right! I knew it." Alice grinned as she increased her speed.

Shaking his head, he lengthened his stride. The sneaky matchmaker had twisted his words to fit her agenda. "Now, I didn't say that exactly. She could be, but I won't know until I spend some time with her. We met all of nine days ago."

"Only takes a second or two for the lust bunny to strike. If the boys are still excited to see her after a week, it's more than a simple itch that needs scratching. Any fellow who knows how many days since he met a gal is downright twitterpated."

Rounding the corner of the main building beside his pink-haired companion, he pulled his keys from his back pocket. With them came Lilith's gloves. "Okay, you made your point. I don't want to scare her off, though, so try not to be too obvious if you mention me. Would you mind returning these to her?"

"You betcha, hot stuff!" She swatted his ass and then grabbed the gloves as she continued along the sidewalk. "Yeah, baby. Buns of steel. Lil's a lucky girl!"

Flynn couldn't hold in his grin. The residents of Montgomery's Crossing had quickly become some of his favorite people, their tendency to speak their minds refreshing. They had nothing to lose by being completely honest. Too bad he couldn't do the same with Lilith.

Slipping into the driver's seat, he vowed to be patient. Her uncle had as good as told him every guy she'd ever dated had treated her like shit. She had a right to be cautious, cynical even. Eventually, she'd have to realize Flynn liked her and would treat her with respect.

Wouldn't she?

*One step at a time.*

He'd never really had to woo a woman into going out with him.

Should he buy her gifts? Maybe flowers or chocolate?

Those seemed kind of impersonal and not terribly original, creative, or thoughtful. A carefully chosen card could be an effective way to show her that he was sensitive—without pushing her to acknowledge their personal encounters. He'd have to make a conscious effort to write so she'd be able to read his message and signature, though.

*What if I deliver breakfast and supper to her office every day? Overkill or concern for her health?*

He'd have to check with Wanda about that. A couple times a week might make a better impression. Too much attention might annoy Lilith and make him look insincere, as would giving her presents that she might perceive as being too intimate. Achieving the proper balance was key to gaining her trust.

Sisterly advice was in order, even if Meredith and Colleen teased him to no end. A chance with Lilith was worth the playful banter and goofy suggestions his sisters were sure to offer.

*Because I don't want to screw up the opportunity of a lifetime.*

# Chapter 16

*I know I shouldn't ask, but what else can go wrong today?*

Tugging on dress pants and a blouse, Lilith glared at her alarm clock. Some mornings it woke her when she could've sworn she'd turned the stupid thing off. Others, it failed to wake her when she needed to get up for work. She should've replaced it weeks ago.

Her sweater caught on the doorknob as she tried to hurry out of the bedroom, nearly sending her sprawling on the carpet. She shoved her arms into the sleeves and jogged to the kitchen to grab a granola bar for breakfast. Spying her keys on the counter, she shoved them into her pocket so she wouldn't walk out the front door without them again.

*Shirt, pants, shoes, sweater. Makeup and hair done. Keys. If I forgot anything, I'll get it later.*

She paused for a brief moment of calm and quiet before pulling the door open to leave. A pale green envelope dropped to the sidewalk, and she rushed to pick it up. All she needed to add to the crappy start of her day was to have a card from one of the residents ruined from falling in a puddle.

Yanking the door closed, she clutched the envelope and then set off toward the main building. Icy wind cut through her clothes, raising goose bumps over her skin. She'd have to remember to wear a coat tomorrow—*if* she managed to get out of bed.

The double doors slid open at her approach, and she sent up a silent thank-you to whoever had arrived before she did.

*Probably Flynn.*

She peeked into the still-dark dining room. The only light shone from the server door window. Maybe she could arrive at Uncle Wade's office without crossing paths with the man she'd almost stripped naked in the cemetery yesterday.

Rushing past the reception desk, she ducked into the office, plunked down in the desk chair, and closed her eyes. Her attraction to Flynn hadn't waned at all over the week and a half since the interview. Two out-of-control tongue wars had turned the sparks into a full-blown flambé. Crêpes Suzette and Cherries Jubilee had nothing on the flames she and her chef had created—and no alcohol had been involved.

*Can I handle getting scorched?*

None of her former boyfriends had triggered that kind of combustibility. Flynn would turn her heart to a pile of ashes if he followed in the footsteps of every other man she'd ever dated. The prospect wasn't a pleasant one.

No, she couldn't take the risk.

She leaned forward, focusing her attention on the envelope in her hand. Someone had printed her name on the front in pencil, but she didn't recognize the handwriting. A careful slide of the letter opener broke the seal.

The scene on the card chased away the stress of waking late and harboring an unhealthy infatuation for a certain Irishman. A pair of calico kittens had unrolled part of a ball of yarn, their furry legs tangled in yards of string as they curled up together for a nap.

*"Life got you tied in knots?"*

She flipped to the inside.

*"Me too. I'll keep you company while we work out the tangles."*

The sentiment chased away the chill from her brisk walk.

Which one of her friends from the complex had known she needed a shoulder to lean on?

Block lettering that resembled a kindergartner's attempts at printing covered one side of the interior. A glance to the bottom of the page made her heart skip a beat.

*Flynn?*

Curious about his note, she started at the top.

*"Lilith, I'm so sorry about the death of your parents. You must've been very close. If you ever want or need to talk, I'll be glad to listen. I lost my oldest sister to cancer a year ago and I'm still learning to cope. Accepting the unfairness of it all has been the hardest part. You're not alone. Flynn"*

His words touched her soul, and his effort to make them legible kindled something more than physical desire. Despite his recent loss, he was offering to help her deal with something that had happened twenty years ago. He also understood one of the most difficult aspects of surviving the death of a loved one.

Since he didn't mention their accidental meeting yesterday, did that mean he'd attributed both make-out sessions to his or her grief?

He must've been at the cemetery to visit his sister's grave. Had their mourning set off the need to connect with each other on a physical level?

*No, I wanted to rip off all his clothes when he stepped into the office for his interview. He just caught me at my weakest moments.*

Under different circumstances, would they have acted on what seemed to be a mutual attraction?

*I wish I knew.*

Tucking the card in the drawer for safekeeping, she powered up her laptop and brought up her calendar. The produce order was due by noon and the Reeds were scheduled to drop by to give her an update on their search for new living quarters. After their visit, she'd make a trip to her apartment, where she kept a stash of greeting cards. For now, she'd carve out a few minutes to formulate an appropriate message.

*Flynn, Thank you for your kindness. Acceptance truly is the hardest part of losing someone you love. I hope each day eases the pain a little more for you as it has for me. The invitation to talk goes both ways. Lily*

She read and reread the words she'd typed on the screen. Did she come across as too impersonal? Too much like a grief counselor? Or would he interpret the last sentence as encouragement for something beyond friendship?

*Do I want more than friendship?*

Her body undoubtedly did, but her ability to judge a man's true character and motives left a lot to be desired. At thirty-two, she shouldn't be naïve anymore. She'd certainly gotten her feelings stomped plenty of times.

She reached for the Delete key as a knock sounded. Her insides somersaulted with the thought that Flynn might've come to see her. Swallowing to wet her suddenly dry throat, she closed the computer. "Come in."

The door swung inward, and Wanda entered, a pleased smirk plastered on her perfectly made-up face and a tray balanced on her right palm. "G'morning, Lily. I hope you don't mind—I brought Bob with me to work today."

"Of course not. Is he doing any better?" Curiosity had Lilith stretching upward from her seat to catch a glimpse of the tray's contents. The tart aroma of cranberries made her mouth water.

"His hair's growing back, but the vet said he needs to wear the cone of shame for a couple more days so he doesn't chew at the incision." Wanda set her cargo on the empty corner of the desk. "Flynn brought breakfast for you. His excuse was that he mis-measured and made too much oatmeal. As if I believe that. I think he's hoping to earn some brownie points with the girl he's got his sights set on. And he wants your opinion on a new tea blend sample he got from his supplier."

Wanda's observation brought a moment of utter girlie satisfaction before Lilith squashed it. Getting her hopes up was a surefire way to add another failure to her dating résumé. Caution and a cool head would serve her much better.

She set the bowl in front of her and then picked up the mug, wrapping her cold hands around the toasty cup. Wisps of steam rose from the surface as she inhaled the fruity scent, and she placed the tea on a coaster near the dish. Spreading the napkin on her lap, she scrunched up her nose. "More than likely you told him I've been eating granola bars at my desk every morning instead of taking time for a *proper* breakfast at home. Please tell him thank you for me."

Rolling her eyes at the dismissal, Wanda pivoted toward the exit. "Well, if you don't want him, I guess I'll turn on the cougar charm. A woman in her fifties may not have the body of a nubile twenty year old, but her sexual experience makes up for it. Oh, and Betsy stopped by on her way to the dining room. The diagnostic came back clear."

"Thank goodness." Lilith refused to rise to the bait, letting Betsy's good news bring a bright spot to the day. If Flynn decided to hook up with someone else, he couldn't have his sights set on her.

Another whiff of the oatmeal and tea snared her attention as the door clicked closed, and she took a bite. The tartness of cranberries mixed with the sweetness of maple and the mild nuttiness of almonds. She savored the bumpy texture of steel-cut oats, thankful she hadn't had to settle for the pasty instant alternative.

Then she sipped the tea, intent on identifying its ingredients. A hint of rose hips teased her taste buds, along with undertones of mint. The subtle essence of something vaguely familiar tugged at her memory in the next sip.

*Raspberries? No. Gooseberries!*

Returning the mug to the coaster, she dug into the oatmeal. No matter Flynn's motive, her empty belly appreciated his gesture. Warmth seeped through her body and settled a little too close to her heart. When the bowl was empty, she lifted the paper napkin to dab at her mouth. Pen markings caught her eye.

*"Comfort food. Enjoy."*

She stared at the words as she flattened the wrinkles from the napkin. Either he was the most compassionate man she'd ever met or he knew exactly how to breech a cautious woman's protective walls. The latter would make him the most manipulative person she'd ever known.

She flipped open her laptop to add to the message she'd composed.

*P.S. Breakfast was delicious and the tea is wonderful. Thank you again.*

Nothing in the note could be construed as romantic or suggestive. Surely he'd realize friendship was all she was offering. Stress had been the instigator of the two hormone-driven kisses, and with the worst day of the year behind her, her willpower to resist him would gain strength.

The phone buzzed, startling her.

She pressed the intercom button. "Yes, Wanda?"

"There's a woman on line one. Eliza Langley. She said she met with you Saturday about one of the singles units. Are you available?"

*What was I thinking about less stress?*

"I'll take the call." After a fortifying swallow of tea to calm her rising temper, Lilith lifted the receiver to her ear and tapped the button for the office's main phone line. "Good morning, Miss Langley. This is Lilith Montgomery."

"Yes, hello. I'm calling to apologize for missing our…appointment Saturday evening. My dad fell, and I spent most of the night with him at the hospital. I'm sorry if I inconvenienced you."

As much as she wished she could be angry, Lilith let it go. "Is he okay?"

"Yes. No broken bones. Just a few stitches and a lecture from Garrett—my son—about not climbing ladders to clean the gutters by himself."

"I'm glad to hear it wasn't serious."

Silence filled the space of several seconds before Eliza spoke again. "I'd like reschedule, if that isn't too much trouble. Are you and Wade free tomorrow after supper?"

Lilith smoothed her palm over the napkin. "To be honest, I'm not sure I should be there. Whatever you're going to tell Uncle Wade is between you and him. If he wants to share it with me, that should be his decision."

"Will you ask him if I can come to his house at six thirty? Please."

His answer was predictable, given his reaction to Eliza not showing up on Saturday, but Lilith had to leave the decision up to him. "Would you prefer to stay on the line while I contact him? Or I can call you back in a few minutes."

"I'll wait."

Retrieving her cell phone from her purse, Lilith stifled a sigh. "Okay. I'm going to put you on hold now."

"Okay. Thank you."

The button for line one blinked when she pressed Hold, and she took another drink of tea before dialing her uncle's number. Each ring brought a mix of relief and aggravation. On one hand, she wanted to protect him from the woman claiming he'd fathered her child. On the other, he deserved to know he had a son—if she was telling the truth.

"Hey there, Lily flower. Calling to beg me to come to work?" His cheery voice triggered a stab of guilt.

Rather than dragging out the conversation, she forged ahead. "No, you're supposed to be resting for another two weeks. I'm calling because Eliza Langley's on the phone and she wants to meet with you tomorrow at six thirty. She said her dad had to go the hospital Saturday. That's why she didn't show up. She's on hold waiting for an answer."

Silence followed. Finally, his noisy exhale revealed that he hadn't disconnected. "Why?"

"Why what?"

"Why should I even talk to her after what she did twenty years ago?"

Lilith wasn't about to spill the beans on that subject. "I don't know. Maybe she's sorry for whatever she did. Closure?"

"I already closed the door on that bullshit. I'm not interested in helping her get through some twelve-step program for liars."

"I think you owe it to yourself to hear her side of the story. If you still believe she treated you like crap, fine. How many times have you told me not to judge people without letting them offer an explanation?" Pulling out one of his adages to use against him probably wasn't fair, but common sense told her that he needed to see his former lover and clear the air.

"You play dirty. Good girl." He cleared his throat. "Okay, I'll meet with her."

"I'll tell her. Oh, and she wants to come to your house—I'm guessing so you can talk in private."

"I don't suppose I can talk you into joining us? Ah, never mind. You should be tending to your own personal life, not mine."

The inevitable push toward her new chef didn't come, but the unspoken implication was there.

"You know I'd do just about anything for you, Uncle Wade. All you have to do is ask."

"I'll be fine. Talk to you soon."

The line went silent, and she set aside her cell to pick up the business phone. "Miss Langley?"

"Yes, I'm still here. Will he see me?" The hope in Eliza's voice didn't fit with a woman capable of breaking a man's heart.

"Yes." Lilith paused at the relieved-sounding squeak in her ear. "My uncle is a very sweet person. Don't make me regret convincing him that you deserve a chance to talk."

"I won't. Thank you."

After a soft click, the dial tone buzzed and Lilith hung up. Glancing at the clock, she reached for her tea again. Even if she'd wanted to avoid Flynn today, she wouldn't have time. Breakfast was over and the Reeds were due to arrive any minute. She hadn't yet started on the produce order. She had to prepare next week's work calendar, scheduling around two requests for days off, one doctor appointment, and a rotating night nurse moving out of state.

*And I have to try not to think about my cousin's mother telling Uncle Wade that he's a father.*

The office door swung open, and Norma Reed stepped inside, with John and Flynn close behind her. "Good morning, dear. Look who John and I bumped into at the restaurant—that handsome husband of yours!"

Flynn shook his head when the older man grimaced. "We're not interrupting anything important, are we, Lily?"

Lilith bit the inside of her cheek to keep from bursting into tears as Mrs. Reed rounded the desk and hugged her. Norma's episodes had never included misrecognizing people. She forgot names on occasion and got lost sometimes if she went out alone. Her behavior made the illness too real now.

Flynn draped his arm around Lilith's shoulders as Norma backtracked to sit down. His breath caressed her ear with a whisper. "You okay?"

Blinking to clear her vision, Lilith nodded.

"Let's play along. No need to embarrass her." He kissed her cheek, his soft lips as arousing as they were comforting.

Norma giggled. "Newlyweds. Still on the honeymoon. How sweet."

Flynn's chuckle vibrated through Lilith, affecting her in places way too private. "I plan on making the honeymoon last for years."

"You naughty young man. Good for you!" The older woman's amusement might be all in her imagination, but that was better than being aware of her gaffe.

Tightening his hold, Flynn met Lilith's gaze. "I need to get back to work. I'll see you later at home."

Pasting on a smile, she rested her hands on the top of the desk so she wouldn't grab him by the front of his chef's coat and give him a kiss he wouldn't forget. "I might be a little late. Lots to do today."

He winked at her. "Not too late, I hope. We have lots to do at home."

Before she could formulate a response, he strode out of the office, closing the door as he left. Besides studying pre-med, going to culinary school, and knowing how to deal with a minor crisis, her chef clearly had acting experience as well.

Norma let out a dramatic sigh. "Now there's a fellow who loves his wife, just like my Johnny loves me."

"More than I can ever tell you." John brushed a wisp of her gray hair from her forehead. "Why don't you tell Lilith about the nice apartment we found?"

Her eyes lit up. "We went for a drive yesterday and stopped at this lovely apartment complex about five minutes from where our oldest daughter...no, granddaughter and her family lives. It's a little smaller than the place we have now, but the security system is state-of-the-art. Meals are included in the rent, so I won't have to cook anymore. All those electrical appliances are dangerous, you know. I worry about them causing a fire."

Smoothing the wrinkles from the napkin on her desk, Lilith tried to cover her distress. "It sounds like the perfect new home for you. How soon will you be moving?"

"In the next week or so. As soon as we finish the paperwork and get everything packed. John, will you write down the address for Lilith so she knows how to get in touch with us?"

He'd no sooner withdrawn a business card from his pocket than his wife rose and started for the exit. Setting the card on the seat of the chair, he hurried after her.

Lilith crossed her arms on the edge of the desk and lowered her head. The tears came faster than she expected, and within seconds, the door clicked closed again. A comforting arm closed around her shoulders.

How had Flynn known to come back?

He knelt beside her. "You don't have to be okay all the time."

# Chapter 17

Flynn scanned the windows of the employee housing a hundred yards from the main building while he slipped on his coat. The fourth window from the right, Lilith's living room window, bore thin stripes of light shining through the blinds. For the first time in his almost two-week tenure, she was home before him. Then again, eight-thirty was late for him—but business came before sleep.

With the day she'd had, he might've dragged her out of her office if she'd still been working. The impulse to take care of her had morphed into a compulsion, her tears setting off a gut-wrenching desire to protect her from the harsh realities of the world. Wanting to carry her off to his bedroom and cook up something hot and spicy was another side effect.

He locked up and then made the chilly trek through the courtyard to his apartment, ducking against scattered raindrops. Considering the progress he'd made that day with his neighbor, a visit didn't seem like a good plan. She'd finally let him hold and kiss her without running away. He would've preferred a less stressful situation, but he'd take any step forward he could get.

With a quick twist of his key, he pushed open his door, jerking away when a rectangular Frisbee came flying at his head. The light-colored weapon balanced on the threshold, the wind rocking it back and forth. He picked up the envelope and then flipped on the lights as he shut the cold on the other side of the door.

Feminine handwriting spelled out his name on the paper, and a bud of anticipation bloomed in his chest.

Not even bothering to remove his coat, he slid his finger through the sealed flap and pulled the contents free. A simple bold "Thank You" graced the front. She could've chosen a card with a birthday cake on it, for all he cared. All that mattered was what was written inside.

He skipped to the bottom of the message to check the signature. The surge of happiness her name brought could only mean one thing.

*"Dear Flynn, I thought to thank you for breakfast this morning, but your comfort and understanding deserve much more than that. The residents are dear friends to me, and to watch one of them succumb to an illness is like saying good-bye to a family member. It never gets any easier to bear the loss. I'm so sorry you had to go through that with your sister. I deeply appreciate your offer to listen if I need to talk, and I'd like to extend the same offer to you. Thank you for helping me through the day. Lily"*

Another read-through had him ready to run next door and insist on an all-night conversation and cuddle session, but one step forward and three steps back wouldn't gain him any ground.

He kicked off his wet shoes at the door as he shed his coat and tossed it on the couch. His next stop was the bedroom closet to retrieve the shoebox from Kate. He sat down on the bed to reread Lilith's message again. If he expected her to take him at his word, he'd have to show her that he wasn't interested in using her like the guys her uncle had mentioned.

Hoping for a trace of her flowery scent, he raised the card to his nose. A faint aroma lingered, and he breathed in the sweet memory of holding her while she cried. If he'd survived without making love to her then, he'd find a way to be what she needed until she was ready for more.

He lifted the lid on the shoebox, placed the card on top for safekeeping, and returned the box to its place. That tiny bit of encouragement from Lilith would be there to boost his confidence and his resolve for the days and weeks ahead.

In the meantime, he had one more work-related task for the night. Alice and CC had insisted he join them for supper, so Flynn skipped his usual after-work meal, opting for a cup of decaf instead. He fired up his computer to tweak next week's menu at the dinette, the pungent brew penetrating his sleepy brain cells.

*Add sautéed cabbage and carrots and baked butternut squash to the vegetable sides. Delete steamed green beans.*

Despite Lilith's assertion that she didn't want to burden him with another responsibility, he'd managed to convince her to let him place the twice a week produce order. If anyone was overworked, it was the temporary boss lady. Maybe by Wednesday, he'd talk her into handing off the other orders to him as well.

Moving on to the breakfast choices, he switched up a couple of the fresh fruit offerings and dropped the sweet potato hash. The residents hadn't been shy about telling him Lilith's version of the dish tasted better than his.

She had to have used a secret ingredient, but asking her what it was bordered on crossing a professional line, and filling his downtime with family had left only a few free hours scattered throughout the week to experiment.

A yawn escaped as he typed in a new category on his spreadsheet template. The colder weather demanded an addition to the supper menu *du jour*.

*Leek and Potato Soup. Chicken and Cannellini Chili. Vegetarian Vegetable Stew.*

He already served French Onion Soup on Friday evenings for what he called "Date Night at Montgomery Crossing." All the residents ate in the dining room, and afterward, they gathered in the party room for music and dancing. By the looks on their faces Saturday mornings, a fair number of them got lucky too.

Saving the changes, he drained his coffee mug and shut down his laptop. His early to bed, early to rise routine prompted another yawn as he headed to the bathroom. The faint shoosh of running water informed him Lilith was probably getting ready for bed as well.

Although he'd planned to deliver breakfast to her office a couple times a week rather than every day, his strategy to look after her demanded daily attention. Wanda had advised him that the nutritionist hadn't been eating particularly well lately. With double duty, Lilith had gotten in the habit of eating a few bites here and a few bites there in between phone calls, meetings, and paperwork, often not finishing what she brought to eat. If she'd consumed an entire meal in the last two weeks, Wanda claimed she hadn't seen it.

Since the teacup had been almost empty when he'd slipped back after the Reeds' departure, Lily must've liked it. He'd pair another mug of tea with a couple muffins made from the leftover oatmeal and some dried peaches for tomorrow's delivery.

Adding that worthwhile task to his mental agenda, he shed his sauce-stained uniform. The intern's first-day nerves had made her slightly clumsy, and from the horrified expression on her face, she'd evidently expected him to transform into a screaming tyrant from *Hell's Kitchen*. His suggestion that he save the slasher whites for a Halloween costume had calmed Shanda enough to complete her supper shift. In fact, they'd worked together quite well after the incident.

Too damn tired to soak the stain, he donned his boxers and crawled into bed, automatically reaching for the wall.

*G'night, Lily. Sweet dreams.*

* * * *

Fumbling for the bedside lamp, Flynn groaned. His body wasn't ready to move after spending the past seven hours tossing and turning. Neither was his brain. If Lilith had been lying beside him, he'd have slept like a rock.

He snorted at the absurdity of that thought.

*Maybe after an orgasm or two. Yeah, at least two for her.*

Then they could lie skin to skin until morning. Before he was able to make it happen, he had to settle for making breakfast for her, which wasn't settling at all. Earning her trust wasn't a hardship.

He blinked at the sudden brightness as the light flickered on. Colored spots danced in his vision, and he surrendered to a jaw-stretching yawn before rolling out of bed. Goose bumps spread over his arms at the brush of cool air, but he grabbed a clean set of clothes from the closet and trudged to the bathroom.

A hot shower woke him up, and he arrived at the main building exactly an hour prior to serving time. A shadow passed over the keyhole as he unlocked the door, his insides doing an Irish jig when a petite reflection looked back at him in the glass.

*Lilith?*

No, it couldn't be. This person was about her height, but short dark hair framed a round face.

*The intern. Shanda.*

Disappointment replaced anticipation.

"Morning, Chef Hastings." She followed him through the door and down the hall.

"G'morning, Shanda. Do you remember what's on the menu today?" Inside the kitchen, he flipped the light switch.

"Yes, sir." Hanging her coat in the closet, she recited the breakfast and supper offerings. Her mouth twitched like she was trying to smother a self-satisfied grin, probably because she hadn't forgotten a single item. The young woman was gaining confidence.

He let her use of "sir" go, knowing that respect for the head and *sous* chefs had been drilled into her brain. "Excellent. I've added muffins to the lineup, but I'll take care of the prep. You focus on the rest. What's first?"

She snapped a hair net into place as she bustled to the sink. "Hand washing. If anybody gets sick from the food, I'm the person who catches the blame."

Waiting his turn for the water, he debated how much praise to bestow on what amounted to his professional slave. Ego and jealousy ran rampant in most kitchens, but good work deserved to be rewarded, if only in the form of an occasional pat on the back. "If you follow directions as well as you know the rules, you'll earn yourself a respectable letter of recommendation when you're done with the internship."

She moved aside, reaching for a clean towel from the stack. "Then I better start chopping."

An hour later, he loaded a tray for Lilith while Shanda carted the last of the food out to the buffet table to refill. Balancing the load on his palm, he left by the hallway entrance and walked to the reception area.

Wanda smirked at him. "Have you asked her out yet?"

"Nope." He set a muffin and a cup of coffee in front of her.

"What the hell are you waiting for, Flynn?" Clicking her fingernails on the desk, she frowned. "Go on in. She has a meeting with the painters at nine thirty, and she'll need all her strength to deal with that bitch of a forewoman. You might want to hide in the kitchen until she's gone."

A whine came from the corner behind Wanda.

"She scares Bob too, huh?"

"Ha! He snarled at her last time." Turning toward the dog, she tsked at him. "No begging for muffins. People food is bad for you. Mommy'll get you a treat in a minute."

Flynn wasn't quick enough to stifle a laugh. "That's probably what he wanted to begin with. He's training you."

"Oh, you mean like Lily's training you?" Peeking over her shoulder, Wanda winked at him. "Pretty soon, she'll have you bringing her breakfast in bed instead of to her office."

He shifted the tray to his other hand and stepped toward the closed door. "Maybe that's part of the plan."

"Don't tease. That girl needs a nice fellow like you to pamper her."

"Who says I'm teasing?" He rapped his knuckles on the door twice and twisted the knob before Wanda could respond. "Room service!"

A squeak caught him by surprise, and he steadied his delivery to keep the hot tea from splashing onto him and the muffins.

Lilith popped up from her chair. "Yikes! Sorry! Let me help."

Waving her off, he lowered the tray to the top of the armchair across from her. "I've got it. Are you okay? I didn't mean to scare you."

Her sheepish expression told him he wasn't going to like her reason for startling. "I'm fine. It wasn't your fault. I kind of zoned out there for a minute."

He transferred the plate and mug to the desk. "You fell asleep at your desk? The almost doctor is telling you to slow down. You haven't been eating right. You're working too many hours, and I'm guessing you aren't getting the rest you need to make up for how hard you're working. Sit. Eat. Please."

Plopping into the seat, she picked up a muffin and peeled away the paper liner. "I'm sitting. I'm eating. Are you happy now, Chef Almost-Doctor Hastings?"

"Not until you finish your breakfast." He dropped into the guest chair and set the tray on the floor. "I got the card you put in my door yesterday. Is the lack of sleep from worrying about Norma Reed?"

Her shrug revealed tension in her shoulders. "Among other things."

"You have to take better care of yourself if you're going help everybody else. How about I handle all the kitchen-related orders to relieve some of the burden? I can put together and print the weekly menus. And I'm glad to listen if you want talk about the other stuff. You've had a rough few days."

She sipped her tea. "More like weeks."

Her offhand remark hit him like a punch to the gut.

"Am I part of the problem?" The question snuck past the sting in his chest, her implication too obvious to ignore.

"No. I don't know." Her cheeks flushed, giving him more than a subtle hint at the true answer. "Norma's illness. The anniversary of my parents' death. Add Uncle Wade's surgery, and...things have been piling up. I'm under a lot of stress right now."

"And you're blaming that stress for what happened in the kitchen last week and at the cemetery on Saturday, right?"

As awkward as outing the elephant in the room was, he preferred clearing the air to letting her hide behind a lame excuse. They'd both been hot for each other already. Worry had only added fuel to raging flames.

"Yes. No. Oh, hell, I don't know. Do we have to talk about this?" The pleading in her eyes nearly convinced him to let the subject drop.

"I think we do. Pretending won't make it go away. I like you, Lilith, and I'm okay with us being friends. But if we were to become more than that, I wouldn't complain." He hoped she appreciated his honesty, because the alternative wasn't a pleasant scenario.

She stared at him, her jaw slowing moving up and down as she chewed. Another sip of tea followed.

Too bad he couldn't read her thoughts.

Her hand trembled a little, making the mug clatter against the stone coaster and betraying her understandable anxiety. Her uncle had warned Flynn that her experience with men might be an obstacle. The lack of conversation stretched out for another minute, but she never took her eyes off him.

Did she think he'd change his mind if she waited long enough?

"The muffins are delicious. What's in the batter?" She broke off a small piece.

Her change of topic would've given him whiplash if he hadn't been prepared for it. He was an expert at avoidance. "I used leftover oatmeal and whole wheat flour. A little bit of honey for sweetener. Dried peaches. Almost any fresh or dried fruit would work as a substitute. Do you want the recipe?"

She finally smiled. "Sure. Thanks."

*Will you trade me a kiss for it?*

Bartering probably wouldn't win him any points. "I'll e-mail it to you. And I meant what I said."

She leaned back in the chair and clasped her hands in her lap. "Flynn, I—"

"Let me clarify. We're friends—with the kinds of benefits that matter. You can knock on my door or come find me in the kitchen anytime you need somebody to talk to, a shoulder to cry on, or a guy to do the heavy lifting. I'm not going to pressure you. Ever." Tucking the tray under his arm, he stood. "If you have time this afternoon, will you stop in to meet the intern? She's doing a good job and the residents seem to like her."

Leaning forward, Lilith jotted a note on the pad beside the phone. "Is four o'clock okay? I don't want to interfere with supper preparations."

"Perfect." He took a step toward the door, slightly discouraged by her evasive measures. "I won't be able to deliver dinner, but you're welcome to call down and let me know what you'd like. I can plate it for the dining room or box it for pick-up."

"Thank you." She sounded almost disappointed that he wouldn't be bringing her room service again later. "For everything."

At the exit, he met her gaze. "You're more than welcome, Lily."

As he pulled the door closed behind him, he could've sworn she muttered, "I hope so."

# Chapter 18

*One, two, three. Knock.*

Lilith nibbled on her lower lip as she waited for Dr. Ito to answer her door. She was safe visiting the psychologist in her apartment, wasn't she? No one would overhear their conversation and send wild rumors stampeding through the complex.

*This is stupid. I should just go back to the office and eat the damn muffins.*

Somehow, peeling away the liner, breaking off tiny crumbs, and fake chewing had convinced Flynn that she'd actually tasted them. Another dose of foodgasmic humiliation was a strong deterrent for eating anything he made in front of him.

Shoving her hands in her coat pockets, she turned to walk away, disgusted with her ridiculous idea to seek out France's advice. Her fingers closed around something crinkly.

*Seeking sexual advice with a strip of Trojans in my pocket. How pathetic can I get?*

A faint click had Lilith weighing her options. She could run away or lie on the couch and reveal her innermost secrets. With her luck, the condoms would probably fall to the ground if she fled.

"Lily! What a nice surprise. Come in, dear." Fingering what had to be her hearing aid volume, Dr. Ito ushered Lilith inside. "Would you care for a cup of tea? I was about to make a fresh pot."

"Yes, thank you." Lilith eased out of her coat as she followed the older woman to the kitchen. "I'm not interrupting anything important, am I?"

*Please say yes. Then I won't have to sound like a lovesick teenager.*

France set the kettle on the burner and then slid the tea canister out from the wall. She picked up the infuser ball. "Nothing is more important than spending time with those we care about, whether the visit is social or professional. Marzipan?"

"Oh, France, I adore you. Yes, I'd love a piece of your fabulous marzipan." Lilith hung her coat on the hook by the back door. "I'll get out the cups."

"You can talk while you're doing that. All that tension in your shoulders will give you a nasty headache. Best to get whatever's bothering you off your mind."

How did Dr. Ito always seem to know when somebody needed an objective ear?

At the cupboard, Lilith set a pair of Japanese teacups on the counter, careful not to chip the fragile porcelain. She had no choice now but to admit the truth. "I don't know what to do. It's Flynn. He wants to be friends."

A boisterous chuckle came from the tiny old woman. "Is that what he told you?"

"Well, yes and no. He said he's okay with us being friends, but he wouldn't complain if we became...more." Shifting to lean against the counter, Lilith rolled her shoulders, trying to relieve the stiffness. "He promised not to pressure me. But if he's willing to accept friendship with nothing else, how can he want a relationship? Or maybe he didn't mean he wants a relationship at all. What if he only expects sex? Men are so confusing."

"And I'll bet he's thinking the same about women." The kettle let out a shrill whistle, and France poured the boiling water into the pot. Steam rose in a cloud around her face. "Are you sending him mixed signals? If he's getting the impression you're not interested in more than being friends, he might be worried about going out on a limb with his feelings. What if you don't like him the way he likes you? Or he could be trying to build a relationship based on friendship, taking his time getting acquainted with you and letting you get acquainted with him. A good strategy if you ask me."

"But is he? How am I supposed to know which it is?" Lilith rubbed at the knots multiplying in her neck.

"Have a seat, Lily. We need to hash out what you're feeling first. Then we can decide what to do about Flynn."

Obeying her advisor, Lilith sat at the dinette table and let out a frustrated sigh. "I'm scared, France. I'm really scared of getting hurt again. Flynn seems like a good person, but you know my track record with men. What if I fall in love with him and he turns out to be another jerk?"

A wrinkled hand closed over hers, and France smiled. "Sounds to me like you're already headed down that garden path, and a precarious one it can be. The question is whether you're willing to take him at his word. Do you trust him not to push you into a physical relationship before you think you're ready? Or better yet, do you trust him—period?"

The lump in Lilith's throat made talking impossible.

Yes, Flynn had taken care of her when she'd fallen, carrying her into her apartment, getting her an icepack, and not taking advantage of the fact that he'd bared her ass. He'd brought her breakfast and helped with errands. All those things covered only the first twenty-four hours after they'd met. Since then, he'd delivered meals to her and comforted her during two incredibly emotional times. Not once had he forced her to kiss him or tried to talk her into sleeping with him.

Instead, he'd given her a card.

The sentiment he'd expressed had seemed genuine, as if he was sincere in his offer to listen to her lament about the great losses in her life. Add to that the residents' gushing comments about his friendliness and likability, and her defenses barely stood a chance.

She swallowed. "I *want* to trust him, France. I think so anyway. But I'm not sure I remember how."

"Nonsense, Lily." The older woman stood, returning to the counter. She opened another canister and placed several pieces of candy on a plate. "You've trusted Wade forever. If you need help, you'd call on Alice or me in the snap of a finger. Same goes for most everyone here at Montgomery Crossing."

"That's different. You're my friends, and Uncle Wade was always there, even before my parents died."

"You seem to be forgetting that Flynn wants to be your friend too. Have you ever known a man as anything other than a boyfriend or a lover? And I'm not talking about relatives and old folks." France transferred the dish of treats to the table and then poured them each a cup of tea.

Considering the question, Lilith shuffled through the memories of her years since college. She'd had a few female friends, but they moved on without her when they'd gotten married and she'd stayed single. Several guys had come and gone from her life, all of them falling into the non-friend, ex-lover category.

Through undergrad and graduate studies, she'd focused on her classes and maintaining her GPA. She hadn't been into weekend partying, drinking, or hooking up for a night. Those six years had simply repeated her high school experience—more brain than beauty and an all but nonexistent social life.

*Aha!*

"In sophomore biology, Stewart Gillhoff and I were lab partners." She scrambled to produce another example. "Oh, and I tutored Brayden

Overmeyer in chemistry my junior year."

Dr. Ito set down the cups and pursed her lips. "Those are acquaintances, dear. I want to know if you've spent time with males your own age because you shared common interests—besides sex."

Crossing her arms on the table and lowering her head, Lilith surrendered. "I've never been good at making friends—and I'm even worse at keeping them."

At France's full-out belly laugh, Lilith frowned at her.

"Lily, you're one of the best, most loyal friends a person could have. I think you just don't like letting too many people get close."

"I—"

"Hear me out. I have a hypothesis about why you work here and why you spend all your time surrounded by us old folks." Settling in the seat across from Lilith, France pushed the plate of marzipan in front of her. "For twenty years, you've been afraid of losing anybody you love. Since we're already close to dying, you know we'll be leaving this world sooner rather than later."

"Don't say that!"

"Hush now so I can finish. It reinforces your belief that everybody's going to abandon you some day. Then you don't have to truly live or trust a man with your heart. It's the perfect rationalization. Have a piece of candy."

With blunt reality staring her down, Lilith wanted to devour every crumb of sweet confection on the dish. "Can you recommend a good therapist? I'm not fit for any kind of relationship."

"Tsk. No pity parties for you, Lily dear. You're capable of working through the problem on your own. Choose a path and start walking. If you don't like where it takes you, make a new one. You decide what your destination is and how you want to get there." France lifted her teacup to her lips and inhaled. "Mm. Roses."

Only conflicting emotions and Lilith's racing pulse broke the long stretch of quiet. Hope struggled against fear. Anticipation tried to overpower trepidation.

Was she afraid of falling in love because she might have to face losing that person?

*Or worse yet—we might have a child and die, leaving her alone in the world.*

What were the odds of history repeating itself?

She wasn't ready to take that dangerous a risk. Friendship, she could probably handle. Romantic and parental love—those were miles down the road. She might never reach that point, but small steps were okay, weren't they?

Shoving a chocolate-covered marzipan cube into her mouth, she tried to calm her churning stomach. The almond flavoring could've been rotten tomatoes for all that she tasted it. A gulp of bland tea washed down the gooey deposit stuck in her throat.

She grabbed for her coat as she rose and pushed in her chair. "I have to get back to the office. Thank you for the tea and advice."

Not waiting for France to walk her to the door, Lilith hurried through the living room. Outside, she set off at a jog, hoping she didn't meet anyone on the sidewalk—especially Flynn. Dr. Ito's diagnosis had left her too exposed and far too aware of her shortcomings.

She'd been sabotaging every potential long-term relationship by allowing her subconscious to make bad choices on purpose. No wonder she'd failed so many times. She didn't even know how to choose friends, and that meant picking a boyfriend was out of her realm.

Wanda wasn't at her desk and Lilith was able to slip into the office unseen. She considered locking the door behind her, but that would probably only come back to bite her on the ass like everything else.

Closing her eyes, she pulled in a slow breath and then blew it out to the count of eight. Tension was clawing its way from her shoulders to her temples.

*Choose a path? How about one that takes me to the nearest mental hospital?*

She didn't bother digging in the desk drawer for the bottle of pain relievers. She'd given the last two pills to Wanda more than a week ago, not that it would be more than a temporary fix anyway.

As she hung up her coat, she checked the clock. She had fifteen minutes until the woman from the painting company came to discuss the details for the upcoming job.

*Bleh. A root canal would be more fun.*

The uneaten muffins beckoned to her, and she carried the plate with her to the window. A slight gap in the blinds gave her a wonderful view of the gardens, the mums still brightly colored in the protected area by the patio. Fallen leaves crowded around their bushy foliage and along the wrought iron fence behind them. The serenity eased some of the stiffness in her spine.

Holding the plate close to her chin, she bit into the muffin, thankful to finally taste her breakfast. Tasty peaches mixed with the lightly sweetened oatmeal. Even cold, it outdid any muffin she'd ever made or sampled. She'd never leave her kitchen again if Flynn shared all his recipes with her.

*That would certainly save me from making a fool of myself.*

Unable to resist, she took a larger bite as she lost focus on the gardens. She savored the hearty goodness filling her grumbling stomach and mused over a delicate spider web sparkling in the sunlight.

She blinked at a flash of white in the background, and the intricate design was gone. Still chewing, she separated the slats a little wider to search for the distraction.

Flynn sauntered toward the employee apartments, his jacket looped over his arm instead of covering his whites. His purposeful stride emphasized his long legs and muscular stature.

She swallowed to keep from choking on her mouthful. A spasm ripped through her middle, sending a rush of pleasure radiating outward. She grabbed the windowsill as she doubled over and shook from the mini aftershocks rocking her inner muscles. A moan escaped.

Juggling the plate, she sent up a silent prayer to save the muffins. They wobbled but didn't tumble to the floor—although no woman in her right mind would allow a bit of carpet fuzz to prevent her from finishing Flynn's divine baked goods.

*I'm so messed up. Orgasms from food.*

She hadn't attempted another one by battery-powered toy since her failure over a week ago. When was the last time she'd gone that long without sexual release?

Even during her short-lived relationships, she'd resorted to masturbation after at least eighty percent of what her ex-boyfriends had thought was "sex." The last year on her own had meant playtime nearly every other night.

Now she had nothing but food to please her. Flynn had ruined her for anyone and anything except his kitchen creations.

A knock sounded a second before the door swung open.

"Lily? You okay in here?" Wanda peeked through the doorway and furrowed her brows. "I thought I heard somebody yelp."

"I'm fine. I almost dropped it." Lilith held up the dish in her hand. She'd have to remember not to make foodgasm noises in the office. "Is my nine-thirty appointment here yet?"

"The forewoman is on the phone saying she needs to reschedule. I'm not sure why we can't just e-mail her the colors, the apartment numbers, and the dates they'll be vacated."

Returning to the desk, Lilith set down her magic muffins. "I'll talk to her."

"Don't let her push you around. Sometimes, you're too nice." Wanda didn't waggle her finger, but she may as well have, considering her warning tone.

"Yes, ma'am." Lilith sat down and picked up the receiver as the door closed. "This is Lilith Montgomery."

"I need to reschedule the meeting with *Mr.* Montgomery." The woman's intimation that she'd only speak to Uncle Wade couldn't have been any clearer.

"Mr. Montgomery is out of the office. I'm acting director and am authorized to make decisions on his behalf." Perhaps a calm explanation would convince the painter to do her job.

"I only deal with Mr. Montgomery." Attitude filled the words.

"We're on a tight schedule, with residents moving out and others moving in a few days later. Mr. Montgomery won't be available before the painting needs to be completed." Lilith tightened control on her flaring irritation, but it was slipping.

"You don't seem to understand. I won't do the job—"

"No, you don't understand." Gripping the arm of the chair, Lilith let her temper loose. "Your contract with Montgomery Crossing is terminated. I'll send you written confirmation by e-mail."

She flipped open her laptop as she carefully set the receiver back in the cradle. With her pulse thumping in her ears, she typed a curt notice of the contract termination, copied her receptionist, and clicked Send.

Next, she pressed the intercom button. "Wanda, please contact the company that painted your brother's house. Ask if they have a crew available beginning a week from Thursday, and tell the owner I'd like to request a written estimate for three apartments."

Wanda whooped in her ear. "I'm on it. You go, girl!"

The sneak had evidently listened in on the phone conversation, but Lilith wasn't about to reprimand her. "Thanks, Wanda."

"Anytime. By the way, Flynn wants to know if you have time to meet the intern this morning. They're working on a special dessert this afternoon, and he thinks four o'clock will be pushing it."

"Fine. When should I come to the kitchen?"

"They're here now. Should I send them in?"

The muffin plate drew Lilith's attention as she fought a wave of panic. "Give me a minute to calm down. I don't want the young woman to think I'm a short-tempered tyrant."

Wanda snickered. "I doubt anyone would ever think that, but you got your minute and not a second longer."

Diving toward the mini fridge, Lilith snagged a napkin from her supply to wrap up the evidence. She had no intention of supplying Flynn with any more ammunition that she hadn't been eating properly.

As she tucked the muffins in the middle desk drawer and drained the teacup, the door swung inward again. Her chef gestured for his new assistant to enter ahead of him.

His bright smile set off a fresh set of tingles between Lilith's thighs. "Miss Montgomery, I want you to meet Shanda Davis. Shanda, this is Miss Montgomery, acting director of the complex. She also counsels the residents on dietetics and nutrition."

Lilith stood, reaching across the desk to shake Shanda's hand. "It's a pleasure to meet you, Miss Davis. I hope you're learning a lot by working with Mr. Hastings."

The girl's firm grasp surprised Lilith, her slight build disguising her strength. Even so, she looked all of about fourteen years old. "Chef Hastings is a terrific boss. I'm sure I'll be prepared at the end of the internship."

He picked up the empty plate and mug, his smile widening. "Apprentice or not, your training speaks for itself, *sous* chef Davis. I don't want to hold up any longer since you need to get going. See you at four for prep."

Shanda's mouth quirked as if she was trying to hide her satisfaction at the compliment. "Yes, sir. Good to meet you, ma'am."

Flynn's eyes seemed to follow her exit. Then he held out the dish as he turned to face Lilith. "Did you enjoy your breakfast, Miss Montgomery?"

*More than you need to know.*

Straightening a neat stack of files, she avoided his disconcerting gaze. "Yes, it was wonderful."

"Good. Would you like Chicken Marsala, Baked Tilapia, Farfalle Primavera, or Roast Pork with Cranberry Glaze for dinner? We're having low-sugar, low-fat gingerbread cake for dessert to celebrate Dorothy's birthday."

She wanted to glare at him, his preemptive question denying her the opportunity to fabricate a reason to miss supper. Other than Uncle Wade's meeting with Eliza Langley, she had nothing on her calendar. "I suppose I'll have the fish, but you have to save a lunch portion of the pasta for me."

Instead of giving her a smug look, he simply nodded. "Not a problem. I'll write your name on the box. Are you eating in the dining room tonight?"

He sounded so hopeful that she hated to deny him, and making up an excuse skated too close to lying. "I can't. I'll pick it up about six fifteen, if that's okay."

"I'll have it ready for you. Want a piece of cake too?"

"Sure." The man could talk her into a triple-size hot fudge sundae with extra whipped cream. "I'm going to have to hit the gym for an extra hour every day for the next week. Some friend you are."

Too late, her words registered.

Flynn was wearing a huge grin as he walked backward to the door. "See you later, *friend*."

# Chapter 19

Four days had passed since Lilith had accidentally called him a friend, and Flynn hadn't seen her for more than five minutes total. He'd expected the dynamics of their relationship to change, but she'd been too damn busy to have a real conversation. She also seemed as stressed as always.

*Enough is enough.*

"Shanda, I need leave for a few minutes. Can you handle refilling the buffet table?" He stopped at the server door.

"Yes, sir! Everything's under control." She pulled the second batch of scones out of the oven and set them on the cooling rack.

"Excellent."

He strode through the dining room, careful to dodge the residents on his way to load a plate for Lilith. She was holed up in her office again, and he wasn't letting her get away with not eating breakfast.

With a rollup between the plate and his fingers, he poured a glass of orange juice with his free hand. By the end of the table, the plate held more food than she'd probably eat, but they could share while they talked.

Alice winked at him as he headed for the hallway. "You take good care of our girl, Flynn."

Beyond trying to hide his interest in Lilith, he winked back. "I intend to."

The office door was ajar a couple inches, so he paused for a quick one-knuckle rap. Easing the door open with his elbow, he stepped inside. "Breakfast is served."

Lilith barely looked up from the notepad she was scribbling on and switched the phone from her right ear to her left ear. "No, I requested movers for *this* Thursday. Whoever I spoke to last week put the wrong date in the computer."

Not wanting to add to her obvious problems, he put the dish of food on the corner of the desk and moved the coaster out of range of her elbow before setting down the glass of juice.

"That won't work. Cancel the order please. I'll have to make other arrangements." She hung up the phone, her frown revealing a wealth of frustration. "Thanks, Flynn, but I doubt I'll have time to eat. I have to try to find somebody to move the Reeds on Thursday."

He unrolled the napkin, freeing the knife and fork to rest on the plate. "I heard. Have you considered renting a truck or a trailer? With my work hours, I can help pack and unpack a U-Haul."

"You can't carry a couch and a mattress by yourself. Well, maybe you can—but you shouldn't." Rolling her head around her shoulders, she yawned. Dark shadows beneath her shuttered eyes suggested she hadn't been sleeping well.

Flynn sat down before the urge to round the desk and massage away the tension could overpower him. "I'll ask Kip to help. The complex can do without him for a few hours, can't it? We'll handle the moving and you can stop worrying."

"That's very generous of you to offer. Thank you." Her voice softened, and some of the tension seemed to leave her body. She yawned again.

"You're welcome—anytime. Feeling a little better now?"

"Mm-hm. But...I owe you a favor."

"You don't owe me anything. Friends don't keep score."

"Friends." She blinked at him as if she was about to nod off.

"Yeah. Friends. People who help each other with the tough stuff and celebrate with you when you have good news."

Her eyes slid shut and her head lolled to the side. A few seconds later, her breathing deepened. Solving her sleep deprivation issue seemed to be at the top of the agenda.

*Sweet dreams, Lily. You deserve them.*

He stood to spread the cloth napkin over her breakfast and stow it in the fridge. She could reheat it if she was hungry when she woke. A nap was more important than food at the moment.

Her lips curved upward, pulling his attention to her perfectly shaped mouth as he stepped toward the desk. She was cute when she frowned and downright beautiful when she smiled, but she didn't smile often enough to suit him. He'd have to change that.

*Damn, I have to get out of here before I do something stupid like kiss her.*

He'd finally made progress with her. A kiss could be misinterpreted, sending him back to square one if she thought he was pressuring her to take things to the next level. He had to remember the long-term goal.

Writing a note prolonged his visit, but he didn't want her to wake up thinking she'd imagined their conversation. When he got back to the kitchen, he'd call the maintenance guy and make a reservation for a moving van. Then he'd pop back in later to update her on the details.

*Quit stalling.*

The walk back to the kitchen was harder than the one to his apartment the night he'd plowed into her on the sidewalk. He hadn't known her very well then. Two weeks had given him time to watch her interact with Alice and CC, John and Norma, and the others. She was kind and generous almost to a fault, neglecting her own needs to help the old folks she cared about.

"You're back too soon." Alice narrowed her gaze at him and pursed her lips. "How do you expect to make any headway with Lily if you cut your visits short?"

Flynn shrugged. "She fell asleep while I was talking to her. What was I supposed to do?"

"Now, I know you're not boring, so that girlie must be working too hard again."

"Again? Does she ever stop?" He automatically scanned the buffet table as he took a step toward the server door. "Sorry to rush off, but I need to make a couple calls. See you at supper? Or are you hosting euchre club tonight?"

"I'll be here." She rose on her tiptoes and leaned closer. "Don't tell Margie I snitched. We decided to play cards in the game room so nobody has to miss your cooking on Saturday nights."

"That has to be the best compliment I've ever had. If I wasn't so crazy about Lilith, I'd snag one of you ladies for a girlfriend. I'll see you later, Alice."

"Later, hot stuff." She blew him a kiss as he turned toward the kitchen.

Without a doubt, he'd ended up in the greatest job he could've found.

As he entered the kitchen, Shanda was bagging several containers on the center island, presumably for a delivery to Dorothy in 4C. "Mrs. Payne's order is ready to go."

Continuing to the phone at the far end, he glanced at the clock. "Excellent work this morning. You can drop it off on the way to your car. See you at four."

"Um, okay. Yes, Chef Hastings."

He punched in Kip's extension while the intern pulled her coat from the closet. She slipped her arms in the sleeves, eyeing him like she thought he might suddenly realize he was letting her leave ten minutes early.

As she shuffled out with the delivery in hand, the maintenance guy walked in, a tool belt hanging at his waist. "Got any of those fruit biscuit things left?"

Flynn gestured to the cooling rack as he hung up the phone, not surprised by the visit. "Help yourself. I was just trying to call you."

"Yeah?" Grabbing a clean plate, Kip chose a scone. "Something wrong in here or your apartment?"

"Everything's fine. I'm hoping you have some free time on Thursday to help me move the Reeds to their new apartment. The moving company screwed up the dates and Lilith had to cancel. I'm going to rent a truck for the day."

"Works for me if it's okay with the boss lady."

"I already talked to her about the possibility, and she doesn't have a problem with it." Flynn made a mental note to book the U-Haul as soon as he got home and then forward the reservation to her. "You don't happen to have a tow dolly and tie-downs, do you?"

"Sure do. I think I have some furniture pads too."

"I still have a few from my move, so we should be in pretty good shape." Pulling a bakery bag free from its package, Flynn stepped toward the racks to wrap up a couple more scones. "Here, take these with you. I'll let you know when I'm picking up the truck."

Kip took the offered package and headed for the hallway exit. "Sounds good. Thanks for breakfast."

Within half an hour, Flynn was hurrying home to complete the arrangements. A golden opportunity to prove his dependability had landed in his lap, and he wasn't about to let it slip away. Lilith would have to see he wasn't a user and a loser.

Eventually, he'd persuade her that her trust wasn't misplaced and he'd be there every time she needed him.

* * * *

"Lily dear, that husband of yours is a real keeper."

Lilith poured more tea for her and Norma while she nodded and cursed the butterflies in her stomach. The pale amber liquid was far more calming than a discussion about Flynn Hastings. "He always seems to be there whenever someone needs a hand."

"You're right about that." The conviction in Mrs. Reed's voice set off a warning bell, and Lilith turned her full attention to the woman across the table from her. "I got confused this morning at breakfast, and he helped me...remember. Treasure every moment you have with him. Someday you might forget who he is or who you are. Flynn's a good man, like my John."

Considering the mistake Norma had made about her relationship with

Flynn, Lilith was unprepared for the lucid observation. The older woman wasn't living entirely in a strange world brought on by broken links in her mind today, and her insights struck a chord.

She wasn't gone yet, even if some things were forgotten.

Tears stinging her eyes and grief tightening around her heart, Lilith grasped her companion's wrinkled fingers. "You're very wise, and I'll miss seeing you every day."

Norma laughed, sounding more confident than she had in weeks. "I'm losing myself, Lily, but I appreciate the kind words. Try to remember me the way I used to be. I might not recognize you next month, or maybe even next week. Thank you for being such a wonderful, caring friend to me."

The lump in Lilith's throat didn't budge with a forceful swallow, and blinking only made the tears come faster. Words wouldn't form to express how attached she'd become to the first resident she'd met five years ago.

Giving Lilith's hand a squeeze, Norma leaned closer and kissed her cheek. "I didn't mean to make you cry. Be happy for me. I've lived a long and fulfilling life. My only regret is—no, not regret. I don't wish to be a burden to my family and friends, but I know they'll take good care of me until my time comes."

Lilith finally managed a whisper. "I want to be like you when I grow up."

"You're much better the way you are. Flynn wouldn't have fallen in love with you if you weren't you, and I've never seen a man more in love with his wife. Have you talked about having children?"

The moment of clarity and reality had evidently passed, and Lilith struggled to regain her composure.

*Children?*

That idea was far outside her comfort zone. Too much could go wrong to bring a child into a sometimes cruel and unpredictable world.

"I'm not ready to share Lilith with anyone else just yet."

She jerked her head up at Flynn's voice. His assessing gaze captured hers, his sky blue eyes stripping away the barrier she'd been clinging to since his interview. No man had ever looked at her with such intensity—or lit the kind of fire in her veins he did by simply standing in her kitchen doorway.

He crossed the room, stopping directly behind her chair and resting proprietary hands on her shoulders. His fingertips moved in small circles, as though he meant to soothe the fear and anguish. "Moving's done. Did you have a good visit?"

Setting down her teacup, Norma fiddled with the saucer. Her lips flattened into a grim line. "We had a wonderful visit, but I've changed my mind. I don't want to move to Arizona."

Flynn seemed to sense Lilith's confusion over the bizarre mistake, and he massaged a little firmer. "Lily and I can go with you and John if you want us to. Or would you like to go for a drive to think about it some more? John should be here any minute."

The front door clicked closed, and Lilith let out a slow breath. Maybe Norma's husband could explain that they weren't leaving Ohio.

Where had Arizona come from?

John appeared in the doorway a few seconds later, his questioning look now typical for when he returned after leaving his wife in someone else's care. Although she couldn't see Flynn's response, Lilith guessed that he'd frowned or shaken his head, given the older man's almost imperceptible nod.

After quickly draining her cup, Norma pushed back her chair. "Would you mind if we went for a drive, Johnny?"

The expression of insecurity and disorientation was back, and she hurried to her husband, practically dragging him through the living room as if she was trying to escape. Within a couple heartbeats, the front door closed again.

Without releasing her, Flynn leaned around Lilith's shoulder. "Are you okay? You've been crying, and your muscles are about to pop."

Needing to pace, she stood, easing out his grasp. "She seemed so...*here* one minute, and the next, she thought they were moving to Arizona. Why Arizona?"

On her return lap, he stepped into her path. "The new address. The facility's on Sedona Drive."

She buried her face in her palms, frustration and utter helplessness threatening to overwhelm her. "It's not fair."

Strong arms wrapped around her, holding her close in a cocoon. His strength seeped into her, and she rested her cheek against his chest. No man had ever comforted her besides her father and Uncle Wade.

She closed her eyes and focused on the steady *thump-thump, thump-thump* beneath her ear. The sound grounded her. Thankful for his unwavering support, she eased her arms around his waist and ignored the annoying panic button going off in her brain.

What harm could come from two friends sharing a consoling hug?

As long as she kept her lips to herself and her clothes on, she was safe. He'd promised not to pressure her for more than friendship. All she had to do was control her sexual attraction to him.

*And I've done that incredibly well, haven't I?*
*Shut off, brain. I'm tired of thinking about it.*

A slow inhale didn't bring relaxation, only the wonderfully masculine scent of the outdoors—nothing artificial. The fragrance filled her mind, reminding her of the woods and nature.

He smelled like silent strength and true reliability, but how many times had her subconscious misjudged men on purpose?

How was she supposed to see beyond sabotage and wishful thinking to the real man?

He loosened his hold, and her stomach sank at his withdrawal. Then he guided her chin up with his finger, forcing her to look him in the face. Worry lines furrowed his forehead. "Will you take the rest of the day off work? You're too wound up to get anything done, and if you don't find a way to reduce your stress, you're going to make yourself sick."

"I'm fine." The terse reply came before she considered how defensive it sounded.

Raising his eyebrows, he gave her a skeptical look. "Okay, I'll put it another way. Shanda asked for tonight off for a family emergency and I need help in the kitchen. Instead of going back to the office, you're assisting me with supper prep."

For half a second, she debated telling him to make her, but she was too tired to pick a fight. Besides, he was right. "Do you trust me with a knife when I'm this tense?"

He grinned, looking pleased that she hadn't argued. "How do you know I won't sit you on a bucket to peel twenty pounds of potatoes?"

"Because you know better than to serve mashed potatoes to my low-carb diet residents."

"And I know when the boss lady needs to de-stress. Now is one of those times." Taking a backward step, he shoved his hands in the rear pockets of his jeans. "I should get cleaned up and change clothes. I'll meet you in the kitchen in fifteen minutes."

She nodded, trying not to read anything into his action.

As he left the kitchen, he glanced back at her over his shoulder and seemed to hesitate before continuing through the living room. He'd kept his promise not to pressure her. He'd even treated her like a friend, caring yet platonic. He hadn't kissed, groped, or seduced her.

Why did his behavior bother her so much?

\* \* \* \*

Flynn scanned the menu, his mind far too distracted by his yet-to-arrive assistant to focus on his job. As much as Lilith needed some downtime, insisting she help with supper preparations was beyond foolish, especially when he'd come so damn close to stepping over the invisible line he'd drawn. Having her arms around him had almost pushed his wavering willpower to the limit.

*I can't break the promise I made to her.*

The door swung open.

"Reporting for duty, Chef Hastings." Lily snapped a hair net over her ponytail and then snagged an apron from the stack of clean laundry. "What are we making?"

Intent on sticking to business, he paused at the entrance to the walk-in cooler. "Chicken Marsala, Asian Stir-fried Vegetables, Broiled Lemon-Pepper Mahi Mahi, and Baked Pork Medallions. We have a full house tonight and everybody pre-ordered. The counts are on the whiteboard. We'll add two extra servings of each for the carryout fridge."

By the time he returned to the center island with the chicken and pork, she'd pulled a roaster pan and the wok from the cabinet. "Do you want me dredge the chicken or start chopping vegetables?"

"Chicken first. What do you think about using a chickpea coating instead of the traditional flour?"

At the sink, she turned on the water and squirted soap into her palm. "Sounds good, kind of like a pakora batter. Will we need to dip the chicken in a wash before the flour?"

"Let's use a light spray of olive oil. Chickpea flour's in the walk-in. I'll get that and the vegetables while you transfer the pork to the roaster."

She rinsed the bubbles from her hands. "Okay."

Although her gaze seemed to linger on him, he returned to the cooler. Trying to read her thoughts would most likely lead to trouble.

*I made two steps forward today. I'll be damned if I'm taking one back.*

He carted out the produce and other supplies while she set to work removing the meat from the cider-and-cinnamon-stick marinade. Before he had a chance to instruct her on the next task, she washed the apples and then prepared a bin of garbanzo flour for the chicken, anticipating his needs as well as someone who'd worked with him for months.

She said little as they chopped, sautéed, and filleted, but her mood seemed brighter. Their natural choreography in the kitchen couldn't have been more synchronized. Hopefully, she'd realize they were in perfect harmony with each other and could build on the framework of their friendship.

As he plated the first of the meal deliveries to the dining room, he served up an extra portion of the stir-fry. "Take a short break to eat while I play waiter. While you get the desserts ready, I'll take a turn."

"Eat?" The spoon she held clattered onto the counter. "I can just take it home with me after we're done with cleanup."

He shook his head. "I already dirtied a plate, so sit down and relax for a few minutes. That's an order."

"Fine." She plopped down on a stool at the far end of the center island.

A stealthy glance at her made his insides tangle. Besides blinking like she was nervous, she was also chewing on her lip and squeezing her fingers.

Why did she dislike eating in front of him?

Or did eating in front of anyone make her uncomfortable?

That could explain her decision to cut short the taste testing during his interview.

"Just so you know—friends don't use the F-word on friends. Enjoy your supper, Lily." He gave her plate a gentle push across the countertop.

Her lips twitched when it stopped a few inches from the edge. He lifted the tray to his shoulder and turned toward the server door instead of calling her on the show of amusement. She couldn't be angry with him for bossing her around if she's was trying to hold in a laugh at his attempt at humor.

When he entered the kitchen several minutes later, her dish was half empty and she stood near the sink pouring a glass of milk. Half a dozen steaming entrées were already loaded on another tray. Her innocent smile didn't fool him for a second. He raised his eyebrows at her, but kept his mouth shut.

On the next return trip, her dishes were gone and another six plates were ready to go.

She was every bit as efficient with dessert, allowing him plenty of time for a dinner break. With only cleanup and boxing the remaining servings left on the to-do list, he followed her into the dining room to clear the tables. The task might've been simple, but spending a little more time with her made him treasure the opportunity.

His job complete for the night, he walked her to the double doors and locked up behind them. Though the air was chilly, warmth flowed through him because of her presence next to him on the way home.

At her apartment, he racked his brain for something to say that wouldn't send her running. "Hey, um, thanks for helping tonight. You did a terrific job."

She turned the key in the lock and pushed the door open. Before he could wish her a good night, she gave him a quick hug. It was over almost as fast as it started. "Thank you and you're welcome. I guess we make a good team. And thanks for the distraction. I'm lucky to have you as a friend."

Her words filled him with hope and love. "Me too. Sleep well, Lily."

She smiled over her shoulder at him as she stepped into her living room. "I think I will."

# Chapter 20

Standing with her face turned into the shower's spray, Lilith pretended the moisture on her cheeks was only water. If she admitted tears were mixed in, she'd also have to admit she was shallow and ungrateful—and jealous of a person she'd never met.

After a week of Uncle Wade's stonewalling every time she asked how his meeting with his former love had gone, he'd finally shown up on Lilith's doorstep this morning. She hadn't even had a chance to chew him out for driving before he'd spilled the beans. Already knowing about Eliza's son didn't take the sting out of her uncle's revelation that he'd fathered a child. The wonder in his voice and joy in his eyes should've pleased her. He'd found happiness.

Instead, the realization that he now had a family of his own had sparked a sense of betrayal and loneliness like she hadn't experienced since the moment she'd learned her parents were dead.

He didn't need her anymore.

She'd pasted on what had to have been a horribly fake smile, expressing delight at the reunion with his true love and discovery of fatherhood. Then he'd left to spend the day with his family—and she wasn't the same part of it she used to be.

How would she face the world today?

Crawling back in bed and burrowing under the covers had been the most inviting proposition, but guilt had forced her into the shower. Her job came before pity parties. Uncle Wade's happiness took precedence over her insecurities and envy.

Life would go on, and she'd have to live with the changes.

The alarm clock read nine thirty when she trudged into the bedroom to dress. That Wanda hadn't come searching for her meant Wade had probably spread his news all over the complex. The moment Lilith stepped out of her apartment, every resident of Montgomery Crossing would descend on her, telling her how lucky she was to have a cousin and a soon-to-be aunt. If she was normal, she might consider herself lucky.

*I've never been normal.*

Her cell phone buzzed on the nightstand, the rhythmic vibrations making it creep closer to the edge.

"What now?" Dropping to the bed, she picked up the phone to check the caller ID. She tapped the screen. "Hi."

"Are you okay?" Flynn always asked the one question she didn't know how to answer. "Do you need someone to talk to? I can be there in two seconds."

"I'm fine." Her vision blurred as more tears formed.

"Friends don't lie to each other. And what did I tell you about using the F-word? I'm at your kitchen door. Will you let me in?"

Was allowing him to comfort her wise under the circumstances?

As much as she wanted him to console her and tell her everything wasn't crumbling around her, she was too weak to resist temptation if he tested the waters. She'd barely survived three hours of supper duty with him last week. Sharing a kitchen should've emphasized their differences, not proven how well they worked together.

She yanked a tissue from the box to dab at her eyes. "Really, I'll be okay. It's Tuesday. You have an order to get ready and another to put away."

"And I have a friend who needs to stop being so damn independent all the time." He sighed in her ear. "I'm sorry. There's nothing wrong with relying on yourself. If you want me to go away, I'll go."

The weariness in his tone brought on a fresh wave of guilt. "No, *I'm* sorry. You're only trying to help, and I'm being a pain in the ass."

His cough didn't hide the chuckle beneath, which most likely meant he agreed with her assessment. "So you'll let me in?"

"Has anyone ever told you you're persistent?" A tiny burst of satisfaction spread through her chest at his unwillingness to give up on her. "Give me two minutes."

She could almost hear his smile through the phone. "I'll be here waiting for you."

\* \* \* \*

Flynn crossed his arms, shoving his fingers in his armpits. He wasn't about to complain about the cold. Lilith was well worth standing in the icy mid-November rain, and he'd endure a blizzard to make sure she was okay.

A shadow crossed the curtained window of her kitchen door, sending his pulse skipping. The lock clicked and then the door opened.

The welcome in her eyes made him forget the chill. "You realize it's raining, don't you?"

He nodded. "I can handle a cold shower now and then."

Rosiness bloomed on her cheeks, his Freudian slip evidently not sneaking past her, and she gestured for him to come in. "I don't have any coffee, but I can make tea."

Even with the latest upheaval in her life, she still put others before herself. She was also an expert at evasion.

He shoved his dripping hair away from his face. "How about a towel? And maybe a mop? I'm leaving a puddle on the floor."

Her lips twitched, but she maintained control. She pointed to the half bath off the kitchen, the layout a reverse of his apartment. "There's a towel on the rack. I'll clean up the puddle."

He pried off his soaked shoes. "My mess, my cleanup. Why don't you start the tea?"

Aiming for the bathroom, he dodged the rebuttal that had to be on the tip of her tongue. She probably would've claimed the mess was her fault since he'd come over to check on her. At least he'd almost gotten her to smile.

He closed the door as he flipped on the light switch, not at all surprised to find a spotless vanity, mirror, and sink. The snowy white towel brought second thoughts about drying off, but he preferred buying her new hand towels to going home.

His sweatshirt was drenched, so he tugged it over his head, using the one dry spot to soak up some of the water from his hair. The towel took care of the rest. At least his T-shirt was only damp. If he'd been home, he would've stripped out of his damp jeans too—an idea that wouldn't earn him any points with Lilith. Returning to the kitchen in boxer briefs would undoubtedly put him on her shit list.

He hung his wet socks on the rim of the sink and then returned to the kitchen to wipe up the puddle. The sight of her bending over stole his breath for a second. "Caught ya. Give me those paper towels."

Popping up, she frowned at him. "You got wet because of m—"

"I chose to go out in the rain. Don't you dare try to take the blame for my decision." He held out an open palm and wiggled his fingers. "Gimme."

She stuck her tongue out and tossed the neatly folded paper towels at him. "You're awfully bossy."

The layers separated as they floated to the floor, fluttering away from their target.

Waiting until they settled on the floor, he slid them to the puddle with his bare foot. "I'm trying to take responsibility for my actions and you don't want to let me. That isn't me being bossy. That's you taking care of everybody and everything. Don't you ever let anybody look after you?"

The teakettle whistled, and she whirled around toward the stove. Steam rose as she filled the mugs on the counter. The spoon clinked as she stirred first one cup and then the other.

Her silence lasted for almost a full minute, leading him to believe she wasn't going to answer. She finally shrugged. "I'm self-sufficient. What's wrong with that?"

He picked up the wet paper towels and carried them to the wastebasket. The delay didn't change his mind about encouraging her to be honest with herself.

Leaning against the counter, he studied her stiff posture. "Nothing—except I think you do it to avoid having to depend on someone else. Take this morning, for example. You find out your uncle has a son, and instead of telling me the truth, you say you're okay. He's been a father to you for the last twenty years. I know you, Lilith. You're thinking you should step out of his life so he can have a *real* family."

She swung around to face him, her green eyes flashing with anger, hurt, and something he couldn't quite define. "I'm thinking you should leave."

"Damn it, talk to me. Please." The tears welling up and over her eyelashes almost broke his heart. "I walked away from my family for an entire year after my sister died, and it's the biggest regret I have. Don't do what I did, Lily. Let me help you through this."

"You don't understand."

He barked a laugh. "I understand better than you'll ever know. God, that feeling of betrayal and abandonment. They all knew Kate was going to die, and no one told me. She made them promise not to. My mom was talking to Kate's husband about it after the funeral and I overheard. I walked out without saying good-bye and didn't speak to my parents or my sisters and their families until you hired me to work here. A whole fucking year. Don't tell me I don't understand."

Her shoulders slumped and she lowered her gaze. "I'm sorry."

The need to touch her had him drawing her into his arms and resting his chin on her soft hair. He breathed in its familiar and tantalizing scent. "I know, but I don't want you to be sorry. I want you to tell me what's going on in that head of yours and listen to my advice. Whether you follow it or not is up to you. Please let me be your friend. Let me help you."

Her body melted against his, and he closed his eyes to savor the closeness for as long as it lasted. More than likely, she'd put distance between them again soon. He only hoped his patience held out until she was ready to become more than friends. Preparing the evening meal with her last Thursday had given his emotions a hefty nudge toward love, and he preferred not venturing there alone.

She shifted, her breast brushing against his bicep. "Uncle Wade's getting married. He still loves Eliza, and they have a son. They belong together."

"Yeah, they do. But he has room for all his family, including you. Do you honestly believe he doesn't give a damn about you anymore?"

"No, but—"

"No buts. He isn't choosing them over you, just like you wouldn't push him aside if you started seeing someone—" *Like me.* "—or got married." *To me.* "You're gaining an aunt and a cousin, not losing an uncle." He rubbed one hand up and down her spine, wishing the silky texture beneath his fingertips was her skin instead of a sweater. "No matter how busy my sisters were when I was growing up, they always made time for me. Even after the weddings and babies, they still came to visit me in Cincinnati as often as they could manage. And after a year of shutting them out, they told me how glad they were to see me, when they had every right to tell me I was a selfish jerk. I'm willing to bet you and your uncle have the same kind of relationship."

The tension in her back seemed to ease, and she reached around his waist like she had on moving day.

"Flynn?"

"Hmm?" He slid his palm down to her lower back, stopping directly above the curve of her bottom.

"Did your sister have children before she got sick?"

"Yeah. She had two girls, Kristin and Hannah—ten and six. Drew says he wouldn't have survived the last year without them."

Lilith tensed again. She didn't pull away, but her attention seemed focused more on his response than on him. "Drew. Her husband? Their father?"

"Uh-huh. Great guy. He started working from home so he could be there before and after school. When he has a meeting or a business trip, one of my other sisters or my mom helps out. My mom retired from teaching this past spring, and my dad cut back on his patient load to spend more time with the girls. My sisters Colleen and Meredith are both married with two kids each and live within twenty minutes of Drew. Finding somebody to watch Kristin and Hannah is as easy as a phone call."

With every word, Lilith tightened her grip around his waist. Her whisper carried two decades of grief. "Uncle Wade and I only had each other."

"You still have him."

Looking up at him, she sighed. "Do you know how lucky you are? I would've loved to come from a big family, but my parents couldn't have any more children."

He brushed his fingertips across her cheek. "I'm incredibly lucky."

Not only did he have his parents and sisters to be thankful for, he'd gotten Lilith to talk to him and reveal some of her personal demons.

"Our tea's probably cold, and you have things to do." She stepped out of his arms, leaving him longing for the day she was ready for more from him. "I should've been in the office a couple hours ago."

*I don't have anything more important to do than spend time with you, and you should be taking the day off.*

He shoved his hands into his damp pockets to keep from pulling her close for one more hug. He'd promised no pressure, and he wasn't going back on his word. "I already sent today's order and the delivery won't be here until eleven. Wanda can handle anything that comes up while we reheat and drink our tea."

Carrying the mugs to the microwave, Lilith shook her head. "If I was paranoid, I'd think you two are conspiring to keep me out of the office today."

"Good plan. I wish I would've thought of it." Flynn sat down at the dinette table. The e-reader was nowhere in sight, but his brain immediately conjured an image of Lilith tangled up in his arms. "I've been working on a German chocolate mousse recipe. If I drop off a serving on my way to check in the delivery, will you tell me what you think?"

Her earlier blush was nothing compared to the color of her neck and face now. She had to be thinking about the erotic story as well.

Had she read it?

Did the idea of food play turn her on?

She cleared her throat. "I, um, sure. Would you mind if I save it for after lunch and e-mail my feedback?"

"Not a problem." Although he should've expected her to delay the tasting, he didn't understand why she wouldn't eat in front of him. She'd pretended the few times he'd brought breakfast for her and hung around for a few minutes. He hadn't noticed at first, too busy worrying about her taking care of herself to realize that a crumbled muffin didn't mean she'd actually taken a bite. "If you like it, I can bring over another helping tonight."

The microwave beeped, and she took out the mugs. "You really are trying to make me fat, aren't you?"

He laughed at the ludicrous accusation. "You're a long way from being fat, and I'll insist you go for a walk with me every day."

Setting the tea on the table, she raised her eyebrows at him. "First you feed me, then you force me to work it off. I'm beginning to question the wisdom of having a friend who's a chef *and* a fitness freak."

He smiled at her use of "friend" again, her lighthearted tone assuring him she was teasing. "You're hardly a terrible cook, and you exercise almost every day already. Friends are supposed to have things in common."

As she sank into the chair opposite his, she grimaced. "That would explain why Erin and Bonnie don't invite me to go out with them anymore."

"The part-time nurses?"

"Yeah."

He lifted the mug, taking a careful swallow of hot tea. "They come across as a little brash to me. Just a personal observation here, but you're a really private person. I can't see you hanging out with them at a strip club or a bar."

"Geesh! They told you about inviting me to the male revue, didn't they? Or was it the speed dating thing?" She buried her face in her palms. "I had to lie so they wouldn't try to make me go."

"If you lied, it was to avoid hurting their feelings." Reaching across the table, he peeled away one hand, keeping it tucked in his. The perfect opportunity to get the truth out of her had presented itself. "Do you mind if I ask you a question about my food?"

She lowered her other hand, her half smile straightening to a grim line. Her tongue snaked out to lick her lips. Then she nibbled on her lower lip. "I—I guess not."

Caught between wanting to take a turn licking and nibbling her sexy mouth and suspecting she didn't actually like his cooking, he huffed out a breath. "During my interview, you said I was a phenomenal chef, but unless I deliver a meal to you, you don't eat. Well, that's not true. You've eaten the boxed portions from the fridge a few times. Only the fish or pasta dishes, though. Are you a vegetarian? Or did you think the chicken and pork entrees were so bad that you're afraid to eat in front of me?"

Her teeth dug into her lip hard enough to turn it white. A tiny dent remained when she released it. "I, um, everything you've prepared has been delicious. And, no, I'm not a vegetarian. Or a vegan."

*The fake tongue-biting incident.*

He rubbed his thumb over her knuckles, not quite sure how to ask his next question. "Lilith, I promise I won't judge you. I only want to help. Do you have an eating disorder?"

She leaned her head back and laughed, the sound echoing off the kitchen walls. After several long moments, she glanced at him and erupted into laughter again. He hadn't made her cry, but the meaning of her reaction eluded him.

Finally, the giggles tapered off. "No. No eating disorder. Well, not exactly. Your food gives me…"

"Gives you what? Cramps? Indigestion? Gas?" He was at a loss to comprehend the problem.

"Your food gives me…" Her lips twitched like she might succumb to another round of hysterical laughter. She cleared her throat and glanced away. Her face was as red as he'd ever seen it. "Orgasms."

# Chapter 21

*I'm having a crazy dream. It's gotta be a dream.*

Flynn would've downed a gulp of hot tea to wake himself if he had a prayer of swallowing without choking. His heart hammered in his chest and the urge to cook for Lilith almost overwhelmed him. He sucked in a deep breath to settle his equilibrium, only to get another whiff of her flowery scent.

*Orgasms? From my food?*

*Damn, I wanna see that.*

"Well, aren't you going to say something?" Her cheeks still glowed. She probably hadn't intended to share her naughty secret with him.

What could he say?

*I'll gladly give you the real thing.*

*Yeah, that'd go over well—like a lead balloon.*

Too flabbergasted to speak and too aroused to risk touching her, he pushed back the chair and stood. Only one option came to mind.

He strode to the door, opened it, and stepped barefoot onto her back stoop. As he pulled the door shut, the steady drizzle changed to a monsoon. Icy rain poured down, soaking every inch of him. He shivered, but he didn't bother trying to shield himself from the downpour. A cold shower was exactly what he needed.

*I give her orgasms—by feeding her. How cool is that!*

A flash of movement caught his eye, and he peered through the deluge at the woman looking back at him from the other side of the glass. Her silent giggles set his pulse racing even faster, and love tightened its hold on his heart.

He offered a wide grin in return.

She might be laughing at him for standing in a downpour, but at least he'd brightened her melancholy mood. The ability to gift her even a single moment of happiness gave him immeasurable joy.

He'd found the love of his life—and he may have finally discovered the way to her heart.

* * * *

*Burgundy Pot Roast or Apricot Glazed Shrimp Kabobs.*

In either case, Flynn's mastery would please Lilith's taste buds and more—especially if she snuck a bite as he left her office. With Uncle Wade back at work today, she'd returned to her consultation room. When she left the door open a few inches, she could catch brief glimpses of Flynn while he worked in the dining room, guaranteeing her a rapturous meal, morning and night.

He hadn't missed a breakfast, brunch, or supper delivery since her accidental revelation almost a week ago. His room service meant every meal came with a side of adorable dimple and a dash of obvious male satisfaction. He never mentioned her admission or stepped beyond the boundaries of friendship, and his vow not to pressure her into more than friendship was quickly becoming annoying.

France's advice had been stewing in Lilith's mind, bringing her sexual awareness of Flynn to a slow simmer. His character hadn't turned rancid or moldy. Nor had she found a rotten core beneath the layers he revealed. The only flaw she'd discovered was his endless patience.

Was he waiting for her to make the first move?

*Not exactly the first since we've already kissed. Twice.*

No man had ever let her decide when, how, and where she wanted to be ravaged. They'd followed their dicks' lead, pushing her for sex sooner rather than later—on *their* terms.

Flynn was different.

A knock on the door sent her tummy flip-flopping. "Come in."

Her uncle poked his head through the narrow opening. "You have a minute, Lily?"

Self-reproach replaced the flash of disappointment. "Sure. How are feeling? You need to be careful not to overdo it the first day back."

He narrowed his eyes as he sat down across from her. "I'm fine, squirt. In fact, I feel great."

"Okay, but if you get tired, you need to rest."

"Didn't I tell you to stop mothering me and have some babies? Speaking of which, you realize the chef has the hots for you, don't you?"

She sorted through the stack of files on her desk to hide her giddiness. "I doubt you're here to discuss Flynn Hastings' temperature. Do you mind if we get to the point? I'm expecting Mr. Langley in a few minutes for a new resident appointment."

"Work, work, work. Thursday's Thanksgiving, and you're damn well taking the day off." The stubborn crease between his eyebrows warned her not to argue. "Since Eliza's father is all settled in, we've decided to have a big dinner here like always. She wants to help you with the cooking. It'll give you a chance to get to know each other better."

"Tell her I appreciate the offer. I'll get a headcount and pick up what we need at the grocery store later."

"I asked everybody at breakfast this morning, and Flynn's donating the turkeys. He says he's spending the holiday with his family, but he wants to contribute too." Wade popped out of the chair. "You done good, Lily girl. That Hastings fellow is just what I had in mind."

"The residents like him a lot. He's friendly and polite to them, not to mention he's a fantastic cook."

Uncle Wade leaned across the desk to tap her on the nose. "But do *you* like him?"

He sounded so hopeful that she gave up any pretense of a strictly professional relationship with Flynn. "I do. We've become friends."

Giving a nod, he stood. "Good. I'll stop in before I head home. Love ya, Lily flower."

"I love you too." She waited until he strode out the door to sniffle.

Flynn had been right. Family dynamics might've changed, but her connection to the man who'd helped through the worst days of her life was no different. If anything, he seemed more affectionate and far happier than she'd ever seen him. Reuniting with his lost love had healed a part of him she hadn't known was hurting.

She peeled a sticky note from the pad by her phone.

*Flynn, The shrimp sounds delicious. Thank you for thinking of me. Lilith.*

Maybe finding the message on the refrigerator would brighten his day the way he lit up hers.

* * * *

As he delivered the Carlton's supper entrees, Flynn glanced across the hall toward Lilith's slightly ajar door. Whether she'd been honest about his food giving her orgasms or not, he'd done his part by providing meals to her. Making her come twice a day was a fantasy like no other.

His body was raising hell at the lack of participation, though. If she didn't make a move on him soon, his balls would shrivel up and die.

*Damn, I wish she'd let me watch her eat.*

"Uh, Flynn, I have the shrimp and CC has the pot roast." Alice's chastisement carried a hint of amusement. "You know, I bet Lily would say yes if you asked her out. The way you two dance around each other is getting everybody hot and bothered. You better be packing a fire extinguisher as well as those horses France gave you. The whole place is gonna go up in flames by the end of the week."

He could only shake his head and grin as he returned to the kitchen for the next batch of plated meals. His progress with Lilith had been slow and steady. Caution beat rejection.

In fact, her mood had improved a lot since their discussion last week. She seemed more relaxed and easygoing, like she was okay with their friendship slowly developing into something deeper.

*I made her laugh.*

Even in the cold, seeing her happy had warmed his insides. He'd gladly endure icy November cloudbursts to see her smile. Comforting her while she cried over the loss of her parents and Norma Reed's downward spiral into delusion had almost ripped out his heart. Inspiring the intense physical pleasure of food ecstasy was satisfying but frustrating. He was ready for the real thing—the whole enchilada.

Balancing four more plates, he made another delivery. His focus strayed again, but no one complained. If anything, they seemed amused—except Harold and Marge. They'd been oblivious to his mistake. Since moving into their new apartment on Friday, the couple paid a lot more attention to each other than the others in the dining room. At eighty-something years old, they were as much in love as young newlyweds.

*I can be patient for my turn.*

He had no choice. Lilith was The One.

So what if he'd known her a month?

Returning to the kitchen, he gave Shanda a thumbs up as she rounded the work island to deliver the last three meals. They'd swapped jobs, with Flynn giving her head chef duties for the meal while he played *sous* chef. She'd performed well under the pressure and had earned a pat on the back. Plus, her pot roast had been a hit.

Of course, he'd prepared the shrimp since Lilith had chosen that entree. He wasn't short-changing her double dose of pleasure unless he was on his deathbed.

Two sharp raps on the server door had him turning toward it as it swung inward.

Lilith stepped into the kitchen, the curve of her lips and sultriness in her eyes telling him she'd thoroughly enjoyed her supper. If the center island hadn't been between them, he wouldn't have been able to resist kissing her.

She held out her empty plate and water glass. "I need to talk to Uncle Wade about giving you a raise."

Taking the dishes, Flynn couldn't decide whether to laugh or groan. He'd never known a chef who was jealous of the food he created. Soon, the desire to give her the ultimate pleasure on his own would overpower him, and if luck was on his side, she'd become as addicted to him as she was to his cooking.

He shrugged. "Money's okay. I'm close to my family again, I'm enjoying my job, and I've made a lot of new friends—including you. Those things matter."

Her smile changed, taking on a softer, more thoughtful shape rather than dimming. "Maybe even a lifetime contract."

A swell of hope rushed through him as he caught the door swinging open out of the corner of his eye.

*Damn. She finally hints at what I want to hear, and we get interrupted.*

"I need an apple dumpling and three cobblers, one *a la mode*." Shanda hurried to the freezer. "How was your dinner, Miss Montgomery?"

Without taking her gaze from him, Lilith shuffled backward to the exit. "Excellent, Shanda. Thank you. I'll get out of your way. See you later."

She hesitated for a second before hurrying from the kitchen, leaving Flynn to wonder what would've happened if they'd had a few more minutes alone together.

For now, he'd have to settle for serving up dessert.

Shanda peeled the lid from the carton. "I didn't interrupt anything important, did I?"

Transferring the four bowls to a tray, Flynn tried for a nonchalant tone of voice. "Nah. Lilith was just dropping off her dishes."

She skimmed a scoop across the top of the ice cream, forming a sphere and then releasing it on the cobbler's golden crust. "Do you mind taking these out? Mrs. Carlton asked me to box up a shrimp dinner for Mrs. Underwood."

"Vivian prefers cabbage and carrots to asparagus." He slid the tray onto his palm. "Lenny gets the *a la mode*, right?"

"Yeah. How'd you know?"

"You learn your patrons' habits after a month of feeding them every day." The predictability was comfortable rather than monotonous. "Alice always orders the apple dumpling and Betsy loves the cobbler, no matter the fruit. I'm guessing Harold and Marge are sharing the last cobbler."

Shanda's eyes widened. "Wow. I want to be able to do that."

"Pay attention to your customers and get to know them." Raising the load to his shoulder, he took off for the dining room.

He moved from table to table, making deliveries and small talk. As he set down the last dessert in front of Alice, France crooked her finger at him. He swallowed a laugh at the suspicion she might want to give him another strip of condoms.

She clasped her wrinkled hands on her lap. "Will you join me for a minute, Flynn?"

"Sure." Sitting in the adjacent chair, he waited for her to lecture him on safe sex or chastise him for not pursuing Lilith more aggressively. Almost all of the residents had done that at some point during the last week. "Did you enjoy your dinner?"

"It was delicious. Thank you." Her intense stare made him wonder what she was trying to see. "You're developing deep feelings for Lily. Be there for her when she needs you most and she'll realize she can trust you."

"I care about her a lot." Stating the obvious didn't erase the unease wriggling up his spine.

Did Dr. Ito believe something bad was going to happen to Lilith?

France nodded. "Take good care of her. Never doubt the strength of love."

"Okay." He refused to worry about things beyond his control. He'd live like Kate had, treasuring every second. Five minutes with Lilith was a thousand times better than nothing. "I'll do my best."

She patted his shoulder. "That's why you deserve her heart."

The small dose of encouragement gave his patience a boost. "I hope she thinks so too."

Easing up from her seat, France levered her cane against the floor as if to steady herself. Her pace seemed a little slower than usual, maybe because she paused to speak to her friends on her way out of the dining room. The cold weather had been playing havoc with several of the residents' arthritis. Hopefully, she wasn't in too much pain.

He stacked her dinner dishes on the tray instead of insisting he help her back to her apartment. The residents were a stubborn bunch, wielding their independence every chance they got. She probably wouldn't whack him in the shins with her cane like Alice or Marge would, but she'd let him know she was no invalid.

*No wonder Lilith gets so attached.*

Everybody at Montgomery Crossing had touched him in some way too. They were family, blood relatives or not.

Adding more plates to the stack, he worked toward the server door. He hadn't signed on for cleanup, but bussing tables for thirty when the part-timer called in sick was a cakewalk compared to his previous job. His gut had steered him right.

A vaguely familiar voice came from behind him. "Just the chef I was looking for. Let me get the door for you."

Lilith's uncle swung the door open and gestured Flynn through the entrance.

He carried his load into the kitchen. "Thanks, Mr. Montgomery."

"Call me Wade. And you're welcome—if you can spare two minutes." The older man followed Flynn. "I have a proposition for you and your intern. That would be you, young lady. Am I right?"

Spine straight and eyes wide, Shanda nodded. "Yes, sir, Mr. Montgomery."

The older man snorted. "I'll have none of that. It's Uncle Wade to you. We're family around here. Now, about that proposition. Eliza and I want you culinary experts to cater our wedding reception. You'll both get bonuses, of course, and a couple extra days off for Christmas and New Years. What do you say?"

"I'd do it for free!" Shanda slapped her hand over her mouth. She evidently hadn't meant to show her enthusiasm.

Grinning at Wade, Flynn shrugged. "I guess that's a yes. What kind of function are we talking about? A formal dinner? Buffet style?"

Wade rubbed his hand over his mostly bald head, patting it as if he expected to find hair there. Then he pulled a paper from his inside jacket pocket and unfolded it. "Eliza suggested an assortment of appetizers. Vegetable and fruit trays. Nothing too fancy. And cake, of course. We decided on a civil ceremony, with our son and Lily standing up for us. Afterward, we'll come back here for the party. Maybe fifty people."

"Sounds doable. I'm guessing the residents are invited and the reception will replace supper?"

"Exactly. Oh, and you have nineteen days. Wedding's on the twelfth of December." Handing Flynn the paper, Wade turned toward Shanda. "Lily tells me you're interested in the catering business. I want to see what you can do."

Her knuckles turned white from her grip on the counter. From panic or to keep herself from bouncing off the walls, Flynn could only guess.

"Yes, sir. I mean, Uncle Wade. Would you like to have a tasting? I can make a list to choose from."

"Good plan. Eliza will be here Wednesday evening to help Lily make pies for Thanksgiving. The three of you can decide what to taste test and when." Wade reached for his forehead again and grimaced. Was he missing the carrot-top toupee he'd worn to the cemetery? "Speaking of Thanksgiving, I know you already have plans, Flynn, but I want to extend the invitation to join us, Shanda. We'll eat about twelve thirty."

Shanda glanced toward Flynn, failing to hide the relief that she had a place to go for the holiday. Her family emergency on moving day had turned out to be an unexpected cutting of ties. "Do you mind if I bring a friend?"

"The more, the merrier. You sure you can't stop by for a little while, Flynn?"

As much as he wanted to share some off-the-clock time with Lilith, he had other commitments, especially after staying away last year. "I wish I could, but my family has a longstanding tradition of breakfast, a huge dinner, and hours of hanging the outside Christmas lights."

If he didn't think she'd beat a hasty retreat, he'd ask Lilith to come with him for part of the day. Meeting his parents and sisters would probably scare her off, though.

Wade pulled his keys from his pocket and jangled them in his fist. "Sounds like a damn fine tradition. Shanda, you're in charge of the kitchen until Flynn gets back. We have another matter to discuss in private. Walk with me, young man."

He strode out the server door, leaving Flynn to trail after him. They walked in silence until they exited the building, and only one possible subject circled Flynn's mind.

Wade wanted to talk about his niece, but about what specifically?

Did he think Flynn was the wrong guy for her now?

Was he moving too fast? Too slow?

"Lily's happier than I've seen her in a long time. You keep doing whatever you're doing."

The older man's words raised Flynn's spirits, making him more determined than ever to bide his time. "I'm being her friend. She's been through some tough stuff."

Wade kept pace as they followed the sidewalk toward the parking lot. "Finally, a man who understands her and is willing to build a relationship with her. You're a good guy, Hastings. Thank you for giving her hope."

Flynn's tight throat prevented him from answering, so he offered his hand and tried to swallow.

Ignoring Flynn's hand, Wade gave him a backslapping hug. "Modest too. Lily's found herself a keeper. Don't you dare disappoint her."

Lilith's uncle was backing out of his parking space when Flynn found his voice. "I won't."

# Chapter 22

Tapping the pen against her chin, Lilith wracked her half-asleep brain for something intelligent to write in Flynn's card. He deserved a personal message after all the meals and orgasms he'd delivered over the past eight days. Actually, she owed him much more than a Thanksgiving greeting, but she hadn't worked up the nerve to drag him into her office and lock the door.

*Dear Flynn, I hope you have a wonderful holiday with your family.*

Good gravy, could she be any more generic?

*Dear Flynn, I'll miss seeing you today—and not just because of your food.*

He'd probably think she only cared about getting sexual satisfaction from his divine creations.

She adjusted her hold on the pen.

*Dear Flynn, I'm thankful for you. Happy Thanksgiving! Lily*

The short sentiment truly expressed what she wanted to say. She tucked the card into its envelope as she slipped on her shoes. If she wedged it between his apartment door and its frame, he'd find it when he left to spend the day with his family. She'd probably already be knee deep in dinner preparations with Eliza by that time.

Shrugging on her coat, she checked the pockets for her keys. At their jingle, she hurried outside to make her delivery.

The crisp air froze her lungs for a moment, but she focused on her task, balancing the envelope in place. A gust of wind made it flutter and then settle back in position.

*Please stay.*

She stuffed her cold hands into her pockets and set off for the main building. As she withdrew her keys to unlock the entrance, a door clunked closed behind her.

Her stomach somersaulted. She locked her gaze on the reflection in the glass instead of giving in to wild hope. As she peered into the fuzzy image of security lights and the faint garden area, she searched for a hint of her tall, handsome chef.

Everything beyond the garden was a blur.

The muffled crumpling of paper almost lured her into looking back, but she inserted the key in the lock and turned it. Even as she entered the hall, she strained to hear muted footsteps on the walkway. Only the quiet swish of branches blowing in the breeze broke the early morning silence.

She closed the door behind her, finally glancing up when she skimmed her fingers along the wall for the light switch. A distinct silhouette stood out against her neighbor's beige apartment door. He looked in her direction, holding something that resembled the card or a book in his hand. Then he pressed it to his chest.

Too nervous to listen to the instinct urging her to go to him, she waved and compelled her feet to carry her to the kitchen. He could've interpreted her message a dozen different ways.

Did *she* even know what she meant?

Five weeks had passed since the interview, and her hormones still went into a tailspin every time she saw him. She hadn't panicked until he'd appeared. That she'd lasted a month without falling ass over teakettle for him was a miracle.

*Who the hell am I trying to fool?*

Flipping the light switch as she entered the kitchen, she strode toward the walk-in fridge. She could ruminate over her indecisiveness while she cleaned and stuffed the turkeys. Besides, the sooner she got them in the ovens, the sooner she could run home for a quick shower and breakfast. Then she and Eliza would meet up at eight thirty to prepare the side dishes while Uncle Wade and Garrett hung the outdoor Christmas lights at the complex.

By noon, Lilith's stomach was growling from the intoxicating aroma of freshly baked yeast rolls, sweet potatoes, and the main dish. Her kitchen partner added to the mouthwatering combination as she ladled homemade noodles, corn, and green beans into chafing pans for the buffet table.

They'd worked well together, a few recent visits smoothing out the bumpy start to their awkward beginning. Lilith had promised her uncle she wouldn't hold a grudge against Eliza if he didn't, and liking the other woman had come easy. She made him happy.

A dozen of the twenty residents and employees sharing Thanksgiving with her and her family had arrived and claimed seats by the time Lilith wheeled her deliveries into the dining room. She unloaded and then rolled the cart back toward the kitchen.

"Lily dear, will you join me for dinner?" Dr. Ito's request was almost too quiet to hear over the lively conversation at the neighboring table.

Lilith paused at her friend's chair to give her a gentle hug. "I'd be honored, France. I'll be back as soon as I set out all the food."

The old woman smiled, the laugh lines around her eyes deepening in her paper-thin skin. She never seemed to lose her positive outlook and love of life. "You're the sweetest girl I know. I'm happy to wait for you."

Deep affection filled Lilith's soul, and she gave France's arthritic fingers a light squeeze. "I adore you."

Before tears had a chance to leak past her eyelashes, Lily set off toward the server door to transport more of the feast.

Eliza followed with the last pan on the return trip. "Are you sure you don't want to share a larger table with us? Wade doesn't want you thinking you mean any less to him now than you did before I told him about our son."

"It's okay. Dr. Ito invited me to sit with her." Placing the noodle pan into its holder, Lilith glanced at her soon-to-be aunt. "I know he still would've welcomed me into his home if you'd already been married when my parents died."

"Yes, I would've insisted on it. Wade's an extraordinary man for having done that by himself. I'm grateful he had you in his life while we were apart, like I had Garrett." Eliza dabbed at her eyes, triggering Lilith's tears again. "We're a happy family now—all of us."

Lilith leaned in for a quick hug, too choked up to speak. Parking the cart against the wall, she scanned the room, noting the only two empty seats belonged to her and Eliza. Everyone was present and accounted for.

Her uncle rose, his grin wider than usual when he locked gazes with her for a long second. He had to be truly content. "Welcome, everybody. First off, I want to thank our two beautiful and amazing cooks. Ladies, dinner smells delicious."

A chorus of similar sentiments came from the residents and their guests.

He wrapped his arm around his fiancée as she joined him. "I have so much to be thankful for this year. Let's have a moment of silence to each give thanks in our own way."

Flynn's silhouette in the early morning darkness appeared in Lilith's mind as she closed her eyes. He was worthy of much more than a single moment of thanks.

"Let's eat!"

The image dissipated with Wade's enthusiastic announcement, but the sense of freedom lingered. Someday soon, she'd muster the courage to act on her attraction. In the meantime, France deserved her full attention and a well-disguised reason to remain seated.

Lilith placed her hand on France's shoulder. "I'll go through the line for both of us if you'll pour our drinks."

The old woman's eyebrows rose as if she was well aware of the motive, but she didn't protest. "Would you like apple cider or lemonade?"

"Cider please."

Lilith made her escape, picking up two plates at the end of the buffet line and adding a little of everything to each dish. Edging along the table behind Dorothy, she couldn't help but notice the other woman's slow steps and shaking hands. Her friends were aging before her eyes.

Weaving past Harold and Marge, Vivian, and the Carltons, Lilith relaxed her hold on both plates. Her dinner companion was an expert at spotting tension, and today was supposed to be about positive reflection and thankfulness, not worry.

She delivered dinner as she sat down next to France. Although the food looked and smelled delicious, Lilith wasn't in the mood to eat.

"You're missing Flynn, aren't you, Lily?"

Lilith spread her napkin on her lap to avoid looking at France. "I see him every day. Why should I miss him?"

Dr. Ito pursed her lips. "The heart knows what it wants. Denying won't change it."

Noodle broth forged a tiny river along the edge of Lilith's mashed potatoes, aiming for her turkey. She set her fork in the liquid, temporarily damming the flow. Then it washed over the obstacle in a miniature waterfall. "I'm not denying. I just don't understand how I could see him when he was leaving this morning and still spend almost every minute since then wondering when he'll be home. I've never missed a man before."

"Maybe today. Maybe tomorrow. It'll happen. You can't fight what's meant to be." The calm confidence in France's words also showed on her face. No matter the state of her body, she always seemed to have a contented soul. "It'll happen whether you're ready or not. The trick is to take it in stride."

The advice struck a chord, giving Lilith the boost of bravery she so desperately needed. Tomorrow, when her chef brought breakfast, she'd tell him she was ready to take their relationship beyond the friends with foodgasm-benefits level.

She'd take the next step and let go of her doubts.

* * * *

Washing the last of the big pots, Lilith gave her imagination free rein. Somehow, she managed to survive dinner and cleanup without collapsing in a fit of giggles or suffering from orgasm withdrawal. Her wayward thoughts had steered into dangerous territory while she'd considered how best to convey her deeper interest to Flynn.

Rewarding his patience by taking a bite of Fried Oatmeal in front of him had triggered the memory of him standing in the ice-cold rain with a self-satisfied grin, setting off a flurry of butterflies in her belly.

Every day, without fail, he gave her a helping of sexual satisfaction—except today.

They'd better experience the real thing together very soon or she might lose her mind.

"Lily? Are you in there?"

She turned toward the server door as Eliza's father pushed it open far enough to poke his head into the kitchen. "Hi, Mr. Langley. Come in. What can I do for you?"

He hobbled inside, the dexterity with his cane slightly better than a week ago. "Lenny and I found a glasses case on the floor when we were helping Betsy with the tablecloths. She said it belongs to France."

A glance at the object in his hand confirmed it.

Gesturing to the center island with a nod, Lilith held her soapy hands over the sink. "You can leave it there. I'll drop it off on the way to my apartment."

"Okay." He set down the flowered case. "I want to thank you for making me feel welcome and for being friendly to Eliza. She was worried you might think badly of her for not telling Wade about Garrett."

"I'm glad you're comfortable here." She dropped the scrubber into the pan and then dried her hands on the dishtowel. "As far as Uncle Wade knowing or not knowing about his son, whatever happened between him and Eliza is their business. He's okay with it and she makes him happy, so who am I to hold a grudge?"

"No wonder Wade speaks so highly of you all the time. You're a smart young lady, and he has good reason to be proud." Pivoting his cane, he limped to the exit. "Happy Thanksgiving, Lily. See you at breakfast tomorrow morning."

"Happy Thanksgiving, Mr. Langley."

Turning back to the sink, she rinsed the pot and chastised herself for thinking her job was expendable. Even if she was basically Montgomery Crossing's cruise director, the residents and her uncle appreciated her presence. Leaving would be selfish—not that she really wanted to anyway.

She perched the pan in the draining rack before checking the island and counters for dirty utensils and dishes she might've missed. The kitchen was nearly as spotless as she'd found it at last night's meeting with Shanda about reception appetizers and the pie-baking marathon.

Glasses case in hand, Lilith set off toward France's apartment, shivering as she stepped outside. Mr. Langley's comments had distracted her from putting on her coat. Goose bumps sprang up beneath her sweater, and she shuddered with the sudden blast of frigid air.

Picking up her pace, she took a shortcut through the fenced patio. She stopped at 2C and knocked.

A full minute passed with no answer.

She knocked again before tucking her fingers under her crossed arms.

Betsy came out of her apartment two doors down, looking ready for her afternoon constitutional in an orange jogging suit and orthopedic walking shoes. She added a rainbow-striped stocking cap to her ensemble. "Lily, you should be wearing a coat and gloves."

"Yes, I should. Have you seen or talked to France? She isn't answering her door."

"Not since I walked home with her after dinner. Didn't she say something about taking a nap?" Pressing her glove-clad palms to the wall, Betsy adjusted her stance for a runner's stretch.

France *had* mentioned she was ready for a rest. Still, she was usually intuitive about her visitors, her sense of knowing sometimes a little unnerving. If she'd fallen, she might not be able to get up, or she could've bumped her head.

"She left her glasses in the dining room." Lilith held up the flowered case. "She'll be missing them when she wakes up. I think I'll go get the master key."

Setting off along the sidewalk, Betsy waved over her shoulder. "Put on a coat while you're at it!"

At the main building, Lilith retrieved her jacket and the spare keys from the coat closet. As she walked back out the double doors, she sighed at her suddenly empty hands.

*Where did I set down the glasses case?*

She made a quick trip back to the kitchen, this time checking for the eyeglasses and her keys before she headed outside.

At the apartment, she knocked again and counted to thirty. When no one opened the door, she unlocked the deadbolt and knob.

"France?" A gentle push gave her a clear view into the living room. She took a tentative step inside. "France, it's Lily."

She walked to the bedroom, peeking in the open doorway. The bedcovers were slightly askew and a telltale lump confirmed France's choice of a nap, even if her lack of response was out of character.

"France, it's Lilith. You left your glasses in the dining room." She moved closer to the bed.

The older woman's eyes were closed and her skin a little pale, but her expression was peaceful. She was normally a light sleeper, but she didn't appear ill.

Had she taken something to ease the pain in her hip?

*She isn't on any medications that would make her sleepy.*

France was too quiet, too still.

Lilith rubbed at the sudden ache in her stomach. She placed her index and middle fingers below the curve of the old woman's jaw, praying for a pulse—even a weak one. No blood thumped through the artery under her fingertips.

"No. Oh, please, no." She repositioned her finger lower, hoping to find the faintest of beats. Failing, she rested her palm beneath France's nose, but no breath caressed her skin. "Come on. Breathe."

Panic crept up Lilith's throat, and she drew in a slow, shaky inhale to calm her fears.

*Focus, dammit! CPR.*

*No. Call nine one one first.*

She pulled her cell phone from her coat pocket, almost dropping it in an effort to hurry. As soon as she'd tapped in the numbers and switched to speaker, she folded down the covers to put her ear to France's chest.

"Nine one one. What is your emergency?"

The question echoed like it came from a cave against the backdrop of her own shallow breaths. She knelt on the bed and set her clasped hands on Dr. Ito's breastbone.

*Wait.*

*Living will. DNR.*

She lifted away her hands and squeezed her eyes shut. "This is Lilith Montgomery at Montgomery Crossing Retirement Village on Water Street. I have a ninety-year-old female with no pulse and no breathing. We have a do-not-resuscitate order on file."

# Chapter 23

As she stared out the office window into the deepening dusk, Lilith wiped another tear from her cheek. The necessary phone calls had been made and all the residents had finally returned to their apartments. Even Uncle Wade had gone home.

More than anything, she wanted to rest her head on Flynn's shoulder and find comfort in his arms. He'd know the right things to say, and he wouldn't allow her to blame herself for not arriving in time to save France.

His apartment windows were still dark, though.

She returned to the desk to shut down her computer. A generous slice of pumpkin pie might distract her from missing her chef and put her into sleep mode. Then she wouldn't have to pretend to be strong.

Not bothering with the overhead lighting, she followed the dim corridor to the kitchen. The exit signs above both doors cast a dull reddish glow off the stainless steel appliances. Faint scents of roast turkey and the trimmings still lingered, reminding her of the last time she'd spoken with France.

A quarter circle of light flooded the floor when she opened the refrigerator, and she blinked against the brightness to find her target. The pie plate held a lone wedge of spicy goodness in a flaky crust. She grabbed the only remaining can of Reddi-wip from the shelf and set both on the counter to get a fork.

The metal utensil clinked against the glass dish, blending with the quiet hum of the freezer and fridges as she popped the lid off the can. She squirted a swirling glob on the pie to bury the orangey-brown filling in fluffy whipped cream.

She'd have to skip dessert and add an extra twenty minutes of cardio for the next week to make up for one day of gluttony, but the exercise might help chase away the weariness, too.

*No, Flynn is the only solution to that problem.*

The kitchen door banged open, and she was momentarily blinded by the sudden flash from the florescent lights blinking on. A large, indistinct body came rushing toward her.

She raised her hand to block the brightness and tightened her grip on the can as it tried to slip free. A short burst of leaky-tire noise warned her she'd pressed on the tip.

"What are you doing in the dar—"

The shape with the familiar voice stopped in front of her, sending her stomach diving to her feet.

Flynn chuckled. "Raiding the kitchen, I see. Hell of a greeting by the way."

*Good thing I wasn't holding a can of mace.*

Her vision came into focus, and his irresistible mouth drew her attention as it curved into a kissable smirk. White speckles dotted his face from cheekbone to jaw.

She set the can back on the counter and then reached up to wipe the spatters from his cheek, too weak to resist touching him. "Sorry. You surprised me."

He cupped her face between his palms, looking down at her with concern in his eyes. "Are you okay? I saw Alice when I got home. She told me what hap—"

She pressed her finger to his lips. "I don't want to talk about it right now. I just want you."

He sucked her index finger into his mouth, triggering a quick spasm in her lower belly. His tongue pulled with gentle suction, and the wet heat of his mouth made her long for an action much more intimate.

He was exactly what she needed—and wanted.

Closing her free hand around his, she led his thumb through the snowdrift on her pie and lifted it to her face. A rush of desire drowned out the warning signals from her brain, and she licked the airy cream from his messy hand. She let her eyes drift shut as she savored the treat.

Forgetfulness took precedence over caution. As thankful as she was for all she had, today's loss outweighed it all.

Friendship wasn't enough anymore, either.

He slipped his thumb from her mouth and leaned forward. The tentative press of his soft lips against hers and tender lap of his tongue along the corner of her mouth stole the last of her control.

Clutching at his shirt, she chased the would-be invader back to his own welcoming home. Too much time had passed since the last time he'd kissed her. She wasn't about to settle for a neighborly peck on the lips.

Every forceful glide set off a tangled struggle for more. A simple meeting of mouths wasn't satisfying the desire building inside her. Even with her heart hammering in her ears and her lungs drained of oxygen, she couldn't break away from him. Ending it might mean she'd have to wait days, weeks, or months for another taste of him—something she wasn't willing to risk.

She wanted to skim her hands over his bare skin, tracing the sculpted body he hid beneath his chef whites every day and discovering where he liked to be caressed. If she stripped for him, would he run his calloused fingertips across every inch of her body?

The temptation to find out won, and she tugged at his shirt, pulling it loose from the waistband of his jeans. She could only hope he'd assume she was giving him permission to remove her clothes as well.

Slipping her hands beneath the stretchy cotton, she slid her palms up his spine. Smooth skin covered rigid bone and strong muscle, and she followed the upward-sloping curve of his shoulder blades to his spine. Instinct and his throaty groan had her gently raking her nails down his back. She flattened her palms when she reached his pants, continuing southward to cup his tight butt inside his jeans.

He arched into her as he tightened his hold on her waist. His hard length lay nestled against her lower belly, and she rocked her hips forward to encourage him.

Jerking away from the kiss, he panted and met her gaze as she finally opened her eyes. His whisper spoke of a man on the edge. "You're not going to run away, are you? Because I'm not sure I can take that again."

Too speechless and short of breath to answer, she shook her head. She'd never been kissed so passionately before, Flynn's desperation seeming to match her own. Lifting his shirt to his chest, she waited for him to raise his arms.

He took hold of the hem and rested his forehead against hers. "Are you sure, Lily?"

How many men in her life had cared enough to ask her that question? *None—until now.*

She nodded once. "I'm sure. I want you. Right here. Right now."

After a quick brush of his lips on the tip of her nose, he yanked off the shirt and tossed it aside. The movement sent his muscles rippling under his skin and desire burning in her veins.

Flynn had waited weeks for those words.

Today alone, he'd spent hours analyzing the brief note in Lilith's card, when he should've been enjoying the holiday with his family. He'd tried not to read too much into the message, imagining the painful disappointment he'd experience if he happened to be wrong.

Her four-word sentence had given him new hope anyway.

He was drawn to the passion in her sultry gaze and the kissability of her full lips, but he was none to anxious to race through what he hoped would be their first time making love. "I want you too."

A faint blush stained her tear-dampened cheeks, and she tried to look away.

Lightly grasping her chin, he guided her head up again. "If you're not ready, tell me. We don't have to do this now. No pressure. Ever."

Her fingers skimmed his stomach, making his abs shudder and his cock fight harder to find a way out. She popped open the button of his jeans. "Shut up and undress."

He stepped backward out of her reach. Removing his pants wasn't conducive to the slow exploration of her body he had in mind. "Ladies first. I've had to suffer through what my food does to you without getting to participate, so I'm going to give you orgasms that'll make you forget Raspberry Chicken, Campanelle with Ports, and Apricot-Glazed Shrimp Kabobs even exist. I want to make you come with my hands and my mouth, Lily. And then, when you're ready, we'll share the pleasure."

Her eyes never left his face as she took a step toward him. "But I want to touch you."

He moved with her, the admission testing his willpower. "I won't last five minutes. Besides, I owe you for missing breakfast and supper today."

Her slight frown suggested she wasn't thrilled with his reasoning. "Next time, we do it my way."

*Next time.*

She could do whatever the hell she wanted to him next time—and the time after that and the time after that. Hearing she wanted more than once with him was a wish come true.

He nodded, too aroused to speak.

Easing the sweater up and over her breasts, he stayed an arm's length away from her. If she put her hands on him again, he'd probably explode on the spot.

He was tempted for less than a second to use the sleeves to trap her hands behind her back, but he'd be an idiot to risk her trust after the effort to get to this point. Instead, he let her sweater drop to the floor.

Yet another layer still covered her skin. The T-shirt clung to her curves, outlining the spectacular body she hid beneath baggy sweatshirts and ruffly blouses. If not for the glimpse of her stepping into the hot tub, he wouldn't have been prepared for her stunning hourglass figure. Unable to stop himself, he gently cupped her breasts, brushing his thumbs over the fullness in search of her nipples. The bra's padding blocked all but a hint of them.

She stiffened, curving her shoulders forward. Her lower lip faded to white where her teeth bit into it.

Did she dislike nipple play?

Was he moving too fast? Too slow?

He forced his hands downward, following her ribs to her waist. "Something's wrong. Do you want me to stop?"

The color returned to her lip as she released it. She sighed, her tension and frustration evident in the sound. "No. It's just that…my breasts are really sensitive. Not that I don't want you to touch me there, but…I don't know how to explain it."

*Okay. A problem I can solve.*

He'd overheard enough of his sister's sex discussions to have a distinct advantage over other guys. "You need foreplay before foreplay. Maybe something like this."

Bending toward her, he lifted the hair out of the way to kiss directly below her ear. The softness of her skin had him going back for more as he slid his palm lower to trace the seam running up her inner thigh. He switched to other side, careful not to get too close to the intersection in the middle. Letting go of her hair, he cradled her shapely ass, memories of the night they'd met making him wish for bare skin.

She trembled against him and moaned. "Yeah, something a lot like this."

"Mm, not a problem from my perspective." Slipping his fingers into her back pocket, he kissed his way along her jaw, enjoying their fore-foreplay as much as he hoped she was. "What does dirty talk do for you? Turn-on or turn-off?"

The low growl that vibrated through her throat to his lips gave him a pretty good idea of the answer. "No experience, but I'm pretty sure it's a turn-on. I'm getting wet thinking about you saying you want to go down on me."

He tensed his gut to try to halt the tightening in his balls. "God, Lily. You're gonna make me come in my pants talking like that."

She panted against his bicep. "Then I'll just have to make you hard again."

"I like the way you think. You deserve at least two orgasms for that. *Real* ones."

Her lips formed what was obviously a fake pout. "Only two?"

"For now." He'd do his damnedest to give her another one when he got around to taking off his jeans. Diving in for a chaste kiss on the lips, he trailed his finger up the inside of her leg, stopping short of the center seam.

"I can't wait to taste you, Lily."

Her breathing changed from rhythmic inhales and exhales to irregular shallow pants when he nibbled a path from her earlobe to her chin.

Smoothing one palm along her hip, he eased the other closer to the apex of her thighs. Then he traced her lips with his tongue. "Do you want me to kiss you?"

"Yes." Her whisper sounded needy and urgent.

"Here?" He moved his fingers past her zipper to the thick crisscrossing seams he'd avoided. Next, he licked her lower lip. "Or here?"

"Anywhere." She squirmed against his hand. "Everywhere."

A kernel of satisfaction tried to take root, but he ignored it. His long-term objective wasn't to get laid.

Taking a cautious turn, he skimmed across her firm stomach to the undersides of her breasts. "And here?"

She arched toward him. "Maybe."

Her answer wasn't as enthusiastic ad he would've liked, but an object on the work center caught his eye, sparking a delicious inspiration.

A second later, he popped her jeans button open. Kneeling at her feet, he dragged down the zipper and tugged on the hems. As the denim slipped lower, he pressed his lips to the frilly edge of her panties and breathed in the intoxicating scent of her arousal. "I'll take Lily for dessert over pumpkin pie any day."

She whimpered, but didn't retreat.

Guiding her hand to his shoulder, he pulled one pant leg free and then the other. Red lace barely covered his first destination.

Was she wearing a thong like the night he'd accidentally felt her up?

*Except that one was blue.*

He'd remember that night for the rest of his life.

Beginning at her ankles, he blazed a slow path upward, letting her curves set the course. Not a stitch of clothing hindered his travels to her beautifully rounded ass and the narrow strip of lace running down the middle. He kissed the tiny red triangle staring him in the face as he caressed her hip.

Her body quivered beneath his fingertips. She had to be on the verge of orgasm number one. A few well-placed licks would take her to heaven, and then he'd try for a second trip.

The skimpy underwear had to go first.

With patience dug up from deep in his soul, he worked the barely there panties down her legs inch by slow inch. Her squirming and soft moans were his rewards. His aching balls sure weren't thanking him.

He hooked her knee over his shoulder, giving him the perfect view of tight strawberry-blonde curls and damp pink folds. As much as he wanted to dive straight in, he called on every ounce of self-control.

Dipping his tongue into the valley at the top of her thigh, he licked down one side and up the other. Her low groan became a gasp when he blew against her moist lips.

He finally gave her what he hoped would send her over the edge— several slow laps through her wetness. She tasted sweet and tangy and salty, and he savored her flavor as he found her clit and gently sucked.

She bucked against his mouth. "Oh!"

Holding her in place, he flicked his tongue back and forth, prolonging her long cry and the trembling of her muscles. She went limp above him, and he scooped her into his arms. He stood, biting the inside of his cheek to divert the pain of his cramped erection.

She frowned and struggled against him. "I'm too heavy. Put me down."

Shaking his head, he sat her bare bottom on the center workspace and stepped between her thighs. "You're not heavy."

"Then why were you grimacing?"

Blunt honesty seemed best. "Because my hard dick's trying to get out of my pants. Kind of a tight fit at the moment."

He laced his fingers through her hair and leaned in to kiss her before she offered to solve his dilemma. With the can of Reddi-wip handy, he still had another opportunity to achieve his goal.

# Chapter 24

Lilith might've choked if Flynn hadn't distracted her with a soul-deep kiss. The man didn't mince words, and he'd done far more in ten minutes than her favorite vibrator had been able to accomplish in over a month.

He withdrew, his lips blazing a trail along her cheekbone. "Stop thinking and lift your arms."

Could he read her mind?

She couldn't help but try to analyze why this experience had been different from the rest. Her brain was wired to overthink and question everything, and men had a tendency to assume all women enjoyed the same types of touching.

He'd find out the truth soon enough.

What she wouldn't give to be normal.

Dreading the obvious next step, she obeyed his request.

He peeled off her T-shirt. "You're tense. If you don't like what I'm doing, tell me."

The urge to become defensive was strong, but she studied his eyes, looking for any hint of impatience or annoyance. Only concern and a hefty serving of lust reflected back. All she had to do was be honest with him.

She took a calming breath, trying to release the pressure to perform. "I don't know if I can come again. My body's a lot more sensitive and my nipples—"

"Let me worry about that." He touched his lips to her shoulder as he unhooked her bra. Rather than pushing the straps down her arms and grabbing her breasts, he kissed his way across her collarbone. "I promised you two orgasms, and I don't intend to let you down."

All the nerve endings above her waist tingled from his soft caresses. Unfortunately, that was no guarantee he'd manage to send her flying to the moon again. Outdoing his entrées and the few guys who'd used her didn't mean she could—or should—expect more.

He gave a slight tug as he tucked his thumb under the slender strip of satin joining the cups. The bra slipped free, baring every inch of her. He grinned and tossed it on top of her clothes. His wink sparked a shiver up her spine and made her nipples tighten to achy buds.

What wicked scheme did he have planned?

He picked up the can of whipped cream, shaking it several times. "Payback time."

Before she realized his intention, he squirted her left breast.

"Oh! That's cold!" Although the topping was chilly, it sent a surprisingly delicious flash of heat southward. She wriggled from the sensation.

"You need a matching set." Flynn applied another fluffy cloud, setting off more flaming arcs before he set aside the can. "Mm, you're my kind of dessert."

He licked away a few spatters from her belly. Fingertips stalked past her knee to skitter up the inside of her leg, sending an anticipatory quiver to the very heart of her body. A slow pass through her wet folds made her arch against his hand, and he sank a finger inside her.

She gasped at the unexpected sensations. "More. I want more. I want *you.*"

Circling her cream-covered breast with his tongue, he moved closer and closer to the taut tip. Ripples of pleasure had her muscles quavering and her lungs refusing to work.

As he finally reached the outer edge of the white mound, he stroked a spot deep within her. A wave of sheer rapture fanned the fire building in her center, and she nearly doubled over at the deep contraction. He switched to her other breast, licking through the middle of the topping. His mouth closed over her nipple, and he rubbed a calloused fingertip against her G-spot again.

Everything burst apart. Relief and joy flooded her veins as her breath caught in her throat and her soul floated out of her body. She cried out, not caring if the world heard.

How could she hold in such utter bliss?

The tension in her body rushed away, leaving nothing but satisfaction and elation.

"Damn, I can't wait another minute to make love to you, Lily." Taking a step backward, he shoved his jeans to his knees. "Condom! Wallet."

A few seconds later, he straightened with a foil packet in his grasp and his purple cock jutting out at her. He fumbled with the wrapper.

"Let me." Holding out her open palm, she didn't even try to hide her eagerness. "I want to touch you."

He shook his head. "I'll never survive if you put your hands on me. I'm only gonna last a minute or two as it is."

The desperation in his voice convinced her that he wasn't too happy about it, either.

She snatched the package out of his grip. "We have all night to test your stamina. I won't complain about a quickie this time."

She guided the protective layer over the head of his penis and down his thick, hard length, earning her a moan.

"It's on." He helped her shimmy to the edge of the counter. Hooking his hand behind her head, he pulled her close enough to kiss. As his tongue met hers, he found her entrance and pushed.

She gasped at the sudden fullness of his erection filling her completely. None of her sexual experiences compared to simply having Flynn inside her. He fit like he'd been made for her, his shape and size allowing him to caress every part of her.

"Hard and fast." She pressed her nipples against his lightly furred chest. The remains of the whipped cream spread over his skin, and his coarse hair triggered wonderful zinging pulses from her sensitive nubs to her inner muscles.

Following her directions, he rocked in and out of her in an increasing rhythm, his panting breaths attesting to his claim of a short-lived ride. With every advance, his cock swelled inside her. "God, Lily, you feel so damn good. Will you come with me?"

The smooth thrusts and his frantic words dragged her toward another orgasm, this one more powerful than the first two. "Yes. Oh, yes, Flynn."

She lost her ability to speak as a swift current bathed her in ecstasy. Only unintelligible cries escaped her raw throat to blend with his hoarse yell.

After a last pair of forceful pushes, he wrapped his arms around her and stilled, holding her while she clung to him. She'd never experienced anything like the oneness of being connected to this man. His heartbeat matched hers, and she wanted nothing more than to lie in his arms until she took her last breath.

Her pulse gradually slowed and her breathing returned to normal. Being with Flynn was how she'd always imagined sex should be—how she'd hoped it would be.

She leaned against his bicep, too comfortable to move. "By my count, you gave me three orgasms instead of two. What do you think a fair punishment is?"

His chuckle vibrated through her. "Letting me do it again tomorrow. And the next day. All weekend. Next week."

"What about tonight?" Confusion rushed in, and the words were out before she could censor them.

Didn't he want to share the rest of the night with her?

She hadn't made yet another mistake, had she?

Flynn closed his eyes and counted to ten.

The quiet hurt in Lilith's question exposed more of the insecurities he hadn't been able to thwart. Even if she considered him a trustworthy friend, she doubted his sincerity and steadfastness as a man.

She'd probably treat him to a massive dose of sarcasm if he announced that he'd settle for fifty or sixty years of tonights with her, right before she hightailed it out the door. The woman had advance down pat, but she was an expert at retreat.

He had to tread lightly and honestly.

Number ten long past, he opened his eyes and leaned back to met her gaze. "I'd love to stay with you. Do you want me to spend the night?"

At the moment, she didn't need to know he'd gone to sleep with his palm against the wall between them every night since he'd moved in next door to her. That fact would likely scare her off rather than soothe her fears.

She blinked at him, opening her mouth as if to speak and then closing it. Her tongue snuck out to wet her lips. "I want you to come home with me."

Hiding his relief wasn't an easy task.

Her jaw tensed. "But I'd like you to use the kitchen door."

He didn't need to ask why. After all the blatant matchmaking attempts, neither of them would hear the end of the teasing if the residents found out. Well-intentioned comments and a skittish woman didn't mix.

Giving a nod, he conceded to her wishes. Square one was finally behind him. He wasn't going back.

He skated a finger through the whipped cream decorating her breasts, careful to avoid her nipples and a reminder of their sensitivity. "I'll grab a towel. We can clean up a little here, but I think we're going to need to shower together when we get to your apartment."

"Together?" She spasmed around his cock and then blinked as if the reaction surprised her.

"Yeah, together." Holding the condom in place, he withdrew from her. He wasn't taking any chances on slippage, even though she could easily make him hard again in no time. "I squirted you with whipped cream. I should get to—I mean, *have* to—wash you."

Pulling up his jeans, he tucked in his latex-clad self rather than leaving evidence of his liaison with Lilith in the trash. He wasn't about to jeopardize the progress he'd made by being careless.

She remained on her perch while he wet a clean towel and wiped the dabs of white goo from her chest.

After a rinse, he mopped the worst of the Reddi-wip from his own skin. "How about if you get dressed while I clean up the kitchen? Then we can go."

"I think we should leave separately."

Setting down a spray bottle of disinfectant beside her, he shook his head. "I came looking for you. We'll draw a lot more attention by walking out five minutes apart than by going together."

"Okay. You're right."

The concession wouldn't be the end of her attempts to keep the new dimension of their relationship under wraps—of that he was certain. A little reassurance couldn't hurt his cause, though. "Nobody's going to question why I'm with you. We're friends, and today's been a really rough day for you. They'd be a lot more suspicious if I left you alone. It'd be completely out of character for me after two weeks of delivering breakfast and supper to you every day." A sniffle had him easing back, and his gut twisted at the tears pooling in her eyes. He might've diverted her thoughts from France's death for a short while, but she needed his comfort now. "Get dressed. We'll talk or whatever you need when we get you home."

He helped her down from the workspace, holding her close for a long minute.

"Thank you, Flynn." Her arms tightened around his waist and she rested her damp cheek over his heart. "I don't know what I'd do without you."

"You'd survive. You're an amazingly strong person." He stroked the shallow valley between her shoulder blades, hoping his touch brought her solace. "But I'm glad I can be here for you."

If they'd been in his or her apartment, he would've carried her straight to bed, enveloped her in his arms, and held her all night. Instead, he kissed her forehead again and then picked up her clothes. As she donned her bra and panties, he forced his mind to putting on his shirt, disinfecting the prep area surfaces, and checking the kitchen for any other signs of their presence. Shanda probably wouldn't say a word, even with their semi-casual rapport, but he preferred safe to sorry.

Snagging a box from the shelf, he glanced at a now fully dressed Lilith. "Give me a second. The pie's going with us."

She grimaced. "I only wanted it for comfort food. I don't *need* it."

Transferring the wedge of pie to the container, he winked at her. "We'll share, and I can think of a fun way to work off the calories."

Her smirk made his pulse skip a beat. "Ah, the universal male solution to diet and exercise. Good thing I know there's actually some truth to it."

"Actually, I want to find out if your food does for me what mine does for you." He waggled his eyebrows at her as he fastened the lid on the box. "You made the pie, didn't you?"

"Yes, I made the pie, but you might want to try that when you're not wearing pants."

"Hmm, you're right about that, except for one problem. If I'm in the same room with you and my pants are off, I'll want the real deal, no matter how good your pie is." He grabbed their snack and slipped his hand around hers. "Ready?"

She didn't try to pull free of his grasp, as he half expected her to. "Yeah."

Leading her out of the kitchen, he savored the ability to finally show her what he doubted she was prepared to hear. He'd have to bide his time and prove his trustworthiness one day at a time. Then he'd say the words. That day needed to come soon.

She veered toward her uncle's office. "My coat and keys are in here. I had to make phone calls and everything."

"You should've called me. I would've helped." He'd been preoccupied anyway, his mind stuck on the card she'd given him.

Shrugging into her jacket, she yawned. "I didn't want to ruin your family holiday. It was your day off."

"They wouldn't have had a problem with me leaving early for that, and today was supposed to be your day off too, other than making dinner with Eliza." Spying her keys on the desk, he pocketed them. "Come on. You've got to be exhausted."

She yawned again. "Just a little tired."

He draped his arm around her shoulders and headed for the exit. When she leaned into him, joy spread through his heart. Every second of the wait had been worth this moment. They'd reached an important milestone in their relationship, and he had no doubts they belonged together.

Content with that simple show of affection, he led her outside and along the sidewalk toward her apartment. Her pace slowed, but he didn't rush her. Most likely, she was thinking about the many times Dr. Ito had sat on the patio, enjoying the flowers and the birds.

He unlocked her door, flipped on the light, and guided her inside. "I'll be back in less than two minutes to wash your back. And your front."

He set the pie box on the coffee table and then cradled her face in his palms to kiss her. An intimate meeting of lips and tongues would only delay his return, so he kept the kiss short and sweet. It still stole his breath.

"I'll unlock the kitchen door for you. Hurry." Her husky command brought a moment of deep satisfaction.

"A minute then?"

"Or less." She gave him a gentle shove toward the front door. "Meet me in the shower."

"Yes, ma'am." With a salute, he strode outside.

The door clicked shut behind him, but he kept going. Time waited for no man, and he had no intention of being late to the party in Lilith's bathroom.

"How's our girl?" Mrs. Carlton's low voice came from the corner of the building, making his pulse shoot into overdrive.

"Geez, you about gave me a heart attack, Alice." He turned the key in the lock, hiding his face to avoid giving himself away. "She's doing okay. Exhausted more than anything else. She said she was going to take a shower and go to bed."

"You should be in there with her, young man. She needs a strong shoulder to lean on."

He shrugged. "She knows I'm here if she needs me. I better get to bed too. Five o'clock comes awful early."

Giving a nod, she set off at a brisk pace toward the couples building. "See you at breakfast, handsome."

A twist of the knob had him inside his apartment and aiming for his bedroom for a set of work clothes. With his duffle bag open on the bed, he checked for his shaving kit and deodorant before stuffing in his whites and shoes.

Ten seconds later, he was at his neighbor's back door letting himself inside. The sound of running water drew him to her bathroom, but he continued to the bedroom to set his bag near the closet. At least a full minute had passed, probably two.

He jogged to the bathroom before he lost his nerve. If she wanted him to leave, she'd have to tell him.

"What took so long?" She peeked out at him past the shower curtain, the lovely curve of her bare shoulder calling to him.

Stripping off his clothes, he struggled not to trip on his pant legs. "Alice caught me as I was unlocking my door. She wanted to know if you were okay."

The older woman's remark that he should be with Lilith was best left unsaid. The less outside pressure on their budding romance, the better.

Lily grimaced. "She didn't tell you to take care of me, did she?"

"No." It was the truth, sort of. He dropped his second sock on the floor as he advanced on his target. A carefully aimed toss sent the used condom into the trashcan. "I don't want to talk about Alice anymore."

Pushing back the curtain, he stepped into the shower. The warm spray formed water droplets on his lover's hair, and tiny streams flowed over her feminine curves.

He picked up a bottle of reddish liquid, reading the label to discover the scent that drove him crazy ever time he got near her. "Berry Blossoms."

"Wash me?" She handed him a wet washcloth.

The shadows beneath her eyes reminded him that she needed rest more than another round of sex. Besides, after a couple hours of sleep, they'd both have the energy to truly enjoy each other again.

He squirted a generous glob onto the cloth, squeezing it to create fragrant suds. With a careful touch, he rubbed the stickiness from her chest, breasts, and belly. Surprisingly, she didn't pull back when he passed over her pert nipples, but logic urged him to move on.

Reaching around her, he slid the washcloth up her spine and over her shoulder blades, caressing and massaging until she melted against him. "Time to rinse."

Bubbles followed the graceful length of her hips and legs to puddle at her feet. He turned with her, ducking under the spray to let the water sluice between them. As pleasurable as standing with her naked belly pressed to his cock was, he reached to shut off the shower. A little restraint might work in his favor.

He snagged the towel from the rack to dry them both. After a few gentle pats, he carried her to the bedroom.

As she wriggled under the covers, she folded back the edge closest to him. "Come to bed with me."

Too crazy in love with her to resist the invitation even if he'd wanted to, he crawled in beside her. She lifted his arm over her waist, settling against him so his erection lay in the crease of her ass. They fit together like a pair of spoons, a perfect match.

For the first time, he cupped her breast in his palm instead of touching the wall between them as he closed his eyes to sleep. "Sweet dreams, Lily."

Her relaxed exhale brought him peace.

# Chapter 25

Comforting heat surrounded Lilith, and she burrowed deeper into the blankets. If she refused to wake, maybe the wonderful dream wouldn't end.

*Please don't disappear, Flynn.*

A glide of her fingertips along his bicep confirmed she hadn't imagined last night's gourmet escapade. He'd given her more pleasure in twenty minutes than every man from her past combined. One orgasm was hardly fair to him after his generosity in the kitchen—and weeks of his divine food.

He deserved some payback.

Slipping beneath the covers, she kissed her way from his chest to his stomach. The light smattering of hair tickled her chin, but she soon reached the shallow dip directly above his thigh. He smelled clean yet musky, like virile male, and good enough to eat.

She traced a path along what had to be his hipbone, following the lean lines of his muscles to a thatch of coarse down. Her target was only inches away. A short glide to the left brought her fingers to the base of his semi-erect penis, and a groan from above brought a burst of satisfaction.

Was he awake? Or was her exploration bringing him out of a deep sleep?

Either way, she planned to give him a generous serving of oral delight. Turnabout was fair play, after all.

She rubbed her cheek against his hardening length, the silky texture as delicious on the outside as it'd been inside her. Cupping his scrotum, she licked the vein that ran from the encircling rim to the thick root.

Flynn groaned a little louder. "What're you doin', Lily? Come up here so I can have some fun too."

"I'm having a snack. Ah-ah-ah! Be still. You got to feed your hunger. Now it's my turn." As she gave his balls a careful squeeze, she closed her lips around the head of his cock. A drop of fluid seeped from the slit to coat her taste buds in his tangy essence. "Mm."

He arched his hips upward, his thigh quivering against her. "You're not going to make me embarrass myself, are you? Thirty seconds of your mouth and I'm—"

She fluttered her tongue on the pleated skin directly below his smooth cap.

His gasp gave her a moment of utter female satisfaction. "God, you're killing me. But in a good way. Really good."

A giggle bubbled up in her throat, and she released him to explore a bit lower. She sucked one lightly furred ball into her mouth and smoothed her palm over his taut abdominals, earning her a loud moan. It set off a swift contraction in her lower belly. Wetness pooled at the juncture of her thighs, a first for her. No man but Flynn had ever caused her body to react with such anticipation.

Desire almost compelled her to forgo the appetizer and move on to the main dish. He was more than ready.

She, however, had barely sampled all he had to offer. One particular part of him had tempted her day after day, sometimes camouflaged by loose-fitting chef whites and blatantly discernible in snug jeans at others.

A long, slow lick up his cock prepared her for the third course. "Roll over."

"What are you up to now? I'm okay with skipping foreplay, just so you know." Despite his admission, he obeyed her instructions.

"I'm not." She placed her hand on his lower back, reveling in the contrast of solid muscles and soft skin. A glide southward yielded more of the same. She pressed her lips to his right butt cheek and gave the firm flesh a nibble. "Yummy."

The whole bed shook with Flynn's wiggle. "I'm dying here. I think I need some mouth-to-mouth resuscitation."

Switching to the other side, she nipped at his tight rear instead of halting her teasing. "You have a delicious ass. What else should I taste before I take you for a ride?"

At her nudge, he flipped onto his back, grasping her shoulders and tugging her upward as he turned. "Do I have to beg for a kiss?"

She landed on top of him, thrilled to have a man in her bed with more on his mind than a quickie. A day's worth of beard stubble rasped her fingertips when she cradled his jaw. "No begging."

Straddling his waist, she bent forward to grant his wish. He met her halfway, the initial kiss gentle and sweet. Not satisfied with a lone chaste peck on the lips, she went back for another, seeking entry with her tongue.

His hearty welcome wasn't rushed, and he let her lead their adventure from playful to passionate as she swiveled her hips forward and back to glide his erection through her wetness. She was dying to take him inside her, but a tiny shred of common sense stopped her.

"Condom." His raspy appeal voiced her thought and tickled her lips.

Reluctant to give up any skin-to-skin contact with him, she reached for the nightstand, sliding her hand over the edge to find the knob. She opened the drawer with an impatient tug, need threatening to take control. With the box in her grasp, she ripped it open, sending a whole strip of Trojans flopping on the bed. She tore off a single packet and stowed the rest under the pillow.

Why hadn't she had the foresight to go back on contraception?

Unable to wait any longer, she sat up, rolled on the condom, and lowered herself onto him. He rose up to meet her, curving into her G-spot and filling her to the hilt.

His hands closed over her breasts, lightly brushing her nipples. "Damn, you feel amazing."

She had no idea whether he referred to her double Ds or her trembling inner muscles, and she didn't care. He was the only man to ever use the perfect amount of pressure on her breasts. The way he rolled her tight buds between his thumbs and forefingers triggered pulses of electricity to her very center. He could probably make her come without her moving an inch, but she was determined to take him along for the ride.

"You make me feel amazing." She slid her hands over his pecs to tease his pert little nubs. Rocking her hips, she set a steady rhythm, his cock stroking all the right places.

He didn't grab her ass to guide her or thrust upward to take over the tempo. Her reaction to his careful caressing evidently hadn't gone unnoticed, either. She'd finally discovered a man who didn't mind sharing the lead role in bed, and he put as much into pleasing her as himself.

Every in and out motion made her breath hitch. His expanding girth told her that he was closing in on the same blissful point she was. She arched back, taking him deeper.

"Time to come, Lily." He vibrated beneath her, and his husky tone washed through her veins to feed her desire.

She thrust downward, plunging onto him, and then jerked upward to repeat the movement. Lightheadedness flowed over her as she raced toward the same unbelievable satisfaction he'd given her earlier.

Her insides coiled tighter and tighter until they couldn't hold the tension anymore. A scream erupted from her, drowned out half a second later by his hoarse yell. Suspended from the clouds, she floated on a wisp of pure nirvana, with not a care in the world.

She melted against him, his heart thudding against her chest. His arms closed around her, and she savored the wonderful afterglow of being held and cherished.

His drooping penis almost slipped out of her, but he reached down to halt its progress. "I love being inside you, but I should get rid of this before we fall asleep again. Got a Kleenex?"

Still drifting back to reality, she had to think about the question for a moment. "Um, yeah. On the nightstand. Next to the lamp."

In less than a minute, he'd disposed of the potential problem and shifted so her head rested on his chest. He threaded his fingers into her hair, slowly massaging her scalp as he kissed her forehead. "I usually wake up before my alarm goes off on weekdays, but I set my watch for five just in case. I'll try to be quiet when I leave so you can sleep in."

A tiny jolt of panic seized her. "You'll go out the back door, right?"

He was silent for several ticks of the clock on the wall. "Sure."

His curt answer held a note of irritation, but she didn't call him on it. He'd seemed to understand her concern about their sweet but nosy neighbors. Advertising that they were sleeping together was only asking for unwanted interference, encouraging or otherwise.

Had he changed his mind about going public?

Maybe he was simply tired. They'd gone to bed fairly early, but she'd awakened him when he was used to sleeping through the night. Plus, he got up by five most days of the week.

*Or maybe I'm reading more into it than it means.*

He hadn't stiffened beside her. His breathing was still slow and even, and his body heat soaked into her like a living electric blanket.

She tucked her hand around his waist a little tighter. "Goodnight, Flynn."

His exhale caressed her cheek, assuring her he'd already drifted off to sleep.

Closing her eyes, she draped her leg over his thigh, touching as much of his bare skin as she could manage. It would have to last in her memory until night came again, because when she woke, he'd be gone.

\* \* \* \*

A glance at the clock confirmed Flynn's guess that he had to roll his way-too-comfortable body out of Lilith's bed. Last night had been a dream come true, except for her insistence about keeping their tryst a secret. He wanted to shout it from the rooftops, telling the world he'd found the woman he planned to marry.

Instead, he had to sneak out the back way and keep his mouth shut about having spent the night with her. He didn't necessary like it, but he understood her reasons and would tolerate it for now.

Light from the courtyard filtered through the blinds, spinning her hair to gold. She looked more relaxed than he'd ever seen her, her lips curved upward and her arm still wrapped loosely around his waist. Life couldn't get much better than a night of making love to her and sleeping next to her without a wall between them.

*Duty calls.*

Easing out from underneath her hold, he levered up to sit on the edge of the mattress. Her contented expression waned, but she didn't wake. She had to be exhausted from their activities, especially after dealing with the death of Dr. Ito. Catching up on her rest while he worked his morning shift would be the best thing for Lilith.

He probably wouldn't last the day without a catnap. The coffeemaker would be his first stop in the kitchen. After breakfast, his number one priority was making sure grief didn't overwhelm her, even if all he could do was send her the occasional text message.

He pushed to his feet, suppressing a shiver from the lack of shared body heat. Then he leaned down to kiss her cheek as he adjusted the covers.

*See you soon, Lily. I love you.*

Speaking those words aloud at this point in their relationship would probably bring the whole thing to a screeching halt. She was far too wary right now. When he gained her trust, he'd tell her exactly what he felt for her. He'd come up with the most romantic proposal any man had ever made to a woman. The biggest challenge would be persuading her to say yes.

*Patience.*

He might be certain of his future with her already, but she wouldn't dive in so quickly. He'd have to remember the ultimate goal or risk losing her.

A quick trip to the bathroom with his duffle bag made him presentable enough for work, his stubbly face shaved and his wild hair tamed. His whites were a bit wrinkly, but they'd have to do. Next time, he'd take them out of his bag before he crawled into bed with Lilith.

*Next time.*

In the kitchen, he forced his scribbly handwriting into submission to write her a brief note. Unless she had other life-or-death plans for tonight, he was claiming her. He'd prefer to spend his half-day holiday with her, but she'd never agree to meet his family yet.

The best gift he could give their relationship was time and space to grow.

He slipped on his shoes at the back door and then locked it behind him as he left. Dropping off his belongings took only the few seconds he needed to walk from his kitchen to the bedroom to the living room. A glance over his shoulder at the wall that separated him from Lilith slowed but didn't halt his momentum.

The busier his day was, the faster it would pass and the sooner he'd have her back in his arms.

* * * *

Lilith paced from one end of her apartment to the other before stopping at the front window to peek through the blinds. Vivian and Betsy were out for a walk, but otherwise the courtyard was empty.

Flynn had been gone all afternoon, spending the half-day off with his family while she'd had lunch with Garrett and his grandpa. Planning a memorial service with several of the residents had dampened her mood, but she'd restocked her kitchen and spent over an hour in the gym to distract herself.

Now, absence was making her suffer from withdrawal. She wasn't about to analyze the disconcerting emotions that went with it.

She'd slept through the day-after-Thanksgiving breakfast—not that she would've trusted herself to maintain an ounce of professionalism when Flynn delivered a plate to her office. Locking him inside for a midmorning helping of sex would've been too much temptation to resist. He'd turned her into a wanton woman.

Returning to the couch, she opened her laptop to check the next week's schedule. The squares blurred, her focus not on the calendar but on the unchanging numbers of the clock instead.

Another minute finally passed.

*Clunk.*

Her heart did a jumping jack at what sounded like a door closing. Unable to sit still, she closed her computer, plunking it on the coffee table as she scrambled to her feet. A quick jog took her to the kitchen.

Flynn stood at the back door, grinning at her as if he knew she'd been anxiously waiting for him.

She snatched her keys and tote bag from the table on her way to the one man who'd ever given a damn about her sexual satisfaction. Checking the lock, she swung the door open. "Do you mind if we stay at your apartment tonight?"

His eyebrows dipped into a deep vee, concern written on his handsome face. "If you want to. Is something wrong? Do we need to call Kip?"

"No, nothing's wrong. Well, except your mattress is bigger and I'm planning on some major payback for the bruise it gave me." Ducking past him, she trotted to his patio entrance.

He chuckled as he caught up with her at his door. "I can't wait to see that. Did you eat supper yet? I brought a couple entrées over from the kitchen."

Stepping aside to let him unlock the door, she snorted. "You just want to watch what your food does to me."

"Yeah, there is that, but I thought we could share a meal." With a turn of the key, they entered his kitchen. "Kinda like, maybe, a date."

She put the tote and keys on the counter, hoping the unease prickling her cautious brain didn't show on her face. In her experience, dating equaled a curse on her love life.

Lifting her ponytail out of the way, he settled his lips on the nape of her neck, seemingly diverted from calling their rendezvous a date. "Mind if I have an appetizer first? I've wanted to kiss you all day."

His light nibble sent a delectable shiver through her whole body. "Appetizers are good."

"Good doesn't begin to describe how you taste." He turned her in his arms as he kissed her temple and then her jaw. "Delicious. Intoxicating. Addictive."

She clutched at his shoulders, trying to guide him to her mouth, but he moved lower. When his lips caressed the sensitive skin below her ear, she whimpered and laid her palm against the fly of his jeans. "Much more of that, and you're going to be the main course. Kiss me, damn it."

His low chortle rumbled through her bones. "So bossy and impatient."

He touched his lips to hers, and she slipped her tongue past his teeth, taking the kiss to the depth she'd craved all day. Each stroke erased hours of waiting to spend another night with him. She didn't care that he was right about her bossiness and impatience, only that he surrounded her and made her desire soar.

Combing his fingers through her hair, he eased back too soon. "How about supper in bed? Then I can be inside you while I feed you. Two for one special."

"Interesting plan. I think I like it."

"Glass of wine to share? I can open a bottle while dinner's in the oven." He lifted the lids on the entrées.

"Sounds wonderful. Is that Spinach Lasagna? And Raspberry Chicken? Yum." As he reached for the third box, she placed her hand over his and shook her head. "Don't make me choose."

His smirk was too mischievous for her not to laugh. "Shanda and I experimented with cheesecake pops for the wedding reception this morning. I grabbed a few."

A weak groan escaped. "Cheesecake. That sounds divine."

"Why don't you go get comfortable while I reheat the food and pour the wine?" She almost insisted on helping him, but he directed her toward the doorway to the living room and gave her a pat on the rear. "Don't even think about offering to help. I'm taking care of you tonight, and you're going to let me."

No one had offered to take care of her since Uncle Wade had promised to stay with her twenty years ago. The knowledge made her slightly giddy. She'd have to watch her step, because falling madly in love with him would be too easy.

Giving in to his directive, she left a trail of her clothes as she moseyed to the bedroom, hoping sex would distract her from the prospect of another broken heart.

# Chapter 26

With the serving tray resting on his dresser, Flynn poured a glass of wine and handed it to Lily. He couldn't keep from grinning. She was nestled among the pillows in his bed, right where he wanted her to be. His life was finally on track and moving in the right direction.

"Lasagna or chicken first?" He carried both plates to the nightstand, balancing the dessert box on the flat of his forearm.

The covers slid down to reveal the swell of her breasts as she put the wine glass on the other night table and waved a foil packet at him. "Naked chef."

Pleased that she preferred him to his entrées, he set down his delivery to strip off his clothes and slip in beside her. "All yours."

She straddled his legs and stroked his half-erect cock down and up. The touch of her hands on his bare skin had him hard enough to tenderize the toughest cut of beef in less than half a minute, and the seductive way she licked her lips tempted him to forget feeding her in favor of giving her his own version of an orgasm. Her teasing slowness as she rolled on the condom had him more than ready to go.

Rising to her knees, she guided him to her entrance. "Chicken first."

He grasped her hips, stopping her descent before she started. "No foreplay?"

She leaned forward, dragging her taut nipples along his chest as she eyed him with a captivating stare. "Foreplay was waiting all afternoon for you to get home."

Gratification blazed through his veins. "You missed me?"

"Yeah." Pressing her lips to his, she rocked downward out of his hold.

Her body swallowed him in a single smooth glide, and he growled at the riot of sensation in his balls. "Damn, I missed you too. You feel fantastic."

He sat up straighter to kiss her again, first with a gentle brush against her soft mouth and then with all the passion she inspired. Her tongue glided along his, and he savored her response. His patience was paying off. He could only hope she was developing the same feelings he was—a love that grew deeper and stronger every day.

She arched against him and gasped as she broke off the kiss. "Feed me, Flynn."

Reluctant to loosen his hold on her, he leaned toward the nightstand, taking her with him. Luckily, he'd had the foresight to cut the chicken. He poked a small piece and dragged it through the raspberry sauce. "Ready?"

Her sly smile sent a shiver of anticipation up his spine. "Are you?"

"I'm always ready to make you feel good." Bracing for her body to tighten around his, he lifted the fork to her mouth.

Her lips parted, and she slid the bite off the tines with her teeth.

He held his breath as she chewed and then swallowed.

She blinked at him, her expression not even close to that of woman who was experiencing the level of sexual pleasure he'd expected—nor the disguised surprise of an employer interviewing a potential employee. "Nothing happened. Are you sure you made the chicken?"

"Yeah." He stabbed another piece. "Let's try again."

"Okay." Although she didn't sound convinced it would work, she opened her mouth.

Each movement of her jaw seemed slow and deliberate, as if she wasn't sure she wanted to participate in their experiment anymore. He may have been a little jealous of his food for the past two weeks, but he'd also taken a certain amount of pride in the fact that his cooking had a sexual side effect.

Finally swallowing, she closed her eyes.

Her snug fit around him didn't change—no twinge or spasm.

She shook her head, sending her hair cascading over her bare shoulders. "I'm sorry. It's not working."

Tucking a finger under her chin, he brushed his thumb over her lower lip. "You have nothing to be sorry about. If it's anybody's fault, it's mine. I'm the one who prepared the food."

"But my body isn't normal. What if I can't—"

"There's nothing wrong with your body, and I'll prove it to you." He rolled with her toward the middle of the bed, putting him on top. Careful not to crush her under his weight, he guided her legs around his waist one at a time. The action allowed him to sink even farther into her.

They fit together perfectly.

Her breath hitched, assuring him he'd found the right position to make up for the failed entrée. She planted her hands on his ass cheeks, holding him in place.

In no hurry, he glided partway out and then back inside her. The easy rhythm allowed him to cradle her face as he kissed her forehead, her cheeks, her nose. He pressed his lips to each side of her mouth before settling on his final target.

She invited him in with a soft sigh and a teasing caress of her tongue.

Accepting her invitation, he matched the smooth in-and-out tempo he'd set for their lovemaking. She met each advance and followed his retreat. They were equal partners this time, with no pressure to perform or "debt" to repay. Grief wasn't a motivation, either. She might not love him yet, but they were lovers in every other sense of the word.

*Or she might.*

The possibility gave him hope.

Her thighs squeezed his hips, and she pulsed around his erection. Even with a layer of latex between them, her tiny rhythmic tremors drew him along the path into paradise.

She pulled her mouth from his and panted against his cheek. "Like that. So much better than food. Don't ever stop."

Burying his face in her hair, he rocked forward again. The friction brought him another step closer, and he tensed his abdominals to keep from rushing toward the point of no return. As he withdrew, her fingernails dug into his skin, stealing the last of his control.

He'd treasured their unhurried pace, but her responsiveness made it impossible to maintain. His only recourse was to show her the truth.

With four quick thrusts, he had her trembling and crying out beneath him. Her sleek tunnel tensed, milking him as his balls contracted. The world splintered apart with the sweet sound of her sexual release, and he let out a yell with his own eruption. Spasm after spasm drew out the fulfillment of having shown her how perfect she was.

His muscles shook from the heady sense of weightlessness. They were ready to give out even as he floated. Her legs loosened their hold, and he shifted sideways to keep from collapsing on her. He slid free with the movement, sparking a moment of regret. Gathering her in his arms, he closed his eyes and waited for his breathing to slow to normal. A post-lovemaking cuddle with her was worth the loss of being inside her.

She rested her head on his shoulder, her warm breath feathering across his chest. "Mm."

Opening his eyes, he smiled against her hair. "I think your body likes the real thing better."

"What? No 'I told you so'?"

He skimmed his palm along the curve of her hip to her waist, enjoying the silkiness of her skin. "Nope."

"You're entitled to it, you know."

"Entitled? I don't think so. 'I told you so' is for people who have to be right all the time. Besides, you deserve more attention than the time it takes to poach an egg."

She wiggled closer, draping her leg across his thigh. "Why go for hard-boiled if both of us are ready in three minutes?"

Grinning, he tightened his hold on her. "I guess that means we cook well together. Want another bite of un-orgasmic chicken? Or we could try the spinach lasagna."

"I'm not sure it can measure up. Not that I don't like your food, but you were right about the real thing being better. Maybe that's why your food isn't working this time."

"Sustenance is good, though." He savored her softness for another minute before she rolled to her side and reached for the fork.

"Bite?" She offered him a piece of chicken.

Burgundy-colored sauce dripped onto her hip and rolled along her butt cheek.

"Don't mind if I do." Swooping in, he licked away the dribble and then nipped at her bottom.

"Ooh!" In an instant, she was standing beside the bed with her left fist perched on her hip.

Was she angry at his attempt to bring some play into their lovemaking?

She shook her head and tsked. "If you're going to bite the hand that feeds you, I'll have to take steps to make sure you can't."

Humor danced in her eyes and in the slight curve of her lips as she snitched his bite of chicken, letting him know she'd been more surprised than angry by his playful nibble.

"That wasn't your hand, Lily." He winked at her. "What kind of steps?"

Did he dare mention his candy stash?

Hints of pink on her cheeks suggested her thoughts might not be far off from his fantasy. "Securing you to the, um, bed."

A twinge of excitement in his lower belly had him shifting against the pillows, and he licked his suddenly dry lips. "You mean like tying me up? 'Cause I don't have a problem with that. Not as long as you're here with me anyway."

She turned toward the nightstand as she cut off a corner of the lasagna and slid it between her lips. After an eternity of eyeing him while she chewed, she set down the fork.

Once again, his food failed to give her an orgasm and disappointment failed to beat out satisfaction.

Then she opened the drawer that held his secret reminder of the day they'd met. "What's this? Do you have a sweet tooth, Flynn?"

The way she dangled the long rope of strawberry licorice over her fingers made him go from sated to half hard again. He snagged a tissue from the other nightstand to remove the used condom before it popped. "You have no idea."

"Maybe I do." She looped the red length around his wrist when he reached past her to toss his trash into the wastebasket. "I have a sneaking suspicion your adoration of licorice ropes comes from a certain story on my e-reader. It was marked as read before I opened it the first time a couple weeks ago."

His breath seizing in his lungs, he froze. The chastising tone of her voice didn't match the amusement in her eyes, but he had only one choice, whether she was mad or not. "The night I knocked you down with the mattress... When I went in the kitchen to close the blinds and turn off the lights, I bumped your tablet. The screen lit up with one of the covers. I was curious, so I read the dessert book. Plus, I was worried about you. I didn't want to leave."

She knelt on the edge of the bed and guided his captured hand to the spindles of the headboard. "And did you enjoy Meg and Aidan's story?"

The succulent breast hovering inches from his mouth tempted him to take a taste, but he lifted his other arm to join the first instead. "Enough to read the whole thing and buy licorice ropes. I never would've guessed prim and proper Lilith Montgomery liked to read naughty sex tales."

The bindings tightened around his wrists, ratcheting his desire up another notch.

"I didn't even know erotic romance existed until Erin added them to my library. They've given me some interesting ideas."

"I noticed. What're you going to do with me now that I can't get away?"

She poked a piece of chicken, this time offering it to him. "I think I'll finish what I started last night. Some *crème de* Flynn sounds yummy."

Anticipation made him lightheaded. Every drop of blood in his body had to have been drawn to his cock. "I don't have any vanilla bark or lemon glaze."

She held the bite to his lips. "I'm sure you'll taste just as good without any toppings. Eat. You're going to need your strength."

This wilder side of her was a welcome addition to their lovemaking. If she was willing to share her fantasies, her trust—and feelings—for him had to be growing, and he wouldn't take it lightly.

"You're incredibly sexy when you're bossy."

A slight smile shone through her sultry expression. "Open."

Mesmerized by the intensity in her gaze, he barely tasted the now lukewarm chicken. A sample of her sweet lips would satisfy his hunger much better. "How about a kiss for my good behavior?"

The fork clinked as she set it on the plate.

"Sounds like a reasonable request." She puckered her lips as she climbed onto the bed, but instead of aiming for his mouth, she angled a couple feet lower. "How about right here?"

Before he could respond, she connected with the head of his erection. Her tongue lapped up the drop of fluid rolling free of the slit, sending an earthquake through him and triggering a release of more pre-sex lubrication. He had to force his eyes to stay open through the ripples of pleasure wiggling up his spine. "Last night. Gonna finish what you started, huh?"

She licked a path from the base to the tip. "Yeah. I want to make you feel as good as you make me feel."

Would she believe him if he told her giving her pleasure brought him pleasure? Or that hearing she loved him would please him more than an orgasm right now?

"You do." Easing deeper into the pillows, he braced for the next lick.

Her fingers crept up his hip to rest on his lower belly, and her soft exhales caressed the patch of supersensitive skin directly below the cap of his dick.

He managed not to shift forward toward her face, but it took all his willpower. Sucking in a lungful of air, he held the position until his muscles shook. "Are ya plannin' ta torture me?

A wicked giggle sent another puff of her breath along his length. "Interesting. Your Irish brogue becomes more pronounced when you're under stress."

"D'ya like it, lass?" He couldn't keep his voice from squeaking on the last word.

"Mm-hm." Her hair fell forward as she took him in her mouth.

The slow, wet glide almost had him yanking his hands free so he could gather the curtain out of the way to watch. He closed his eyes and sank into the bed, hoping the pounding pulse in his ears didn't mean his heart was about to give out. Whether the licorice ropes could hold him or not was beside the point. A little kink might make her realize he wouldn't put his wants before hers, that she could trust him to keep their needs in the relationship on equal standing.

He almost choked when she smoothed her tongue along the lengthwise ridge. Her teeth scraped ever so lightly over his skin, and he groaned at the zips of electricity the action sent to his balls. Maybe closing his eyes wasn't the best way to enjoy the experience.

Raising her gaze but not her head, she rubbed her cheek against him as she peered through the narrow opening in her hair. "Feels good, does it?"

"Och, aye, love." She seemed to tense at the accidental endearment, warning him to be more careful with his words. He'd made too much progress to ruin everything now. "If ye swing tha' lovely bottom around, I'll be glad ta return the favor."

Not surprisingly, she raised her eyebrows at his suggestion. "And distract me from this delicious treat? I don't think so."

In the next second, her mouth closed around him again and her palm cradled his sac. His concentration broken, he arched up to meet her, savoring the rising euphoria. If she wanted him to lose control, he'd gladly surrender to her, give her the same power she'd given him in the kitchen.

With every gentle tug of pressure, the world drifted farther away. Soft humming vibrated through his cock, and he let it carry him closer to paradise.

Her grip on his scrotum tightened, triggering a burst of hot fluid rushing from his body. He shuddered from the deep contractions, his release every bit as forceful as the one he'd shared with her earlier. A roar escaped his stinging raw throat, and he forced his gaze on the love of his life.

She jerked forward, as if she'd felt the thunderous jolt he'd experienced. A high-pitched cry cut through the fog—her cry.

Had she simply exchanged foodgasms for sympathetic orgasms?

He smiled all the way to his soul as she collapsed on top of him. If he hadn't found true happiness with her, he never would.

# Chapter 27

Lilith took another sip of her champagne as Harold made a toast to the bride and groom's happiness. The cheery bubbles still did little to chase away the dark cloud that had settled over her yesterday morning at France's memorial service in the courtyard. Nor did they distract her from the handsome Irishman laughing with Alice and Vivian. Flynn drew her attention whether he wore chef whites, jeans, or a suit and tie.

*Or nothing at all.*

After sharing a bed with him for two and a half weeks, she'd missed him last night. No matter that she'd been the one to recommend they both get a full night's rest for today's preparations and activities. He hadn't argued the point, even if he hadn't seemed thrilled with the suggestion.

Their relationship, or whatever it was, was moving too fast anyway. His invitation to Sunday dinner tomorrow with his family had come as a shock, and she had yet to decide if saying yes was a smart idea. At least he hadn't pressured her to go.

She pushed away the plate of half-eaten hors d'oeuvres and emptied her fluted glass. Only Flynn could satisfy her current hunger. Maybe if she lost herself in a night of decadent sex, her mood would improve.

Shanda stepped into Lilith's line of vision, bringing her wondering thoughts back to the party. The intern's confident posture and bright smile were fair indications she was enjoying her caterer status. "All finished?"

Trying for an upbeat tone, Lily nodded. "Yes. Everything was delicious. If you're interested, I'll be happy to recommend you next time I hear of an event."

"Thanks. That'd be great." Practically glowing, the young woman loaded the dirty dishes onto her tray and then headed toward the kitchen.

A light stroke on her shoulder made Lilith jump. Flynn had somehow managed to sneak up on her while she'd zoned out and back in.

He dropped into the chair next to hers. "Things are starting to wind down. Mind if I walk you home?"

His intense stare said he was looking forward to getting naked as much as she was.

A slight twinge between her thighs was all the prodding she needed. "Not at all. I think I'll go to bed early tonight."

"Probably a good plan after the last few weeks. Don't want you getting overtired." As she stood, he offered her his hand. A subtle wink was his only hint at something more than sleep.

She allowed him to help her up before heading across the room to the newlyweds. Although she welcomed his touch, releasing her hold on him would keep anyone from teasing them about burning up sheets or mattresses. Thankfully, most of the residents had already left, giving her a few minutes to congratulate her uncle and his wife again in private and wish them a happy and safe honeymoon.

Wade enveloped her in a bear hug. "Thanks for being a part of our wedding, Lily flower. It means the world to me. Now, go home and rest. You looked tired underneath that pretty face. You'll make sure she goes straight home, Flynn? No stopping at the office?"

Her chef chuckled. "I'll carry her if I have to."

She swallowed hard to thwart the sudden bout of cold sweat. Every ounce of self-control would fly out the window if Flynn swung her into his arms. He'd also put their secret at risk for discovery by going caveman on her.

Clucking her tongue, Eliza shook her head. "You're one to talk about being a workaholic, Wade. I've heard stories of your long hours."

Her uncle snorted. "Who? Me?"

Not up to bantering, Lily kissed Wade's cheek as he released her. "You two should get on the road. The weather forecast is calling for freezing rain later. Have a great time at the cabin." She turned toward her new aunt. "Congratulations again."

Grasping Flynn's forearm, she encouraged him toward the exit. He didn't resist, simply shaking his employer's hand and offering best wishes before setting off for the hallway.

When he slowed and started to shrug off his suit coat at the sliding doors, she kept walking. His gentlemanly behavior could wait until she wasn't in dire need of him inside her. "I'm warm enough. Hurry."

She trotted along beside him as he lengthened his stride to trek past the patio and gardens. Evidently, he'd believed her and taken her request to heart.

At her apartment, he hovered next to her until she unlocked and opened the door. "My place or yours?"

"Yours. I'll be over as soon as I grab a change of clothes."

"Meet you in the kitchen." He jangled his keys and turned toward the end of the building.

Anxious to make up for last night's deprivation, she closed her front door as she switched on the light. A quick trip to the bedroom yielded yoga pants and a sweatshirt. Half a minute later, she was back outside.

He met her at his back door, the jacket and tie gone and his dress shirt unbuttoned. Dropping her spare clothes on his kitchen floor, she drank in the sight of him. Then she shoved the shirt from his shoulders as she used the high heels to her advantage by diving in for a much-needed kiss.

His tongue came out to war with hers, attacking and retreating. He toyed with the zipper of her dress, sliding it down her spine while her pulse skyrocketed with the aggressiveness of his kiss. Every uncompromising demand for a response reminded her why she'd taken a risk with him.

She didn't have to pretend with him. He brought her body to life.

Tossing aside his shirt, she targeted his waistband next. The button slid free with too much effort, but she focused on getting him naked. Maybe if she connected with him, the desperation would disappear.

He released her mouth, pulling in panting breaths. "Wallet. Condom."

Nodding, she reached around to his rear pocket, fighting to remove his wallet from the drooping pants. It caught on the seams twice before she finally yanked it loose. The task of finding the foil packet was much quicker. She tore it open while he shoved his suit pants and boxers down his legs.

Not missing a beat, he worked her dress into a puddle around her feet. Her nipples tightened at the brush of cool air on her skin, heightening the urgency to welcome him inside her. Her bra's coarse lace only added to the sensory overload.

His hungry stare made her shiver, and goose bumps rose everywhere his gaze touched her. "Heels and stockings are staying on. So hot."

He lifted her from the pool of fabric, holding her close as she wrapped her legs around his hips. The short shuffle to the table didn't give her near enough time to enjoy the up and down motion of his erection against the front of her thong and what lay directly beneath it.

She tensed at the chill as he sat her on the edge of the table, but his lips on her neck erased all but the fire between them. She'd waited the entire day for the stolen hours she'd get to spend with him. Hiding their relationship from her uncle and the residents today hadn't been easy with Flynn in the same room, the draw to lean on him for strength a constant temptation.

Now they were alone and she could forget her weaknesses.

Feeling her way to his cock, she unrolled the condom onto him as he nuzzled her ear and shoved her panties past her bottom. He changed in her hand, growing harder and longer—exactly how she wanted him.

He groaned, the sound vibrating through her throat like she'd been the one to voice pleasure. Hooking her knee over his arm, he dipped a finger inside her. Then he glided out and over her clit, setting off a rapid series of anticipatory tremors and a wave of lightheadedness. "You're so wet. Are you ready for me, Lily?"

A whimper was the best she could manage.

She closed her eyes to stop the stinging tears and nodded. Ready didn't begin to encompass what he inspired in her. He'd saved her from a life of believing a man couldn't satisfy her.

He could, only him.

Skimming his palm along her stocking-clad leg, he placed her ankle on his shoulder. Light pressure against her entrance signaled the moment she longed for had arrived. "Look at me, Lily. I want to see what you're feeling when I'm inside you."

A droplet rolled from the outer corner of her eye to her hairline when she conceded to his wishes.

*Don't notice. Please.*

He brushed away the moisture, but he didn't comment. The concern on his face—the slight frown on his lips and the furrow across his forehead—spoke for him.

Pushing inside her, he bent forward. His sweet kiss made her chest ache, even as her body sang at the fullness of having him deep within her. They were intimately connected, and he caressed the very heart of her. A mix of joy and relief had her blinking back more tears.

She was safe.

The pain in her chest subsided with the steady rhythm of his slow in-and-out strokes. She wasn't in danger of falling too fast or too hard. They were friends first and lovers second. If the flames sputtered, they'd simply return to friendship. She'd hide the pain of losing him behind the knowledge that he'd never truly leave her.

Each slow thrust increased in speed and force, Flynn's cock rubbing back and forth over her G-spot. He slipped his hand between them, his thumb finding her clit. "You first. I want to watch you come."

He found the perfect spot, as he always did, and his gaze never strayed from hers. The building tension coiled tighter and tighter until a scream tore at her throat. Her abdominals seized, release crashing over her with the power of a violent storm. Aftershocks thundered through her body as he continued to pound into her, his erection swelling to fill every inch of her.

"Yes! God, yes!" He threw his head back as he came. His joyful expression blurred from her tears, and he slumped over her, her leg sliding from his shoulder to catch in the crook of his elbow. His shallow breaths tickled her chin. "I love you, Lily. I love you so much."

The tender statements took a second to register. Then they sucked every bit of oxygen from her body, stealing her ability to speak. The musky scent of sex set her stomach churning, and his hot skin scorched hers everywhere they touched.

She wanted to push him away, but she couldn't make her hands move.

*It's too soon. I need more time.*

He jerked back, as if suddenly aware that she hadn't responded to his declaration. Or maybe he hadn't really meant to say those words. Furrows creased his forehead and his mouth straightened into a grim line. "I think we have a problem."

At least he didn't mince words—and she wouldn't have to explain her reluctance to rush into a serious relationship.

Withdrawing from her, he dropped his chin to his chest. "Yep. The condom broke. Not that it's really a problem. I mean, I want to be with you, and I'm ready to start a family if it happens."

Spots danced in front of her eyes, made worse from the inability to breathe. Her arms and legs went numb, and the churning in her stomach hit blender speed. A trickle of fluid seeped along the crease of her ass. If she hadn't been lying on the table, she would've collapsed in a heap on the floor.

"Are you okay, Lily? You know I'd never leave you to deal with this by yourself. Right?" Grabbing a paper towel from the counter, he removed the damaged condom. "What are the chances of—"

"Zero. My period's supposed to start tomorrow." The words tumbled out as she finally found her voice. Clamoring from the table, she scanned the room for her clothes.

"Oh. Okay." He sounded almost disappointed.

What had she gotten herself into?

She teetered to the pile of sweats, her equilibrium too off kilter for heels. Kicking them off, she grabbed the pants. Her foot caught twice on the elastic waistband in her hurry to dress. The sweatshirt went on much easier, and she didn't bother sliding the hood off her head.

"Lily, are you okay?"

How many times in the past seven and a half weeks had he asked her that question?

Snatching up her dress and shoes, she faced the truth. "No."

He took a step toward her, and she retreated to the kitchen door.

"Please don't run away. Talk to me." His quiet plea reminded her why her resolve had weakened.

It also reminded her that she'd been too swept up in fantasy to recognize reality when it stared her in the face. "I don't want kids."

He stopped mid-shuffle, his pants still around his ankles. His stunned expression might've been comical if she wasn't ready to lose wedding cake all over the dress bunched under her arm.

Clutching at the doorknob, she lifted her gaze to his and steeled her battered emotions. "It was fun while it lasted."

# Chapter 28

The door clicked closed behind Lilith as she left, her casual dismissal far colder than the chilly December evening.

*Dumped. Fucked and dumped.*

Flynn toed off his shoes and squeezed the crumpled paper towel in his hand. He'd said he loved her, promised her the torn condom wasn't a problem, and basically told her he wanted to marry her and have kids.

*And she fucking dumped me!*

Ignoring the ache in his gut, he yanked off his suit pants and tossed them over the milky smear on the edge of the table. She'd given him a hell of a parting gift.

He shuffled to the bathroom, the scent of their lovemaking too horrendous to bear.

*Lovemaking? Ha! What a joke.*

A month of playing hard to get had led to a couple weeks of raunchy sex for sweet Lily, the poor waif who'd been hurt by every man she'd ever dated.

*What a load of bullshit.*

After a quick shower, he pulled a pair of jeans and a shirt from the dresser, his only goal to put as much distance as possible between him and Montgomery Crossing. A few shots of Jameson would hit the spot too.

Thumbing through his contacts, he searched for Drew's number. As the call connected, he tugged on his clothes.

"Hey, Flynn. What's up?"

Not wanting to go into details on the phone, Flynn kept the conversation light. "Not much. Just wondering if you want some company?"

"Sure. The girls went to see a movie with Merie and Colleen and the kids. Is every—"

"Okay. See you in twenty minutes." Flynn disconnected, pocketing the cell as he eyed his duffle bag.

Considering tonight's fiasco, he'd rather sleep in a too-short bed than spend the night with the wall between him and his ex-not-girlfriend. To the world, they'd been nothing more than friends. He wasn't interested in pretending they were even that much anymore.

He stuffed a change of clothes in the bag and then jerked on his coat. A quick check of the back door's lock sparked his still smoldering anger, but he shook it off. She wasn't worth the energy.

Fifteen minutes later, he parked in his brother-in-law's driveway. A fast departure had seemed wise since a run-in with one of the residents would delay leaving. He was in no mood to tolerate any mention of him and the boss's niece getting together. Alice and the others were delusional to think Lilith Montgomery could ever love him.

He shouldered the overnight bag as he locked the truck, the weight heavier on his mind than his body. Walking away from his apartment had him wondering if he'd go back. His job was there, but it could be gone tomorrow morning when he went to prepare brunch. He had the best supporting evidence in the world for keeping business and pleasure separate.

"You coming in or standing on the sidewalk all night?" Drew's teasing tone was irritating instead of welcoming.

"Depends on if you have a bottle of whiskey." Following Drew to the front door, Flynn gave his mouth free rein. "And a room for the night would be good. I can check the Holiday Inn if you don't."

They walked past the living room to the kitchen, and Drew retrieved a couple shot glasses from the cabinet by the sink. "What happened? You strike out with your boss?"

Flynn laughed. "No. I'm probably quitting my job, and that means I have to look for a new apartment as well as a new job."

Drew's eyebrows rose as he poured amber liquid into the squat glasses. "Okay, drink this and let's hear the whole story."

Tipping up the tiny serving of painkiller, Flynn swallowed it in a single gulp. The alcohol coated his throat, the burn hidden beneath its smoky flavor. "We've been sleeping together since Thanksgiving, and tonight she dumped me."

"Ouch. Did she give you a reason?"

"Well, for starters, since I told her I love her and all she did was lay there gawking at me, I guess I'd have to say she doesn't feel the same."

"There's more?"

Flynn downed the other shooter. "The rubber broke and she doesn't want kids."

"Whew. Not good." Drew poured another round, holding on to one glass this time. "What're you going to do if she's pregnant?"

"Her period starts tomorrow. She said it's impossible."

"You mean, you…finished and then she told you to take a hike?" Sipping the whiskey, Drew settled onto one of the bar stools.

"More or less. Except she got dressed as fast as she could and left." *She left me.* Anger faded at the harsh truth, pain creeping in to take its place. "I practically asked her to marry me, and she walked away. I thought she was The One. We were perfect together. I would've sworn she loved me too."

Grabbing the bottle, Flynn poured himself another dose. He'd always been able to read people, but Lilith had snowed him somehow. She'd hacked his hopes and dreams into extra-fine dice with the sharpest blade in her cold, sterile soul.

Drew refilled his shot glass. "Life doesn't turn out how you expect it to sometimes. You can love somebody who feels the same and still end up alone."

"We're pretty pathetic, aren't we?" Tossing back the whiskey, Flynn hoped it drowned the pity party moving into full swing in his head. He had less excuse to feel sorry for himself than his dead sister's husband.

"I wouldn't trade the years I had with Kate for anything, especially if it meant not having Kristin and Hannah. I have a lot of good memories."

"Yeah, well, at least you have something to show for falling in love. I've spent the last two and a half weeks sneaking around with a woman who never gave a shit about me. And you'd think I asked her to throw herself into a hot wok when I said I loved her."

The ache in Flynn's gut spread to his chest. He could've handled Lily telling him she wasn't ready yet. He might've resorted to quitting the best job he'd ever had, but he would've gotten over it. Instead, he'd still have to give up the chef position at Montgomery Crossing and he'd have to spend who knew how many months or years trying to forget her. Hijacking the Jameson and hiding in the guest room until morning sounded like the best plan.

As he reached for the bottle, Drew shook his head and screwed on the cap. "You've had enough. Getting plastered won't change a thing, and the hangover'll only make it worse. Besides, the girls are due home soon."

"How do you do it?" Flynn rolled the empty shot glass between his palms, the repetitive motion not quite forcing his attention away from the thought that an hour ago he'd been holding his lover in his arms.

"Do what?"

"Hold it all together. Get up every day, knowing Kate's gone."

Drew rubbed his finger—his bare ring finger.

When had he taken off his wedding band?

"She probably would've come back to haunt me if I'd given up after she died. The kids need me, and I had time to prepare. If it'd been an accident, things might've been different. But it wasn't."

"Why didn't I see this coming?" Running through the last several days, he analyzed every word and action he could remember. The trail of breadcrumbs was easier to spot in hindsight. "Maybe I should've. Damn it, she didn't have to blindside me."

"Did you say something else that could've set her off? Unless she's a manipulative bitch, a woman doesn't usually toss a guy to the curb for saying he loves her."

"I kinda dropped some hints about taking our relationship public a couple days ago. She didn't comment, so I didn't think she picked up on them. Then yesterday, we were talking about dessert options I want to add to the menu. When I told her she'd get along great with my sisters, she got quiet. I asked her to go with me to Mom and Dad's for dinner tomorrow. Why didn't she just drop the bomb then?"

Why had she waited until he'd handed her his heart on a silver platter?

Setting the shot glass on the counter, he swallowed against the lump in his throat. "Mind if I borrow the spare room for a week or so? I'm giving notice Monday morning."

"It's yours for as long as you need it." Drew patted him on the back. "I'll make sure the munchkins leave you alone tonight."

"Thanks."

Flynn hefted his duffle bag again, wishing he'd brought more than a single change of clothes. He'd have to stop for his whites before heading to the kitchen to make brunch tomorrow. With his luck, Lilith would come out her door as he passed her apartment. Pathetic fool that he was, he wouldn't be able to prevent himself from drinking in the sight of her and begging her to reconsider.

*When something seems too good to be true, it usually is.*

He'd learned that lesson the hard way.

The floor and walls wobbled slightly as he weaved down the hall. The night of Kate's death was the last time he'd drunken himself into a stupor. Having the love of his life relegate him to her reject pile was a close second to the gut-wrenching pain he'd experienced that day, but Irish whiskey wasn't the cure.

No cure existed.

Fumbling with the light switch, he entered his temporary living quarters. Nothing had changed since he'd stayed there when his sister was alive and well. The full bed was still going to be a tighter fit than he was used to and the same frilly doilies decorated the dresser and nightstands.

Kate would've followed him into the room with an armload of clean towels for the bathroom, laughing and chattering as she mothered him.

What advice would she have given him?

She'd told him a couple times to jump back into the dating pool, that a woman who didn't appreciate him wasn't worth the time or the effort.

What would she think of Lily?

*It doesn't matter. Whatever we had is over and done, whether I like it or not.*

Splashing water on his face didn't change anything, and neither did crawling into bed. Tomorrow, he'd get up and go to work, putting in his hours until his time at the retirement complex expired.

Then he'd pick up the pieces of his shattered life and move on—again.

\* \* \* \*

Prying open his eyes, Flynn squinted at the clock until the red block numbers came into focus. He'd tossed and turned most of the night from sleeping alone. No matter that he'd slept alone most of his thirty years, he'd reached for Lilith over and over, never finding her beside him.

Four thirty in the morning was far too early to make breakfast for Drew and the girls, but he got up anyway. The breakup hangover dragging him down was a thousand times worse than the pounding pain any amount of whiskey could've induced. His head hurt from rehashing yesterday's scene at least a dozen times, and his insides were imitating a bad case of the stomach flu.

*Why?*

Why had she let him believe they had a future together?

He'd never pressured her for more than friendship, even when he'd already fallen in love with her. The slow progression from friends to lovers had taken a lot of patience, but he'd always kept his end goal in sight—making her happy.

Shouldering the cloud of depression, he slogged to the bathroom for a hot shower. The steam did nothing to clear his thoughts. Her words continued to replay in his mind.

*"Zero. My period's supposed to start tomorrow."*

*"I don't want kids."*

*"It was fun while it lasted."*

He could live without having kids if it meant having her, couldn't he?

What if she was wrong about not being able to get pregnant? Would she tell him if her period was late?

Had she worried about him not wanting to be with her during her time of the month? Was that why she'd dropped him like a hot potato?

He rinsed the shampoo from his hair, more questions than answers forming. No woman had ever shoved him in the deep end and left him to drown.

His reflection in the mirror as he shaved gave him no insight. He'd figured he had a better than average understanding of females, having grown up with three older sisters, but Lily defied explanation. He had to stop grasping at possible reasons for her betrayal. She'd thrown him out with the day's garbage because she didn't want him, plain and simple.

Resorting to the one thing in his life that had never gone to hell, he trudged to the kitchen to make breakfast. Cooking had helped him survive losing his sister. It'd take his mind off his current problems.

He flipped on the light over the sink before padding to the fridge to take a quick inventory of the contents. The bottom shelf held a nearly full carton of eggs, half a loaf of bread, and half a stick of butter. If he didn't know better, he'd almost think Drew had been expecting him to call.

"Did you find the ingredients, Uncle Flynn?"

He straightened at the whisper from behind him. Sharp pain shot through his skull on impact with the freezer handle. Trapping a chorus of obscenities with sealed lips, he grunted. "What're you doing out of bed so early, squirt?"

After a few pitter-pattering steps across the tile floor, Hannah perched her hands on her hips beside him. "One time, Daddy did that and he said a bad word. He had to put a quarter in the naughty jar. If you say bad words while you're here, you have to give me and Kristin a quarter each to put in the jar."

"Oh yeah? How do I know you aren't scamming me?" Handing her the bread, he winked at her. "You're not trying to fund your college education, are you?"

"You're silly." Her giggle made him smile.

"So are you, munchkin. I found the ingredients. What are we making for breakfast? Scrambled eggs and toast?"

She scrunched up her face and stuck out her tongue. "Blech! I don't like scrambled eggs. They're slimy. We're making French toast. That's why I got up, and to see you. Daddy wouldn't let us bother you last night. He said you had to get up really early for work. Do you have to work all day?"

"I'll be done about lunchtime today. Do you want fancy or regular French toast?"

Her eyes widened. "You can make it fancy?"

"Yep. We could use apples or peaches. Or let's see what we can find in the pantry." He picked her up as he stood. "Bread delivery to the counter.

Light switch please, Miss *Sous* Chef."

"My name isn't Sue!"

He laughed at her affronted frown and set her on her feet in front of the pantry. "*Sous* is French. It means you're my assistant. Where's the canned fruit?"

She pulled open the louvered door and pointed to the middle shelf. "Right there."

Six cans of pineapple rings formed the first row.

"You and Kristin must like pineapple a lot." A memory awakened at the sight of the cans. They'd both requested Pineapple Upside-down Cake for their birthdays after he'd taken it to a family dinner a couple years ago. "Want to make Pineapple Upside-down French toast?"

"Oh, can we? It'll be like having dessert for breakfast!" She stood on her tiptoes, reaching for the closest can. "Help me, Uncle Flynn!"

He gave her a boost up and then grabbed a jar of maraschino cherries. "Can't forget these."

Prep took a bit longer than if he'd done it himself, but he wouldn't have traded the experience for anything. He adored his nieces and nephews, planning for the day he'd become a father somewhere in his mind. His earlier assertion that he'd sacrifice having children to be with Lilith wasn't exactly cut and dried, not that his willingness or unwillingness mattered.

She'd made the decision for him. They weren't getting married. They wouldn't grow old together, and she wasn't going to be the mother of his kids.

Reality crept in once again as he set the timer for the oven. "Thanks for being my assistant, Hannah. You did a great job."

"No, she didn't." Kristin frowned at her sister from the doorway. "She was supposed to wake me up if she got up first."

Hannah slapped her hand against her cheek. "Oops, I forgot."

Not in the mood to watch his nieces argue, Flynn crossed the room to the older girl. "Since Hannah got to help with breakfast, you and I will make supper together tonight. Right now, I need to go to work."

Kristin heaved a sigh, clearly not happy, but willing to compromise. "Okay."

"That's my girl. The timer's set for breakfast. Be sure to let your dad take it out of the oven. I don't want to see any burned fingers when I get back. Deal?" At her nod, he leaned down to hug her. "We'll do something fun this afternoon after lunch at Grandma and Grandpa's too. A game or whatever you feel like doing."

"Shopping for Daddy's Christmas present?"

"Works for me. Hannah should probably come along. Get it all done at once."

"You're braver than I am." Drew shuffled to the coffeemaker. "I was planning to ask your mom or one of your sisters to handle shopping with them and write a check for the damage. Please tell me I smell breakfast. If I have to eat another bowl of cereal or a frozen waffle, I think I'll go on a hunger strike."

Hannah crossed her arms in front of her, looking so much like Kate that Flynn had to stifle a laugh. "But frozen waffles are *good*."

Kissing Kristin on the head, Flynn covered his grin. "French toast in the oven. Timer's set. I'll meet you at Mom and Dad's about noon."

Drew poured a generous amount of ground coffee into a filter, making Flynn wish he'd thought to brew a pot. "Sounds good. And thanks for breakfast. I owe you."

"Nope. We're even." To be truthful, he owed Drew and the girls much more than they owed him.

His brother-in-law nodded, likely understanding Flynn's gratitude at having a place to lick his wounds.

Heading to the bedroom for his keys, he made a quick stop to kiss Hannah's cheek. "See you later."

The short drive to the complex added to the gnawing agitation in his gut, and Flynn almost drove past the entrance to avoid a possible meeting with Lilith. Shanda and the residents were expecting him, though, and he wasn't about to let his dismal personal life turn him into an irresponsible jerk. He had a job to do, at least until his two weeks' notice was up.

A survey of the dark courtyard yielded no one out and about yet, so he made a beeline for his apartment. Rather than switching on the lamp, he used his cell phone to navigate to the bedroom. He worked by the closet light to fill his suitcases, packing all but a single set of whites. Several pairs of jeans and a handful of shirts filled the larger one near to bursting.

After a quick change into the last of his chef pants and jackets, he hooked his computer bag on his shoulder and hauled the overloaded bags to his truck. As soon as brunch was over, he'd take off, with no need to return for anything other than his shifts in the kitchen.

"Going on a trip?"

His heart jumped at the voice coming out of nowhere in the early morning dusk. "Geez, Alice, are you trying to give me a heart attack again?"

"You didn't answer my question." She stepped out from the shadows, her arms folded across her chest. "And don't you try pulling that blarney crap on me."

With his initial thought to fib shot down, he shrugged. "Blarney's all I have."

"That's bullshit, young man. You couldn't lie to save your own skin. Now, what's up?"

"Sorry, I can't talk about it. I made a promise." He closed the passenger door, ready to make a run for it.

Alice's face brightened, her mouth curving into a wide grin. "You and Lily. You're eloping, aren't you?"

Her teasing query sliced a serrated hole through his already stretched-thin emotions. She'd managed a direct hit on the most vulnerable spot in his damaged ego.

"Nope." Setting off at a good clip toward the main building, he prayed his legs were long enough to leave Alice and her inquiring mind in his dust.

How would he last two weeks of everybody asking what had happened between him and Lily?

He sure as hell didn't intend to act like they were still friends. She didn't deserve his loyalty or an easy way out. Grudges weren't his style, but he'd also never had his heart sliced, diced, and puréed after having table sex and declaring his love.

Jamming his key in the lock, he couldn't keep himself from staring at the employee housing in the glass expanse. All the windows were dark, including the ones next to his apartment. He forced his attention back to gaining entrance to the main building. If he didn't hurry, Alice or one of the other residents would pounce on him again. Worse than that, Lilith might decide to make an appearance.

He retreated to his domain, diving into the prep work he usually left to Shanda. The sooner the meal was done, the sooner he could compose his letter of resignation. He'd write it while his intern handled the dining room tasks.

When she arrived at seven thirty, he was pouring egg mixture over the vegetables for a third quiche. She raised her eyebrows at him, but she only offered a good morning and followed the routine he'd taught her for the days she was in charge. She didn't push him to talk or chatter on about nothing, seeming to understand his need for silence and solitude.

As she wheeled the cart out the server door with the last of the scones and muffins, he pulled out his laptop. He owed Wade an explanation, some sort of reason why he was walking away. Somehow, he had to do it without revealing the details of his and Lily's association, because he'd promised not to tell anyone—and no matter the circumstances of their breakup, he wouldn't go back on his promise.

Half a dozen false starts finally led to a short and somewhat vague letter. Copy and paste moved it into an e-mail, and one click sent the message to his boss. A few seconds later, a response popped up in his inbox.

*I'll be out of the office from December 12 to December 16 and will respond as soon as possible upon my return. If you need immediate assistance, please call the office and ask to speak to Lilith Montgomery, Acting Director. She will be handling all urgent matters during my absence.*

*Wade Montgomery*
*Owner/Director Montgomery Crossing Retirement Village*

Flynn massaged his forehead, hoping to relieve the tension headache creeping in to make him even more miserable. He'd already forgotten that yesterday's bride and groom were taking a short honeymoon. Their wedding seemed days ago. The only positive side of Wade's out-of-office announcement was he hadn't set up the account to automatically forward all his messages to his acting director. She'd probably get a good laugh out of Flynn's inability to maintain a business relationship with her. By the time she found out he'd quit, he'd be gone.

In any case, he was sticking to December twenty-seventh as his last day—if he managed to hold out that long and not simply walk off the job sometime over the next fourteen days.

*Or maybe in the next four days.*

Who gave a damn if she thought he was a wuss?

He had difficulty caring about her perception of him when she'd used him for nothing more than a temporary fuck buddy. Self-respect and knowing when to cut his losses were hardly signs of weakness.

Shutting down his computer, he glanced at the clock. Brunch was nearly over, and he could leave as soon as he helped with cleanup and stowed the extra portions.

His assistant came rattling through the dining room entrance, empty dishes stacked on the cart. Her quick look toward him then away poked at his conscience.

"Great job today, Shanda." He tried to put some enthusiasm into the compliment, but wasn't sure he succeeded.

"Thanks." She began transferring the load to the sink, and he joined her. "Everybody wants to know if you're sick. You don't usually hide out in the kitchen."

"Just having a tough day."

He hoped Alice hadn't shared their conversation in the parking lot. He wasn't up to dealing with the gossip mill.

"Must be a case of post-wedding exhaustion going around. Miss Montgomery was a no show, and she never misses Sunday brunch in her office."

He bit the inside of his cheek to hold in a snide remark. Throwing fuel on the possible rumors would only end with him getting burned worse than he already had been. "Your hors d'oeuvre spread was a hit. Why don't you bring in the rest of the dishes and I'll load the dishwasher?"

If she noticed his avoidance of a certain topic, she didn't comment on it as she nodded and headed to the dining room again. She was an excellent coworker and would make a damned good head chef. Too bad his failed love life would mean orphaning her. He doubted he'd get lucky enough to find a job that would let him bring her with him. He'd probably have to go back to working the same disgusting hours he'd put in at The Westerville House.

With the last of the dishes in the dishwasher and all the self-serve portions in the fridge, he slung the computer bag over his shoulder and trudged to the exit. The short reprieve until tomorrow morning was better than having to come back to serve supper tonight. Maybe by then he wouldn't feel like he'd been run through a meat grinder.

A check of the hall gave him the all clear—no ex-girlfriend, no senior citizens out to play matchmaker, no weekend staff.

*Almost outta here.*

Breezing through the double doors, he finally relaxed. The gardens were empty, as were the sidewalks.

At the patio, he turned left instead following the path to the employee apartments. The home stretch was no place to risk running into anyone, especially Lilith. He passed the scattered tables and chairs where Dr. Ito had loved to sit, her death seeming like months ago with all that had happened since Thanksgiving.

*Less than three weeks.*

A door closed, drawing him from the memory of France enjoying the sunshine on the patio. Lilith stood on the sidewalk with her back to him. His scant breakfast climbed to his throat and his stomach dropped to his feet.

As she turned, he pulled his cell phone from his pocket, tapping the screen in search of anything to keep him from looking at her. The sweet scent of her hair filled his senses, nights of holding her in his arms having planted it in his brain.

How much time had to pass before the imprint faded?

He lengthened his stride, the prickles between his shoulder blades suggesting she'd seen him, but he forced his eyes forward. He'd had to watch her walk away without a backward glance last night. She deserved no better today.

# Chapter 29

"What did you say to that young man, Lilith Montgomery?"

Lily almost jumped out of her skin at the admonition. "What are you talking about, Alice? *Who* are you talking about?"

*As if I don't know.*

The older woman propped her fists on her hips and looked down her nose at Lilith. "You know damn well who I'm talking about, young lady. Flynn, the sexiest chef this side of the Pecos. He hasn't said more than a handful of words to anybody since right after Wade and Eliza's wedding. And he's all but moved out of his apartment."

*He hasn't spoken to me at all, so consider yourself lucky.*

Straightening the stack of papers on the desk, Lily bit the inside of her lip to ease the ache in her chest. Although she'd noticed the lack of noise next door in the evenings and mornings, she hadn't wanted to think about why that was the case. "Maybe he's dealing with a family issue."

Her tapping tennis shoe and pursed lips said Alice didn't buy that excuse for a second. She threw her hands up in the air and marched out the door. "Fine, don't tell me. Stubborn Irish missy."

Wade stepped out of her path as he entered his office. "What's got Alice's feathers ruffled this morning? Did you hire an all-female painting crew while I was gone?"

Frowning at his implication that Alice's mood was her fault, Lilith walked over to greet her uncle. "Nothing important. How was your honeymoon? We have an applicant for the empty singles unit, and the part came for the whirlpool. Kip had it up and running Monday afternoon. Would you like a cup of coffee?"

He gathered her in a hug and kissed the top of her head. "You're not my gofer, Lily girl. I'll get my own coffee. The honeymoon was wonderful, and thank you for being so damn efficient."

Tears stung her eyes at the comfort of his embrace. She missed being able to climb on his lap and have a good cry, but she was all grown up now. Her problems were her responsibility now. She'd created them, after all.

"I have an appointment with Vivian in a few minutes, so I should probably go." She gave him another squeeze before easing away. "Are you free for lunch? I started vegetable soup in the slow cooker this morning."

"I was hoping to meet with you and Flynn today sometime. Do you mind if he tags along?"

Her stomach somersaulted to her knees. She'd spent the past four days and nights waffling between apologizing to Flynn for her abrupt behavior and letting time erode the sharp edges of their split. A clean break seemed wisest since he wanted something she couldn't give him. Reconciliation wasn't even a remote possibility. They were both better off suffering now than after they'd assumed their relationship would last forever.

She was meant to be alone. That much was clear.

"Today? Um, I guess that's okay. Let me put it in my calendar." Tapping the icon on her phone, she wracked her brain for a reasonable excuse to avoid the meeting. It popped up in the day's agenda. "Today's out. I signed up to teach a nutrition class at the hospital this afternoon. Rain check?"

"Oh. I'll check tomorrow's schedule and get back to you. Maybe we can fit it in then."

"Okay." She hurried past him to the hall, relieved that Wanda was on the phone and unable to continue the interrogation she'd attempted the last three days.

At least she hadn't had to lie to Uncle Wade. The class had been on her calendar for two months, even though she'd forgotten it somehow.

*Because I've been drowning in hormones.*

With that thought, she walked to the closest restroom. Her period had arrived like clockwork on Monday, instigating the most confusing pang of regret. She wasn't pregnant—the best solution for the situation. She had no cause to interact with Flynn, no motive to discuss her predicament or any other aspect of their failed relationship. That brand of turkey was best served cold.

The class did little to take her mind off having to discuss restaurant business with her uncle and her ex-lover tomorrow. The meeting was bound to be awkward, and Uncle Wade would surely notice the tension. Then he'd want an explanation she wasn't prepared to give.

She plodded to her office to drop off leftover presentation handouts, in hopes of sneaking in and out without crossing paths with anyone. Flynn and Shanda would've started supper prep, meaning neither would see her if she was careful.

As Lilith followed the corridor, a pair of auburn-haired girls sitting at one of the dining room tables caught her attention. They weren't the granddaughters or great granddaughters of any resident. Lilith had met them all. Besides, the folks at Montgomery Crossing wouldn't leave their grandchildren unattended in the main building.

The older girl looked up from her book and smiled. "Hi."

Switching the file to her left hand, Lilith detoured into the dining room. "Hi, I'm Miss Montgomery. I work here. Are you waiting for your grandparents?"

The younger girl stopped coloring and giggled. "No, Grandma and Grandpa are at their house. Daddy brought us. He'll be back at five o'clock."

"He just...left you here?" The concept of dropping off kids at a retirement village, with no supervision, was beyond Lilith's comprehension. Should she call the police?

"Daddy would *never* do that." The older sister's exasperated tone suggested she couldn't believe Lilith had asked that question.

"What about your mom? Would you like me to call her?" At a loss, Lily dug her phone from her purse.

The giggler sobered. "Mommy died. We miss her, but it's okay 'cause we're working on getting Daddy a new wife."

Every drop of blood draining to her feet, Lilith grabbed the chair to maintain her balance. Invisible needles pricked at her fingertips and spots dotted her vision. A chill engulfed her. "Your mom died? And your dad told you to wait here for him?"

"Yep. I'm Hannah. This is my sister, Kristin." Hannah returned to her coloring.

Lilith tried to cover her shock at the girl's nonchalant attitude about being abandoned. Her father had almost certainly left them to their own devices on other occasions. "Don't you have somebody to stay with?"

Kristin set down her book. "Why would you ask that? And the man with the purple tie said we could hang out here."

"Purple tie?" Was the girl referring to Uncle Wade? Didn't he have on a lavender shirt and matching necktie when he came in the office? "Do you mean Mr. Montgomery?"

"Yeah. Is he your dad?"

No, but he'd been a father to her for twenty years. "He's my uncle."

"Well, we're here with our uncle. He makes the best Pineapple Upside Down French Toast in the world."

*Can my life get any more complicated?*

The hair color, their eyes—both girls looked enough like Flynn to be his daughters, except they were his nieces. He was also the only man she knew who would serve a cake version of French toast.

*His sister's children. His sister who'd died last year.*

Even without anything in it, Lilith's stomach lurched. Life was incredibly cruel to have taken away someone so loved and needed.

"Miss Montgomery, are you okay? You're really pale, like when our cousin Cody had the flu. You're not going to throw up, are you?" Kristin scooted forward in her seat. "I should get Uncle Flynn."

"No!" Shaking off the bout of lightheadedness, Lilith steadied herself with the chair again. "I'm fine. Really. I just need to go home and eat."

She took a tentative step toward the exit, hoping she didn't collapse on the floor. The last thing she needed was Flynn taking care of her—not that he would want to.

"There you are, Lily." Uncle Wade marched toward her, his normal happy-go-lucky attitude hidden behind a scowl. "I need to see you in private. Right. Now."

What had happened to put him in such a foul mood?

She nodded, determined to get her bearings. "Okay."

"Hi, girls." Wade's demeanor transformed from boss mode to favorite uncle in an instant. "Would you like a snack or something to drink?"

Kristin shook her head. "No thanks, Mr. Montgomery. Daddy'll be here soon to pick us up."

"If you're sure." He winked at the girls as he took hold of Lilith's hand and headed for his office. "You'd better have a *darn* good explanation, young lady."

Hurrying to keep pace with him, Lilith didn't even attempt to understand what he was taking about. He'd undoubtedly tell her when they arrived at their destination.

As they neared the double doors, a tall man in a suit entered the building. His tie was loose around his neck and the jacket unbuttoned. He looked left and then right.

Wade stopped to greet the stranger. "I'm Wade Montgomery. Can I help you?"

The man extended his hand. "Drew Fulton. I'm looking for Flynn Hastings."

Shaking the outstretched hand, Wade smiled. "Ah, Kristin and Hannah's dad. Pleasure to meet you, Drew. Sweet girls you have. This is my niece, Lilith. You'll find Flynn in the kitchen and your daughters in the dining room straight down the hall and to the right."

"Lilith." Drew nodded at her, but his expression was hardly friendly. "Thank you, Mr. Montgomery. Good to meet you too."

At a loss for how to respond, she offered a fake smile. "Mr. Fulton."

Without so much as a glance at her, he followed Wade's directions.

Uncle Wade, on the other hand, narrowed his gaze at her. "This gets more interesting all the time."

Had she fainted and hit her head?

Flynn's brother-in-law had obviously heard the one-sided story of the breakup, but her uncle's behavior baffled her.

"My office." He tugged on her hand.

Too confused to argue, she set her pace to match his. Wanda frowned at her as they passed through the reception area, one more strange greeting to add to the others.

He closed the door and released her. "Sit."

Her mood had darkened enough to resist his order, but she held her tongue. The sooner he finished letting off steam, the sooner she could lock herself in her apartment and hope for a less stressful day tomorrow.

Dropping in the chair, she crossed her ankles and forced her shoulders downward. The motion didn't help her tense neck muscles.

He sat across from her. "What the hell happened while I was gone?"

The only thing that had happened was reality crashing down around her where Flynn was concerned, and she wasn't about to discuss that with anyone. She didn't have an answer that would satisfy her uncle.

He popped open his laptop. "I expected a few e-mails, but none as perplexing as the first one I opened after you left this morning. I forwarded it to you so you can read it at your leisure. The gist of it is my chef has given two weeks' notice, effective this past Monday morning."

His announcement took a moment to sink in, the words almost incomprehensible. She'd accepted that working with Flynn would be difficult for a while, but she'd figured they'd move beyond the uncomfortable avoidance stage at some point. She wasn't going to change her mind about having children. He'd forgive her for the abrupt end to their sexual liaisons, and she'd learn to deal with seeing him every day.

He was quitting.

*And he didn't tell me.*

*Why would he?*

"Lily girl, I want the truth. Flynn cited personal reasons when I talked to him after lunch, but he wouldn't go into details. Is he leaving because the two of you had a fight?"

She tightened her clasped hands until her fingers hurt. "No. We've always agreed on everything to do with the restaurant."

"I'm not referring to your *professional* relationship." Uncle Wade stared at her until she had to look away.

She'd been so careful.

How could he know she and Flynn had been more than friends?

Perhaps, he didn't.

"Sometimes friends—"

"Don't bullshit me, Lilith. I've got a hell of a lot more practice at stubborn than you do." Pushing up his sleeve, he tapped his watch. "I'm having supper with my wife in thirty minutes. I want the truth and I want it now."

A wave of lightheadedness had her scrambling for some way to pacify him without baring her soul. "It's no big deal. We had a personal disagreement and—"

"Damn it, 'fess up or you're both fired."

She lowered her gaze to her hands and swallowed against the lump in her throat. A tear trickled down her cheek. "We were...seeing each other. He wants more than I can give him, so I...broke things off. I might've been a little harsh, but it's for the best."

"Ah, Lily honey." He rounded the desk and crouched in front of her. "We can only decide what's best for ourselves."

Pressing her lips together, she tried to stem the tears. "But he wants kids, and I don't think I can do that."

Her uncle closed his hands around hers. "I didn't think I could, either. That's what stopped me from asking Eliza to marry me twenty years ago. I knew she wanted a child, but at forty-four, I thought I was too old to start a family. Letting her go was the hardest thing I've ever done. When I found out she was pregnant and getting married less than two months later, I was sure I'd made the right decision. Angry and devastated she could move on that easily, yes, but certain we weren't meant to be. Until six weeks ago, I didn't know she called off the wedding and that I was the father of her baby. We lost twenty years because I took the choice away from her. And I ended up being a parent to you and loving every minute of it."

His story added to the heartbreak already eating at her insides. She leaned forward to rest her head on his shoulder and cry. Whatever chance she'd had at happiness was gone. "I ruined it, and now it's too late."

He lifted her chin and brushed the wetness from her face. "It's only too late when you're in the ground. Are you ready to live, Lily?"

\* \* \* \*

With the coast clear, Flynn pushed through the server door to grill his nieces about their conversation with Lilith. He may have spied on them from the kitchen for the past five minutes, but he hadn't been able to hear a word they'd said. For not wanting kids, she'd been perfectly at ease with them.

"How're you doing out here?" He sat down in the chair facing the hallway.

Kristin shrugged. "Okay. Miss Montgomery stopped to talk to us. She's nice, but I think she was worried about us being in the dining room alone."

Kids tended to be pretty good judges of character, although they didn't know everything. He'd keep his opinion to himself.

Slipping her crayon into the box, Hannah scrunched up her face. "Then I told her about Mommy dying and she looked kinda sick. I don't think she likes talking about dead people."

A startling jolt of empathy tore at his insides. "Her parents died when she was twelve."

He'd be willing to bet their deaths had affected her on a much deeper level than she wanted to admit—sort of like when he'd buried himself in work to deal with the loss of Kate. For all he knew, she'd dumped him because he was getting too close.

Was she afraid of him dying?

She surrounded herself with old people, many of whom had health problems. Even then, Mrs. Reed's illness and Dr. Ito's sudden passing had brought incalculable grief to Lily.

Could the fear of losing a child have influenced her decision not to have kids?

"Hey, Flynn." Drew's voice pulled him from his disconcerting thoughts. "Thanks for taking care of the girls for me."

"Anytime."

Hannah and Kristin both jumped from their seats to hug their father. "Daddy!"

The joy in Drew's smile diffused the fog in Flynn's mind. Lilith mourned the end of her friends' lives, but, more than that, she hated being one of the survivors. She'd always been a survivor. Dying was easy. The living were left behind to get through day after day and year after year without their loved ones.

*She doesn't want her children to go through what she did.*

He'd let her toss him aside because he hadn't understood that part of her. By giving her up without a fight, he'd played into her plan, the vicious cycle that had begun when her parents had died. In her wounded soul, leaving a child parentless was worse than suffering a horribly painful death.

Had she ever gone through the normal stage of thinking she could do anything without worrying about the consequences? Or had she always had a realist's view of her mortality?

No wonder she'd been so reluctant to venture past friendship with him. Conscious or not, sabotage was her way of protecting herself, and she'd done a damn good job of making him think twice about his feelings for her.

*I love her.*

Unless he was a complete idiot with his armchair psychoanalysis, she loved him too.

"I might be late tonight." Unfolding out of the chair, Flynn made up his mind. "Or I might stay here. I'll let you know."

Drew grimaced. "You're not thinking of—"

"I need to talk to her." Whether or not she'd actually agree to it remained to be seen.

"Are you sure you know what you're doing? Sometimes trying for closure doesn't work out for the best." He gave his daughters a quick hug. "Pack up while I talk to Uncle Flynn."

Motioning for Flynn to follow, Drew walked to the windowed back wall of the dining room. Surrendering to the request seemed easier than explaining. Flynn would allow him his say.

When they were out of earshot, Drew looked him in the eye. "I saw her. I met her when I came in the building, and I get it. She's hot and as innocent looking as any woman I've ever seen, but the heartbreakers usually are."

"Heartbreaker?" Flynn snorted. "She's afraid if she has kids she'll die and leave them to grow up without parents. Just like what happened to her."

Drew rubbed his fingers back and forth across his temple. "Okay, say you're right about the not wanting kids part. What about the baggage she must be carrying around? Do you really want to deal with that?"

Flynn hoped like hell he wasn't wrong. "Do you honestly think she has more baggage trailing behind her than I do? And what about you?"

"*Touché.*" Juggling his keys, Drew sighed. "You know you're welcome at the house if things don't work out."

"Yeah, I know. Thanks. And sorry about the baggage comment."

"No problem." Drew offered him a grim smile. "You're right. We all have issues."

Flynn had evidently hit a sore spot. For his brother-in-law claiming he was ready to date, the guy didn't seem too sure about it now. "I should get back to work."

Drew turned toward his daughters. "Good luck."

"Thanks." *I'm gonna need it.*

Summoning every ounce of hope he could muster, Flynn waved to

Kristin and Hannah as he returned to the kitchen. He had some thinking and planning to do before he cornered Lilith. Convincing her to hear him out was only the beginning. He'd rather not find himself staring at the end again when he was done.

The habitual task of preparing meals with Shanda provided plenty of time to think, an adequate amount of time to plan, and few ideas of how to talk Lily into listening to what he had to say.

Taking her an entrée would make him look like he was trying to use sex to win her back—not that his food was likely to give her sexual pleasure anymore. Sleeping with him had put a stop to that.

Offering her flowers was out of the question unless he wasted a half hour or more going to the grocery store. No respectable florist would be open at seven thirty in the evening.

Gourmet chocolates probably weren't an easy commodity to find, either.

With the single-serve meals stowed and the kitchen clean, he strode to the exit before he lost his nerve. The double doors gave him a clear view of Lily's apartment. Her windows were dark, but he refused to let her off the hook that easily.

The short walk across the courtyard was a chilly one, and he increased his pace, anxious to see Lilith and get out of the cold. He stopped in front of her apartment to knock and wait.

No lights flicked on and no one came to the door. She seldom went anywhere on weeknights, so he knocked again.

He waited another minute. Still, no one answered.

Impatience tried to surface, but he took a calming breath. If her car was in the parking lot, she had to be somewhere on the grounds. He only had to find her.

Setting off at a jog, he headed toward the lot, almost afraid to face the fact that he might have to delay their confrontation. At the end of the sidewalk, he slowed to a walk, scanning the area where she usually parked. His racing pulse steadied at the sight of her sedan. He had a shot at talking to her and correcting her belief that children were the deal breaker.

*Where to look for her?*

She could be anywhere in the complex, including hiding in her dark apartment.

A slight movement near his truck caught his eye. The security lights silhouetted a hunched form sitting on some sort of box by his passenger door.

Light-colored hair shone under the eerie glow, and his heart leapt to his throat. Hope lifting his spirits, he hurried to his truck.

*Please let it be her.*
"Lily?"

# Chapter 30

Lilith wiped her eyes as she raised her head. After the way she'd treated Flynn, he should've climbed in his truck and driven away, leaving her like she'd left him. He'd actually spoken her name, the first word he'd said to her since she'd walked out on him four days ago.

His chef whites were too thin to keep him warm in the frosty temperatures, but he didn't seem to notice, and he was even more handsome than the first time she'd seen him.

Why had she ever thought she could live without him?

She waited for him to make his getaway now that he knew she wasn't some homeless waif hanging out in the parking lot. Using her overstuffed suitcase as a seat had to convey that pathetic image. She didn't dare get her hopes up that he'd forgive her.

He crouched in front of her and grasped her gloved hands. "What're you doing out here? You're gonna freeze. And it's dark."

She'd all but thrown his declaration of love back in his face, and he was worried about whether or not she was cold?

"I was waiting...for you." She swallowed past the lump in her throat. "I realize it's probably too little too late, but I'm sorry. The things I said to you. I—"

"You panicked. I get that." Standing, he tugged her upward. "Can we go someplace to talk?"

"Talk. Yes. Um, my house? Do you want to drive?"

They'd have complete privacy, with no interruptions by well-meaning neighbors.

"Your house? You mean you're moving?" Too bad his face was shadowed, or she might've been able to judge his mood from his expression. He didn't sound terribly thrilled with the prospect.

*That's a good sign, isn't it?*

She reached for her suitcase handle, but he picked up the bag and set it in the bed of his truck. The action brought him closer, and he hesitated, as if he might kiss her.

She missed his lips.

Unfortunately, she had a lot to tell him before she wrapped herself around him and hoped he didn't let go, no matter the ache. "It's sort of a complicated story. Do you mind if I tell you on the way?"

"Works for me." He opened the passenger door. "Where are we headed?"

"South past the reservoir." She climbed in, reminded once again why she liked him.

He was polite and kind, when he had every right to be angry. No wonder she'd gone off the deep end. Unlike the other men she'd dated, Flynn possessed the power to truly break her heart—not that he'd ever do it on purpose.

Exiting Montgomery Crossing, he cast a glance at her. "Are you moving because of me?"

"I suppose indirectly." She tucked her fingers under her legs and stared at the dotted center line on the road as it zipped toward them. "But it isn't your fault. Uncle Wade moved in with Eliza, and he insists I go live in his house. My house. It belonged to my parents. I grew up there."

"You've been paying rent even though you own a home?" He switched on his turn signal. "Too many painful memories?"

"Just one—the police coming to say my mom and dad had died. I wanted my uncle to be able to have a life after taking care of me until my eighteenth birthday, so I moved out when I started college. He dropped everything to come live with me. Now that he's married, the house will set empty if I don't move back in."

"Do you want to live there?"

"Yes. I don't know. It needs a family." She shifted to study Flynn's profile. "Uncle Wade evicted me from my apartment. He threatened to fire both of us if I don't make a real attempt to live there. With you."

"He knows about us." His jaw flexed. "Or knew. Not much us, is there?"

Shaking her head, she forced her gaze out the side window. A few dim lights shone through the trees, but mostly utter darkness surrounded her. "No, but I wish there was."

He was silent for too long, leading her to wonder if she'd finally made the biggest mistake of her life by walking out on him. He wasn't going to forgive her—or if he did, a reunion wasn't in his plans.

Why had he agreed to take her home? Did he want her to beg him for another chance so he could laugh at her audacity?

He probably wouldn't laugh at her, but she'd been a fool to think she could right the wrong she'd made. Some things couldn't be fixed.

She squeezed her eyes shut to stop the stinging tears from becoming a pitiful crying jag. She'd cried far too much in the past four days. "Turn right at the next road. Then left on the third street."

His fingers closed around hers. "I wish there was too."

A tiny spark of hope fluttered in her chest, and she bit her lower lip to keep from demanding an explanation.

Did he want to renew their relationship? Or did he mean he wished they could, but they couldn't?

Releasing her hand, he made the turn. He flipped on the high beams and continued along the winding road as if he'd driven it a hundred times. Even in the dark, he found the next turn-off without slowing. "Where to now?"

Her insides pitched, her nerves strung tighter with every turn. "Right at the end of the street. Fourth house on the left."

Less than a minute later, gravel crunched under the tires as he made the turn into the driveway. He stopped in front of the garage and shut off the engine, but he made no move to get out of the truck. "My brother-in-law lives about three blocks from here. I've been staying with him since Saturday night."

At a loss for a response, she pulled her keys out of her coat pocket. Not only had he given two weeks' notice, he also preferred sleeping at Drew Fulton's house to staying at the apartment next to hers. Whatever delusions she'd had about getting back together were gone. He'd already put as much distance between them as he could without quitting his job outright—and she'd caused all of it.

Should she even bother inviting him inside?

He opened his door as she lifted the handle on hers. "I'll carry your suitcase."

"You're coming in?"

"Yeah. Unless you don't want me to." Looking over his shoulder at her, he halted halfway out of the truck and frowned. "Actually, just yes. I have some things I need to say."

Without giving her time to comment, he climbed out and shut the door. He was already lifting her luggage from the bed when she climbed out of the passenger seat.

Hefting her suitcase, he started toward the mudroom entrance. "Would you mind grabbing the duffle bag behind the seat? I'd like to change clothes."

She fiddled with the latch, not bothering to acknowledge his request since he'd already walked away. Spotting the overnight bag, she tugged it free from the compact space and then followed him.

As she unlocked the back door, she tried to dispel the seesawing thoughts from her brain. She switched on the lights and gestured him inside. "Are you thirsty? Hungry?"

"I'm fine for now. Where's your bedroom?"

She almost choked as she spun around to stare at him. "What?"

His cold-pinked cheeks flushed a deeper shade of red. "For the suitcase. And the bathroom so I can change clothes."

*Get your mind off sex, Lilith Montgomery.* "Oh, um, this way."

Kicking off her shoes on the rug, she adjusted her hold on Flynn's bag and then strode through the mostly dark kitchen to the living room. Only a few rays from the outside light lit her way. She paused only to turn on a lamp as she crossed to the stairs, steady footsteps trailing after her.

At the top of the steps, she dropped off his change of clothes in the main bath. "Help yourself to whatever you need. Towels are in the closet if you want to shower or wash up."

The dark red spatters on his sleeve hinted that his Burgundy Pot Roast had put up a fight—and she'd missed out on every one of his delicious meals all week. She hadn't even had the guts to sneak a single boxed entrée. Instead, she'd gone into hiding, surviving on leftovers from her freezer.

She continued along the hall to the next room, the decor still perfect for a teenage girl. "This is my bedroom. Or it was when I was growing up. I'm thinking of moving into the master suite."

"Your mom and dad's room?" Flynn's soft voice assured her he understood her misgivings.

"Yeah. I slept in their bed the night they died. I couldn't go back in after that."

He slipped his fingers through hers, linking them together. A gentle squeeze gave her more comfort than she'd experienced in years. "I'll put your suitcase in there. I can move it later if you decide you're not ready."

Leaning against him, she sniffled. She'd missed having his arms around her and being able to spend the night wrapped up in his strength. "Thank you."

His whisper caressed her forehead. "You're welcome."

* * * *

Stripping off his stained jacket, Flynn studied his reflection in the bathroom mirror. He looked the same as he had yesterday, last week, and two months ago, but he'd never had to exercise as much self-control as when Lily had leaned into him.

He'd wanted to haul her closer, until he couldn't tell where she ended and he began. One kiss would've led to another and another, and he wouldn't have been able to resist making love to her right there in the hallway. He'd missed her so damn much. That simple touch of her hand in his had almost defeated his restraint.

With the cold water turned full blast, he put his head in the sink and tried to cool his lust.

*It's more than lust. It's love.*

Their relationship was based on more than desire. Attraction may have been the initial reaction, but friendship and mutual caring had built something far stronger. If he could convince Lilith that he really loved her, she might be willing to say the same.

He shivered at the drips running down his back and chest as he dried his face and hair. A long talk about their expectations and true feelings had to come before a hot and heavy session in the master suite's inviting bed.

Of course, she could decide to send him home.

Donning jeans and a shirt, he shook off the negative thoughts. She wouldn't have invited him to her house if she didn't think they could work out their issues.

Would she?

He scuttled down the steps, ready to argue his case. He'd let her go too easily Saturday night, and he had to correct that.

The living room was empty when he reached the bottom of the stairs, and he followed the sound of dishes clinking to the kitchen. Lilith was half hidden behind an open cupboard door.

"Uncle Wade, you sneaky Irishman. You leave every plate, pan, and speck of food, but you take the damn whiskey." She banged the cabinet door closed, grimacing when Flynn stepped into the kitchen. "It isn't funny."

The urge to laugh was almost overpowering—in a sympathetic way. Under the circumstances, he could use a shot or two of liquid courage himself. "Am I so scary that you need alcohol?"

She shook her head, sending her ponytail swishing back and forth. "I'm scared of what you make me feel."

"Want to talk about it?" He held out his hand, hoping she was ready for him. Her fingers were icy against his palm, and he rubbed them between his hands.

"Yeah." Tightening her hold on him, she led him to the living room couch. "Sit with me?"

He settled next to her, leaving enough space between them that he wouldn't be tempted to drag her into his arms. Four nights without her had seemed like an eternity.

"Uncle Wade was really upset with me when he found your resignation letter in his e-mail today. He wanted to know what happened to make you quit." Her voice cracked on the last word, and she blinked like she was trying not to cry. "Everybody knows we were…you know."

Curious as to what "you know" meant to her, he stayed quiet, hoping she'd expand on the generic description.

She glanced toward him. "He knows we were more than friends, even before he made me tell him the whole story. He said he warned the residents to mind their own business and let us figure things out by ourselves. Not that it did any good. I overreacted and threw away the best man—the best *friend*—I've ever had."

Turning to face her, he lifted her chin so she'd have to look at him. "You can't take all the blame. I dropped the L word in your lap *and* we had a condom mishap. I was so worried about making sure you knew an accident wasn't necessarily a problem that I didn't consider how you might feel about having kids after what you went through."

Her shrug didn't fool him for a second. Losing her parents had scarred her, and she'd learned to wear armor.

He wrapped her in a hug. "I love you—no matter what, Lily. I'd like to have children, but I *have* to have you."

Her arms tightened around his waist. "I do too."

He was reluctant to pull back, but he did it anyway. He needed to see her eyes when he asked his question. "You what?"

"I love you." She kept her gaze locked on him. "I need you in my life."

"You have no idea how glad I am to hear you say that." He couldn't hold back a satisfied grin.

"And we can talk about kids at some point."

"I'm serious. I'm not going to pressure you to—"

She pressed her finger to his lips. "I know you won't, even though it's what you really want. Uncle Wade and I had a discussion about parenting, and how sometimes it chooses you when you thought you couldn't do it. I can't let fear of what might happen take all the enjoyment of what is and what could be."

Kissing her finger, he pulled her close again and inhaled her purely feminine scent. "Still, no pressure. We can talk about it, but I don't want you to do it for me. I'm okay with the two of us if that's what makes you happy."

"Are you sure?"

He set her against the back of the couch as he stood. "Do you trust me,

Lily?"

Staring down at her, he studied her face for any sign of doubts, second thoughts, or regrets.

Only a flash of anger darkened her eyes, and she popped to her feet. "Yes! Do you trust me?"

He had her right where he wanted—ready to fight for him. He dropped to one knee in front of her. "I trust you with my heart and soul. Now, will you trust yourself and take a leap of faith with me? Will you marry me?"

She opened her mouth as if to speak, but shut it before so much as a whisper escaped. Surprise could've been the culprit, although he'd told her Saturday night that he wanted to be with her and was ready to start a family.

Kneeling across from him, she hooked her arms around his neck and touched her lips to his.

Love and hope soared through his veins.

Not a single doubt shadowed her bright eyes. "Yes. And yes. Will *you* marry *me*?"

Leaning his forehead against hers, he grinned. His white lie from the night he'd spied on her in the whirlpool actually had some truth to it. "Yes, I'll marry you. What do you think about getting married Christmas Eve?"

"There's no hurry. I'm not pregnant."

The lack of disappointment caught him off guard. In fact, he was pleased. "Good. We need some time alone together."

"Are you worried I'm going to change my mind? Because I won't." She nipped at his lower lip.

"Worried? No. Ready to tell the world how much I love you? Absolutely." He brushed his fingertips along her cheek. "I told a complete stranger I was going to marry you on Christmas Eve. You wouldn't want to make a liar out of me, would you?"

"I have a feeling that's an interesting story. You realize that only gives us a week, don't you? I don't need some big event, but a dress and some flowers would be nice."

"Wade told me to take the day off tomorrow. We'll go shopping after breakfast."

Her raised eyebrows warned Flynn she wasn't letting that piece of news pass without a question or two. "Why would he tell you to take the day off if you were quitting in a week and a half?"

"He wasn't too pleased with 'personal reasons' as an explanation for why I was leaving. When he demanded specifics, I said it was none of his business and threatened to quit today. He's known all along how I feel about you, and he told me to take the day off to deal with whatever problems we were having."

"That devious—"

"He was just trying to help. You're a daughter to him. He wants to see you happy." Flynn stroked his fingers through her hair. "Are you happy, Lily?"

She leaned into his hand, her lips curving into a beautiful smile. "Almost."

Although she looked and sounded like she might be teasing, he wasn't taking any chances. "What can I do to make you truly happy?"

"Show me how much you love me. And let me love you."

He pulled her to her feet as he stood. "I'm all yours for as long as you'll have me. How about we celebrate our engagement by making love? Sort of a private housewarming party."

With a nod, she led him upstairs to the master bedroom. Filtered light shone from the bedside lamps, giving the space a welcoming glow.

Her hesitation at the doorway had him wondering if she was ready to claim this house as her own. "My mom and dad held hands and kissed a lot. Not a day went by that I didn't see how much they loved each other. I remember hoping I'd find someone who'd share that kind of love with me."

Had she ever thought about the happy times with her parents before tonight? Was she finally allowing herself to heal from their loss?

Gathering her in a hug, he kissed her forehead. The familiar feel of her body against his had him closing his eyes to fully enjoy the sensation. "We have that. It might not be as strong as what they had just yet, but we'll get there. I promise."

She tightened her hold around his waist. "Let's go christen the bed. I've missed you so much."

He met her gaze as he scooped her into his arms, treasuring the sweet satisfaction of her words. "Me too."

With four long strides, he reached the bed and laid her down on the covers. As much as he wanted to strip off her clothes and bury himself inside her, he didn't. Instead, he stretched out beside her and loosened her ponytail. Threading his hands through her hair, he combed it away from her face. The love and trust in her eyes were true gifts.

She pushed his shirt toward his chest, sliding her palms over his stomach and triggering a chain reaction from his quivering abs to his tightening balls. "I want to be skin to skin with you."

Her soft declaration hijacked his intent to go slow. As much as he wanted to appreciate every motion and moment, demonstrating the depth of his feelings for her took precedence.

He sat up long enough to send both their clothes into a pile on the floor. Tossing her second sock at the heap, realization dawned and he swallowed a mouthful of swear words. "I don't have any condoms."

"Outside pocket of my suitcase." Winking at him, she trailed the arch of her bare foot along his calf.

His heart skipped a beat. "Another reason I love you. Always prepared."

The trip to her luggage and back gave him the perfect view of her shapely form reclining on the bed. Tonight was the beginning of their life together, and he couldn't wait to get started.

Lilith reached out to Flynn as he knelt on the bed, confident that she'd spend the rest of her life with him. The fear of loss was nothing compared to the love in her heart and the future they'd share. She'd taken a risk, fighting for something—and someone—worth having.

Linking her fingers with his, she relished the simple connection. "Let's apply for the marriage license before we go shopping tomorrow."

He leaned down, touching his lips to hers. "Excellent plan."

She looped her free arm around his neck to pull him closer. Meeting him halfway to a kiss, she opened herself to him, inviting him inside. The first caress of his tongue against hers sent desire rushing through her body, and she arched against him. Coarse hair rubbed over her nipples, triggering a surge of wetness between her thighs.

His fingertips lit a flaming path from her shoulder to her hip as she savored the taste and texture of him—the minty flavor of his toothpaste, the softness of his lips, the rough stubble of his day-old beard. She treasured the chance to experience them again.

Dragging her mouth from his, she panted to catch her breath. "I'm ready for you, Flynn. Make love with me."

His eyes locked with hers as his hand brushed past her ribs. He slicked a finger through the dampness, making her gasp when he paused at her clitoris. A flutter across the bundle of nerves had her groaning. "Mind if I play down here next time?"

"Next time. Yes. Or now." Yes, she wanted it now.

"How about both?"

Another flurry brought a torrent of pleasure, an orgasm overwhelming her faster than ever before. She cried out with the sudden release of tension and reveled in the exhilaration of sweeping along in the current. He didn't stop until she sank into the comforter, her muscles shaking and her mind floating.

She blinked up at him. "Mm-hm. Both."

His satisfied grin was well earned. "Beautiful. I love making you come."

"Your turn." The pounding rhythm in her chest mixed with the drifting feeling in her head, making her unsure if she'd spoken the thought.

Her lips had moved, hadn't they?

Crinkling sounded and then he rose over her, hooking her legs over his arms and pressing his cock to her opening. "Go with me?"

She cupped his jaw in her palms, grateful to have found such a giving man. Tilting her hips upward, she took him inside her, moaning at the incredible bliss of bonding with him this way. "Always."

Not a single doubt entered her mind. They'd take the journey, short or long, together.

He kissed her as he pushed deeper, stroking every inch of her. The spiral slowly wound tighter with each intimate thrust and petal-soft kiss, taking her to heights she'd only dreamed of.

His pace remained steady, even as he changed inside her. He grew harder, massaging the spot he never failed to find, banishing every thought from her mind except being one with him.

He squeezed her hand a little tighter and groaned. "Now, Lily."

The hoarse sound of her name on his lips sent her flying, and she forced her unfocused gaze on his face. "I love you, Flynn."

Tremors rocked her as he stiffened and let out a growl. "Love you. So much."

Although she welcomed the words, she didn't need to hear them to know what was in his heart. He'd shown her a hundred ways since they'd met, his friendship not the least among them. She'd been blind to it for weeks.

He dropped beside her, cradling her against him while her pulse returned to normal.

She rested her cheek on his chest. "The biggest mistake I made wasn't choosing the wrong guys. It was pushing away the right one."

His fingers tangled in her hair. "But we're okay now, Lily. And we'll keep getting better. Together."

Pressing a kiss to his neck, she savored the steady pulse beating in her ear. "Together."

# Other Books by Mellanie Szereto

Love on the Menu series ~
    Just Desserts
    Iced Latté

Death Benefits ~ A short paranormal romance

The Sextet Anthologies ~
    Volume 1: Sharing
    Volume 2: Dirty Dancing
    Volume 3: Occupational Hazards
    Volume 4: Entanglements
    Volume 5: Mistletoe & Ménage

The Sextet Presents ~
    Playing in the Raine: A Toy Story
    Bound by Voodoo: Legends

Bewitching Desires series ~
    Two if by Sea
    Two Knights of Passion
    Two Fated for One
    Two Pirates to Treasure
    Two Times the Trouble
    Two Roped and Ready
    Two from the Triangle
    Beyond Bewitching

Writing Tip Wednesday series ~
    Writing Tip Wednesday: The Writing Craft Handbook
    Writing Tip Wednesday: The Writing Career Handbook
    Writing Tip Wednesday: The Self-Publishing Handbook
    Writing Tip Wednesday: Books 1-3 Boxed Set

# About the Author

When her fingers aren't attached to her keyboard, Mellanie Szereto enjoys hiking, Pilates, cooking, gardening, and researching for her stories. Many times, the research partners with her other hobbies, taking her from the Hocking Hills region in Ohio to the Colorado Rockies or the Adirondacks of New York. Sometimes, the trip is no farther than her garden for ingredients and her kitchen to test recipes for her latest steamy tale. Mellanie makes her home in rural Indiana with her husband of twenty-nine years and their son. She is a member of Romance Writers of America, Indiana Romance Writers of America, Contemporary Romance Writers, and Fantasy, Futuristic, and Paranormal Romance Writers.

Visit her website: www.mellanieszereto.com
Read her blog: www.mellanieszereto.blogspot.com
Like her on Facebook: www.facebook.com/authormellanieszereto
Follow her on Twitter: www.twitter.com/mellanieszereto
Find her on Goodreads: www.goodreads.com/mellanie_szereto

If you enjoyed this book, please consider rating or leaving a review on the retailer's website and/or Goodreads. Thanks!

www.ingramcontent.com/pod-product-compliance
Lightning Source LLC
Chambersburg PA
CBHW071304250626
47159CB00004B/1299